For Love of Kitty

Julie

Thank you for listening

Kathleen J

Also by Kathleen Judd

The Regency Romance Series

Coming shortly

Saving Rebecca

Finding Diana

For Love of Kitty

A Regency Romance

Kathleen Judd

authorHOUSE®

AuthorHouse™ UK Ltd.
1663 Liberty Drive
Bloomington, IN 47403 USA
www.authorhouse.co.uk
Phone: 0800.197.4150

Published by AuthorHouse   06/03/2014

ISBN: 978-1-4969-8234-6 (sc)
ISBN: 978-1-4969-8251-3 (e)

Prologue

"So we are about to lose you, Jeremy. I have to say it has been a pleasure to have a scholar like you, in spite of all your troubles."

The master handed a glass to Jeremy who sat comfortably relaxed in the chair on the opposite side of the unlit fireplace.

Jeremy, actually Lord Jeremy Wellmore, heir to his father the Duke of Wenton, gave a wry smile. He was a gentle, intelligent young man, not over tall but well built. His hair was light brown, his features were regular and gave him the good looks that suited his character, but he could never be called overly handsome. He was fit enough but not a fighter. He had spent enough time learning to defend himself over his time at Eton.

"I could have wished for a more comfortable existence here for you. Although you seem to have found a way to survive all that harassment."

"I have never found out what antagonized him so. I shall no doubt have it all over again at Oxford. Let us just hope he gets himself sent down."

"I don't see it could be just your academic ability. Did you never do anything to upset him or one of his brothers? There seemed to be a general dislike for you but the others were never so vindictive."

Jeremy took a drink from his glass. He looked thoughtful.

"I really have never figured it out. I have no knowledge of doing anything to anger him, he seemed like that from the first day I arrived. Perhaps his family has had something in their past which made them hate ours. I think he trained his brothers to carry on the tradition when he left. The youngster seems much better tempered although I have had little dealings with him. He has only just arrived after all."

The master laughed a little ironically.

"I only hope that proves to be the case. He does seem more interested in horses and a military career. I can do without more of that family's arrogance." He shifted in his seat.

"Yes, I think I would agree with that assessment, it is not so much antagonism to everyone, it is more arrogance."

"There are many more at Eton with as much of a pedigree as that family, like yours for instance, yet they interact and make friends perfectly easily. I just wish a few more were willing to study like you have, my boy."

Jeremy looked deeply into his glass, a little embarrassed.

"Thank you sir. I only hope I can maintain your academic standards while at Oxford."

Chapter 1

Five years later

"I'm only seventeen Papa and I don't want to get married, at least not yet. I prefer it here with you and Carina, with the horses and my books."

The Duke of Wenton smiled down at the daughter he clearly adored.

"You are almost 18 child, and it is time you went out into society more. Since your mother died I have been selfish in keeping you so close to me." He sighed deeply. "You are far too attached to your books and the estate. If your mother were alive you would feel completely at home with many in ton society by now, not turning into a regular bluestocking. Why, you know no-one of your own age in the haut ton and it is about time you found some friends." he chided.

Kitty opened her mouth to speak but the Duke put one finger gently over her lips to silence her.

"No! I have decided. You must be allowed to have a life of your own whether or not you want it at this moment. You must have the choice. Look at your Aunt Jane, destined to be an unmarried companion to her ageing mother and aunts and given no chance of marrying. Now look at what has happened to her, left alone with no real purpose in life. Is that what you wish to become? Anyway you have no ageing infirm mother, so the question does not arise."

She looked at her papa hopefully, a cheeky smile on her face.

"I could be maiden aunt to all Carina's many children. I could teach them the merits of modern farming, and Latin. Everyone should be able to read the original Latin texts."

The Duke barked with laughter.

"You have just proved my point completely, Kitty. Few young men, let alone young ladies, are interested in Latin texts. Gothic novels are more to their taste."

Kitty wrinkled her nose. "Are women really interested in such dreadful books?"

"How do you know they are dreadful if you have never read one?"

"Oh but I have." She replied, her face showing real disgust. "Miss Phelps made me read one last year, so we could discuss the genre. Why would any young, gently brought up lady, wish to read such gory details? There are enough real stories in the news sheets if that is what interests them. Who encourages them to be interested in such horror, if they saw it for real most of them would swoon with a fit of the vapours, I'm sure."

"Spoken like a true bluestocking. You need to learn more of the real world Kitty. You can assess it and moralise about it to your heart's content, but you will be leaving for London next week. No more arguments!"

Preparing for your come out is an exciting time for a young girl. Or it should be. However Lady Katherine Elizabeth Wellmore was getting rather disillusioned by the whole thing.

Lady Katherine, known to all as Kitty, was a pretty, slim, and elegant young lady with light brown shining hair and pure clear skin which glowed from the fresh air of the life she led. She had spent her formative years at Wenton Hall just outside London, the principal seat of her father the Duke of Wenton.

They were a close family, her father, her brother Jeremy and her younger sister Carina. Kitty's mother had died when she was only seven years old and she had been raised by an army of governesses. She had now reached the elderly age of seventeen and was to be presented for her come out.

But she was bored and lonely.

She knew she should be excited but Aunt Jane did not exactly inspire a young girl. At forty years of age, Lady Jane Marsden was a traditional spinster aunt with no intention of ever marrying and no knowledge of the workings of the ton. She was tallish and extremely thin, almost running to bony, with dark hair and pallid skin, mostly from staying indoors. She was the younger sister to Kitty's mother and had not really spent any time outside the rarefied atmosphere of the elderly ladies she had been bred to assist. She liked to think that she knew about the world and was often heard admonishing any who would listen.

It was not that the Duke thought she was the best person to bring Kitty into society; she was merely the youngest family member available to bring her out.

Kitty missed being at home with her books, her quiet walks and long rides, and she missed Carina's chatter. True, Jeremy was not often at home, but when he was, there was no lack of informative discussion. They discussed the latest books on theology, the ramifications of the government's latest bill, every kind of current thinking, most of which would have been denied to her by anyone except her intelligent and similarly bookish brother.

They were staying at Wenton House in the very best area of London, of course. The house had been altered and updated quite recently and looked more like a main residence than a London base for the occasional visit. It had a pillared portico, tall windows which let in so much light it was necessary for extremely expensive curtains to keep the sunlight from damaging the priceless paintings that hung unnoticed on the walls. It included all the latest in modern comforts which was not the case at the Hall. They were staying there because although Wenton Hall was quite close to London, it was just too far for attending the balls and afternoon visits, not to mention the endless shopping.

Please, no one mention the shopping! Her feet ached at the thought.

If only Jeremy came to London more often, after all he had no bachelor rooms and so stayed at Wenton House when he visited. Or why could Carina not have come with them? Just because she was only fifteen and too young for her come out did not mean she should manage to avoid Aunt Jane's ministrations. No, she was feeling decidedly lonely and isolated. Aunt Jane did not approve of her reading habits and had no interesting conversation. What was there to do when she was not allowed out of doors without a maid and at least one footman trailing close behind like a comet's tail? It was not as if the weather was inviting. The air in London was dirty and smelly in comparison to the fresh air of even a few miles away at the Hall.

"Do I really need any more dresses, Aunt Jane? "she complained. "I shall scream if I have one more pin stuck in me."

Aunt Jane merely looked down her nose. "You can never have enough gowns for your come out. Now do keep up, we have shoes and gloves to buy to match the walking dresses and travelling gowns. That green walking dress is a particular shade which is quite difficult to match and we need to finalise your wardrobe before the balls begin. You will be too tired when the season starts properly."

Kitty thought Aunt Jane might be rather more tired than her. She was champing at the bit to be doing something. "And do not forget we have Mrs Fitzgerald to visit this afternoon."

So Kitty went to Mrs Fitzgerald's and Mrs Fitzwilliam's and Lady Fitzherbert's and any other Fitz Aunt Jane could find. She also went to Lady Hewlet's, and everywhere she went she drank endless cups of insipid tea and talked the same meaningless talk to the same uninteresting people.

"Really, Kitty you should make at least a little effort." Never having been in this position herself she was having trouble understanding her young charge.

"This afternoon we go to Lady Waltham's and I want you to make an effort to talk with the young people there. Make some friends."

So Kitty was dutifully ushered into Lady Waltham's salon for yet more insipid tea and indifferent biscuits. The problem with being from such a wealthy family is that you were brought up with the best of everything and that included the biscuits.

As usual the room was overfilled with non matching chairs, an over abundance of objects on every available surface and a lack of fresh air.

She surveyed the company present. Oh no. Robert Fitzwilliam, him she could do without.

"Ah, good afternoon, Lady Katherine. Deigning to honour us lower mortals with your exalted presence, yet again. How good of you!"

Kitty stared at him with all the disdain she could muster. *Think of something to say.*

"But of course, Mr Fitzwilliam. Every worm should have something to look up to before it crawls back into the ground to avoid being trodden on."

A giggle erupted near her elbow. Robert Fitzwilliam bristled and she could see his mind trying to form a reply. He was not quick witted, he just worked out in advance what to say to look intelligent, and waited until the right time arose. He opened his mouth to speak but the voice came from beside her.

"Oh stop being a pompous ass, Robert."

Kitty turned to the pretty young woman beside her and saw the irrepressible mirth on her face. She was a slightly plump but pretty young lady of about Kitty's age. She wore a dress of apricot muslin with ruffles at the neck and hem and puffed sleeves. Kitty thought she would have looked better without the ruffles, as she was not overly tall.

"Take no notice of Robert, he always was too full of his own importance. I'm Emily Weston, Robert is my cousin, much to my disgust. Do you have any disgusting cousins, Lady Katherine?"

Kitty beamed a genuine smile.

"Miss Weston, I am very pleased to meet you. No, I have no close cousins, disgusting or otherwise." and with a cheeky smile asked "Tell me Miss Weston, are all the young men in London like Mr Fitzwilliam?"

Emily laughed, she seemed to do that a great deal. How nice. Kitty had no idea that such friendly people existed in the ton.

"Oh no, Robert is quite unique, I am very glad to say." She turned a laughing face to her cousin who looked decidedly put out.

Emily took Kitty's arm and steered her across the room to a quieter corner.

"You are not acquainted with the bucks of the ton, Lady Katherine?" she speculated.

"No, indeed, we have not long arrived in London and previously I stayed at the hall most of the year. I have met a few friends of my brother, but they are deeply serious bookworms in the main. Few of them would have the opportunity to visit a ton ballroom, even if they wished it. I have to admit I was happy there and not too keen to come to London."

Emily looked a little bemused.

"Forgive me Lady Katherine, but I know nothing about your family, although I know of it, of course. You have a brother?"

"Yes, Jeremy is five years older then me. I also have a younger sister who is fifteen years old."

"Do you stay there with your parents all the year?"

"My father is there most of the year, although he comes to London on business and for parliamentary votes occasionally. My mother died ten years ago so we have had governesses. Carina and I have hardly ever been away from the estate."

"Oh how sad. No wonder you know no-one in the ton. I will be your friend and introduce you to everyone, Lady Katherine."

"Please, will you call me Kitty, I am not used to being treated so formally and I would love to have a friend."

"I will call you Kitty only if you will call me Emily"

Kitty beamed at her, it felt so good to have met someone as kind as Emily.

In this way Kitty made her first and very important friend in London.

At first Kitty thought the balls would be lonely and difficult. She expected to be bored, but balls were less than boring, even quite exciting sometimes as she had Emily to talk to, and through Emily other young débutantes and young men. She also made friends with Jane Arbuthnot, not the brightest specimen in Kitty's eyes, but a gentle and genuine young friend. Now the chatter took on discussions about various young men and who they appeared to prefer. She learned about rakes and roués, which Kitty had never heard of before. How could she have lived to this great age without learning all this important information? Her governesses had taught her what to think, how to behave but never about men not to be trusted.

She wondered why she had to have so many outfits with matching shoes and gloves but was only allowed to wear white, the same as every other débutante, at the balls. She longed to wear something a little more colourful. It was not that white did not suit her; it was just that colours were so much more interesting.

Then came the day a week after the balls had started when they attended the Wilmots' ball. The room was overcrowded, and there were so many candles the air was thick with the scent and smoke of them. The flowers were everywhere making it difficult to find a wall to hide against and there was a buzz in the air that the débutantes were not acquainted with. Suddenly the ball was disrupted by the arrival of His Royal Highness the Prince. He never stayed long on such occasions, but looked around and spoke with a few of the aristocracy known to him. He asked to be introduced to any of the débutantes who warranted his attention. Thus it was that Kitty, as the daughter of the Duke of Wenton, was presented to His Highness.

"Wenton, good fellow. Met your brother not long ago, ..." a long pause, until the ever helpful Kitty supplied "Jeremy, Your Highness."

"That's right. Very sound fellow, extremely learned."

The Prince smiled, Kitty curtsied and he was gone.

Everyone could continue as normal.

The next grand ball Kitty attended was Lady Bertram's. Kitty was attired in yet another white dress which seemed to match the colour of the décor. The débutantes just blended in. The ballroom was, as usual, far too crowded and the heat became quite steamy with the smell of overheated people and overpowering perfume. A small knot of young ladies, plus their ever growing court, grouped themselves in a corner away from the main dancing, in an area occupied mostly by flower arrangements. The smell was heady but at least it was only flowers. Those who gave balls tried to outdo each other with exotic ways of decorating their ballrooms that included the use of unusual flowers to show their wealth.

"We don't have these at home, does anyone know what they are called?" Jane Arbuthnot queried.

"I should know but I am not completely sure." Eliza Binton looked thoughtful. "I have seen them before, but they are hothouse flowers. I think I saw them at Kew."

"Who goes to Kew these days?" Robert Fitzwilliam thought he was being superior.

Eliza stuck her nose in the air. "Some people should find something better to do than gambling and drinking." She was far too polite to mention anything else she was not exactly sure about. He had dipped his toe in the other pursuits that young men indulged in but was not really dissolute yet.

Robert looked a little chagrined.

Jane Arbuthnot looked up sweetly into his face. "I have never been to Kew, Mr Fitzwilliam, have you?"

"I admit I have not." He was rather taken with Jane. She was quieter than his cousin Emily and quite adorable. Pale blond hair and a clear alabaster skin, she was an English beauty and would be an asset on any man's arm, he thought.

"There you are then!" Emily leapt in with encouragement to both of them. "I suggest we get up a party to visit the hothouses at Kew."

There were various opinions given, some of the girls were a little nervous at visiting such an unusual place, some of the young men were reticent, but between them an outing was arranged to Kew for a few days later.

Kitty found herself with a varied party of young people, gazing at a very large and strange looking plant.

"It grows so large because of all the rain in the rainforest." self appointed expert Eliza Binton expounded. Kitty listened half heartedly. It was very steamy in the hothouse but at least they were not outside, where the weather was rather changeable. A sudden pounding of rain on the glass roof brought an influx of gentlemen. Their loud voices prevented the small group from concentrating on Eliza's speculative information.

"Good afternoon ladies and gentlemen. The weather seems to have driven us undercover."

He walked forward followed by three others including the official foreman.

Consternation reigned as the young group recognised the Prince and curtsied and bowed, struck utterly dumb by the royal proximity. The Prince looked from one to another until he saw a recognisable face.

"Ah, Lady Katherine, are you enjoying your visit to Kew?"

"Indeed, Your Highness, it is most instructive."

"And what have you been discovering?"

"Well Your Highness, Miss Binton was telling us about this very large specimen and why it grows so tall." She had not actually taken in anything else Eliza had said. Kitty looked at Eliza and the others for some support but rigor mortis could have set in for all the help she was given.

The Prince was somewhat amused by the spectacle and inclined to enliven this enforced change to his planned itinerary.

"Come, Lady Katherine, shall we see what else we can find to enlighten you." At which he encouraged Kitty forward to another exhibit. He waved the foreman forward to impart his genuine knowledge and beckoned the silent group to join them.

A full ten minutes later, when the rain had ceased enough to venture outside, the Prince took his leave and with his friends departed amid bows and curtsies from everyone there.

Robert Fitzwilliam was the first to gain his voice. "I was unaware you knew the Prince so well, Lady Katherine."

"I don't." Kitty exploded. "I was introduced to him at the Wilmots' ball last week."

"Well you seemed to keep the conversation all to yourself."

"I didn't see any of you willing to speak. I tried to encourage you to help but you all looked away."

Emily was the one who came to her aid. "Leave her alone, Robert, what was she supposed to do, ignore him? I didn't see you joining in."

So, a little shaken, the visit continued. But for Kitty the pleasure was gone.

Chapter 2

It was hard to say exactly when she first noticed the attitude of some of the ladies. They seemed to be casting glances while they had their heads together. Conversations ceased when she walked past and less young men asked her to dance. Even her young friends seemed reluctant to include her in their group. Aunt Jane told her she was imagining it.

* * *

"I think I shall give Lady Filbert's garden party a miss." The Prince was feeling bored with the expectations put on him. He was irritable for some reason and had no desire to be pleasant to the general ton.

"If you are sure, Your Highness." His valet brushed down his sleeves and straightened his shoulders while Sir William looked on with amusement.

"I suppose it would be best given the rumours."

The Prince looked pointedly at Sir William.

"What rumours?"

"Your latest little plaything. Although I must say you are not usually interested in virginal seventeen year olds."

"What plaything? What are you talking about, man?"

Sir William raised his eyebrows.

"The Duke of Wenton's young chit. It's all over the ton. Some even say you are setting her up as your mistress. I would advise against it, Your Highness. As a single young woman, any child she produced could become a problem for the crown."

The Prince stared in horror. "Where have these rumours come from? Who makes up such lies? Good God, man, you don't believe them do you?"

"Well you did seem rather taken with her."

"Taken, what do you mean, taken? I have only met her a couple of times. She seemed pleasant enough, not quite the normal silent panic I usually meet, but that was all it was. You were there with me when I met her."

"Well the ton seems convinced. Perhaps the young lady herself has ambitions. She is the daughter of one of the senior dukes after all. She might have ideas to raise her station."

The colour rose in his face as his anger rose.

"Does she, by God! Well she is just about to learn what happens when you try to manipulate me."

Sir William inclined his head. "As you say, Your Highness. Are you going to the garden party?

"Will she be there?"

"Oh I imagine so."

"Then I will be going" he bit through his teeth.

* * *

Kitty was looking forward to the garden party although she was a little apprehensive. Emily would be there and she would not be left with only Aunt Jane. She wore pale blue muslin with darker ribbons. Her bonnet was trimmed with a matching blue ribbon. She carried a parasol with her to which she was very attached.

Everything suddenly turned to a nightmare for Kitty at the garden party. It had been unusually good weather for early May, such that Lady Filbert's 'at home' had expanded to an outdoor gathering. The sun shone so strongly that most of the ladies were carrying parasols, some for the first time this year.

About half way through the afternoon the Prince arrived. Everyone remarked they had never seen him in such a temper.

Kitty had been walking with Emily and Jane Arbuthnot and they sat to rest on a bench under a tree. Jane was loath to stop and exhorted Emily to walk with her, probably because she had sighted a young man both wished to become acquainted with. Emily complied but Kitty preferred to sit quietly alone.

The first she was aware she was not alone was the sound of angry breathing behind her. She turned to find the Prince glaring at her. She quickly stood and curtsied to him.

"Your Highness."

"Perhaps, madam, you care to tell me the reason for this? If you think to gain any standing by it you are sadly mistaken. All you have succeeded in doing is to ruin your own reputation!"

Kitty looked stunned. He radiated anger and it was all directed at her.

"I do not understand, Your Highness." she stammered. "What have I done to make you so angry?"

The Prince glared at her.

"Why did you start such rumours, or are you claiming innocence? If so it will do you no good!"

Kitty bit back the tears that welled.

"If you could tell me what rumours, Your Highness, I may better understand your anger."

The Prince's anger seemed to diminish in confusion.

"I am assured that we are intimate, madam, and that I am setting you up as my mistress."

Kitty's senses reeled, her face blanched and her knees started to buckle beneath her. She leaned against the bench for support. How could he think such a thing of her? For a few moments her head spun but as she gained control of her wits the shock was replaced with anger. Forgetting who she was speaking to she pulled herself to her full regal height and retorted in a highly emotional voice "How dare you sir! I am not and have no intentions of ever being any man's mistress. I will not be accused of such an unconscionable action by anyone. Even if you were the King of En........Oh." She stopped and the colour rushed back to her face if only for a moment.

The Prince blinked. He was unused to being spoken to this way and came to sit on the bench in shock; perhaps she was as innocent as she appeared. He was genuinely confused.

"Please sit, Lady Katherine, before you fall down."

Kitty subsided onto the far end of the bench with relief.

"Do I understand that you know nothing of these rumours?"

"No, Your Highness, I have heard nothing. Although I have noted a change in the way some of the ton react to me." Her voice was thin and quavered. The Prince looked intrigued.

"In what way?"

"There are not as many young men asking me to dance and other debutantes seem to be too busy with their mamas to speak to me. If there is anything I can do to prove them false, sire, only tell me what?"

She stared at the floor as he sat thoughtfully, taking in all she had said, then anger began to show in his face again.

"If this is true, Lady Katherine, then someone has planned a very evil joke on both of us. My advisors have 'advised against me taking a young girl as a mistress' as if they believed it to be true."

"What can I say or do, sire? I am at a loss."

He thought for a moment.

"It is useless to deny rumours, it only makes them more eager to believe it is true. For the sake of both of us, but especially for you, the rumours must be allowed to die quickly. How long that will take I cannot tell, but we must never be seen speaking. It would be better if I never acknowledge you or speak to you again. It will give this whole problem a better chance of being seen for what it is, a malicious rumour."

He stood and turned to her.

"I apologise if I have distressed you with my anger. I wish you well in the future, my lady. I would not have your reputation ruined in this way. You have my assurances our association is at an end. You will never hear from me again, ma'am. Good day to you."

The Prince gave a small bow and departed, leaving a stunned Kitty still sitting where he had left her.

Some time later when she had calmed herself, she rose to leave the shade of the tree. The sun still held warmth and she realised she no longer had her parasol. Returning to the bench she searched but could find no trace of it. Systematically she searched every place she had visited during the afternoon in the vain hope that she had left it somewhere, but there was no sign of it. Anxiously she sought out her aunt.

"Aunt Jane, I cannot find my parasol." Tears were welling in her eyes. The ladies sitting near her aunt took great interest in her discomfort, attributing it to the confrontation with the Prince. Aunt Jane was unconcerned.

"Pull yourself together, girl. Stop getting yourself into such an unseemly state over a parasol that is easily replaced."

Quietly Kitty replied "No Aunt it cannot. It is the first time I have used it, it was my mother's."

* * *

Over the next two weeks Kitty's distress increased. Many of the ladies gave her the cut direct; she received few invitations to 'at homes' and the essence of her partners changed. Now they had a look and feel about them that made Kitty's skin crawl and her stomach curl into knots. She wanted to refuse them but Aunt Jane insisted. When they asked her to dance it was Aunt Jane who replied. Her aunt kept to her side to direct her and in doing so prevented her from being totally alone.

By the time those two weeks had passed a small ray of hope and relief came into her life in the guise of her brother Jeremy.

Jeremy surged over the doorstep and reached to hug Kitty.

"Kitty, it's good to see you. And how is my little sister, taking the ton by storm I expect?"

Kitty looked up into his face and opened her mouth to speak but all it emitted was a sob.

"My God, Kitty, whatever is the matter?"

Still no words would come. She clung to her brother's hands as if he were her only lifeline.

"Peters, where is Miss Marsden?"

"I believe she is visiting a friend, my lord."

"Have some tea sent to the library will you."

Peters bowed. "Yes, my lord." and retreated tactfully as a good butler should.

"Now Kitty, come into the library and tell me what is troubling you."

Some little time later when tea had been drunk, or hiccupped over in the case of Kitty, Jeremy had heard about the Prince and the rumours, the ton ladies and the loss of dance partners. Jeremy sat stony faced.

"And no-one has said anything to you?"

"No, the only conversation is with the horrible men Aunt Jane makes me dance with. Most of the time I don't understand what they are talking about."

It took Jeremy a few minutes of intense encouragement to extract the information he needed.

"Kitty, do you know what a carte blanche is?"

"No, not really. I have heard the name before but I never understood what it meant."

"It means, little sister, that they are asking you to give your body to them."

15

Kitty still did not fully understand. "Give, you mean like a courtesan?" Horror filled her voice.

"Even worse than that."

Silence reigned for quite some time as she tried to understand quite what was happening. The tears streamed down her face until it was red and blotchy and her eyes were red rimmed. Eventually Jeremy broke the silence.

"Does Aunt Jane know?"

"Most of it she does, but she doesn't think anything is wrong. She says I am imagining it. I haven't told her what the men said to me, I thought she would laugh at me."

"I doubt she would have understood what they meant." His face was twisted with anger. "I told father she was the wrong person to bring you out. She is not capable of chaperoning you. It's my fault, I should have come with you. I knew there was liable to be a problem at some time, but not this bad. From now on Kitty, I will be staying with you and I will sort this out."

He moved restlessly around the room trying to work out what to do next. The first thing he needed was information. He needed to know just what the rumours were and why the ton was taking them so seriously.

Jeremy walked into Whites to be greeted by ribald laughter from one of the tables. A group of his friends sat quietly at a table in the corner contemplating their glasses, aware of his progress across the room.

"May I join you?" He was directed to an empty chair. The steward moved forward to take his request.

"A very large brandy, your best, if you will. And just for the record, fighting is not allowed in Whites is it?"

"No, my lord." The steward departed with haste. Jeremy turned slowly to his silent friends.

"So, it seems you are safe from me here. When I decide who is going to get killed I will need to wait until we leave. Morton, cat got your tongue?"

Phillip Morton, one of Jeremy's closest friends from Eton spoke in a slightly higher voice than usual.

"Wellmore, good to see you. You seem a little aggressive, friend."

"Are you my friend. Morton? Who is? Can I trust any of you? Should I just call out the whole ton, because I am going to need convincing that there are any gentlemen I can trust any more."

The steward arrived with his brandy and placed it on the table. Jeremy took it in his hands and took a large swallow.

"So who is going to tell me?"

Carstairs turned to face him.

"What do you want to know?"

"What are these rumours, and don't tell me you don't know. It appears the whole ton both knows and believes them."

"We were rather loath to upset you. We hoped they would die down but it seems they are getting worse." Carstairs felt the need for brandy. It was Phillip Morton who began.

"It started with a rumour she was involved with the Prince. We ignored it as spite from someone. The next, he was setting her up as his mistress. That was so unlikely we presumed everyone would ignore it. The worst are the latest." he stopped too embarrassed to continue.

"Go on, you have my complete attention."

Carstairs looked pointedly at him.

"Don't vent your anger on us, Wellmore. We have nothing to do with them."

"Did you deny them? She's my little sister, for God's sake, why did none of you get in touch with me?"

Morton started at his glass.

"We didn't know what to believe, especially the latest rumours. Half say she turned him down, the other half say he threw her off. We do know they had a very public argument at Lady Filbert's garden party. Most of the ton saw it."

Jeremy sipped at his brandy.

"Well then, you and the ton should be extremely pleased with themselves. It is just what they love to do. One totally naïve innocent has had her whole future destroyed by them. Need I say, nothing of the ton's rumours is true? And yes I know I am her brother, but there is no doubt about it. She has not understood any of what is going on, and I may yet call out several of our more adventurous acquaintances.

How would you feel if your frightened little sister was offered a carte blanche by half the ton. She is seventeen years old and a complete innocent. I am more than likely to kill someone!"

"Wellmore….."

"It's a bit late to become a caring friend, isn't it? I shall take her home and deal with the ton one man at a time. Maybe I should start

17

some rumours about prominent ladies of the ton. They at least would be believable, and probably true!"

Jeremy drained his glass and stood to leave. As he turned, Victor Penwold, a rather unpleasant specimen of manhood, rose from his chair and approached him, a smirk across his face.

"How is your delightful sister, Wellmore?" he sneered.

Jeremy walked to face him.

"Are you referring to my innocent seventeen year old debutante sister who you offered a carte blanche to, you even offered to teach her how to satisfy a prince, and all in the middle of the ballroom?"

Penwold smirked. Jeremy took a deep breath and half turned away his right shoulder. He brought his fist into Penwold's face with all the strength he had. His hand would hurt like hell later, but it was worth it to see Penwold on the floor, blood streaming from nose and lip.

"Anyone else? Later perhaps."

Jeremy turned to all around, made a small ironic bow. "Good afternoon, gentlemen." At which he walked out.

Chapter 3

It was starting to spit with rain when Jeremy left Whites. Although it was a long walk home he considered he needed the time to be calm enough to deal with what he must when he arrived back at the house. The increasing rain helped to cool his temper and time spent walking allowed for his hand to stop hurting quite so much. While fairly fit, he was, after all, a classical scholar not a prize fighter. He very rarely went to Jacksons Boxing Emporium as he was never in town.

He rapped the door with his left hand, not because he did not have his key, he did, but he needed Peters in immediate attendance.

"My lord, you are extremely wet. Shall I call your valet to prepare a bath?" Peters looked quite concerned.

"Take my coat if you will and ask Swanson to bring a dry shirt and smoking jacket to the study. Dry feet would be good also." He let the butler help him out of his coat with difficulty.

"My lord, your hand is hurt."

"Self inflicted and in a very good cause. Where are Lady Kitty and Aunt Jane?"

"Lady Kitty is in her room refusing to go out, Lady Marsden is in the parlour insisting she does."

"Ask Lady Marsden to join me in the study, will you. I am loath to drip on the parlour carpet."

"Of course, my lord, a wise choice if I may say so."

Jeremy retreated to the study to drip until his valet arrived with dry clothing. He poured himself a brandy. Settling himself in the leather chair behind the desk, he awaited Aunt Jane.

"Good grief, Jeremy, you are soaking wet, go and change at once." Aunt Jane arrived with her usual dictatorial verve.

"Indeed I am, Aunt Jane, all the better to cool my temper."

He never moved a muscle as he sat holding his glass, staring at her.

"Perhaps you could explain what has happened with Kitty, as you are supposed to be her official chaperone."

"What do you mean, what has happened? I have no idea, she just refuses to go out. There is no understanding her." Jane sank stiffly onto an upright chair close to the door. "She gets such silly childish ideas."

"Ideas, what kind of ideas?" His sarcasm showed.

"She is too sensitive, she lets things upset her too easily."

"What kind of things, Aunt Jane?" His voice was not the normal Jeremy, his face taking on rising colour. Aunt Jane was beginning to sense his anger.

"You know young girls, nobody wants to dance with her, her friends are ignoring her. Just silly ideas."

His voice was unusually cold for the jovial Jeremy she was used to. It made Jane stop and narrow her eyes into a frown.

"Who dances with her Aunt? Young men of good family or older men of indifferent honour? And what do they say to her?"

"Most of the time it made no sense. I have no idea what she was complaining about."

"Tomorrow morning I am taking Kitty back to the hall. Whether you come is up to you, but I can assure you that you are no longer her chaperone. You may be required to answer for your behaviour to father when you choose to call. I suggest you consult with your closest friends if you do not know how badly you have served my sister. For make no mistake, Aunt Jane, Kitty's reputation is ruined through no fault of her own. If you ever believe a word of what the rumours say, I would suggest you do not try to visit the hall again."

"What rumours?

"The ones you should have rebutted." He was almost shouting now. Luckily for Jane the valet tapped on the door, bringing his dry clothes. She made a grateful escape.

"Are you sure you would not prefer a bath, my lord."

"No. Swanson, I have too much to do for now. Maybe later, although I would like something I can eat with one hand." He lifted his right hand and gave his valet a rueful look."

"I will fetch something for your hand, my lord."

"Can you also tell Aleen, Kitty's maid, I would like to see her, and Swanson, pack our bags. We are leaving in the morning."

The valet looked surprised "We have only just arrived, my lord, I have barely unpacked. I will of course attend to it right away." he finished hastily.

The rest of the evening was full of arrangements. Kitty's maid was instructed to pack all Kitty's belongings as she would not be returning to London. A tearful and shaken Kitty was relieved at not having to face the ton again, whatever the cost. The explanation had been painful but Jeremy was as gentle as possible and home offered peace of mind and a return to friendly faces and normal routine.

The following morning the travelling carriage conveyed a strangely silent Jeremy and an increasingly pensive Kitty the short distance from Wenton House to Wenton Hall.

Their arrival caused something of a stir as Jeremy had only just left, and Kitty was not expected at all.

Jeremy spent the whole afternoon closeted with his father in the study discussing the details as known, the cause and the ramifications for Kitty and for the rest of the family. Carina also could be substantially damaged if this scandal were allowed to remain.

The Duke was thoughtful and reserved when he spoke to Kitty later.

"This is a sad business, my dear. We will find some way to clear your name but it may take some time. Unfortunately the mealy mouthed tabbies like their scandal, no matter who it hurts.

"Why me, papa? I did nothing wrong and I was only there for a few weeks before it started. I have to admit I had no idea what was going on. When I queried things with Aunt Jane she kept saying I was imagining it."

"Yes, well, I am afraid Aunt Jane was my mistake. I should have listened to your brother. She never had a come out herself but I thought she was sensible enough. Obviously not sufficiently to understand the ton workings." He rubbed his hand down his face, as if trying to wipe away the thought of it.

"I asked Jeremy to discuss having a ball or party in London for your birthday next week, but I suppose that is the last thing you would want."

"Indeed, papa, I would rather be quiet at home here with the family, if you please."

"Whatever will please you, my little one. Shall we have a family dinner with just those we can trust?"

"Thank you, papa, that would be best."

So arrangements were made for a family dinner at Wenton Hall the following week with just a few close friends. There were a couple of the Duke's friends invited, but Kitty was never to be told of the Duke's ulterior motive which was to show his damaged daughter as the innocent she was, thereby hopefully starting the rebuff of the rumours.

The day of Kitty's birthday, the sun shone and the air was fresh and warm and the outdoors inviting.

"Good morning, and a happy birthday, Lady Kitty." Aleen, Kitty's maid was bright and breezy. Quite excited for her mistress's special day.

"Good morning, Aleen, is that hot chocolate?"

"Yes, my lady. I know you usually rise for breakfast but today is your birthday and cook thought you should have a little treat."

Kitty laughed. "You are all trying too hard to cheer me up. I assure you, Aleen, I am not down in the least." She swung her legs out of bed. "Come, let me drink it while you lay out my birthday morning attire. Then I will go down to breakfast, no doubt to be fawned on by the others."

There had been so many dark and dreary days but today was so lovely and bright that Kitty put on a pale yellow morning dress with deeper yellow ribbons. Her hair was in a loose chignon at the back of her head and threaded with matching yellow ribbons. She looked like sunshine herself, as her father remarked when he greeted her at breakfast.

Jeremy was just rising from the table. He strode forward, beaming, to plant a kiss on her forehead.

"Happy eighteenth birthday, not so little sister."

Carina rushed to give her a hug. "Come and have breakfast and then you can open all your presents. Miss Phelps is expecting me upstairs, so hurry before I have to go."

"I am afraid I will have to forego the pleasure of watching you, Kitty." Jeremy said. "I have to ride over to the Ballstons' place to give the vicar a theology book he especially wants to work with before the weekend. But I will not be gone very long and then the rest of my day I am at your service." He grinned and waggled his eyebrows.

"I shall hold you to that Jeremy. It is after all my day."

"Indeed but do not keep me, the sooner I leave the sooner I will be back."

Jeremy strode out as Kitty chose her breakfast, toast with a little conserve.

"Tea if you please Wilkins." She smiled up at the footman, who could not help but smile back.

"What are you going to do after opening your presents?"

"I have not yet decided, papa, but it is such a beautiful day it must be out of doors."

"Good, enjoy whatever you decide to do, but do not overtire yourself, for we have your birthday dinner this evening. I imagine our guests will be arriving quite early." He had a quite conspiratorial look on his face as he left the breakfast room and a laughing Kitty.

The first present Kitty opened was from Jeremy. A beautifully tooled leather bound diary. Carina was almost jumping with excitement as she opened the present from her. Three beautifully embroidered handkerchiefs.

"Oh, Carina, these are so beautiful, they must have taken you ages. You are far better at embroidery than I am." Carina hugged her again.

"Do you really like them?"

"Of course I do. How could I not? They are just delightful. Now I want to finish my breakfast, so off with you. Go on to Miss Phelps or she will give me black looks and I will not permit that today of all days. It is only for the morning, today."

Carina fairly skipped to the door, then remembered she was supposed to be a demure young lady. She slowed to a stately walk, nose in the air and a twinkle in her eye.

The next present Kitty opened was from her father. She had wanted to be alone when she opened this one. A beautiful set of diamond and pearl ear bobs, set in gold filigree. It was all she could do not to cry in pleasure. Finishing her breakfast she set off to find her father, but he was busy with his steward. She would thank him later.

As she started up the stairs to her room, the butler spoke to her.

"Excuse me, Lady Kitty, this has just been delivered for you." He held out a package. The only writing on the parcel was her name.

"Who delivered this, Wilson?"

"A servant in a black carriage, my lady. He was dressed in livery but not one I was able to recognise."

She took the parcel and carried it to her room where her maid was waiting for her.

"Look, Aleen. This has just arrived for me."

She untied the string and opened the brown paper. Inside was a parasol. It was made of silk of the most beautiful colours which shimmered in the light. The handle was ivory and the shaft was made of metal instead of wood. The silk was frilled and must have been very frilled inside as the shape was extremely bulbous to the point of being almost round. Around the spokes and the lower edge of the silk was a fine string with a label attached. Kitty lifted the label and read it.

To Kitty on your eighteenth birthday
HRH

Kitty let the label drop, a cold shiver running through her. Anger then followed. How dare he! He said no contact. How will everyone react to this?

"I don't want it!"

"But it is beautiful, my lady."

"It is the parasol of a Paris courtesan. I have never seen anything so expensive in all my life."

"Can I just open it to see, my lady?"

"You can keep it. I want nothing of it, it is an insult!"

Aleen tried to untie the fine string but the knots were too tight and the string too thin.

"I shall have to cut the string, my lady. Do you have your needlework scissors here?"

Kitty looked at the string. "They will not cut that. You will need a sharp knife from the kitchen."

Much against her better judgement Kitty went with Aleen and the parasol downstairs to where the butler was giving instruction to a footman.

"Can I help you, my lady?"

"We need a sharp knife from the kitchen, Wilson. We will walk around to the sundial, it you could send someone to us there." The butler was surprised by her manner, on this day in particular. She had been so bright earlier. "Of course, my lady."

Turning to the footman he said "You heard Lady Kitty, Simpkins, a sharp knife to the sundial at once." Simpkins made a quick bow and left at speed.

"Shall we go?" Aleen was very excited. After all it may not have been sent to her, but it is not often a lady's maid gets to own a parasol sent by a prince, and such a beautiful one.

The sundial was on the south side of the hall on the terrace by the large dining room, where there was much activity for the evening dinner. The terrace was a fairly spacious square area bounded on three sides by the house. The fourth side was grass which reached down to the lake and was dotted with ornate topiary bushes at various points. She had chosen this area because it was not far from the kitchens, plus Aleen would be able to lean the parasol on the base of the sundial to cut the string.

Kitty liked the sundial. It was quite newly installed, a plinth with an ornate filigree metal sundial of quite a large size. It must be heavy, hence the strong base, big and tall enough to lean on.

While Aleen was impatient, Kitty was trying to deal with her feelings. Anger mostly. If anyone knew of this they would think the rumours true. She was cross and tearful that it should spoil a day which started so well and confused, how was she going to deal with this? She wished Jeremy was there.

The kitchen maid came running from around the side of the house, fearful she would be chastised for having taken too long. Kitty walked away wishing she had let Aleen come alone. She stood on the grass some feet away.

The kitchen maid gave the knife to Aleen and backed away to wait for it to be returned. Aleen placed the parasol on the plinth and they both watched as she cut into the cord. What happened next only Kitty could ever relate.

As the knife cut into the string, black powder started to spill from inside the parasol. The knife struck the metal shaft and the gunpowder exploded.

To Kitty, everything seemed to happen in slow motion. She could feel she was in the air moving backwards, her feet not on the ground. The windows of the house shattered inwards and the screams of those inside as they were showered with glass were as if from another world. The kitchen maid was also blown backwards, but she hit the wall of the house and slid to the floor like a broken rag doll. But Aleen, her maid, her friend!

Aleen's hands moved outwards with the blast, but kept moving away from her body, not attached any more. The sundial flew upwards from its plinth and sliced into her neck making her head fall back and the blood… Oh God, the blood.

At that point Kitty hit the topiary bush and was impaled on and in it. Her senses gave out and blackness slid over her.

That was the point at which Kitty's life changed completely. She stopped being the naïve Kitty, her innocence was gone. From now on she would be an adult woman who needed to learn to deal with her own life. For no-one would ever be able to take those images from her memory.

Chapter 4

It was a gardener who found Kitty about half an hour after the blast. The house was in uproar, the kitchen staff and maids coping with those covered in shards of glass, the footmen and butler with the Duke found the dismembered remains of Aleen on the terrace and the crumpled form of the kitchen maid at the foot of the house wall. Kitty was nowhere to be seen.

The Duke sent to her room to check she was safe. When his wits returned from the shock, the butler remembered Kitty had been outside with Aleen. Footmen and gardeners were dispatched in all directions in case she had run in horror and was somewhere in deep shock.

Eventually they came to remove Aleen's body and a young gardener who could not cope with the horrific spectacle, turned and faced away from the house. He registered the yellow flowers on the topiary bush which seemed odd. Topiary bushes did not have flowers. Closer inspection revealed Kitty, unconscious and deeply embedded in the bush, the branches wrapped around her like arms holding her close.

It took a small team of gardeners a great deal of time with pruning cutters to free Kitty from the bush's clutches. Her hair was so wrapped into the foliage and the branches so embedded in her skull they had to cut off her hair to free her.

The doctor had already been called to help the staff with glass cuts when Kitty was eventually freed, laid on her bed face down and tended by the housekeeper, Mrs Alford and Kitty's old nanny Binny, now otherwise employed in the house since Kitty and Carina had grown up. Her clothes were cut from her and under the supervision of the doctor, the sharp twigs were gradually removed from her back and head. As each area was cleaned the doctor checked for splinters and the wounds were washed and salved. It was a long job. At one point Kitty regained consciousness but her pain was so great the doctor gave her laudanum to send her back into a kind of sleep.

It took two hours after which the wounds were covered to keep off the air and Kitty was left to sleep. A small fire was lit to prevent a chill as it would have been too painful to lay covers over her.

Jeremy and the Duke turned away guests as they arrived with as little explanation as possible. Later in the library they sat with drink in hand, the Duke silent and frowning with shock, Jeremy getting gradually drunk to drown the pain. Carina was given a potion to help her sleep and was tended by her maid and Miss Phelps who strove to deal with her hysterical bouts of sobbing and pleas to be allowed to go to Kitty.

The next morning, the Duke went out to assess the damage. The windows on the ground floor had been boarded up for security, but the terrace was badly stained. A builder must be found to repair and replace the windows and the terrace must be re-laid. First the stains must be removed to limit the evidence of what had happened to any of the outside world.

The gardeners, glad to be of real use at this terrible time, were set to remove the evidence from the terrace ready for re-laying the area. A message was sent to a builder who had previously worked on Wenton House in London, with an urgent request for assistance.

Some time in the early afternoon, the Duke sat staring into empty space in his study, when Wilson the butler tapped gently on his door.

"Beg pardon, my lord, but what should be done with the non human items from the terrace area?"

"Non human? What items, Wilson?"

"There is some twisted metal and silk fragments from the parasol she was carrying. It may have been the cause of the blast, my lord."

"Parasol, Aleen or Kitty?"

"I believe it could have been a birthday present for Lady Kitty, but Aleen was carrying it. They also found this."

The butler put out his hand which held a piece of burnt card attached to a piece of singed string. It read.

To Kitty on y
   HRH

The Duke was silent for a few moments as the butler waited.

"Wilson will you have my valet pack an overnight bag and arrange for the coach to be brought round in half an hour, I shall be going to London immediately."

It was a stone faced Duke who went to check on Kitty's health before finding Jeremy brooding deeply.

"I am going to London in a few minutes. I should be back by tomorrow night. You will have to deal with any problems which arise. Keep an eye on Kitty and don't let Carina get hysterical again." His cold determination showed in his every feature.

"What are you planning on doing?"

Holding out the card he answered curtly.

"Getting some bloody answer to this!"

The Duke's arrival in London brought initial delight to his staff. Aunt Jane, he discovered, was still in residence but preparing to leave. His manner of questioning and his demeanour soon brought a sombre mood on the house. No intelligence of the explosion had reached London so at least he was spared having to discuss it at home.

His first action was to send a message to the Prime Minister asking for an urgent meeting of the highest importance, preferably first thing in the morning. The Prime Minister, whilst not a close friend of the Duke, knew him well enough to read the importance and acquiesced to his request.

Dinner that evening was a chilly affair, with Aunt Jane unaware of her brother-in-law's reason for his icy disdain. She tried to explain what she had eventually learned and how distraught she had been. To think, all her closest friends knew what was being said but never spoke to her on the matter.

The Duke reminded her that as chaperone she should have been aware of the problems, have been looking for them, that a little response from her could have denied the rumours and saved them from all this trouble.

Neither of them ate much, the cook was in despair.

The following morning the Duke was admitted to the PM's office by a sharp eyed young man. The Prime Minister strode forward, hand outstretched.

"Wenton, to what do we owe this precipitous meeting?" The Duke looked at the retreating young man.

"Don't worry about Willoughby, he always looks that way, he says it frightens off malingerers." He gestured to a chair.

"Do come and sit down."

"How much do you know about the on-dits. The rumour-mongering of the ton?"

"Too busy to listen to the tittle tattle, but my wife did mention there had been a bit of a problem. I'm not sure how I can help with that."

"None of it is true, she only met the Prince twice and in public with others there. The third time at the garden party, His Highness was angry when he arrived and accused her of starting the rumours for some reason. Apparently he swore not to speak to her or contact her in any way, to let the rumours die down. She was upset because someone took her parasol."

"Her parasol?" The Prime Minister's face held a bemused question.

"Yes, after the accusations of his highness the loss really upset her. Apparently it was her mother's parasol."

"Your late wife's. I can imagine it would distress her in that case." He still looked bemused.

"So if there is to be no connection with His Highness, perhaps you could tell me what to do about this?"

The Duke handed him the tell tale card with its message. The Prime Minister took it and raised his eyebrows.

"This was the label attached to a parasol sent to Kitty for her birthday. It was filled with gunpowder and has blown out half the windows of the hall, killed Kitty's maid and a kitchen maid and impaled Kitty in a bush with major damage to her back and head. She is lucky to be alive. That is if she recovers."

"My God, Winton. This isn't just a minor on-dit problem is it? I can go to the Prince, of course, but the workload is heavy for the next week and this definitely must not be delayed. Let me get Willoughby to bring up some coffee and we can think this thing through."

He went to the door and looked into the outer office. "Coffee please, Willoughby."

"Already on its way, sir."

"Good man."

The Prime Minister returned to his seat and held his forehead with one hand.

"While I can ask questions, Wenton, I don't have the time or the ability to follow through with any awkward scenarios. How would you feel if I suggested someone from the Foreign Office to look into it for you?"

"An official investigation, you mean."

"Not exactly. There is someone I know of, more or less retired from the Foreign Office now, good man, very discreet."

Willoughby arrived with the coffee. He poured a cup for both of them, then sensing the pregnant silence, left with all speed.

"When you say discreet, do I take it we are talking ex- spy?"

"Not exactly, more in the way of ex-spymaster with men and connections he can call on. On good friendly terms with the Prince too. Gets to speak to him alone if necessary!"

"How soon can you arrange it?"

"If he is in town, I am sure he will respond very promptly if I send him a note. I can have Willoughby deliver it. How do you say?"

"Yes, with grateful thanks! I had no idea how to proceed."

The Prime Minister took out a sheet of paper and opened his inkwell. It was a short note and to the point.

"Willoughby, have this delivered immediately, will you." and turning to the Duke. "Have you breakfasted?"

"No, had no stomach for it."

"I suggest you go and avail yourself of some food or at least a fortifying drink. Call back in an hour or so and see if we have a reply."

The Duke clasped his hand, too full of thanks to speak. He left with just a ray of hope that had not been there before.

Outwardly the Duke appeared calm but his stomach churned. Maybe the coffee had been a bad idea. Finding a table in the least dubious looking inn, he ordered a slice of pie and a pint of porter. A pity it was too early for brandy, whisky was not normally to his taste, best keep to something lighter. Even so, swallowing took concentration. Maybe the Prime Minister was right. His stomach did begin to settle.

A little over an hour later he walked into Willoughby's office to be greeted with an affable smile. "The Prime Minister is in a meeting, but asked me to give you this, my lord."

The note read 'Will be at Whites from 11 a.m. Please tell Lord Wenton I would be pleased to take lunch with him. Danvers.'

"Willoughby, please give the Prime Minister my most grateful thanks. I will no doubt be in touch in the future. I may not take an active part in politics, but if he ever needs an extra vote for a bill, I will be more than willing if I am available."

Leaving the Prime Minister's office, he went in search of his coachman, much quicker than sending a boy. He was eager to meet this ex-spymaster.

Danvers was intrigued. What had the Prime Minister's note said, 'utmost discretion needed, innocent murdered, Prince involved. Duke of Wenton needs urgent help', well the war was over and what was there to occupy his ever active brain. Perhaps a small intrigue would help stave off the boredom of ton life.

The Duke of Wenton, now wasn't that his daughter caught up in the rumours about Prinny? This could just prove to be amusing, given the Prince's appreciation of a pretty face,

Barely had he ordered a coffee from the steward when a gentleman of around fifty years old was being ushered in his direction. He stood to greet him.

"Wenton, good to meet you." He held out his hand. The Duke shook it.

"Danvers. Not good to meet you in these circumstances, but grateful for any help you can give."

The Duke settled into a chair and waved the steward away.

"I have, of course, heard the on-dits about your daughter. I presume that is the basis of your problem."

"That is the start of the problem. I had no idea what was being said and her aunt seemed totally blinkered. Where and why the rumours started I have no idea, but let me assure you they are all totally untrue."

"What about the argument with the Prince?"

"He thought she had started the rumours and was extremely angry as you may imagine. She had not even heard them. Her distress was not only the Prince's anger but someone took her parasol. I now believe it to be a deliberate act. She was understandably distressed as it had belonged to my late wife."

"That I can imagine. How long ago is it you lost your wife?"

"Over ten years now."

"So your daughter has had no mother for quite some while. She is obviously missing her at this time in her life. Why do you think the parasol was taken with a purpose?"

The Duke struggled to keep his composure at this point. Danvers paid attention to his coffee to give him time to settle.

"Because of this." He handed Danvers the label and watched him raise his eyebrows in surprise.

"Two days ago it was Kitty's birthday. Just after breakfast a parcel was delivered. When opened, it contained a parasol tied closed with string and this label."

"The label is incomplete, what happened to it?" Danvers interest was now fully engaged. A present from Prinny after he had been so angry. He thought a visit to his friend might just be useful.

The Duke could not stop now or he would never manage to finish what he had to say.

"Kitty's maid cut the string. The parasol was filled with gunpowder."

The Duke now definitely needed something to calm him. Danvers signalled to the steward and ordered brandy for both of them. They sat in silence until the steward returned and the Duke took a swallow.

Danvers frowned, knowing he was not going to like what came next.

"Was anyone hurt?" he asked quietly.

Best get it over with.

"A kitchen maid was killed, Kitty's maid was... dismembered, half the house windows blew in and it took half an hour to find Kitty. She is alive but she may not ...." Danvers reached out a hand and laid it on his arm to offer comfort. Good God? This was more than he had imagined. Even after all the atrocities of the war, he was shocked.

Danvers asked a few more questions and then assured the Duke he would find out all he could. He also borrowed the half label. It was not just the Duke who left Whites in turmoil that day.

It was a couple of days later when Sir Peter Danvers was shown into the receiving room where the Prince sat in a state of boredom.

"Danvers! Thank God, someone with a brain to talk to. The Prince rose from his chair to meet him in an act of genuine pleasure.

"What brings you here today? Any more traitors to be uncovered, eh?"

"Well if it is intrigue you want, sire, that I can offer, but very much in private."

"Of course, of course. Shall I show you my latest acquisition in the adjoining chamber?"

"How kind, Your Highness." They made for the corridor to the adjoining room, the prince waving away the footman and onlookers.

"I heard a few rumours about Wenton's chit" Danvers steered the discussion lightly as they walked companionably.

"Don't say even you believe those malicious rumours. I had thought better of you, Danvers. I just feel sorry for the girl."

"So none of it is true?"

"Decidedly not, although I did vent my anger on the girl, quite unlike me." Danvers thought otherwise. He continued "Even my advisers believed the rumours. The poor girl had no idea what I was shouting about. She is quite ruined, of course, and for what? Tittle tattle of some old ladies."

Danvers watched the prince's face closely. He was genuinely angry.

"You haven't spoken to her since?"

"No intention to. Let the whole matter die down and she may recover some standing, though not what it was. Diamond of the first order, Duke's daughter etc. It makes me angry to think about it. What use is it being a prince when I can do nothing to help her except keep away?"

They reached the area where the Prince had been intending for them to talk in private.

"So, what intrigue is afoot?"

Danvers took a deep calming breath and held out the label. "Can you enlighten me about this?"

The Prince took the label and stared at it.

"What the devil is this? And how did you come by it?"

"Did you send it Your Highness?"

"Send it? No, to whom may I ask?"

"It was attached to a parasol sent to Wenton's daughter. It was filled with gunpowder."

The Prince stared in disbelief. He walked to a chair and subsided onto it. It was some minutes before he spoke again.

"Is she …?"

"Lady Katherine is alive, just, for the moment. I do not yet know how badly injured she is. Two others were not so lucky. Wenton Hall seems to have suffered too."

"I want whoever did this caught, Danvers. You have the contacts, call them back. Find whoever did this."

"I have every intention of doing so, Your Highness. Starting with the ton and who started these rumours. We have enough contacts within the ton to work without detection. I have a feeling this was done for a purpose and not just jealousy of a young girl. The ramification could be huge."

"Keep me informed, Danvers."

"I will, Your Highness. One point. Did you know Lady Katherine had lost her parasol?"

"Yes, one of my advisers told me a few days later."

"One of your advisers who believed the rumours?"

The Prince stared hard at Danvers but his thoughts were looking into his memory.

Danvers prodded. "It could be …."

"You can't think…"

"Perhaps we should keep this strictly between ourselves, Your Highness."

"Indeed." said a thoughtful Prince. "Indeed."

* * *

It was late in the day when the Duke returned. His first question was about Kitty. So far she had drifted in and out of a troubled sleep, helped by the laudanum. The doctor had called twice and Binny changed the covering every two hours and used more salve.

The Duke closeted himself in his study until Jeremy could bear it no longer. He tapped gently on the door. "Papa, do you have any news?"

It was a hollow eyed Jeremy who put his head tentatively round the door.

"Come in, my boy." Jeremy sank rather than sat in the only other chair in the room.

"Yes, I have as it happens. I don't know what will come of it, but there is an investigation starting.

"By Bow Street?"

"Good Heavens, no. Much more discreet. I met Sir Peter Danvers who works for the Foreign Office, or did. It seems he was employed to run certain operatives during the wars."

"Good grief, a spymaster!"

35

"Indeed. Let's hope he can discover what is behind all of this."

"You look tired, Papa."

"But not half as bad as you do, I'll warrant."

"I can't sleep, it's true. I live in fear of the next few days."

"Brandy is not the answer, Jeremy. Get cook to give you one of her remedies and see if that helps.

"I will. At least there is some hopeful news."

The following day Kitty's condition never changed. The doctor called twice and inspected her wounds when Binny changed the dressings. Some areas were very inflamed.

As the day slid into night, Kitty began to take fever. The doctor was recalled and potions were given but to little avail. Through the night and all the following day the fever raged. Kitty tossed and tried to turn. Each movement made her cry out in pain. By the following day she was shouting in her delirium, with bouts of total silence where she hardly seemed to breathe. Binny stayed by her side only being persuaded to leave for a few moments at a time. Always someone was there. Sometimes Jeremy sat, his head bowed as if in prayer. Carina could not be allowed to visit for more than a few seconds, she was too distraught.

The Duke looked in occasionally, but not for long, his hopeless heartache was too great. He tried to keep busy but it was an impossible task. The days seemed to be unreal, like looking in from another place.

The builder arrived from London to arrange for the restoration of the hall. The discussion was fairly one sided, the Duke's senses being tuned only to the upstairs bedroom where his beloved Kitty fought for her life.

Six days after the horrific birthday, around mid morning, Danvers arrived in the hope of speaking with Kitty. Not understanding just how ill Kitty was, he stressed the importance of her view of everything that had happened.

The Duke could barely speak with him. Instead he took him out to the terrace, to the topiary bush that caught Kitty in its arms, to the dining room that was being prepared for her birthday dinner. All round the house he saw maids and footmen with evidence of glass cuts. The staff were silent or whispering. He stayed only until the end of lunch and suggested he came back at another time.

"My lord, My lord, you must come now!"

An upstairs maid with tears streaming down her face turned and ran back towards the staircase. The Duke followed slowly. Danvers stood for a moment and then followed the Duke.

Danvers watched the Duke go to the open door of his daughter's room. Binny appeared before him, crying and laughing at the same time.

"My lord, the fever has broken!"

Danvers stepped forward to support the Duke and propel him to a chair on the landing. It is not pretty to watch a grown man cry, but even Danvers could have wept, for the palpable relief that began to wash through the house. Maids ran, a not normally allowed occurrence, spreading the news. The normally stoic butler leaned behind a potted plant while he removed his handkerchief from his pocket. Jeremy appeared from somewhere and would not be denied access, as if he had to see it to believe it.

When everyone, especially Carina, had cried themselves happy, Kitty was left to rest. The men adjourned to the library and broke out the best brandy the Duke had.

Danvers was invited to stay, and dinner that evening was served with as much champagne as anyone wanted. Some of the staff awoke the following morning with very sore heads.

The following morning the full discussion of what had happened was started. Danvers spoke at great length with Jeremy about what he knew. His own reaction to the attitude of some of the ton's men matched Jeremy's reaction at Whites. The only difference being, if it had been him it would have been more than just one fist in the face, and probably outside in a back alley. Not surprisingly, Jeremy and Peter Danvers struck up a firm friendship, in spite of their vastly different backgrounds and interests.

Chapter 5

The following day a weak and increasingly uncomfortable Kitty talked to anyone allowed to visit her. All women, of course. Now she was lucid, the only member of her family allowed in was Carina.

"I don't think I can stand much more of laying face down. Even laying on my side is uncomfortable. Later in the day she was allowed to sit up to eat and drink, but pillows at her back were painful. In the evening she was helped out of bed to relieve herself and sat on one of the straight backed chairs. She wished she could talk to Jeremy and meet that Danvers fellow who had arrived to investigate.

The weight of the covers was still more than she could take, but she was allowed a nightgown. Hers were too tight for what was required, so a larger one belonging to her papa was fetched.

It pained her wounds a little to do it, but by pulling her knees up under her, with her bottom in the air, she eased some of the ache in her back.

While Binny was sent for her dinner, Miss Phelps stayed with her. She requested she sent a footman to fetch one of the straight backed chairs from the nursery - the larger size, not the baby ones.

The next time she was helped out of bed, she insisted on sitting on the nursery chair backwards, the way Jeremy often had. This meant she could lean on the back of the chair with her arms. It worked wonderfully. The seat was a little uncomfortable, but with a pillow to sit on she was content to stay that way as long as she was allowed. She would happily sleep like that.

The next day, Kitty wore the most voluminous nightshirt and a simply huge dressing gown, and bullied her helpers to take her to the private sitting room attached to the bedroom normally belonging to the duchess. They installed her backwards on the chair with a pillow to sit on and one for her to lean her arms over the top of the wooden chair back.

For a while Carina kept her company and read to her, but then Miss Phelps decided she had missed too much study over the last week and she should return to the schoolroom. Binny stayed with her until luncheon. She leaned her head down onto the pillow and slept.

She awoke when the door created a draft. Jeremy crept in.

"I am awake."

"How are you?"

"Well, all that dancing last night wore me out. How do you think I feel?"

"God it's good to see you recovering, Kitty. You gave us all such a scare."

"Not on purpose, I assure you. I could do without this."

"Do you need to sleep or would you like company?"

"What I would like, Jeremy, is to talk to this Danvers fellow who has arrived."

"Dressed like that, not allowed, little sister."

"Excuse me while I put on a fitted morning gown. Not possible for a long time yet. You can come as well, but I need to get this over, so I can relax a little better. I need to talk, Jeremy, and Danvers is the best person to talk to."

A short while later, the two entered the sitting room. The maid had been dismissed but Binny was there. Danvers looked with concern at Binny.

"Mr Danvers. Is it Mr or Lord? Please excuse me for not rising to meet you." Her voice held a playful sarcasm.

"I am indeed pleased to meet you, Lady Katherine, would that the circumstances were different. My name is actually Sir Peter Danvers, but you may call me whatever you will."

"Then I am pleased to meet you, Roderick!"

Danvers barked with laughter, as did Jeremy who was well aware of her sense of humour.

"Lady Katherine, if you could" he got no further.

"Oh, for goodness sake, call me Kitty and I will call you Danvers. How formal can we be when I am sitting her in my night attire - well papa's night attire, actually."

Jeremy joined in the conversation. "Kitty, don't tire yourself too much."

"If I become tired, big brother, you will know because my head will droop and I will cease to answer. Can we get this done while my nerve holds out, please?"

"Lady ....sorry, Kitty, tell me what you can, so I can see your understanding of what happened. If you could start from what happened in London, please."

So Kitty started from her arrival in London. As she said, anything anyone had said to her may be a part of why it happened. She detailed everything the Prince had said, especially at the garden party. She mentioned the cooling attitude of the ton before the garden party, and the appalling treatment afterwards. She left nothing and no one out. Especially she stressed the Prince promising there would be no contact of any kind again.

Danvers was impressed. "Lady Kitty, your understanding impresses me. I must say it merely adds to the knowledge I have already been given and to what I have found out. I have spoken to the Prince, who I know quite well, and he is genuinely shocked. I have his full backing to use any means I can to deal with this. He did know you had lost your parasol but not until days later. Someone close to him told him. I am hoping he can remember who it was. I would like to speak with him.

"It was because he had broken all contact between us to allow the rumours to end, that I was so angry when the parasol arrived."

"You were angry, I am not surprised. I know it will be painful but if you can be as detailed as before it will help. For this period of time there is no-one but you to give me the details I need."

Jeremy looked a little worried in case the memory was too much for her. But she started clearly enough.

"It started after breakfast when the butler announced a parcel had been delivered. You will obtain a better description of who delivered it from him than I can give."

Danvers made a note in his pocket book.

"I was angry, especially as it was a parasol. I rejected it, but Aleen, my maid went into raptures over it." Danvers nodded to her.

"Can you describe it?"

"I described it to Aleen as the kind a Parisian courtesan would carry. Not that I have ever seen one, you understand, but no lady of the ton has such a one, and nowhere in my shopping have I seen anything as exotic."

Jeremy intervened "What made you feel that way?"

"Well the silk material was so expensive, with various coloured frills over it. We presumed it had even more frills inside as it was so bulbous."

"Bulbous, it was that fat?"

"At least twelve inches across at the widest point, possibly more."

"Go on, Kitty." Jeremy was fascinated.

"The shaft was metal but not painted, the handle was carved ivory. It was the most spectacular item a lady could ever own. Then I read the label."

"Yes, the label. The prince did not send it, but someone wants everyone to believe he did."

"It would have been even worse if you had been in the house when you opened it." This from Jeremy who envisioned how much of the hall could have been damaged causing the death of untold numbers of staff. Kitty most definitely would not have survived.

"I was so angry I told Aleen she could have it. She tried to open it but it was tied too tightly. The only way was to cut it with a very sharp knife."

"That is why you went outside."

"Yes. On the way we asked Wilson to send someone for a kitchen knife to be brought to the sundial."

"Why the sundial particularly?"

"It needed somewhere flat and not too low. The plinth is rather like a small table."

"You gave it to Aleen?"

"Yes."

"That is why she cut the string?"

"Yes." Tears welled in Kitty's eyes. Her voice was low and quiet. "It was supposed to be me."

Jeremy turned to Binny.

"Tea, My lord?"

"I think so, don't you Binny."

"We will let you rest a little until after tea and then you will perhaps feel a little more able to finish this interview."

"Thank you, My lord -er- Sir Peter -er- Mr Danvers, perhaps I will."

Jeremy moved his chair close to Kitty and went to put his arm around her shoulders, pulled back just in time and laid his hand on her arm, his forehead touching hers.

"It's too much for you to cope with, Kitty."

"Well who can cope for me, Jeremy? I see what happened over and over in my head. I can tell you about it, but no one can take it from my memory. This is something I will live with for the rest of my life."

The air was heavy with emotion and everyone stayed silent, until tea arrived.

They all relaxed a little over tea. There was some almost light hearted banter. Kitty talked about the dreadful insipid tea and indifferent biscuits in London, as compared to their cook's. Her look dared anyone to criticise them.

Tea taken and the tray removed, Jeremy stayed close. A glance at Binny plus the nod she gave him showed she understood how bad this would be for her.

Kitty described waiting for the kitchen maid to arrive with the knife and how excited Aleen was. But then the time came to describe exactly what happened. The feeling of a dream as she was weightless in the air, the flight of the kitchen maid and the screams from the staff in the dining room.

"It just started when the string broke. All this dark powder spilled out. I saw when the knife hit the metal shaft and there was the spark and the nightmare began. It was as if Aleen was a doll. Her hands want sideways, torn off. The sundial flew up."

She stopped to gain some control. They waited silently.

"The sundial hit her neck. Her head fell back and there was a fountain ....a fountain of blood."

Kitty began to quake uncontrollably. Binny ran to her. Jeremy grasped her but it seemed impossible to touch her anywhere that was not damaged.

They all felt their helplessness to assist her in any way.

"Back to bed, Lady Kitty." Binny tried to chivvy her up.

"No, Binny. I will be well again in a moment. Just leave me be. This had to be told. Now it has, I can begin my life again. A different life than I originally expected, Mr Danvers. Anything more you will have to ask someone else, as I remember nothing after this."

Her voice was quiet and shaky but at least she had managed to speak. She was proud of herself.

Neither Jeremy nor Danvers could speak. Jeremy, heartbroken for his sister, but Danvers was filled with admiration for her strength under such circumstances. His thoughts were more on the lines of 'My God, what courage this woman has'.

* * *

Richard Trevane, fifth Earl of Pengarron, watched the horses race down the Newmarket straight with little interest. Viscount George Bellars, his friend, stood by his side in deep concentration, following their progress avidly.

"You don't care to wager much, do you Pengarron? You're not low on funds are you?"

"Not at the last time I checked, although my mother is doing her best."

"How is Lady Pengarron, I have not had the pleasure of seeing the lovely Lady Amelia for some time?"

"Lucky you, George. I see far too much of her these days."

"I thought you were on good terms with her. Not had a falling out, have you?"

"No. I just wish she would stop throwing eligible young débutantes at my head. I have hardly settled back into English life. It's bad enough avoiding the matchmaking mamas, at least I should be safe in my own home!"

"Oh, that kind of problem. At least I am safe from that kind of trouble. Married life is not so bad. You could try it, you know."

"I am not averse to marriage, George, I would just like to make my own choice. Life is difficult enough. Settling back into ton life after so many years behind enemy lines in France takes time."

"That's the problem, Richard. You have no interest in settling back into ton life."

"After the life I led for the last few years the inane stupidity of most of the ton is more than I can handle."

"It would not be so bad with a woman at your side."

"The right one, yes. The bland, mindless misses being pushed in my direction, most definitely not."

"If you are not enjoying the races, may I ask why you are here?"

"What else is there to do around here? With the London house off limits because of mother, I have been spending time at my box near

Thetford Forest. It is necessary to visit my properties from time to time to check them. Trevane Lodge was sadly neglected while I was away at the war, and is rarely used. Mother thinks a visit to the lodge would be a punishment. Perhaps I should instruct her to make this her home."

"As if you could."

"True. It would be impossible to make her do anything. Apart from the season, when she is in the London house, she seems to move between friends' houses. I just have to survive to the end of the season!"

Another gentleman, of middle years and superbly dressed, joined them. He was obviously known to both.

"Carvon, enjoying the races, or have you had a bad run?" Having just seen a horse he backed win the race, Viscount Bellars was in a chatty mood.

"No, quite good, as it happens. Been looking at a nice quiet little filly for Elizabeth. Her mount is getting a bit old in the tooth and I thought I might surprise her."

"Lucky Countess. Many husbands need a strong push from their wives before they even consider it."

"Do we have to talk constantly about wives, Bellars? Anyone would think you were in league with my mother."

"Amelia being persistent, Trevane? There are plenty in your position now they have returned from the war. If they have a title and more or less all their limbs, the mamas are hounding them. Dunlabe was trapped by two of them last week, he's taken himself off for Scotland, and he is missing an eye."

"I am finding life in London a strain. After the solitary life I've led for so long it is a little difficult to settle. Away from London keeping abreast of my new investments, plus parliamentary discussions, is well nigh impossible. I may have to take rooms, or live in a hotel for a few weeks."

"That sounds rather drastic, old man. Are you sure it is that bad?"

Richard, who was the youngest of them at twenty nine, objected to the 'old man' but was too polite to take issue.

"I am afraid it is."

"If Newmarket is not to your taste, when parliament rises, come down to Highborne. We can go to Newbury races, quite a different crowd there."

"You know, I might just take you at your word, Carvon."

"Yes, do. I can look forward to some sensible young company."

"Not enough young company at your place?" Viscount Bellars queried.

"Plenty, with my family, just not yet at the sensible age. "Carvon moved away to leave. "How is Danvers, these days? You were one of his weren't you?"

"How do you know Danvers?" Richard moved over to him, away from Bellars.

"Oh, you would be surprised who I know. Took in a few of the French refugees you rescued. Good work that. Plenty hold you in high regard, lad." With that he patted Richard on the shoulder and left. Richard looked around at Bellars, but he was involved in the race.

Eventually a quiet voice said.
"Who is Danvers?"
"My ex boss, and no one you need to know about, George."

Chapter 6

Danvers returned to London with fresh areas of enquiry.

Each day Kitty grew stronger and more cheerful. Sitting back in a chair was still not possible, but if she sat on the end of a sofa and leaned into the side she was quite comfortable. She had lost quite a little weight so her simple dresses were wearable, although getting into and out of them was still uncomfortable. Binny had taken up the post of maid to Kitty and that suited both of them very well.

By the time another week had passed, Kitty was again walking in the garden and taking up all her pastimes, all except riding. She was even taken into the village in the small carriage, and fared quite well.

However in London things were not proceeding that well. New rumours had started saying that the Prince had arranged for Kitty to be killed, one that she was dead. Quite a few of the ex operatives now part of the ton, searched and questioned but could find no one source for the rumours. Again Danvers visited the Prince and spoke privately with him. He had not been told of the new rumours yet, but would take note of who informed him.

Fear now raised in Danvers' mind as to whether the rumours were directed at Kitty or the Prince. Having tried to kill her once, would they try again? He rode out to Wenton Hall with some qualms.

The Duke was confused by the news, Jeremy was horrified and Kitty was not told.

How to keep Kitty safe became the main topic of conversation between them. It would be safer if she were not at the Hall. Of course, she would not take kindly to being sent away, but then a way to convince her arrived with the builder.

The builder had arranged for the repairs to be started on the damaged downstairs wall and windows. Half the house would be unusable. It must be put under Holland covers and even then the floor and the air in the

Hall would be full of plaster and stone dust. It was the ideal situation. Kitty could go to his aunts, plural. He had a plethora of aunts of one sort or another. They all knew Kitty as they were invited for occasional parties, and usually came for Christmas.

The closest were Aunt Fay and Aunt Hinchcombe. Aunt Fay was a little timid and cowed beneath Aunt Hinchcombe's opinions, but no doubt they would care for her well enough. If not she could go on to Aunt Lynch, a cousin married to a baron, and with teenage daughters, she would be a good choice. If not then his sister Lady Phillipa Shrobisher. A strong minded widow with an impoverished distant cousin, Aunt Hetty, as a companion. They were three days away, probably too far for Kitty in a coach.

The Duke wrote to all three including as few details as possible, but impressed the need for Kitty to recuperate in a quite untroubled household.

Kitty was made as comfortable as possible with piles of pillows in the unmarked small black coach. She took Binny and Ferguson, a trustworthy man for anything needed, from under butler or footman to general help and security. With William, the Duke's favourite coachman, she was sent to Aunt Fay and Aunt Hinchcombe a day or two after the letters were delivered requesting their assistance.

A short visit to the village in a carriage was somewhat different to a day's travel. The coach was filled with soft pillows and comfortable wraps and at first Kitty leaned against one side of the coach with her shoulder. Then she moved and tried the other side. She sat forward but her balance was such that Binny had to lean forward to hold her on the seat. She laid on her stomach with her hands under her chin and her feet up. Eventually she put her head down and tried to sleep. It was rather an ungainly way to lay but the carriage was not wide enough for her legs, which seemed to have nowhere to go.

Binny remarked that if they were stopped by a highwayman he would not take her for a lady, and ride away in disgust. The ducal travelling coach would have been somewhat more comfortable, but she was not to know the only reason she was in this smaller coach was because it bore no coat of arms. In the discussion between the Duke and Danvers the considered outcome was that her identity should be withheld to disguise her progress though the countryside, thus keeping her as safe as was possible.

Thus it was necessary to make several stops to rest and walk about and progress was slow. Kitty became more dishevelled as the day wore on. At one point when Kitty was sprawled on the seat, a curricle travelling too fast caused William to pull the horses over quickly to avoid an accident. He was obliged to pull up sharply, which unceremoniously dumped Kitty and Binny and all the pillows and wraps onto the floor of the coach, amid squeals and eventually much laughter, as they sorted out whose legs and arms belonged to whom.

William was contrite and worried Kitty had been hurt, but Binny was adamant he should not take on so. As she pointed out to him, it had been the first time in a long while that Kitty had laughed.

They eventually arrived at six pm just as the aunts were sitting down to dinner. Kitty was shown to her room and quickly washed off the dust of the road. Binny tidied her hair as fast as possible. When she was shown into the dining room she found dinner had not been held for her and they were halfway through the second course. She had to make the best she could without the first course and as much of the second as there was time to eat. There was not the usual number of dishes she was accustomed to at the Hall.

It would not be correct if she had told Binny they were unfriendly, but they were cool. The first evening she presumed it was her late arrival that had caused this, but the following two days the atmosphere was chilly and formal. Kitty told Aunt Fay of the carriage journey and the descent to the floor which had caused much laughter. Aunt Fay looked amused but glanced at Aunt Hinchcombe, who frowned severely and the laughter died in Aunt Fay's eyes.

How best to overcome this? Kitty decided to take the most direct method.

"Aunt Hinchcombe, you do not seem pleased to have me here."

"Your papa asked and we will, of course, accommodate him."

""What have I done, Aunt, to displease you so? We have always been amiable together in the past. I do feel you are in some way angry with me."

"You know what you have done, girl. It seems the whole of England knows what you have done."

Kitty stared in disbelief.

"I have done nothing wrong, Aunt Hinchcombe. I would not have expected family to believe the lies of spiteful people."

"Your conscience is between you and your God.

"My conscience is clear, Aunt. It is also clear that I am not welcome here. I will leave first thing tomorrow morning. You can have the pleasure of informing the Duke of the reasons for your lack of hospitality."

Kitty spent the rest of the day and evening in her room with Binny.

"The problem is, Binny, we have no way to refute the rumours. Papa gave very little detail to anyone about my birthday; I don't expect he mentioned the rumours. He probably never realised they would have heard what London was saying."

"But these are family, Lady Kitty, why did they not ask you about anything?"

"I don't know, Binny, they have their set ideas and will never change them. Until Mr Danvers can find some reason, I will have to live with people's prejudices."

The next day the little entourage moved on to Aunt Lynch's. The journey was a little easier; her back was giving her less pain.

They arrived at Aunt Lynch's to a flurry of excitement from the twins. Emily and Jane were fifteen years old, the same age as Carina. They were both lively, blonde and beautifully dressed, Emily in a pink muslin morning dress with an edging of deeper pink ribbons, Jane in lemon with frills around the neck and sleeves. They almost dragged her out of the carriage in their eagerness to see her.

"Kitty, I am so pleased you could come. Mother said she had received a letter from Uncle Wenton, but was not expecting you to come." Jane was bursting with pleasure.

Emily was a little more concerned about why Kitty had pulled away from her hand. "Kitty, what is wrong with your back.?"

"There was a terrible accident at Wenton Hall and I was hurt. That is why I have been sent into the country, to recuperate."

They were entering the house by now, with both girls asking questions and wanting to know how long she was staying. They could imagine various delights and escapes from the schoolroom.

Kitty was received by the butler and shown into the parlour where Aunt Lynch sat sewing.

"Kitty, whatever are you doing here?"

"Papa wrote to you, Aunt Lynch. I have been injured and need to heal. He thought a visit to family would help. Did he not tell you?"

"Well, yes, of course he did, but I thought ......"she stopped in confusion.

"I will have a room arranged." She rose in a flurry to pull the bell chord for the servant and gave instructions.

"I am sorry if it is an inconvenience, Aunt."

At which point Emily joined the discussion. "She has been injured, mama, she is in pain. I can see it in her face. Can she not sit down?"

"Yes, of course, what was I thinking."

Aunt Lynch was definitely flustered.

Kitty subsided onto a chaise and leaned on the end. Jane was feeling a little deflated by her mother's reaction. Emily being solicitous for Kitty's comfort sat on the chaise by Kitty and put a hand on her arm.

"Are you very much in pain, Kitty? Can you not lean back and rest?"

"I am afraid that leaning on my back is what pains me, although it becomes easier as the days pass."

Jane was finding her voice a little more. "What happened to your back, Kitty?"

Lady Lynch leapt in to stop the conversation.

"Not now Jane. Fitch will take her up to her room. We will not get into gothic details."

So Kitty was shown up to her room to wash and change her travelling gown for a loose day gown. Having hardly any hair except at the front made preparations much quicker, although she would be thankful when her hair was sufficiently grown and her head sufficiently healed to leave off the white caps she was forced to wear.

There was no one about as she went down to the dining room. Did they keep country hours or later town hours for dinner?

Finding nobody in the entrance hall, and having only a vague memory of the layout of the house, she walked down the hall to where she heard voices. It was Aunt Lynch's.

"I can't have her here polluting the girls. If it is known she was here their future could be ruined!"

"Well if you feel that way, my dear, you must ask her to leave. But be very diplomatic. We would not want to upset the Duke."

"He must know, after all he sent her away to get rid of her. He can't be angry if I put my girls first."

"Surely a couple of days won't hurt. She may not be well enough to leave straight away. She is physically damaged. The girls might not understand why she has to go."

"I shall tell them the truth. I expect her back is from the beating she was given for her dreadful behaviour."

Kitty had not wanted to eavesdrop; after all, they say you never hear well of yourself. In this case that was most definitely true. She returned to her room and rang for Binny.

"Binny, I fear was must move on again tomorrow."

Binny was so distressed she wrung her hands and her head went down. "So soon, Lady Kitty. Have they no heart but to turn you away?"

"No, Binny. They have said nothing to me as yet. But they do intend to lie to the girls. I think I have to start defending myself a little more."

"Defend with everything you have, my lady!"

"We will still leave in the morning. This time I will leave them with the rejection. Do you happen to know what time they eat here? This is about to be a very interesting meal."

Binny looked at her mistress, noted the look on her face, and smiled.

"It will be my pleasure to find out, Lady Kitty."

Dinner was not a very formal affair, after all it was just family and there was no concern shown for Kitty's presence.

Talk at the table was very stilted. The girls obviously wanted to ask questions but had been forbidden to do so. Around the dessert course, Kitty prepared for her onslaught.

"I shall be so glad when I no longer need this cap, but that may be a few weeks yet."

"Why must you wear the cap?" Jane was bursting for information but kept one eye on her mother's disapproving looks.

"Why because my head was damaged in the blast."

"What blast?" came from everyone.

"Did papa not tell you? The blast which damaged the hall and killed my maid and a kitchen maid." Kitty said it with such innocence. She must learn to be good at this if she was going to survive this life.

"I know papa was so upset over the whole affair. It will take weeks for the hall to be repaired and papa wanted me to recuperate without the noise and dust of the builders."

Kitty peered at them.

"I still have few clothes loose enough to accommodate the dressings on my back. The topiary branches went quite deep, especially on my shoulders and head. They thought I should die from the fever afterwards."

"But I thought....." Emily stopped herself.

"What, Emily?" Emily was looking at her mama.

"I know," Kitty continued "It is so difficult to see the truth when you are happy to believe lies." Her aunt bristled.

"Let me tell you girls about evil people. They don't look evil, they look like ordinary people." Aunt Lynch tried to break in.

"No, Aunt Lynch, the girls should hear the truth if it will help them understand what happens in their future. Which are the most evil people, those who tell nasty lies to hurt someone, or those who believe them and ruin someone's life?"

Jane answered "Both."

"Indeed, Jane. Horrible people told lies about me and now others believe them. I was not beaten for my sins, Aunt Lynch, I have none of the sins I am accused of. The blast is real, the damage and death is real. You wish me to leave because you believe what is not true but do not believe what is. I will leave in the morning." and to the girls she said "I wish you both well for the future whatever your mama thinks. I will say goodbye to you now as I am retiring. We will possibly never meet again." She arose to leave. It was Emily who tentatively said "But won't you be there at Christmas?"

"I hope I will, Emily. However you will not. I think the link with my family has just been irrevocably broken. You see, my papa knows my innocence. He is trying to stop the lies, not carry them on."

Here she looked pointedly at her aunt and uncle.

Turning with all the poise of a duchess that she could muster, she left everyone in the dinning room stunned.

When she reached the stairs she stopped and waited. It was some few minutes before the argument erupted. Everyone seemed to be shouting at once. Kitty turned and climbed the stairs to her room. This was the first encounter she had won in the battle against the ton rumours and it felt good.

The next morning they loaded the coach for an early start. Breakfast would be taken on the road. As she went out through the hall she heard footsteps coming down the corridor. The baron came out behind her.

"I just wish to apologise, Lady Kitty. I understand how it is for you."

"Do you really, sir, I doubt it. The greatest brains in England do not understand. After all this involves the Prince. All the undercover operatives from the foreign office are working to understand. If they do not, how can you? Unfortunately until it is solved I am destined to be treated like a leper. I did not expect it from my family. Neither did the Duke, my father, or he would not have sent me here."

She went to the carriage and turned before alighting.

"Goodbye to you, sir, and I thank you for trying to intercede. I was not intentionally eavesdropping, it was quite by chance I was passing when looking for someone to speak with."

With that she climbed into the coach and they pulled away.

The housekeeper bustled up. "They have not had breakfast, sir."

"Do you know, I doubt she could stomach it. It would probably choke her." and quietly added "And I don't blame her in the least.

Chapter 7

The next part of the journey was taken in gentle stages with several stops. They were off the main road and would not reach the coach road until shortly before the turning to Burton Hall where her Aunt Phillipa, Lady Phillipa Shrobisher lived, with her companion Aunt Hetty

They took an evening meal at the coaching inn on the road, it was still light until quite late and she could not be sure they would be there in time for dinner, at which they were not expected.

Their arrival was treated with calm efficiency as one might expect from the household of the sister of a duke. As they were not to dine, Kitty was able to go to her room as soon as it was ready. In the meantime she was given tea and fussed over by Aunt Hetty. Aunt Phillipa hovered regally until all was prepared and then bade Kitty goodnight.

The first week was heaven for Kitty. Nobody accused her, nobody required anything of her and nobody expected explanations. She was there because she needed tending, and she would he allowed to heal. Aunt Hetty was the one who surprised her most. She came to see her in her bedroom and asked Kitty about the injuries and how they were healing. She fetched a new salve of their cook's and insisted on helping Binny apply it. She devised ways to sit for her to rest in a chair more easily, but the best was that she talked about the blast without asking questions. She only asked just enough questions to start Kitty talking. Eventually, by the time the first week ended, Hetty know all there was to know.

In the beginning Kitty thought the London rumours had not reached so far away, but that hope was dashed in the second week when the vicar and his wife came to visit. Vicars come in various types; those who are pushed into it for financial reasons; they have no real interest, those who are brought up knowing it is their destiny as a second or third son, many of whom learn to respect the calling and those who take it up with a particular zeal to reform mankind. This was one of the zeal kind, as was his wife.

At their first meeting she realised she was being inspected. Did he not approve of ton ladies? Did he object to her clothes, they were loose and ill fitting as she could only wear light clothing? Her dress did not have a low neck, fashionable was not possible with her back still salved and wrapped. They could not fault her hair, she had little and her head was covered with a cap which resembled a bonnet made of white cotton. It did not have lace and only one frill at the front. There should be nothing to complain about in her appearance, but obviously they had a problem with her. They lectured her on the Bible, on original sin, on confessing your sins to God in prayer every day. She felt sorry for their parishioners. Could it be that they had heard the rumours and if so, how?

That afternoon the first of the local ladies came to visit. Two spinster ladies, the Misses Williams. They quietly surveyed her with what appeared to be disapproval.

"We hear you have been ill." A statement not a question, and administered with a sniff.

"It is more than admirable that your aunt should take you in, given the circumstances."

"What circumstances would that be?" Kitty was getting to expect misunderstanding but was not yet able to cope with it.

The second Miss Williams was a little less vitriolic in her attitude.

"Why the circumstances of your ......" she fought for a word "..illness."

"You are hiding your condition with loose clothing, I see." The first Miss Williams.

"I am unable to wear fitted clothing until my back heals." Kitty retorted, becoming a little angry.

"Oh, is that what you are calling it?

Kitty was angry and mortified at the same time. Her Aunt Phillipa took no part in the conversation and seemed not to feel the slight to her niece. Aunt Hetty tried to help.

"It was such a dreadful accident. I fear it will leave many scars. She will probably never be able to wear off the shoulder dresses to a ball. Such a shame for such a pretty girl, and the daughter of a duke." The last sentence held a little emphasis.

"Don't be so melodramatic, Hetty, I doubt Kitty will ever have need to wear such dresses." It was a strange statement from her Aunt Phillipa.

It certainly felt as if it were meant to chastise Aunt Hetty into keeping her place as a companion, as much as to be about Kitty.

The Misses Williams merely nodded in agreement.

By the time the second day had brought the same disapproval from visiting neighbours Kitty was feeling quite depressed. She retired to her room. She had not intended to wallow in her misery, but she did have a few tears. An unexpected knock on the door brought Aunt Hetty.

"You seem a little low, child. I thought you could do with cheering up."

"I have no notion how anyone in my position could ever be cheerful."

"Kitty, it is hard to turn your back on a painful past and ignore it when everyone is always referring to it. But it is possible."

"I am so sorry, Aunt. I should have remembered, life has not been kind to you. Aunt Phillipa is always making comments about it. Is it because she has no children and you did?"

"No, I believe Phillipa does not realise what she is saying could be hurtful. She has never had to bear the loss of her family. Even when her husband died the estate was not entailed as ours was. Like you I had a double tragedy, that of losing husband, son and my home. Following the death of my daughter in childbirth and being asked to leave her husband's house, I can only be grateful Phillipa took me in."

"It may have been good of her, but she is hurting you with her remarks. I could not live like this, Aunt Hetty."

"And where would I go if I upset her?"

"I want to cry for me, and I want to cry for you too, Aunt Hetty."

"Do not cry for me, child, I shed enough tears of my own."

"Do you still cry?"

"Oh yes, child. I often wake with my pillow wet from tears. Then I get up and look for ways to fight back."

"Are there ways to fight back? I never see you arguing about anything."

"You have no need for anger Kitty. You just have to put your brain to good use. When you confuse their understanding, you can feel contentment. Sometimes you can use innocent conversations to make them angry at themselves. That can make you feel elated. Do not despair, child, I will teach you. It will be like a game between us."

Kitty threw her arms around her and hugged her. To Kitty she felt like she had a mother again. To Hetty, it felt like the love of the daughter that she so missed. To them both it felt as if they had sealed a pact between them.

"The squire's wife comes to call every Wednesday. How do I deal with her?" Plans were made for every visitor who came.

"The squire's wife is very well dressed. She will have heard about you and your loose clothing and will make up her mind in advance. These neighbours listen to the rumours and then add their own opinion when passing it on. By now you are probably with child and due to go into confinement at any time soon. Binny, how is Lady Kitty's back now?"

"Doing well now, ma'am. No more salve, only covering to stop clothing from rubbing."

"So, Kitty, do you think you could try a tight dress for an hour or so?"

"I doubt any of my dresses are tight. I lost so much weight and we only brought loose ones anyway."

"Which dress makes you look slimmest, especially your front?"

"Oh, the blue muslin, but it is still loose. Maybe Binny could take it in at the sides. Would it take long Binny?"

"Oh no, my lady. It's quite an easy dress to alter. We can have it done in no time at all."

"Now" Aunt Hetty studied her head. "Your lack of hair at the back will be a problem for some time, but we could do something with the front, and with the cap. I believe I will get Milly, the girl who acts like a maid to me, to cut the front a little tidier. She is quite good at hair, even if she is only a housemaid."

"You should have your own maid, Aunt Hetty!"

"Hush, Kitty, don't get angry again. If she can alter the front of your hair, cut it shorter and make it frill up, you could have a smaller cap. Shall we see how to alter one? Some lace would be very becoming.

When the squire's wife came to call she was received by Aunt Phillipa. Kitty was summoned to join them, arriving with Aunt Hetty.

The squire's wife was not the only one surprised.

Kitty's loss of weight made her look taller and more regal. She held herself like a duchess, although mainly because of the tight blue muslin which made her feel thinner, but was a little restrictive after the last few weeks. Her hair was cut short and curled at the front giving her face a softer, rounder appearance. The cap was attached at the sides and top to her hair, rather than tied under her chin. It now had a lace frill to cover the nape of her neck.

The squire's wife stared. Aunt Phillipa stared.

"When did you become so thin, Kitty?" Aunt Phillipa was genuinely puzzled.

"I have always been this size, Aunt, I just wore loose clothing and padding on my back until it healed." Aunt Hetty was right. It felt good to cause confusion.

Kitty sat bolt upright on a chaise and received her tea. She had intended to refuse a biscuit, mainly because it was difficult to lean forward. Aunt Hetty came to the rescue again, holding the plate close to Kitty while she chose. She gave her a conspiratorial smile, laughter brimming in her eyes.

By the time the squire's wife left, Kitty felt elated. The talk had been about everything and everyone except her. Every so often they would look at Kitty, fall thoughtfully silent for a moment, then resume with another topic.

"If you will excuse me Aunt, now that visiting is over, I will change into something a little more comfortable for my back. This is the first time I have worn normal clothing and I am still a little tender."

Aunt Phillipa grunted her consent. Kitty escaped upstairs, and when Aunt Hetty found her, she and Binny were jumping like children with their delight.

"Do not overtire yourself, Kitty."

"It was such a success, Aunt Hetty. Did you see their faces?"

Hetty grinned.

"Just the first success. There will be times when you feel you have failed, but the better you become at this, the fewer the failures. You will have to be aware of everything they say and do, Kitty, if you are to regain your position in life. It will not be easy."

"Will I ever regain my position, Aunt?"

"It depends on how strong and how good at manipulating the situation you become. When possible, forward planning is the key. Look at the ton harpies who caused this problem. If you can outface them, and then make them feel in the wrong, then you have won."

"How do you make them think they are wrong?"

"That's what we need to practice over the next few weeks. You have to seem innocent and behave as if they are referring to something else, which you then agree with."

"I am confused, Aunt."

"Let's start with something easy, like dinner. If I say I really enjoyed the previous main course, you innocently remark about the starter, as if that was what I was meaning."

"Talk about something different, you mean."

"Exactly. We shall try it at dinner this evening and see how your Aunt Phillipa reacts."

She reacted surprised, then confused. Kitty liked this game. For the first time, possibly in her life, she felt she was in charge.

Kitty wrote to her father of her progress and gave a date a few weeks ahead when she expected to return. She told both her aunts of her decision.

Aunt Hetty smiled, but not with her eyes.

"I shall miss you, Kitty. It has made me feel useful and wanted, almost as if I had my daughter back again."

"Do not be sad, Aunt Hetty. You are not being left out. I shall tell papa what it is like for you here, and how helpful you have been. If no young man of my choosing wants me for a wife, and I have my doubts now, I intend to ask papa for a cottage of my own in which to live quietly. Then I want you to come and be my companion.

"You will find a good husband I am sure."

"Then you will come to live with us and be a special Aunt to all my children. I intend your future life to be happier than this. You deserve more."

Hetty was quite overcome. She looked away to hide her brimming eyes.

"Will you come, Aunt Hetty?"

She felt so full of emotion all she could do was nod, and hug Kitty.

After six weeks of recuperation Kitty was feeling much better, both physically and emotionally. She felt capable of dealing with whatever problems came. The one that arrived was in the guise of the vicar and his wife. They usually arrived in the morning, twice a week, and gave a disdainful lecture on morals and the consequences of your own actions. Normally they gave no chance for her to speak. She had borrowed a cross which she wore around her neck when they came, but it made no difference. Today she felt strong enough to take on anyone, even the self important vicar.

"Good morning, vicar, ma'am. I see my Aunt is occupied elsewhere as usual."

"Your Aunt is a good, God fearing woman, Miss Kitty." Kitty interrupted.

"Kitty is a name only used by my family or those I give permission to. I do not permit you. And I am not a Miss, I am Lady Katherine Wellmore."

"A lady is as a lady does, my dear." His voice was cold.

"This lady is exactly as a lady should be, sir. And before you start your misplaced lecture yet again, today I intend to speak."

She sat as tall as she could.

"Firstly, your condemnation of me is as misplaced as are the rest of those sinners who consider themselves above me. Second, I see no Christian offer of help or redemption as the Bible offers. As it happens, I need no redemption, but you, it seems, do require it. A less Christian person I have never met, vicar. I have done my Christian duty and forgiven you your totally wrong condemnation of me, for several weeks. I would suggest you read your bible, vicar. You have preached at me in this house, you have preached at me in church, and all your parishioners have believed the lies against me that you have been perpetuating. I suggest that you go to your church, get on your knees and ask God for forgiveness for what you have done. It might be an even better idea if you confessed to your parishioners, they could do with a little humanity too."

The vicar and his wife were staring at her. He was beginning to go a little red with his ire. Before he could speak she concluded.

"I will pray for you, vicar, but I do not expect to see you here again, spouting your venom. Good day to you."

With that Kitty left the room. She closed the door and leant back on it breathing heavily. She had done it. She had said everything she wanted. It felt so good.

The butler approached. She waved her arm toward the parlour.

"The vicar and his wife are just leaving. If you would see them out, please."

She walked like a duchess to the bottom of the stairs and when out of sight of the butler she fled up to her room, her heart pounding.

At lunch, Aunt Phillipa was going over everything she had done that morning and berating Aunt Hetty for not doing something she had not been asked to do.

Kitty was angry on Aunt Hetty's behalf.

"Aunt, did you specifically ask Aunt Hetty to do it?"

"That is immaterial, girl. She should know that I would need help."

"What were you doing Aunt Hetty?" Kitty's eyes laughed at her.

"I was arranging the flowers, as instructed." She said a little too innocently.

"There you are Aunt. She could have helped you if you had asked me to do the flowers."

"You had to see the vicar."

"Ah yes. It was to listen to the vicar's twice weekly diatribe. Well at least that is over, he will not be calling on me again."

"What do you mean?"

"I eventually managed to get to speak, and could tell him the truth. He will not be back, and if he comes, I will not see him."

"What are you talking about now? You had better be in a more amenable state this afternoon. Lady Jerman is to call. She has just returned from the London season."

Chapter 8

After lunch, in her room there was a tactical plan being discussed.

"She is going to be full of the rumours. Those Aunt Phillipa has not heard she will tell her. Do I just say she is lying, be aloof, or ignore her? What do I do Aunt?"

"First you need to know about her. Lady Jerman is the wife of a man of very little consequence, especially around here. She was the daughter of the vicar from a neighbouring parish who was not from a noble house, just a local squire's son. Lady Jerman feels she needs all the airs and graces she can put on. She is very obsequious to your aunt. I do not think she will come straight out and accuse you, so you will be able to misunderstand her."

"Misunderstand, yes that sounds good. Perhaps I will be able to tie her understanding into knots."

"Do not try to be too clever. Be honest, but leave out anything that would not look good. That should do."

"And of course, I must look my best, Binny. This is a blue muslin day, I believe." That caused some laughter.

Lady Jerman was indeed obsequious, also dressed in the latest London fashion, the better to enforce her worth. Kitty was sitting with both aunts when she arrived. She greeted them both, at the same time casting glances at Kitty.

"This is my niece, Lady Katherine Wellmore, the Duke of Wenton's daughter."

Lady Jerman knew exactly who she was, that was why she was there so soon.

"I received your note this morning, of course. I did not realise you had returned. When did you arrive?"

"Last evening, my lady, but I felt I had to come and pay my respects to let you know I was returned."

She wasted no time, Kitty thought. She could not get here quick enough.

There followed a little conversation of what had been happening in the surrounding area, who was at home, who was ill, who had argued. All the usual inane chatter that goes on at tea parties.

The tea was brought in and Kitty handed round the teacups. She was aware of Lady Jerman continuously glancing at her waistline. Aunt Phillipa asked a little about London but the conversation soon died out. As the teacups were collected and the tray removed, she was amused to see Lady Jerman take a calming breath, readying herself to speak.

"Lady Katherine, I understand you are in the country because you have been ill." She could say that, but everyone knew what she was referring to.

"Indeed, Lady Jerman, I have."

"I am surprised to see you looking so well." So thin she means.

"Well it has been eight weeks now." How far should she push her? "I expect the ton know of it now, of course."

"Well you know the ton, they like to be informed."

"Are they informed? Are you, Lady Jerman?"

"Well, of course, I know what they say, but if you want to talk about it, to help put things into perspective." Wonderful, she walked right into this. Thank you Aunt Hetty. Misunderstanding comes no greater. Aunt Phillipa was looking rather uncomfortable, as if about to stop the conversation. Not a hope, Aunt Phillipa. This was her moment.

"It was so terrible. I had no idea what was happening." Lady Jerman nodded, she was hooked.

"At first it felt like a dream. I could not take it in. Everything seemed to be happening in slow motion. First the blast."

"The blast?" Lady Jerman looked confused. Good, Aunt Phillipa began to look angry.

"Yes, it was huge. A part of the wall to the dining room crumbled in and all the glass in the windows all around flew into the rooms. They were preparing the dining room for my eighteenth birthday dinner and I could hear the maids screaming as the glass showered them. The little kitchen maid was flying though the air. She hit the wall hard, it broke her neck and she fell to the floor like a rag doll." Lady Jerman was beginning to look a little green. Aunt Phillipa was staring in disbelief. Kitty stood and moved to the window.

"While all this was happening, I was flying backwards through the air. But the worst part was my maid, Aleen. She was the nearest. Her arms flew off and blood came out. The metal sundial flew off the base and cut her throat. Her head fell back and the blood squirted out like a fountain.

Oh God, the blood!" Kitty had no need to pretend at this point in the telling. Remembering this always brought tears to her eyes. "At that point I reached the topiary bush and was embedded in it. I knew nothing until later. It took an hour to cut me free. I nearly died from my injuries. The nightmares are the worst, I see it every night."

She turned to see the back of Lady Jerman leaving through the hall door. The next moment she heard her being sick into the flowers.

Aunt Phillipa was incandescent with rage.

"Really Kitty, that was disgraceful. How could you be so nasty, I thought you better than that? You will apologise immediately, and I will deal with you later."

A very pale Lady Jerman was being helped back into the room by a footman.

"A drink of some kind for Lady Jerman." Aunt Phillipa barked.

The footman bowed and retreated down the corridor at great speed.

"My dear Lady Jerman, Kitty wishes to apologise for upsetting you."

"Indeed I do." She must keep control of this situation, this was the greatest test.

"I would not upset you for anything, but I know the ton, and as you knew about what happened I thought you had hurried here for all the gory details. The ton does love their gothic novels."

Lady Jerman stared. A drink was put in her hand and she took a sip. "But all that ….."

"Yes, Lady Jerman, it was exactly what happened. I was sent away to recuperate in the country while the builders restored the damaged area of Wenton Hall. Papa thought the noise and dust would be bad for me."

Lady Jerman laid back in the chair and sipped her drink. When she was a little recovered, her coach was called for and she returned home.

Aunt Phillipa could not contain her rage.

"I had no idea I had taken in a viper. Your lies are so outrageous I see I shall have to punish you until you come to your senses."

"What lies, Aunt Phillipa? You had never asked me what happened, if you had you would have known all this. I do not expect papa told you much, he was too distressed to talk about it. Why did you think he sent me away?"

"Well, because of your behaviour in London. We presumed you were with child. After all, this story is just a fabrication. You made the error of adding so much horrific detail that it became unbelievable.

"No Aunt, it is not a fabrication. Not one word of it. The rumours from London, they are a fabrication, none of them are true. I am still a maid, but a ruined one because of people like you. Does everyone around here know of the rumours?" Her aunt did not answer. "Do they Aunt? Who told them? Was it you? Did you tell the vicar to come and sermonise at me for weeks because of a lie? Why don't you answer, Aunt?"

"How do I know they are lies? You appear very good at lying."

"Did you ever come to see my back, my head? Did you never wonder how I came by my injuries?"

"Well in the circumstances...."

"You mean that like Aunt Lynch, you presumed my father had thrashed me to within an inch of my life and then disowned me? Is that the case, madam?" Aunt Phillipa looked dumb.

"You obviously do not know your brother." She turned to pull the bell for a servant, with whom she sent a message for Binny to pack her belongings.

"We will be leaving in the morning, very early. Thank you for the use of your house, if not your hospitality. I doubt I shall ever see you again."

"I will no doubt see you at Christmas." She was a little more contrite now.

"No, I think not. If you are invited I will not be there. I wonder which of us papa will prefer to have at his Christmas table?"

Kitty went to her room, buried her face in her pillow and sobbed. It was like this that Binny found her. She was still there a little later when Aunt Hetty arrived.

Hetty pulled her into her arms and hugged her.

"All this time she thought that badly of me." She had trouble getting out the words.

"You must be strong now, my love. When you leave here I will not be able to help you. Tell your father everything and he will protect you from these lies."

"I just want to go home, Aunt Hetty. I just want to be among people who believe me and do not judge me by these lies."

While Binny packed her boxes and laid out her travelling clothes for the morning, Kitty talked with Aunt Hetty.

"If things remain as bad as this, Aunt, I will never be part of the ton or have a suitable husband. I will not marry someone I do not care deeply for, and the only men who will offer for me will be wanting my dowry. I shall ask my father for that cottage, and then send for you. Will you come?"

"Of course I will. It would be my greatest pleasure to be your companion. I think between us we would rule the surrounding countryside, or at least make them very confused."

"What a wonderful idea. But Aunt Hetty, if Aunt Phillipa is angry with you and tells you to leave, promise me you will let me know, or come to Wenton Hall. My father would accept you as part of his household, I know. When I have spoken with him, he may even insist you come."

Kitty had dinner in her room that evening. She spent some time with her man, Ferguson, discussing the journey back. She needed to keep to the post roads to have as smooth and fast a journey as possible, but she did not want to change her horses. Ferguson escorted her down the servants' stairs to see her coachman, William, who was eager to be on the move again. If the roads were good and they travelled slowly but for many hours, the horses would not tire as much as if they drove them hard. Speed meant having to change the horses, so a route was agreed that would be less strenuous for the horses and a time set. They would start by seven in the morning.

Chapter 9

Although it no longer hurt her back, long periods of travelling were still tiring. This was not the luxurious, well sprung travelling coach, so a gentle trot was best for the passengers as well as the horses.

The routine planned was that they travelled for three to four hours, then stopped at a coaching inn for at least one hour while the horses rested. If all worked well, they would be home in three days. Long days, to be sure, but the fewer days the better. Of course, this did mean that they would be staying overnight at two coaching inns, but then anything was preferable to visiting the aunts again.

They left that first morning at seven o'clock as had been decided. The first part of the journey, though short, was on poor country roads and had to be taken very slowly. Once they reached the coach road they were able to move faster and more comfortably. Ferguson rode with William, the coachman, although he was not at home that close to horses, Binny rode with Kitty in the coach. It was a little after ten o'clock when they reached the first stop. One hour for breakfast and to rest the horses. After eleven, the full hour's rest, Kitty was adamant about that, they set off again at a steady trot, reaching the coaching inn at the next timed stop, just before three in the afternoon.

The second stop was a relief for Kitty who badly needed to move around to ease her back. As the day was fine, if a little cool, she and Binny walked outside for a while, whilst Ferguson watched protectively from a distance. After a light lunch and the obligatory full hour rest, they moved off again. William knew the coaching inn he needed to reach to maintain the planned journey. They made it by eight o'clock in the evening and while William saw to the horses, Ferguson arranged rooms, one for the ladies and one at the back, that William could share with Ferguson if he wished. He often slept in the stables near the horses.

The ladies took their dinner in their room, but both men enjoyed the noise and company of the tap room downstairs.

The second day began as had the first. They left by seven in the morning and arrived for breakfast by ten o'clock. One hour later they set off again. The pace was slow as the horses were not quite as fresh as the previous day; however they arrived at their afternoon stop at a little after three. The sky was somewhat overcast although it did not prevent Kitty and Binny from walking to relieve the stiffness. When they resumed the journey it was just beginning to drizzle with rain. After an hour, Ferguson was wet, not having a coachman's cape to keep him from the worst of the rain. William stopped the coach at a small inn and insisted the ladies take Ferguson into the carriage. His wet coat was removed and Binny sat with Kitty to give the large body of Ferguson enough room; even so his legs did seem to cause a problem.

The rain now became much heavier and the journey slower as the roads were very wet. Eventually the discussion in the carriage concluded that they must shorten the day's travel for safety. They pulled into the next available inn. The rain was now so bad it was difficult to see far enough ahead, the road being awash with water. Ferguson retrieved his coat from the corner where it had been banished to drip, and went to secure rooms. Minutes later he returned with the news that there were no rooms free. Others, it seemed, had the same idea as them and had stopped to get out of the rain. The decision was to travel on to the next inn, but wherever they stopped there were no rooms, everywhere was crowded. There was now thunder and lightning and the horses were becoming difficult to manage.

William pointed out that they were no more than two miles from her Aunts' house. Much against Kitty's inclination, it was decided to pull off the road and head towards Aunt Fay and Aunt Hinchcombe's. The road was narrow and difficult in the dark of the storm and the coming night. It was nine in the evening when they made it down the hill, over the bridge and up through the village to the house.

Ferguson hammered on the door which was eventually opened by their elderly butler. He was not enthusiastic about giving them entrance, but Ferguson chivvied him inside as the ladies climbed down and fled into the hallway. William closed the door of the carriage and drove up the road to the livery stables, the old aunts not having their own, as they were without horse or carriage.

With the coach gone and the storm still raging, it was impossible for Aunt Hinchcombe to turn them out. So Aunt Fay, much to the displeasure of her sister, bustled about with the housekeeper and prepared rooms. Kitty was aware of the reticence, but she now had her new found confidence.

"Aunt Hinchcombe, I am aware of your displeasure at having me arrive once more at your home, but there is nowhere else to go. I assure you, I have no wish to be here in your company any more than you have to be in mine, but the circumstances are that I must impose on you for the night. We will be gone before you rise in the morning."

Aunt Hinchcombe was not quite sure what to say, so she said nothing. Kitty was hurried up to her room by Aunt Fay.

"You must get out of your wet clothes, my dear. You will become unwell if not."

"Thank you, Aunt Fay. I am rather cold and damp."

A small meal of pie and cold meats was prepared, which was all that could be supplied as they had not been expected. Binny put her clothes to warm and dry by the hastily lit fire, and Kitty retired to bed. Binny bustled off to see about Ferguson, who was a great deal wetter than both of them put together. How William fared they could only guess.

The storm abated some time during the night and when Binny woke Kitty, just before eight o'clock, it was to a reasonably clear sky, just the remnants of the disappearing storm clouds. They dressed quickly and prepared for the carriage to arrive. It would be a long day if they were to arrive at the Hall by nightfall. They were already late starting out.

What arrived was not the coach, but William on foot.

"I am sorry, Lady Kitty, but the bridge is impassable because of the storm last night."

"Is there no other way out?"

"It is possible, but quite likely the bridges on the way would also be impassable. It would take most of the day to reach the coach road close to yesterday afternoon's coaching stop."

"Oh goodness. How long will it be impassable, do you know?"

"I am on my way down to the village to enquire, my lady."

At that moment Ferguson arrived from around the side of the house.

"I thought I heard voices. I will walk with you, William. As soon as we have any information, I will return, my lady."

"Thank you Ferguson. Come Binny, we will wait in the parlour."

When Aunt Fay came downstairs, she found Kitty and Binny sitting quietly in the parlour. She was confused.

"Oh, I thought....."

"Indeed Aunt, we would be gone if we were able, but the bridge is impassable."

"It sometimes is quite bad after a storm."

"It was a very bad storm last night. How long is the bridge usually impassable, Aunt?"

"Oh, normally only for a few hours."

Hearing voices in the parlour, a very sour faced Aunt Hinchcombe entered the parlour.

Aunt Fay was eager to placate her.

"The bridge is impassable, sister dear. They must wait until it clears."

"Let's hope it clears quickly, then."

Together they sat in stormy silence for some time, after which Aunt Hinchcombe could cope no longer and found some chores to do.

After a meagre lunch, Kitty stood by the window hoping for Ferguson or William to appear.

"You seem slimmer, Kitty." Aunt Fay suggested cautiously.

"No, Aunt, on the contrary, I am possibly a little plumper than when I came before. I am just able to wear normal clothes now my back has healed."

"But I thought....."

"You thought wrongly, Aunt. You should never listen to malicious gossip. It causes unhappiness for everyone concerned. Oh look, here comes my man. I hope he has good news."

The news was not as bad as it could have been. It would be at least another hour before the bridge was clear. Ferguson suggested that they stay until the following morning, but Kitty wanted to leave as soon as possible.

So at four in the afternoon, the coach stopped outside the door and Kitty took leave of her Aunts and joined Binny inside.

They drove carefully over the country roads, dirty with puddles. Things improved when they reached the coach road, which meant they made good time. At eight in the evening they stopped at a coaching inn closer to home than originally expected, but a day late.

The next morning everyone was in good spirits. The road had dried, the horses were rested and they would be home early in the afternoon.

They actually arrived just a little before three. The butler, Wilson, was overjoyed at seeing Kitty arrive days earlier than she originally stated. The excited voices in the hall brought Jeremy from the library. He threw his arms around her in a bear hug, then pulled back suddenly.

"Kitty. Oh, have I hurt you?"

"No, Jeremy, I am quite healed if a little sore sometimes. You must tell me all the news. Where is everyone?"

"Father is around the estate somewhere, he is not due back until dinner tonight. Carina is about somewhere." He looked hopefully at the butler.

"Indeed, my lord, she is in the small parlour. When the gift arrived for Lady Kitty, she ...."

Kitty turned ashen. Jeremy supported her.

"It is not as you think, my lady, this present was in a basket and making a great deal of noise."

"A puppy?"

"No, a kitten, my lady. A very noisy one, howling like the devil. Lady Carina took it into the parlour to quieten it."

Kitty walked down the hall to the small parlour with some haste.

"Calm down, Kitty. There is nothing to worry about, it is only a kitten." Jeremy put a hand on her arm to quieten her. A footman appeared and opened the door. Kitty walked forward, Jeremy immediately behind her. On the floor was a basket and in the chair sat Carina with the kitten on her knee. From both their mouths and noses the blood had congealed.

They were both stone dead.

Kitty stood frozen in horror with Jeremy clinging to her. It was impossible to know who was supporting whom.

On the floor the basket had a label attached to the handle which read;

A kitty for my Kitty HRH

Chapter 10

For three days Kitty never spoke.

Carina lay in her coffin in the chapel. Danvers was sent for and the Hall waited in almost total silence.

Danvers examined the basket and its label. It was definitely the same hand that penned it.

The kitten was taken away and examined by someone from the Foreign Office that Danvers knew.

The death was announced in the paper and the funeral arranged. It was supposed to be a family funeral but half the ton came. It was quite difficult getting the coffin and the family in and out of the church. Kitty and Jeremy were both silent and in need of support. Jeremy was on one side and Binny supported Kitty on her other side. As the coffin was sealed into the mausoleum Kitty collapsed. She was held by her two supporters. Their father stood alone by the vicar. As they moved away the three went to a side avenue and sat on a bench while the hoards of nosy ton intruders left. They pushed each other aside and made it more like a night at Vauxhall Gardens than a young girl's funeral.

The three waited silently for the crowd to disperse. Some vitriolic lady of the ton passed behind the trees close to them.

"I expect the Prince preferred the younger sister. That's probably why she killed her."

"How do you know she did? I think the Prince had her killed."

"Mrs Farthingale told me, it's all over London. She came back to the house, found her sister had a present from the Prince, so she killed her. It's common sense if you think about it."

Kitty almost stopped breathing. Jeremy whispered "Oh God. What are we to do now?"

Long after everyone had left a few staff still stood at a distance. The Duke stood silently by the mausoleum, Kitty barely conscious, supported by others. By one tree near the exit the ton had taken stood a lone silent figure, Danvers.

Danvers was puzzled, perplexed. Why was this happening? He had heard some of the cruel things the ton had been saying. They also seemed to know about the present. How? Who had told them? Not the family that was certain. What had anyone against this family, Lady Kitty in particular? He needed every scrap of information he could get. Someone was doing this for a reason. They had to make a mistake soon. He would work this out. He had to.

For a few days Kitty never spoke. It was not that Kitty could not speak, it was trying to sort out her mind to decide what to do, what to say and how to make sense of it. There was no time for talk, not yet. She felt like Medusa. Everyone was hating her, wanting her dead, and yet it was those close to her who died instead. Who was next, Jeremy, Papa? Why did they only die when she was there, at the Hall? Was that true or just a coincidence? If she went away could she keep them safe?

A few mornings after the funeral she had the plan in her mind. Could she do this alone? She had to, if others knew they would be at risk.

The first obstacle to overcome was Aunt Hetty. She could not be left any longer. If they killed her, Aunt Hetty could be abandoned by Aunt Phillipa and no one would know to help her.

She wrote a note and gave it to the butler when she left the breakfast room. In it she asked for an interview with her father.

The response was immediate. He was waiting in his study for her arrival.

She tapped quietly on the door.

"Come in, Kitty. Shut the door and sit here." He pulled the second chair, used by his estate manager, to his side of the desk close to him.

"This is a dreadful business, I feel so helpless. Even Danvers has no idea yet."

"I feel like Medusa, papa. Someone wants me dead and others keep being killed instead." The Duke closed his eyes in pain.

"The question is, papa, why did they not kill me when I was in the country? Why wait until I came home to try?"

The Duke opened his eyes and stared at her.

"But you were not at home, Kitty. It happened before you arrived."

"You and I know that, but the ton think otherwise. After all, I was held up by the storm. I should have been home the evening before."

73

The Duke gazed into space.

"Oh God. Someone knew you were coming home."

"I believe so, papa,"

The Duke sunk into deep melancholic thought and barely seemed to register Kitty was still there.

Kitty had come for two reasons and had broached neither yet.

"Papa, I have certain things I wish you to know." He looked up, suddenly back in this world.

"The first is not pleasant but must be said. It relates to my visit to my aunts."

For the next few minutes the Duke could only listen in horror as she recounted the treatment she had received from her Aunts. She was very firm in advocating that she would never be able to be in the same house with them again. If they were invited for Christmas as usual, she would find somewhere to stay, probably a coaching inn. She also told of the wonderful help Aunt Hetty had given her, and how Aunt Phillipa hurt her by bringing up something from her past almost every day. She used it to keep Aunt Hetty in her place.

By now the Duke was open mouthed.

She described her desire for a cottage somewhere with Aunt Hetty as her companion.

"After all, I can never marry now. The only part of me a man will want is my dowry. But that must wait for now. I cannot put Aunt Hetty in danger. I would like you to do something to help her until this is over and it is safe to be near me."

The Duke hardly recognised his daughter. This strong young woman, coping sensibly with the terror she was living through. At the moment he was probably incapable of the rational thinking she was showing.

"The second thing I need is closer to you, papa. When I am away there are no attacks. So I believe I will go to stay with someone for a few weeks at least. I have been invited. I will not tell anyone I am going until the arrangements are made and I am packed and ready to go. Then I will give you the name and address to put in your safe. But only you must know, papa. Everyone must think no one knows. Even the coachman will only know the first direction. While I am away we must hope Danvers makes some progress. You will be able to write to me if he does."

The Duke reached out for her hand and held it between his.

"I feel so helpless, child, and you are so strong."

"No, papa, you feel helpless because you are looking in from outside. I, on the other hand, am in the centre and forced to address the problem in a much more personal way.

If I fell in the river, papa, you would try to get me out or send someone to get me out. If I fell into the river I would fight to save myself, because it is my life."

So Kitty left her father to think over all she had said and turned her mind to the next part of her plan.

The Duke, however, thought deeply about the change in his daughter, and everything she had said. He pondered on her remarks and then sent for Danvers.

The Duke worried how to impress on Danvers the validity of all that Kitty had said. Men like him would not believe a young chit of a girl of having any understanding of such complex matters. However, he was not aware of the high regard in which Danvers held his daughter. Not only did he accept her thoughts, he asked to speak with her to discuss various aspects of her ideas.

Armed with new insights, Danvers arranged a visit to the Prince.

* * *

"Sir Peter, how are you?" Then more quietly "Do you have any information for me?"

"Indeed, Your Highness, I have a little information but not of a positive kind. I need to be sure we are not overheard."

"Then I will arrange it personally." He walked slowly, deep in thought. To divert interest he became very light hearted.

"I am attending a balloon ascent on Hampstead Heath tomorrow. Have you heard about it? Will you be going?"

"I have indeed heard of it." and under his breath "I will attend you and speak with you then, Your Highness."

In such a crowd and surrounded by courtiers and advisers it was not easy to find a private place, but true to his word, the Prince had arranged it.

Sometimes it is easier to be private in a large crowd than in a room with eavesdroppers. The best way to divest himself of his entourage, he had found, was to start a boring discussion which went into great detail. Details of well hashed incidents from the war, yet again, were easy for Danvers to take part in, the others were not interested enough to stay.

"Your Highness, the rumours are even worse than before. They link you with an attempt on Lady Katherine's life. None of which information has come from the family. They merely refer to it as an accidental blast." The Prince looked concerned.

"I gather she was injured."

"Quite badly at the time, and two killed. Did you know about the latest incident?"

"I was told her sister died."

"Yes, Your Highness, but were you informed how?"

The Prince looked his question.

"Can I check something with you?"

"Of course, if it is important."

"Did you send or arrange to send a kitten in a basket to Lady Katherine?"

"Good Heavens, no. I told you before, I will have no connection between us."

"Well someone, the same person who sent the parasol, sent her a kitten with a label 'A kitty for my Kitty, HRH' The kitten had something pushed down its throat which gave off some kind of gas. We can't be sure what. It killed the cat and also Lady Carina."

The Prince paled.

"Be careful, Your Highness, people will notice your demeanour."

"Yes, of course. Always be jovial!" He put on an unnatural smile.

"The problem is, someone knew she was returning home early when they sent the basket. She was delayed by a storm the day before and did not arrive until after it was delivered. The worst part is, she walked in and found her sister dead. They are watching her, using her."

"You have to find them, Danvers. Stop them."

"I am calling in all operatives from the war that I can reach to assist in this. Whatever happens with the Duke of Wenton's family, it now looks as if the main target is you, Your Highness. You and the Crown."

The Prince stopped dead. A few moments passed, then he looked at Danvers.

"It is the rumours, sire. They are brewing up dislike, almost hatred for you. Whoever is doing this is definitely committing treason. We are now involved in a way with someone, or several people who probably want to see the downfall of the Crown. The main problem is why.

"Look harder, Danvers. Use as many men as you need. For God's sake, stop this!"

* * *

Putting her plan into action would take a great deal of organisation. She could tell nobody the whole idea, but some she needed to trust, Binny and Ferguson. She had her first discussion later that day. When walking in the garden with Binny she saw Ferguson delivering a message to the coachman. As he returned she beckoned him over to her.

"Lady Kitty, how are you?" His tone was worried.

"I am as well as can be expected in the circumstances, Ferguson. Are you not afraid to be close to me, you might get killed?"

"I would do anything to protect you, my lady."

"Thank you, Ferguson, I had hoped you would feel that way." She turned to encourage Binny into the conversation.

"I am thinking of going away for some months. I would, of course, need others with me."

"Where are we going, Lady Kitty?" Kitty laughed.

"Thank you Binny, that answered my question to you."

"I should hope you would know I would go with you." Binny answered just a little peeved at being doubted.

"And so will I, my lady." Ferguson joined in.

"Tell me, both of you, could you run a tiny cottage between you? Can you cook Binny, for I definitely have no idea how to, and I do not wish to starve to death?"

"Of course I can." Binny replied. "What do you think I was doing all those years after you had outgrown the nursery? I can cook and clean and wash clothes too."

"Oh Binny you are a wonder." Kitty was delighted.

Not to be outdone, Ferguson began "I can chop wood and make fires and fetch water and clean silver, anything required, my lady."

"I doubt there will be silver to clean, Ferguson. Not unless we steal some to take with us."

"Where do you intend to go, Lady Kitty?"

"That I have not yet decided. But I will tell no one, not even you two, until we are on our way. That way nobody can give information accidentally." She looked serious. "It is a large and difficult undertaking, but I will have no more deaths on my conscience."

"They were not your fault, my lady." Ferguson was adamant.

"They may not have been caused by me." Kitty said "But they were because of me, and I will do everything I can to protect the rest of my family."

So her plan could become reality with their help.

"Just one thing I would ask of you both." She looked at the two seriously concentrated faces.

"From now on, both of you should only call me Miss."

It took a moment to sink in.

"But that would be ……. You are going to hide?" A statement that showed how well Ferguson understood the task ahead.

"Of course, Ferguson, what is the point of going into hiding and being called Lady Kitty? I will pretend to be just a Miss. If you are used to saying it, then you will not give me away."

"Of course, La…..Miss."

Kitty did not sleep well that night. There was so much to decide. First of all, where? As far away from the ton as possible. Wales, no it rained so much and the locals did not like the English. Scotland, they could get lost easily in Scotland. There was too much contact with the ton in the lowlands, it would have to be much further north. Mrs Fitzgerald had talked about the highlands. How did she describe it; she could not understand a word they said; it was cold all the time; they dug up the earth to burn on the fire; and when the sun shone they were plagued by millions of flies which bit her maid and made her ill.

Oh dear, not Scotland and it was so nicely far away. Papa had maps in the library, she would search there.

How would she cope with the coachman? She would need one of them to agree to come. What if all was ready and her father sent a different coachman? So much to work out.

Sleep eventually came but it was very disturbed.

"Binny brought her hot chocolate.

"You look like you had a poor night's sleep, my … miss." She corrected herself.

"You can tell." Kitty remarked ironically.

"Well, you have dark circles under your eyes and your hair, well!"

"My hair is always a mess in the morning, Binny, It is so long at the front now and short at the back."

"The back is growing, but maybe we could cut the front a little shorter. Not too much though or people will think you are a boy.

"Later, Binny, not now. I have too much on my mind this morning."

"If you are only a miss, what clothes will you require? You only have a small amount of expensive black made up."

"Oh Binny. I never thought of clothes. Not black, people will ask too many questions and I wish for us not to tell too many lies. Lies come back to haunt you if you forget yourself. We will discuss clothes while you cut my hair this afternoon.

Nobody was surprised when Kitty left the breakfast table and went to read quietly in the library. Jeremy and the Duke left her to do as she wished, and if she wished to be alone then they would let her.

In the library she took the maps from the drawer and lay them on the largest table. She started with an overall map which included all of England. Scotland was at the top, cold and flies. Wales was to the west with mountains. There seemed to be few roads too, except those to the coast. They would be noted and remembered on their journey. The coast, why did that sound appealing? She moved down to the south coast. Brighton, good grief, the Prince went there, that was too near, most of the ton visited there anyway. Further, Devon, a few towns but a big space called Dartmoor, and one called Exmoor. Beyond that Cornwall with Bodmin Moor. What exactly was a moor anyway? Searching through various travel books she found a description. 'A rocky waste ground covered in heather or stands of trees with sparse grass. Often wet, windy and boggy, prone to mists, mainly deserted of habitation. Dangerous to cross and easy to get lost, be sure to keep to the road. Often inhabited by highwaymen and outcasts.' Well not on a moor then, but if you went beyond the moors into Cornwall, there must be roads in Cornwall, well that sounded possible. The more difficult it was to reach, the safer she would feel. Good, Cornwall it was.

Once the decision was made she fetched a sheet of paper and started to choose roads to use to avoid being seen on the journey, The towns and villages they would go to. She listed those she thought she would go through, plus a few for an alternative route in case of problems, That done, she tidied away the maps and books and went to sit in the garden arbour. She took a book, but only for the look of it, she could never concentrate on reading, not at the moment. She would take a few books with her she thought.

After lunch she and Binny sat in her room and discussed clothing, while Binny cut her hair to look tidier at the front and top. When washed it would lie in soft curls at the front of her bonnet, and the top would curl over the cap to make it less obvious. The back was beginning to grow now, it covered the scars on her head but was not yet long enough to be seen in public.

"We need practical clothes, Binny, not fashionable ones. Most of my dresses are too elegant. No silk.

"Not one, my ....Miss? What if you are invited out?"

I doubt there will be local dances, let alone balls, where we are going. But pack one if it pleases you, plus several muslin dresses. They will not be too unusual. The rest must be practical and warm. We could be gone for a long time, Binny. Winter may be very cold in a cottage."

"I suppose it will. You will need warm cloaks and extra petticoats…..miss. There may be some we could alter stored in the attic."

"Oh, do we keep clothes, Binny, I had no idea?"

"Well, you children used them for dressing up when you were small. Do you remember you and …… did."

The memory of her lost sister cause her sudden pain.

"So we did, Binny. I was going to have a bath and wash my hair now, but perhaps after we have visited the attic!"

"That's best, miss."

So to the attic they climbed, to the nursery landing and the attic room with discarded furniture and trunks. It almost felt like being a child again, opening trunks and pulling out their contents to laugh at and assess. One or two held men's clothes not suitable for the servants. Some were worn too well and some were outgrown by Jeremy. Kitty held up a pair of breeches. "Good gracious, it seems hard to imagine Jeremy was once only as big as me."

A thought entered her head. With her short hair and in Jeremy's clothes what would she look like, a young man?"

"Binny can we take some of Jeremy's old clothes for me to try on?"

"Goodness, you don't intend to pretend to be a man, do you?"

"Only on the way, Binny, not all the while. You have to admit, it is a good way to go missing."

A selection of Jeremy's clothes, plus quite a few items of warm winter clothing and old cloaks and shawls, were removed to Kitty's room. It took Binny three trips to carry it all.

"I am quite worn out miss." Binny leant against the empty fire grate.

"Sit down on a chair and rest. You can watch while I try on these clothes. I can fasten most of these myself. She picked out a couple of pairs of Jeremy's trousers, a shirt, waistcoat and a coat. The trousers were easy to pull on, they were a little loose in places but quite acceptable. The shirt was much mended. It must have been hard work to keep him looking acceptable, judging by the numbers of tears that had been darned. Tucking the shirt into the trousers was a whole new experience for Kitty. The back needed Binny's help.

With the waistcoat and jacket she was just missing stockings and boots. She looked into her mirror and noticed the cap on her hair. Removing it, she turned to Binny who sat open mouthed.

"It's like looking at young Jeremy again."

"Will I pass as a young man?"

"A very pretty one, but yes, you'll do."

In the end two sets of Jeremy's clothes were chosen plus various dresses and petticoats. Most of the dresses would have to be altered to fit but that was no problem as they were so out of date they would need to be changed in any case. Those needing washing were put to one side and a list of what was needed to complete the clothing trunk was written.

This endeavour now began to be achievable. It was time she made a date and wrote her letter.

The next morning Kitty wrote a letter to her friend Emily Weston in Norwich. Emily, of course, was in London, but no one in Wenton Hall knew that. She presented the letter to her father to be franked.

"Her papa is the local squire with arable land and waterways where they cut the reeds for thatching roofs. They are cousins to the Fitzwilliams.

"I know Fitzwilliam. A bit pompous, but not a bad sort."

"His son is pompous too, papa." She pulled a face.

"This is what you wish, child, to be away from us again?"

Kitty felt the pull of home and family, but she had to harden her heart for their sake.

"Yes, papa. I will write her name and direction for you before I go. I met Emily this summer, we came out together. She was with me every time I met the Prince. She knows it is all lies. I wrote to her while I was away and her letter was here when I returned. She tells me her mother is well now, but Emily has missed the season and is bored and would love my company. I have said I will arrive the middle of next week, papa. Is it acceptable for me to leave on Monday next?

"Of course, if you must. I understand your needs, my little one. Promise me you will take all care."

Kitty nodded to her father and leaned in to kiss his cheek.

"I do love you, papa, and Jeremy too. So very much."

The letter would arrive at a home where Emily would not be for some time. She was still in London and was invited to a great house for the summer, together with Robert and others of her friends, plus a young man she did not name, but clearly he was very important to Emily.

William was to take her there and then return to the Hall until called for. This time he was not expected to stay with her.

Clothes were readied and packed. A hat and extras were found, or purchased from the village. Some alterations were made, others could be done when they were needed. Kitty insisted Biddy and Ferguson had sufficient warm clothing themselves.

What Kitty needed most now was money, to rent a cottage and survive for some months. The journey would be very expensive as it would take a great many days to arrive in Cornwall. She still had some money left from the sum she had been given for her journey to her aunts. She asked her papa if she could have all her annual allowance as she would probably need more black clothing in a less expensive material, if she were just at a squire's house. Her papa was impressed by her thoughtfulness. Her allowance would be untouched, he said, as he gave her a hundred pounds, quite a large sum, much larger than she had expected.

The next person she spoke to was Jeremy. She told him papa was upset at her leaving and she did not wish to upset him more by asking for more money. Jeremy, not one to gamble or to spend money often, gave her all he had. One hundred and fifty pounds. Good gracious, she was only used to having a few pounds in her reticule.

At the weekend she spent some time writing to her father. A letter he would not receive until she was gone. She explained why she had gone, but not where.

She had a long talk with Ferguson about how to leave William without him realising. It was Binny who suggested a little laudanum in his ale might put him to sleep for a few hours. Ferguson elected to take on that task.

The Sunday, as the last day together, was very precious to Kitty. She was quite tearful, her father was quiet and attentive and stayed with her all day. Jeremy was more robust about it.

"Cheer up, little sister. You're only going to be gone for three or four weeks. It's not as if you're going for six months." Little did he know.

Chapter 11

Everyone was there to see them leave. Kitty went into the Duke's study and gave him Emily's name and direction. The instructions given to the coachman were to make for the great north road and stop for the night at a coaching inn.

William was intrigued, but kept the horses to a slow pace. He knew Lady Kitty did not like to change her horses, preferring to stop and rest them. The trunks were removed from the coach and placed in the ladies' room. The private dining room was already taken, but a table in the corner of the public dining room was secured. Kitty insisted they all ate together. The men were not comfortable with this, but it was not appropriate for Kitty to eat alone, and she insisted. The ladies retired but Ferguson stayed with William in the tap, Ferguson ensuring that William had a sore head in the morning.

The following morning the ladies took breakfast in their room. Binny went down to see the men who were having their breakfast in the public room.

"Lady Kitty is a little late in rising this morning, William, so make sure you have breakfast and don't rush seeing to the horses."

"Right you are, Binny." Turning to Ferguson he remarked

"This ale is not as good as last night, it tastes quite bitter." to which Ferguson replied "Perhaps you were a little too full of ale to notice the flavour. I would take a rest until needed. Today could be a long day."

"I intend to." William leaned back into the corner and closed his eyes to ease his sore head.

Kitty, dressed as her brother, went out by a different door and around to the stables to have the horses put to.

Binny hustled some barmen to bring down the trunks and they were loaded into the coach. A young hostler was left in charge of the horses while Kitty checked with Binny that William was sound asleep.

Ferguson purchased a coach ticket to London, and between them they put sufficient money to reach Wenton Hall, together with the letter to her father and the coach ticket into the sleeping William's pockets.

Ferguson spoke with the landlord's daughter, the one who had been flirting with William the night before. She was asked to see he woke in time for the London coach at two in the afternoon and assured her that he already had his ticket. She was more than happy to make sure he ate before the coach came.

Now came the tricky part. The young hostler holding the horses was to be their cover. He must tell everyone that two women, one man and the coachman left the coaching inn. It helped that the two women had arrived wearing black. Kitty went to the coach, opened the door and put down the step. Binny bustled forward to the coach. Kitty spoke in her higher woman's voice, put her foot on the coach and rocked it as if someone had entered. Ferguson gave the boy a coin and distracted him while Binny moved back from the coach and walked toward it a second time, this time climbing in. Binny and Kitty spoke to each other. Two female voices. Kitty put up the step and closed the carriage door, grunted something in as deep a voice as she could manage, then climbed up to the box. Nodding thanks to the boy they moved off. Not until they were several minutes down the road did any of them breathe freely.

"Well that went better than I expected, Ferguson."
"Indeed, my...Miss."
"I think I need a man's name for this journey, what shall it be?' You choose."
"Well, many coachmen are called John, regardless of their original name."
"Right, John it is. Just try not to call me my lady."

Now all Kitty's careful planning was to be tested. Two hours later they stopped at an inn further up the Great North Road. From here Ferguson travelled in the coach with Binny. They were now two employees being taken to another house by the young coachman on his first solo trip. According to the map she had studied, there was a road to the west in a few miles, going to Bedford. Somewhere along there they would find an inn to stay in.

She did not push the horses, only keeping then at a slow trot. She needed to keep the same horses, partly because she was extremely fond of them and they knew her, plus they were expensive for carriage horses, but also because if she changed horses anyone following or searching for her would recognise them.

Once on the Bedford road they stopped for an hour as was her requirement, and had a leisurely meal in the inn tap. Just two servants and John, the young coachman. A slow drive brought them to an inn just outside Bedford.

The first problem to be solved was who slept where. Rooms were taken for Binny and Ferguson, but often coachmen slept in the stables or in communal rooms. As John, she could have shared with Ferguson, but if she was seen going into Binny's room it could draw attention to them. She slept in the hay loft that first night, something she was to do several times during the journey. When she went to help bring down the trunk, she washed in Binny's room.

Another problem she had not foreseen was her lack of muscle to lift the trunks. A tale had to be thought up to cover this. They decided John had been very ill and was not physically strong yet, which happened to be true.

That first night none of them slept well. They had not slept that well the night before either. Kitty only hoped that as they moved away from where they might be followed they would be able to relax more. She knew she should not push the horses, but needed to get to the west of England as soon as possible.

After breakfast they set out on the Northampton road. From now on they must be especially alert. William could have arrived back at Wenton Hall and no doubt a search would be instigated. Worst of all, someone may have followed her as they must have done when she went to the aunts'.

When they stopped to rest the horses, Ferguson was to ask for directions to somewhere different, enough that anyone following would be unaware which road they had actually taken. By nightfall at the end of the second day, they were at a small inn on the Leamington road. The days were dry and warm if overcast, so Ferguson now rode in front with her for at least part of the day.

"I wish I was able to take responsibility for the driving, miss."

"John. I would rather be driving with you keeping watch with the pistols at the ready."

"I doubt we shall be met with highwaymen on these roads, …John."

"It is always possible. Soon we will be on less frequented roads and you will need to be vigilant."

On the fourth day, they left the Leamington road and turned south on the much quieter road towards Moreton-in-Marsh. The road was not in good repair but at least it was reasonably straight.

By that evening they found rooms in Moreton and gave the horses to the livery stable to be rested. They would stay there for two nights, a well earned rest for the horses and a needed rest for Kitty. She was barely at full strength for a young lady, four days driving the coach had tired her, her arms and back ached and her hands were sore in spite of the driving gloves she wore.

Moreton-in-Marsh was a pretty place, one used to having strangers visit, and the inhabitants were very hospitable. The following day was market day and it was possible to stroll around the stalls in a way Kitty had never done before, mixing with a great variety of people. Kitty sat outside an inn sipping ale, which was not to her taste, but then coachmen did not drink tea or wine. The slow speed at which she supped gave her time to watch those around her. She had never really had the opportunity to notice how the various levels of humanity looked, dressed, walked and interacted. She had only known the villagers and workers on her father's estate. She fell to judging what people did for a living, who was dishonest. She saw a pickpocket steal a man's wallet and be chased. She noted who helped chase him and who did not, some actively got in the way. She found she could see who made eye contact with someone unexpected, perhaps partners in crime. She noted the demure young ladies who made eye contact with men, that was interesting! Some of the women were not so demure, market day was a good day for their kind of trade.

She was amazed. Who would have thought it; there was a whole world out there she, as a delicate lady, knew nothing of. It was all open to her as young John, coachman.

There was a point when a young lady came to offer her wares to the pretty young coachman. Kitty found it intensely embarrassing, particularly as the men around her were trying to encourage her to partake. Some of the things they said made Kitty blush to her ears, which caused even more amusement.

The following day, Sunday, they continued until just beyond Cirencester, onto the Stroud road. It was rather wet and Kitty dearly wanted a bath to warm her. The coaching inn they picked was very accommodating; they heated water for both rooms. Binny went to Ferguson's room and left Kitty's wet clothes to dry while Kitty bathed in the gloriously hot water. That evening she slept in Binny's room. She was never more appreciative of a warm bed than she was that night.

In the morning Kitty wore her change of clothes but went to Ferguson's room with Binny's cloak to disguise her as she walked down the public corridors. It was a useful ploy as there were others moving in and out of rooms. She was about to call out to him to make sure he was up and ready, and her female voice caused no surprise. Subterfuge was becoming a natural attitude now, and why not. When they arrived in Cornwall her whole life would be make believe.

The days followed on in the usual routine. They managed to bypass Bath where there could be members of the ton who would recognise her. By the time they reached Oakhampton, they had been travelling for almost two weeks, including the extra days when they had rested, which had seemed sensible on a couple of days when rain threatened to soak them.

Once below both Bath and Bristol they were travelling on good roads and hopefully beyond meeting the ton harpies going to take the waters or visit summer house parties, most of which would be in full swing.

At Oakhampton they stayed and rested, listened to the locals and asked for advice about crossing Bodmin Moor. Some were for it, some were not. Some advised stopping at Jamaica Inn overnight, others said to avoid it and go straight through. All advised not to be crossing late in the day, and to carry loaded pistols at all times. And everyone said, beware of the mist.

They moved on to Launceston.

Bodmin was now the next target to be reached. It was only a day's drive, but they faced it with some trepidation. Food was packed to be sure they had to stop as little as possible. Kitty had decided on only one stop that day, Jamaica Inn, for resting the horses. She would not leave the coach, she intended to ask information of riders coming in the other direction.

Ferguson sat up with her, pistols loaded and ready. They left early, soon after seven, now in the middle of August, the days were still long. It was nearing nine o'clock when they felt the barren nature of the moor around them. The road was quite good and there were other travellers in both directions. By eleven they reached Jamaica Inn, an old inn with a reputation she did not wish to prove; she was not keen to spend a night there with the tales of ghosts they had been told.

They rested the horses and she ate some of the food they had brought. Binny and Ferguson went to eat inside but came out as soon as was possible, bringing drink for Kitty, so that Ferguson could be on guard with his pistols. Altogether they stayed for an hour or so, using the second part of the time to enquire about conditions or problems.

A little after midday they set off again. There was mist in some of the lower lying areas where the water collected. At first they had no problem, but after a few miles the mist came hard over them. Kitty was obliged to slow the horses to make sure they stayed safely on the road. The mist seemed endless. In a few places it had cleared and she whipped up the horses to make up some time.

From the mist the occasional rider appeared like a ghost, silently approaching. Coaches could be heard in the distance, but not that often. On one occasion a coach rattled toward them at speed, in spite of the conditions. The coachman was shouting something she could not make out, and pointing backwards. Ferguson sat to attention, his pistols in his hands, eyes and ears straining. A sharp muffled noise brought a rider fast approaching through the mist, a pistol waving in his hand, but it was not pointed at them, it was gesticulating behind him. Had it been a pistol shot they had heard? Kitty whipped up the horses to a fast trot, she dared go no faster. She heard, rather than saw, riders off the road in the mist. She could only just see where she was going but she would not slow down.

Then suddenly the mist cleared completely and they saw the landscape open around them. She put the horses to a gallop, not for safety but mainly to get off the moor as soon as possible.

It was a sudden pleasure to find themselves at Bodmin, to give the horses over to be cared for, while they ordered rooms, one each this time. Kitty needed a bath and to sleep in a bed. She had spent too many nights in strange places and the day had been difficult on her emotions. She thought she was strong but she was overcome with the need to cry in sheer relief.

They did not leave early the next morning because she had no idea exactly where she was going. Late in the morning she drove towards the west, towards the coast, towards whatever fate brought.

Chapter 12

Cornwall was very different from her home near London. The roads were narrow, some leading in odd directions. She met a few strange glances from the locals as the coach, with such a young man driving, squeezed down narrow roads, through tiny hamlets, only to come to a much larger road which seemed to come from nowhere and go to nowhere. She struggled on, westwards, towards the sea and suddenly there it was, a shinning expanse of blue that met the sky and merged into a pale glow. She was mesmerised. She had never seen the sea before. She had seen the river in London, and where it grew wider in its lower reaches, but nothing had prepared her for the sheer scale of this, the feeling of hugeness, or emptiness, of never endingness. It filled her with a sense of freedom, of elation, of total awe.

"Oh my." Binny had climbed out of the coach, "I have never seen the sea before."

"Nor I, Binny. It is much more than I expected, quite overwhelming."

"Are we staying on this road to find an inn to stay in?" Ferguson was being practical and his stomach was having something to say as well.

"I think we should find someone to ask." Kitty said, thoughtfully. "It seems more sensible than just driving. I myself do not fancy sleeping in the coach again as I sometimes have had to on the way, and I am most definitely not sharing it with you two!"

The thought of three of them trying to sleep in the coach brought on a sudden awareness of the time.

It took only ten minutes driving to find a cottage to enquire at, and surprisingly only fifteen minutes more to enter a small town with an inn renting rooms. Tomorrow they would start the hunt for a cottage, but for tonight they had successfully reached the end of their long journey; all they needed now was food rest and each other's company.

The reality of what they had now to achieve began to sink in.

"Ferguson, you will need to take charge from now on." Kitty watched his face as various thoughts and feelings crossed his mind.

"What do I need to do? Have you made a plan, my ….Miss…John?" Kitty smiled.

"Here is the story. We are looking for a small cottage, preferably near the sea, which is off the road; that is important. It is for a very reclusive elderly gentleman who wishes to be totally isolated from everyone. We are his servants. His name is …." She thought. "William Sinclair. He will not see anyone. If you need to have his signature for the rental, then you must take it to him, that is bring it to me, to be signed. We will take the cottage for six months."

"Six months! ……"

"Yes, if he wishes to stay longer he will make another agreement after that."

"What if they wish it for a year, miss?"

"We can only afford to be here for six months, Binny. We have to hope something has been resolved by then."

"It will be cold, miss."

"I know, Binny, now you know why I insisted on all the warm clothing. Now Ferguson, we will require a bedroom each and a stable for the horses. We cannot have the horses in a livery stable where they will be seen. Questions would be asked, people would enquire about us. Besides, it is an expense we cannot afford."

"What if people come to call?" Ferguson was concerned.

"We are not at home." Kitty was adamant. "If we need to, we will live in the early morning and late evening and lock ourselves in during the main part of the day, or go out. Binny looked confused.

"Don't worry, Binny. We must make this an adventure. We are not at the Hall now, things are bound to be different, difficult sometimes, but we will manage, somehow, we have to." This last was said with a quiet shudder; the alternative was too horrible to contemplate.

That first day Ferguson enquired at the inn as to where he could find an agent with property to rent.

"To rent, yer say. Well't depends as what you want, I 'spect. You could ask in Newquay, or a bit past that in Wadebridge. If'n it be good house, I dunnow." The landlord was doing his best.

"Not a house, a cottage or small house." Even Ferguson was hopeful. "Best ask at the Jolly Sailor, they might know." At which point he wandered off, scratching his head.

"What did he say?"

"Ask at the Jolly Sailor."

"Where's that?"

"Goodness knows. It could be Newquay or Wadebridge or anywhere in between, he was not any more forthcoming than that. He walked away."

"I think we pay the bill and move on. It could take us several days to find some kind of agent or estate manager."

"I think an agent is what we need to ask for. If any of the locals think they can get a high rent for a cottage they don't own, it could be disastrous."

"Which way do we head?"

"You choose. He was not that helpful."

In the end they went north through small roads that sometimes threatened to refuse access to even their small coach. Eventually they came to a town.

"Where is this?"

"I have no idea, go and ask."

It turned out to be Padstow. They found a small inn but not with rooms. The locals were difficult to understand. It being late morning, the fishing boats were out and only the old men were sitting outside the inn.

"Agent, wat fer!"

"A cottage to rent."

"Oh. Dunno no agent ere. Cottage up on top you could av. Got two rooms it as."

"Thank you."

Poor Ferguson. Bemused was not the word for it. He put his head in the inn door to ask the innkeeper where there was an inn with rooms.

"That'd be Wadebridge you want then."

"How do we reach there.?"

"You goes up there." He pointed to a slightly different direction than where they arrived.

"What did he say?"

"You go up that road...track to Wadebridge. They have an inn with rooms."

"Oh good, I don't fancy sleeping on the rough ground!"

"There's always the coach."

"Not for all three of us."

So on they went. When they came onto a better road they had to guess at the direction to take.

"Are we going to sit here for long, miss?"

"No, Ferguson, just until someone comes who can tell us the direction. After the débâcle in the inn this morning, I am not prepared to risk it."

It took nearly half an hour but eventually someone came, from Padstow, with a cart. With much cursing he let them know they were blocking the road. Ferguson got down.

"Wadebridge?"

The man gesticulated to the left.

"I believe it is to the left, my lady, if his shoulder can be believed."

"Kitty thought it funny, but perhaps she was not as hungry as Ferguson.

Late in the afternoon they found the inn, after much grumbling and gesticulation of arms and heads had directed to them to several small taverns which were totally unsuitable.

"Oh, you means the coaching inn."

Ferguson was wiping his brow, Binny had her head out of the window asking questions, and Kitty succumbed to a fit of giggles.

Still, a coaching inn, with beds, and proper stabling for the horses, wonderful.

They knew nothing about agents. After eating a hearty meal, lunch and dinner combined, they set about making enquiries. They asked about cottages, they asked about houses, they asked about agents.

Somewhat dejected, they sat at a table in the coaching inn and discussed what to do. A traveller at another table heard Ferguson's exasperated outburst.

"Excuse me." a cultured voice said. "I could not but hear you are wanting to rent a dwelling."

They answered in the affirmative.

"Well most of the housing around here is mere hovels. The only reasonable places are the landowners' property, and you will need to speak to their agents."

"We have been asking for an agent, Sir." Binny said

"But nobody knows of one."

"Well there is one a little way down the coast. You will do better to ask at Newquay. What did I say?"

All three of them were laughing.

"We had a choice of direction this morning, sir, it seems we took the wrong one." Binny surmised.

"Thank you for your valued assistance, sir." Kitty said in her deepest voice.

"Is it somewhere for yourselves?" He seemed somewhat amused by them. She could not allow him to become too interested.

"No, sir. It is for our elderly master who is a recluse."

"Oh, well, you're in the right place here. You can't be more reclusive than living anywhere around here."

"You are not local, sir?" Kitty asked.

"No, I have just been visiting friends. I am returning to civilised habitation."

At that point he wished them well and took his leave of them to continue on his journey.

"I think a visit to check the horses and a good night's sleep, ready for an early start."

"I hope our rooms are around the back, the noise of the coaches in the night can be very disturbing." Binny observed.

"I doubt there are that many coaches." Kitty said. "We do seem to be delightfully isolated here." She allowed herself a smile that was almost relaxed.

The following morning they followed the direction the coach driver indicated, and found a quite reasonable road, to Newquay.

Newquay was, if anything, smaller than Wadebridge, but it did have one thing missing from Wadebridge. It had The Jolly Sailor.

After their early breakfast, the late lunch was extremely welcome.

"No the agent aren't ere." It was not that the locals were unhelpful, just that they only answered the questions asked. They volunteered nothing.

"Where could we find the agent?" *Please do not say Wadebridge.*

"He lives on the estate."

"Where might I find him?"

"Jo, were be Alwood?." the barman called.

"Down on't ard."

"Where is t'ard?"

"Down't path to sea. He be checking a boat pr'aps.

"And his name is Alwood?"

"Aye, that it be."

"Thank you." The barman looked surprised at being thanked.

As the horses were stabled, Binny went to her room and Kitty and Ferguson walked down to the slipway to find Alwood.

Amid the usual old retired fishermen, Alwood was easy to recognise.

"Excuse me, Mr Alwood, I believe you must be he."

Ferguson used his best butler like voice.

"We understand you are an agent for the local landowner. We are looking to rent a cottage or small house for our employer."

"Rent, you say. Well I'm sure we could find something. I have to warn you though, the village houses are only small. It depends on how large you need it to be.

"We have instructions to look for no less than three bedrooms, stabling for the carriage horses, but not in a village. Our master is an elderly recluse gentleman. He sees no one. He is rather fearful of any intrusion into his privacy. We are to look for a six month rental to begin with."

"An elderly gentleman, you say. So a fairly comfortable place, not a hovel. I have several cottages that might suit, but mostly in or near villages."

Kitty joined in.

"By the sea would be a pleasant view for him."

"It would be rather open to the cold winds. Usually such places are only wanted for summer occupation."

He fell quiet for a moment, considering the options.

"Off the road, facing the sea. I have a house which is rarely occupied as it is difficult to reach with a coach when it rains. It is beyond the means the locals can afford. Where are you staying?"

"We are at The Jolly Sailor, sir."

"Oh, staying locally, that is useful. When would you want a lease to begin?"

"Well, right away if possible."

"We have left Mr Sinclair at a coaching inn but he is not happy there." Kitty made up.

"No, I don't expect he is. Come back to The Jolly Sailor and we will talk some more."

So back they went to discuss the terms of the rental agreement, and what the cottage contained. It was arranged that he would return the following morning to take them to see the property. In the meantime, he would send word to have the rental agreement written and, if they deemed the cottage suitable, he would let them take the lease to the reclusive Mr William Sinclair to be signed.

That night, Ferguson drank a little more than usual, and Kitty had to watch he said nothing untoward.

"I do hope it is adequate" Kitty voiced quietly.

"So do I, my...miss. I would rather not have to do this all over again." a slightly inebriated Ferguson mouthed.

It was just right, no, more than right, it was perfect. Facing the cliff top with a view of the sea from all the front windows, It had the three bedrooms needed, two downstairs rooms, comprising a parlour and a dining room. The back of the house was the kitchen and scullery. The stable was small but enclosed because of the winds from the sea, and would house both horses and carriage. There was a small paddock to one side for the horses. But best of all was the lack of road. Only a mud track led across unused pasture land, enclosed by a hedge, from a tiny, empty track road. It was furnished but very sparsely and had definitely not been lived in for some time.

"He will love it." Kitty exclaimed. "It is truly perfect."

So the Honourable William Sinclair of Elms Road, High Wycombe, took possession of the house for six months.

Binny assured the agent that she would clean the house herself, she needed no help. Now it was theirs she had no intention of letting anyone into their hideout.

They made only one journey, to buy linens and basic necessities which included food, candles and wood for a few weeks. The coach was crammed to the brim and Binny had to sit surrounded with her legs straight out. Ferguson had to ride with Kitty.

They unloaded the coach and Kitty and Ferguson pushed it into the stables out of sight, letting the horses into the field to run freely.

Now their new life would begin. For good or bad they were committed to this place for the next six months, God willing no one found them.

Chapter 13

The letter Kitty sent to her father caused emotional panic and total havoc for everyone. A communication was sent to Danvers, who arrived with some speed for a conference, bringing with him John Portman, one of his former operatives who still worked for the Foreign Office. He was second in command of what was now a full scale operation.

Although Kitty sent the letter there was no proof she was not forced to write it. The Duke had already questioned William, who the young hostler had assured that there were two ladies and a gentleman and a coach driver when the coach left. Danvers sent Portman to ask again, and to check the surrounding coaching inns for sightings of the coach. He would send a man to Emily Weston's house in Norwich, in the faint hope that she had actually gone there. Nothing could be done until they had the results of the search. The Duke and Jeremy were left to make a list of anyone in the family she may have gone to visit.

It was an anxious time for everyone. The Duke was almost inconsolable. He shut himself in his study and spoke to no one. Jeremy went to London with Danvers to check the London house, although Danvers warned him not to ask his friends in the clubs. It would cause more problems if the ton knew too soon, and started more rumours.

Four days later they sat in the Duke's library with nothing positive to discuss. Portman had the same story from the young hostler, and from all the surrounding inns they could have visited. There was no sign of them or the coach. The only similar coach to stop anywhere had been carrying only a man and a woman servant with a coachman. They only remembered them because the maid wore deep black. There was no trace of them either in Norwich or on the way there.

"Could she have been kidnapped?" Danvers avoided the word killed. "If so, why, when she was leaving anyway? They never took her before when she went away."

"There was something strange, sir." All eyes turned to Portman.

"If someone kidnapped her, who and why? Someone was asking the same questions as me the day she disappeared.

"Someone asked who?"

"The coaching inn, the young hostler, at most of the inns I questioned. They had all been questioned by a fairly rough fellow. They refused him any information, plus a more cultured man arrived the day before I did."

Danvers let out a whistle.

"Either there are two groups, or our Lady Kitty has indeed managed to evade everyone in an effort to 'protect her family' as she put it."

"Where do we go from here?"

"Give me your list and I will send riders to visit them. Some may have information. What about the family she visited before?"

The Duke answered sourly "I doubt she would go there. They were less than friendly. She would not be welcome."

"If they were family, why would she not be welcome?"

Portman was yet to come to terms with all the ramifications of the ton.

"They knew the rumours, and believed them. She had no desire to see any of them again." He became thoughtful.

"Except Aunt Hetty."

Jeremy cut in with a suggestion.

"If I went to all of them, maybe I could tell them a little and decide who is actively hostile. I could also check with Aunt Hetty for anything she had said that could be helpful."

"Then we cover the family and confer when we have more information. I know it is distressing to you, sir, but I begin to think she is safe. She is intelligent enough to organise this."

It was a small consolation to the Duke. Danvers asked to keep the letter which prompted a question from Portman.

"What paper is the letter written on, the coaching inn?"

Jeremy took the letter from Danvers' hand.

"No, it's yours, father. Show him a sheet.

The Duke went into the study and fetched a sheet from his desk. Jeremy took it and held it towards the light of the window.

"The same watermark, papa. Your paper, your ink. Kitty wrote it here before she left."

"Well done, Portman, that was a stroke of genius."

"So, if the letter is genuine, then she should be safe somewhere. The sooner I leave for Aunt Hetty, the better.

Plans in place, they arranged to meet when Jeremy returned.

* * *

Jeremy set out early the next morning. A single rider could make much better time than a coach, and he was riding a very good strong horse. It was just before lunch on the day he arrived at his Aunt Phillipa's house. She was more than surprised to see him.

"Jeremy, what a surprise. To what do we owe this visit?"

"I need to talk to you, but mainly I need to talk with Aunt Hetty."

"What does Hetty know that I can't tell you?"

"A great deal, I hope. She, at least believed in Kitty's innocence." Aunt Phillipa looked a little shocked.

"We were not to know." she began.

"Did you ask?" Jeremy gave her no chance to finish. "Carina is dead. It was meant to be Kitty, again. Now she is missing. We need all the information we can find, and Aunt Hetty might be able to help."

"Did Carina not die of an illness?"

"No, Aunt. She was murdered. It was addressed to Kitty, just like the first one. Just like the lying rumours in the ton are all aimed at Kitty and no one can find out why."

Luncheon was announced at that moment. Aunt Hetty appeared and they all went into the small dining parlour for a light repast of mostly cold meats and pie.

There was very little discussion over luncheon. Aunt Phillipa hardly ate anything. Hetty, not knowing why, tried to urge her, but to no avail.

"Jeremy wishes to speak with you, Hetty." Phillipa said.

"Hetty looked surprised. "I thought this was a visit while on your journey, Jeremy."

"No, Aunt Hetty. I need a private conversation with you about Kitty."

"Use the library, Hetty. There is brandy in there for him." Aunt Phillipa was definitely affected.

Ensconced in the library, Jeremy mused how to start.

"I would like to thank you for everything you did for Kitty, Aunt Hetty." He held up his hand to stop her speaking. "No, she told papa what happened. What I need is any information she may have given you that could help us." Aunt Hetty looked shocked.

"She is not dead, Aunt Hetty, or at least we do not believe so. Carina is dead, as you probably do know. What killed Carina was addressed to Kitty. I walked into the room behind Kitty when she found her. I need not explain the emotions involved. It was days before she spoke. Now she is missing. She arranged to visit a friend in Norwich, but she disappeared at the first coaching inn. We think she arranged it. Others beside ourselves have been searching for her, so we think she is safe from them. She is not here with you, is she?"

Hetty was trembling. She found it hard to find words.

"My poor Kitty. All she wanted was peace. No, she is not here."

"Did she ever say where she would like to live or to go, what she hoped for her life?"

Tears were now streaming down her face.

"She thought she would probably never be able to marry now. She talked about persuading her father to give her a cottage where I could live with her as her companion. She had no idea where, that would be up to her papa, she said."

"She told my father all that. She even said she had to wait, because she could not risk anything happening to you. She calls herself Medusa. She thinks they want her dead and everyone around her dies in her place."

He stopped and turned away.

"She left a letter saying she was going away to save us." A tear slid quietly down Jeremy's face. He stood and walked away. Eventually his shoulders shook as he gave way to his grief for the first time.

Hetty crossed the library and poured a glass of brandy which she took and placed in his hand. He took a sip.

"I just feel this is all my fault. I said Aunt Jane could not bring her out properly. If I had gone to London with her, none of this would have happened.

"Who knows, Jeremy, Maybe it would still have happened, or maybe not, we will never know. Kitty is a sensible and intelligent girl. If you think she organised this, and if others are looking, then she is probably safe. Wait, and she may contact you. Did she have money?"

"I never thought of that. Yes she did, I gave her everything I had. She said she did not want to trouble papa."

"Would your papa have let her go without any funds?"

"No, I suppose not. So she may have had quite an amount of money."

"I think Kitty planned this very carefully. She has gone to the cottage she talked of, and she will be safe until she contacts her papa for more funds."

Jeremy stared at her.

"Thank you, Aunt Hetty. Now I understand just the kind of comfort and help you gave Kitty. You are the most sensible and understanding woman I know. I wish you had been nearer when we were all growing up. We sorely needed a mother figure like you."

Big as he was, Hetty was not above hugging him, as she had the son she had lost.

Jeremy knew then that if she had gone to anyone it would have been to Aunt Hetty. He need not trouble to visit the other aunts, they had been too hostile. He now had some of the answers they needed, and some hope, however small.

The next day early, he set out for home. If he pushed hard he could make it in two days, although it would be very late when he arrived.

The journey was uneventful. He stopped only when he need to, continued until late, then started early the next day.

It was ten in the evening when he rode through the village to the west of the estate. It was a dark night and as he picked his way carefully along the narrow road, he was met by a group of four men.

At first he did not comprehend what they were about. He drew his pistol.

"Out of my way, or I shall shoot."

"Now, now. All we want is information." It was a cultured voice that spoke behind him. "Just tell us where she is."

"Who, what do you mean?"

"You know perfectly well what I mean. Your sister Kitty, where is she?"

"I don't know. We are looking for her."

"Come now, you've just been to see her, haven't you."

"No. She wasn't there, we can't find her."

"Oh dear. I think we will have to persuade him, gentlemen."

With that they dragged Jeremy from his horse and beat him with something metal. The pain that erupted was intense, and he reeled with every blow.

"Where is she?"

"I don't know." and the beatings went on.

It was some time before they stopped, by which time most of his body was broken and bruised. The pain was so great he was barely conscious.

"Shall we finish him off?" one said.

The cultured voice spoke, Eton accent, then a kick in the head and Jeremy was fully unconscious.

The road returned to silence when they rode away and left him to die.

From the other side of the hedge, two courting young villagers whispered together.

"What shall we do?"

"We best go for the doctor."

"What if he's dead, they'll blame us."

"No they won't, just tell them we found him."

Thus it was that the probably dying Jeremy was taken by the villagers, under the supervision of the doctor, and carried to the doctor's house.

To begin with, nobody could recognise him, he was so damaged. His broken limbs were splinted and his broken ribs were bound, but the bruises would take some time to come out, and the blow to the head had left him badly concussed.

Later the next morning, Jeremy's horse made it back to the stable at Wenton Hall and a search began of the estate and surrounding roads and villages. The young man at the doctor's house was identified and the Duke was informed.

It was several days before the doctor would allow him to be moved at all. They took the travelling coach and fitted it with a pallet covered in soft pillows to lay him on. He was carried with the greatest care to his bed. The doctor was in attendance all of the time, watching over him. He prescribed a sleeping draft, not for Jeremy, but for the Duke.

"Will he live?"

"He may, but I cannot guarantee it. If he does, I have to warn you, he may never walk again. You need a woman here, Wenton. Are there none of your relatives, sisters, cousins who could come to take care of him?"

"No. I can't think of any of them ....Aunt Hetty!"

The following day, the travelling coach with William driving and two armed attendants, took a letter to his sister Phillipa, with instructions to bring Aunt Hetty to take charge of the broken family, including the Duke.

A week later, Danvers arrived for a conference and found a house of invalids unable to cope any longer with the investigation. From now onwards, he must manage this himself from London.

A week or two later, there was an unexplained fire in the stables. Almost everyone from the house rushed out to help save the horses, and to douse the fire. It was the footman and newly arrived Aunt Hetty tending to Jeremy, who smelled the smoke, and the fire in the small parlour was discovered. Help was summoned and it was soon extinguished. The parlour was ruined, but it was at least confined to the one room.

Danvers was informed, and believed the stable fire was a decoy to remove the staff while the parlour fire was set. Whether they intended to burn down the Hall, he was not sure. He thought it possible they believed Kitty was hidden there, and intended to smoke her out.

A Bow Street Runner was sent to the Hall to watch for any intruders or problems, however small, and all the outside staff were put on alert.

This was getting out of hand. He needed all the operatives he could reach to assist. The ton rumours were getting worse and were against the Prince. This was dangerous treason, which could bring down the government, the crown, the whole civilisation of England.

Chapter 14

The first problem was when Binny tried to stop Kitty helping to clean the house. That first night they made up the beds and tumbled into them. It was the following morning when, with the shutters open, you could see the dirt. Ferguson helped Binny clean out the kitchen boiler to light the fire for hot water. The cliff was so high above the sea that a well was not possible close to the house, but there was a spring which fed a small stream some half a mile away. Fetching sufficient water to fill the boiler and the saucepans, took a great deal of time. Kitty made a note that baths were to be few and far between. Buckets of water are heavy to carry any distance, and Kitty was not strong enough to help, so she thought up the idea of tying two buckets, one on either side of the horse. They lost some water as it sloshed about, but all told, it was an improvement. It took them all morning to fetch enough water to fill the boiler and heat the water,

They had a cold lunch, after which the range and saucepans were scrubbed to allow Binny to cook. The fire was lit in the range, but when Kitty went outside to the cliff top she noticed the black smoke from the chimney. Surely that could be seen for miles out to sea, and all around the bay. If they wanted to hide the fact they were there they must light fires only when it was dark.

While Binny started cooking dinner, Kitty took hot water up to her room. Binny presumed it was for a wash, but Kitty had started to clean her room. She washed the windows and the sparse furniture. She stole upstairs with the brush, and swept the floor, depositing the dirt at the top of the stairs.

Then she tied up her skirt and tried to scrub the floor. Scrubbing floors, Kitty found, was much harder than she had realised. The maids at the Hall had always made it look so easy.

Binny was horrified when she realised what she had been doing, but it was a waste of hot water not to start, Kitty said. Binny scrubbed the kitchen table, while Kitty watched her technique. That evening they ate together in the kitchen as the dining room was too dirty. Binny and Ferguson were most upset about it but there was no alternative. Besides, was she to eat alone for the rest of her life?

The next few days were tiring but fulfilling. Kitty had never done any manual work in her life, but the drive there had strengthened her muscles and she was not entirely helpless. During those cleaning days they discussed and planned. It took some serious pushing from Kitty to get Binny and Ferguson to put forward their ideas rather than just carry out orders. As she said, after all, what real idea did she have about how to run a house like this? All she knew was how to order servants to do something, not how they achieved it.

A routine was worked out which would get easier as the nights closed in. Water must be fetched early morning or late evening at twilight. Fires could only be lit when it was dark enough not to see the smoke. All outside work, such as fetching in firewood and water was at a similar time, as was Kitty's job as John coachman to look after the horses. Washing was to be dried in the stables or the scullery, not outside.

After a week, where they all worked very hard, the little household could begin to live a regular life in their hideaway. Their meals were meagre, Binny did her best but they had little and ate simply. Ferguson found a bag he could carry on his back and announced that at least once a week, possibly more, he would walk to the small town and buy food.

Kitty was now reduced to being the Lady of the house once more. With the work she had been able to set aside her fears, but now they all came flooding back. With nothing to do except hide in the house all day, she found sleeping became a problem. Binny watched as the worry and lack of sleep gave her black circles around sunken eyes. The loss of weight from the journey and the cleaning, after all she had lost before, made even her most closely fitted clothes hang on her. She tried to walk in the daytime but was too afraid of being seen.

It was into September now. The weather was still not too cold, but they had taken to eating a good early breakfast and a late dinner. Very little was taken at luncheon, except for bread and a little cheese when available. So when Kitty found the path down to the sea it opened a new interest for her. Instead of sitting in the house looking out at the sea, she could walk down the cliff path to a cave-like indent about half way down. She had only brought a very few of her favourite books, but each day she went early after breakfast, with a shawl, a book and her lunch, and sat in the hollow in the rocky edge of the cliff.

She watched the ships come and go from the little harbour just around the headland. She watched the workman with his horse and dray collect rocks from the cliff face, presumably for some kind of building work. People came to scavenge after the tide went out, and children came to play, running from the waves as they crept up the beach.

One day she was a little later leaving the house. She needed to be 'John coachman' seeing to the horses, and it made her late. A young man with a horse and dray was coming slowly up the usually empty lane.

"Hello, I didn't think you was 'ere yet. Agent Mr Alwood said you might need wood."

"I think we might." she replied. "How do we get more?"

"I brings it, miss. Have you found the water?"

"Yes, down over there." She pointed in the direction where the spring was.

"The'm be nother one over there, tis nearer."

"Oh, is it far, you must show me."

She walked up to the road and followed him a short distance. He pointed through a gate they had presumed was someone's private land.

"See where the wall turns. It be there."

"I am so grateful to you. And yes, we could do with some firewood. But there is one thing I would ask."

"Aye miss."

"Mr Sinclair would like nobody to know we are here. So if you could not tell anyone I would be very grateful, young man."

"Course, miss. Alwood did say as how he was a reluse."

"A recluse, that means he is very private and wishes no one to see him or know where he is."

"I'll tell no one, miss. If ye need owt, I live at the white house down't lane. Just ask."

With that he drove off up the lane towards the town. Kitty, still trembling with fear at having been seen, went back into the house to relate what had just happened.

* * *

Richard returned to London as the season was coming to an end. He arrived one evening when his mother was attending a ball. Settling himself in his study with a selection of cold meats and cheese, with some of cook's special home baked bread he nursed a relaxing glass of his favourite brandy.

"Will you be needing anything more, my lord?" His butler stood quietly by the door.

"No thank you, Elliot, tell Smithson I will be out fairly early in the morning, so if he could make sure some of my town clothes are ready, he can unpack everything else tomorrow." The butler bowed and turned to leave. "Oh, and Elliot, do not inform my mother I have returned, not tonight at least. I will be away from home all day tomorrow. I may be home for dinner, but I can't be sure."

"Yes, my lord. I will see nobody informs your mother until you are ready. Goodnight, my lord."

"Goodnight, Elliot."

The next morning at nine o'clock, Richard ate a good breakfast and left the house shortly afterwards. His first call was to his agent who looked after his investments. He was a good man, Richard had concluded, his having been honest and successful in keeping his funds in good order while he had been away in France. Now he was back, however, Richard was enjoying working with him, making decisions about new areas of investment and new developments that were coming up which could prove to be worthwhile. He stayed there all morning.

At midday he went into his club to take his lunch.

"Ah, Pengarron. Good to see you, Been missing for most of the season. Holed up with a nice little piece, I'll be bound. Making up for lost time, I expect." Wittain was a rather obnoxious acquaintance he would rather not have known.

"No, just seeing to my property." He replied sharply.

"About time you had yourself a little fun. Know a nice piece in need of a protector, if you're in the market."

"I am not Wittain. Thank you for your sentiments but a mistress does not appeal to me."

"He needs a nice little wife, Wittain." Corbin joined in to the conversation. "Come up to stay this summer. I'm sure we can accommodate you. I have two of mine on offer, suit you down to the ground."

"How do you know what will suit me, Corbin? You have hardly seen me in years. Daughters not taken this season?" Corbin looked a little uncomfortable.

"Excuse me, gentlemen." Richard gave a nod to the two of them and removed himself from the club. He would find a decent place to eat, where he was not offered anything except food and drink.

Later he visited his tailor to be fitted for some less formal country wear. Why have all these formal outfits when he had no desire to be in company?

From there he went to The House to see what was being discussed. He sat through several tedious speeches which actually managed to say absolutely nothing. In the foyer he met others on the way for a drink and discussion so he joined them.

While they were discussing parliamentary matters all was well. It was when the first turned to him and asked

"Not married yet, Pengarron?"

"No, nor do I have a mistress, nor do I want either. If you wish to offer me your unmarried daughter, or ex mistress, may I suggest you do not."

"A little sensitive, Pengarron! Is there some reason?"

"I have had a surfeit of offers and attempts to trap me. That includes my own mother."

"Ah, a very persistent matchmaker, your mama, eh?"

"You are not alone in this, young fellow. Any titled gentleman, or for that matter from a good family, with funds, is having a hard time of it. Is there a reason for your aversion?"

"None, except I will choose my own wife. When I meet her I will know."

"Ah, a man of strong intentions. I only hope you can hold out."

The bell rang for Parliament to reconvene and he was spared any further personal discussion.

The bill under discussion in the Lords was of no interest, and the speeches did not inspire him, so he took himself off home, hoping his mother was again out somewhere.

His mother was at home, but was entertaining a few friends. Richard took himself to his study and ordered his dinner served there. Among the few guests was her latest protégé, Miss Penelope Langdale. He spent his evening dealing with his correspondence. There was the invitation to Highborne, for whenever he was free.

The following day his mother managed to corner him.

"That was very poor of you last night, Richard. I hope you are not going to continue to ignore your poor mother."

"If you continue to try to wed me to your latest young ingénue, then I will. When you allow me to make my own choice, then will I be amenable to you, madam."

"You need to marry, Richard. You need an heir."

"And I will, someday, but it will be when I choose. Can you guarantee me that your little empty headed protégés will give me a male heir? No you cannot. Therefore I will marry as and when I choose, someone I can stand to live in the same house with."

"Are you staying in London all summer, can I not tempt you to join me at a house party?"

"I am staying until Parliament rises, then I plan to visit Carvon at Highborne."

"What a stroke of luck, the Earl and Countess have also invited me. I have several offers, but I think I will accept theirs. At least I will have a little time with you."

He knew he should have said nothing. Now he was stuck.

Three days later his mother left for Highborne Castle. She took Miss Penelope Langdale, and his travelling carriage. She also took the smaller London carriage filled with luggage and maids. Apparently her own carriage had been left at some friends' house when they brought her to London. His temper was sorely tried.

He attended few parliamentary debates, but used it as an excuse to stay in London. He worked in his study, or read in his library, but he never risked his club again. What he needed was a cause, and parliament was not giving him one.

In the middle of August he eventually gave in to the boredom of nothing worthwhile to do and set out for Carvon at Highborne Castle. There was another annoyance, he was obliged to hire a carriage to take his valet and trunks.

He rode down on horseback.

His first encounter was no real surprise.

"Walcott, what a surprise you being here." No real surprise, just a little sarcasm on his part. "Why don't you just marry my mother?"

"I would if she would have me. Says she will not marry until you have a wife to run your houses."

"Since when is she at any of my houses except London? I usually fend for myself, I make sure I employ very capable housekeepers."

The company was quite varied, most of them Richard was acquainted with. Dinner was very formal, the ladies especially liked it that way as it gave them an opportunity to wear their beautiful gowns and jewellery. That first evening Richard was seated between Miss Langdale and Mrs Langdale. His mother must have had some hand in that.

"You are not acquainted with my daughter, sir?" Mrs Langdale started.

"No, I have not had the pleasure, but I believe she is very friendly with my mother."

"Indeed she is. We are so honoured at Lady Pengarron taking to Penelope so well." Mrs Langdale simpered.

"My mother likes to take up a cause each season, it seems your daughter is this year's." He was being a little cruel, but wanted to give her to understand that he was not involved. Mrs Langdale was at a loss how to respond.

Miss Langdale had been talking to the elderly scholar sitting at her other side. He only heard short snatches of conversation, but she did not seem to be able to converse with him well, and kept trying to turn the talk to much lighter matters. Eventually she turned to Richard.

"Do you appreciate gothic novels, my lord?"

Was she trying to flutter her eyelashes at him? Good Lord.

"No, I do not." Silence

"What kind of books do you read, sir?"

"I mainly study the latest developments in farming, and the increasing mechanisation with all its ramifications for the future of the countryside."

She blinked.

He was being a little cruel he knew.

She looked a little lost, but was determined to try again.

"Don't you ever read books?"

"They are books. Do you mean novels?"

"Yes, my lord."

"I do when I have the time. I often read Aristotle or Dante. I must confess that I find them best in their original language." None of this was strictly true, but he had no intention of giving her any point to discuss.

"Why do you not like the latest genre of gothic novels?"

"They are stories with no reality. Why would you wish to be entertained with horror?"

"It is real to me, my lord."

Now she was becoming a little belligerent. In her effort to cope with two difficult neighbours, she had been sipping her wine quite freely. It seemed she was not used to imbibing.

"Then you know nothing of real life, madam. I admit at your age it is beyond your comprehension."

The ladies left them to their port and he settled in with a group of his friends, which included Carvon.

"So glad you could come, Pengarron. We seem to have a surfeit of gossipy women. Hard to get a decent conversation going."

"Then I will refrain from speaking with them. While on the subject of women, Carvon, who organised the seating plan? I have a feeling my mother was involved. If so, can you let your lovely wife know that in future if trapped deliberately that way, I will take suddenly ill and retire."

"That bad. I thought you knew them."

"No, I never met them before. I believe Miss Langdale is my mother's latest attempt to marry me off."

"I will have a quiet word. Wouldn't want you to flee so soon after arriving. There is a meeting at Newbury Races in two days time. I shall be getting up a party."

The following day was clear and warm. Richard went riding with several of his friends while the ladies walked in the garden. After lunch, most of the ladies retired ready for the evening, which was to include musical recitals by several of the young ladies.

During the afternoon Richard played billiards with several of the men. One of those present was Mr Langdale. When several were in a deeply argumentative game he was approached by Mr Langdale and pinned into a corner.

"Pengarron, wanted to say, it won't do. Can't have you playing with my daughter's affections. If you intend to offer for her then do. I will not have her reputation damaged by your type." Richard sat quietly trying to hold his temper.

"Mr Langdale. I have no interest in your daughter, I have barely spoken to her. If you believe to corner me into offering for her, I will not. If you try to use your intrigue to shame me, I will not be trapped by you or anyone of your family."

Langdale looked perplexed.

"I was led to believe you were in some way attached to her."

"No."

"I was told you were thinking of courting her."

"No. I never met her until yesterday at dinner. Who led you to believe?" He was belligerent.

"Well, my daughter and my wife."

"And no doubt my mother is at the bottom of all this."

"Why would your mother have anything to do with this?"

"Because she keeps taking up young girls and trying to marry me off to them. And while we are on the subject, I suggest before you make a grave mistake you find out what 'type' I am."

This was beyond acceptable. He took himself out to the stables to find his coachmen. By a series of questions he discovered where his mother's carriage and horses had been left, also her coachman with them. He gave strict instructions, on pain of instant dismissal, that the travelling carriage was not to be used again by his mother. The second carriage and coachman was returned to London via Lady Pengarron's friend's house, where he was to deliver instructions for her carriage to go to Highborne Castle. After this he returned to the library and hid in a corner, determined not to be seen.

"My most formal evening wear, Smithson. Tonight I intend to be the cold, aloof unapproachable Earl, full of my own consequence."

"About time too, if I may say, my lord."

"What! You think I should be higher in the instep?"

"It will do you no harm. People take liberties with you because of your good humour."

"Not at the moment they are not. Are we talking of my mother here, Smithson?"

"Well..." he never finished the sentence. Being transported in a hired carriage of inferior cleanliness and bad suspension still rankled with him.

"Well tonight I intend to be superior and unapproachable."

"Can you do it, sir?"

"If I can fool the French for so many years, I am sure I can fool a few self centred ton ladies with their heads full of scandal."

"Just so, Milord."

When he arrived in the drawing rooms, heads turned to him. He wore black with pristine white shirt and cravat. His waistcoat was pale grey, but with silver thread throughout. His breeches were tight fitting, his cravat held a magnificent stick-pin with a large sapphire stone. In his waistcoat pocket he carried a gold hunter on a chain across his chest, something he never normally did. He stood tall and straight and held his head high, giving the impression he looked down on everyone there.

"Really, Richard, what is the matter with you?"

"The matter, ma'am?"

"Stop looking down your nose. It is not like you."

"And what am I like, madam, I am an Earl after all?"

His mother looked quite shocked. After that she left him alone. So did most of the other guests. Carvon just looked at him and raised his eyebrows. Richard quirked the corner of his mouth, his eyes full of laughter. Carvon just nodded and with a smile said. "I see." And Richard rather though he did.

A party went to the races the next day. A few of the ladies accompanied them, but not his mother. She had intended to take Miss Langdale and Mrs Langdale in the travelling coach to keep them near Richard, but finding the coach not available to her she feigned indisposition and stayed at Highborne.

It was several days before the arrival of Lady Pengarron's coach and driver. By this time there was definite animosity on her part.

"Walcott, why not remove my mother to where she will be happier?"

"I begin to think I have no influence over her."

Walcott was quite serious, his face almost downcast.

"If you want her, Walcott, talk to her. Try to make her see sense. If you can't do that then I see no future for your cause."

Walcott tried, he argued, he lectured, he cajoled, in the end he intimated that he would have his trunk packed and leave. It was only when he actually left that she believed him. A few days later she took herself to another house party, leaving Miss Penelope Langton, Mrs Langton and the unfortunate Mr Langton, to cope alone at the residence of the Earl and Countess of Carvon, somewhat above their usual station in life.

At the end of August the house party broke up. Some gentlemen stayed for Newbury Races, but it was a comfortable male atmosphere that prevailed.

A week or so into September, Richard packed up and left for home, the place he grew up in, Trevane Hall on the west coast of Cornwall.

Chapter 15

"Mrs Pillars, how good to see you again."

"Oh, my lord. If we had known you were coming......"

"Never fear, I shall make do until you are fully prepared. Feed me a little and I shall spend my time with my agent, riding the estate.

"You are most kind, my lord." she curtsied and fled to organise the household.

"Shall I have Alwood fetched, my lord.?"

"No, Witherspoon, I shall take a little refreshment then go and search him out myself."

"Very good, my lord. I will tell cook to bring you a repast." With that the elderly, stately butler retreated. Richard watched him go with amusement. God it was good to be home, why did he ever leave here?

Alwood was surprised and a little confounded by the sudden appearance of the Earl.

"My lord, I was not expecting you. I would have come to the Hall."

"They are rather at sixes and sevens at the Hall. They were not expecting me either. Come, tell me what I need to know and where we need to visit. We can spend a few days out and about touring round, if you are free, that is?"

"Of course I am free, my lord, for as long as you wish."

"Well we can look to the accounts later, perhaps a visit to the fields and a general account of the kind of yields this year. If we start around here today, tomorrow we could start in my study and decide the most important areas to visit first."

"Yes, of course, sir. Before I have my horse put to, we can walk to the village."

They talked as they walked along. Repairs had been needed to one of the older cottages occupied by Tommy Tenford, a woodsman, and his family. The village pump had needed repair. Milly Welford had married Johnny Tenford and they had moved into the cottage in the wood. Him being a woodsman and very handy, most of the repairs there had been done by them and with his father's help. Alwood had allowed them some time during the summer for the works. The woodcutting schedule had not in any way been delayed.

"Another cottage filled. Soon I may need to have some new built. How many more marriageable young men have we?" Richard was laughing at this.

"Oh, by the way, the cliff cottage is let for six months."

"How long ago was that?"

"Only two or three weeks ago."

"I must visit."

"Oh no! I'm sorry, my lord, but no. The gentleman is a recluse, will see nobody. I told young Toby Fuller to see if they needed anything. He said he could not tell anyone was there until he saw a girl yesterday. They never light a fire unless it is dark. He can smell the smoke at night, but there is never any smoke in the daytime."

"How strange. However reclusive he is, I shall make it my business as their landlord to call."

He made his way back to the Hall via the Cliff Cottage, and saw no sign of life. No answer to his knock. For several days he continued to call. The only sign was a decreasing log pile. By the end of a week, he made it a point of finding Toby Fuller on his daily rounds of delivery and collection for the Hall.

"I am to tell no one, I promised her."

"Her, who, the maid, cook?"

"Oh no, sir, a young lady. Talks good like you."

"And you promised not to tell anyone, because Mr Sinclair is a recluse?"

"Yes sir, a reluse, Mr Alwood said."

"Just tell me when I could see someone, they do not have to know I spoke to you."

"Thank you, your Lordship. Early and late, at dawn and dusk. I took em logs, but no one come out."

"Thank you Toby, you have been very helpful."

Toby tugged at his hat and scuttled off.

The following morning he was there before light. He watched the household come alive, the boy putting out the horses, smelled the smoke from the fires heating the water, cooking the food. He stayed until the smell of smoke disappeared, until the life inside could no longer be seen or heard outside. As he stood ready to retrieve his horse, a door opened quietly and a young woman emerged. She was warmly wrapped and carried a basket on her arm. She made her way to the beach path and descended. Now that was interesting. He liked interesting things, they gave him something to ponder over.

A Mr Sinclair rented the house, he had seen two servants, a man and an older woman. So who was this girl? He would find out. He was a retired undercover agent, after all. Finding people was his speciality, if he could not find out, who could?

That evening, before the light was failing, he was positioned close to the house where he could hear, but only partly see what happened.

The young woman returned to the house.

"You're staying out too late, miss. You'll catch cold."

"Stop worrying, Binny. It is enclosed there, unless the wind comes in from a certain direction, it stays warm, and I have my cloak. I promise I will not take cold. Besides I cannot come back before or I may be seen."

"All the same."

"Binny, soon it will be winter and I will be shut in the house all day. Let me enjoy the fresh air while I may." She disappeared indoors. Then returning without her cloak and basket, she helped the older woman fetch the drying from the stable. Meanwhile the man was taking in wood.

"Would you like a bath, miss?"

"Have we enough wood? I can go to the young man and see about more if we need?"

"We have plenty for now, miss. I have a fire laid in the parlour for you."

"Oh Ferguson, you spoil me. Do we need more water fetching? I will help."

"That you will not, miss. You just see to the horses, and I will heat enough water for a bath."

See to the horses, where was the boy?

The girl went into the house and ten minutes later the boy came to take in the horses. Again, that was interesting.

Over his dinner, a very late one which confused his staff, he mused on what he knew.

The only thing he remembered about the house was the layout. Two bedrooms at the top of the stairs, One servant's room, not large. If the servants slept in the small room, the recluse in one bedroom, the girl in the other, where did the boy sleep? Start again.

The man and the boy slept in the servant's room, the recluse in one bedroom, the two women in the other. The woman was a servant, the girl a lady, they would not share a bedroom. Start again.

Who had he seen? A man, an older woman, a boy and a young lady. 'Just see to the horses.' A boy, the same size as the girl. Ah, no boy then. Three people, three bedrooms. If there was no boy, was there a Mr Sinclair? This was getting more interesting by the minute.

The following morning he watched for the early activity, then retrieved his horse and waited to be in the right place to 'accidentally' meet the young lady.

As it happened, this day she was late. Hurrying to the path she was unaware of him until he spoke.

"Good morning."

"Oh. Good Morning, sir." her face showed abject terror.

"Are you staying around here?" Panic but controlled.

"I am visiting my great uncle for a few days."

"Mr Sinclair?" More panic. "This is my land, he is renting my house."

"Oh, good grief. I am afraid I don't know your name, sir."

"Richard Trevane. And yours?" More panic.

"Elizabeth Sinclair, Miss Elizabeth Sinclair."

"And where do you usually live, ma'am?"

Oh dear. "High Wycombe."

"A lovely town is it not? The green is particularly lovely with the old hall to one side."

"Indeed it is." She agreed.

Now that was interesting, Richard thought, she has never been there.

"How long will you be staying, ma'am?"

"I am not sure yet."

The wind caught her cloak and took off the hood. She was quite young, eighteen or nineteen at most, brown hair, very short for a young lady, they usually had it long and piled up, pale blue eyes, hollow and dark rimmed.

Her dress, from what he could see where the cloak had blown back, was ill fitting as if she had been unwell and lost weight.

"If you should need anything, please ask. If you tell young Toby Fuller, he lives just down the road in the white house, he will arrange it. Tell him to come to the Hall and ask for me.

"Thank you, sir, but we are adequately supplied. I wish you good day, sir." And with that she hurried away down the path towards the beach, leaving Richard feeling vaguely bereft.

During the day he inspected the stables. A small black coach, good quality, well used but well maintained and extremely clean. Two horses in the field. Washing hung about to dry, mostly female clothing, lady variety, not maid. Vegetables stored ready for use. The wood store was not that full, coal was much more effective than wood. He would send Toby down with a full dray later, plus some extra vegetables to add to the store.

In the next week he managed to meet her on three occasions. Each time she was distressed but polite. She asked about the coal and thanked him.

By the following week, Richard was tired of playing catch me if you can. He watched to see her go down the path, then returned some time later. Following the path he found the hideout of his youth, the cave like area sheltered from the wind and rain. He also found Miss Elizabeth Sinclair.

"May I join you?" He did not wait for an answer. "I used to hide here when I was young, until my tutor found it and the game was up."

Still not a word.

"There is no Mr Sinclair, is there? Alwood told me he never met him, the paper was taken for signature and returned signed. He was nowhere near, but the signature came within a few hours. Not believable ma'am. If you are in trouble, I would be willing to help in any way I can."

"Keep away from me if you value your life, Mr Trevane. It is not safe to associate with me."

"I doubt that, really I do. Let me see, no Mr Sinclair, not from High Wycombe, black rings under your eyes and a great deal of weight lost. You see, I am observant. You are in some kind of trouble."

"There is nothing you can do for me, sir, except leave me to my seclusion and tell no one."

"Leave you to starve and freeze, which in that house you will do as the winter comes. You light no fires during the day. The house is too cold for your good health."

"I will manage, sir."

"I am offering you friendship and assistance, Miss Sinclair, if that is really your name." A flash of panic in the eyes.

"The best friend anyone can be to me is not to let anyone know I am here. I am Medusa. My life is in danger and anyone who comes close to me dies."

"You read too many gothic novels, Miss Sinclair. Do you have sufficient books? I have an extensive library and can lend you some."

She was definitely ton.

"I have none of the popular gothic novels, I'm afraid."

"I hate gothic novels."

For one so melodramatic that was a strange statement.

"Some poetry then, or Shakespeare?"

"Thank you. It would, perhaps, be helpful." But it was a very grudging acceptance.

The next day he took her a book of poetry, the day after, Shakespeare's 'A Midsummer Night's Dream'. Nothing too heavy for this troubled young lady.

He arranged for Toby to take Ferguson to town to save him the walk, and he could carry more back, and extra meat to have with the vegetables.

It took a week for him to be able to converse with her comfortably.

The days grew colder and rain kept her indoors some days. When she could she went to the cliff hideout. She wore more clothing for warmth. One day, she arrived to find Richard had lit a small fire. It produced so much smoke they almost had to leave their haven and brave the weather in order to breathe.

Richard noted the extra clothing she wore, even a second cloak worn under her grey lightweight one. The inner cloak was very old and damaged, but had once been dark blue velvet, and was lined with fur. This was not a cloak given away to a servant to pass on. Only the aristocracy owned fur like this, and not even all of them. Her family had money, or used to have anyway.

Miss Sinclair still secluded herself to such a degree she never visited the town although, as the boy, she could have ridden there. Even the village just beyond the end of the bay, only a mile away, knew nothing of her existence here.

Richard was becoming beyond frustrated. She was suffering because she was stubborn. Was she being married off to someone she disapproved of or disliked? Why would she think he would kill her? Was it just her way of making sense of something she did not understand? She seemed so sensible in other ways.

The crunch came after their discussion of Dante's Paradise Lost. He was amazed to find she had read the original version, and also other texts in Latin. He looked forward to their meetings more and more; she was a highly intelligent and educated young woman. If only he could break through her reserve. Perhaps! Just perhaps!

* * *

The parcel was sitting on the logs out of the rain. Ferguson found it when he went to make up the fires that morning. It was just a parcel addressed to Miss Elizabeth Sinclair. Kitty stared in horror. They had found her; they even knew her assumed name. It was not signed, but that was perhaps a new ploy. Kitty took it in shaking hands.

"Open the door, Binny." She walked carefully to the edge of the cliff and with great effort threw the package over the cliff. She crouched to the ground, holding her head, waiting for something to happen. Nothing did.

That day they locked the door and closed the shutters. Even in the evening they lit no fires. Nobody was home. After several days they were hungry, frightened, and shivering with cold.

Ferguson checked, but nothing else appeared. Kitty made a decision. She would go back to the cliff whatever the weather, and if they came for her she would throw herself over the cliff. No more deaths would be laid at her door.

She was trembling as she heard someone approaching. It turned out to be Richard. She would willingly have thrown herself into his arms. She checked herself, what was she thinking of, Richard was just the local squire, no more than that. Wasn't he?

"Have you been away?"

"No, Mr Trevane."

"You have taken in no fuel, lit no fires, why not? What has happened?" He sounded concerned.

"Nothing that need concern you, sit." There was a definite change in her attitude. Well now what? Had he become a fool to hope for something more? Perhaps she was trying to keep her distance and the book had been too personal.

"I hope you were pleased with the book."

"What book?" She looked surprised.

"I sent you a gift. A very old and precious copy of Dante's Paradise Found." He had hoped it would send some kind of message, and appeal to her intellect in a way other ladies appreciated jewels.

"I received no book." She was looking a little pale.

"I left it in the log store out of the rain. It was addressed to you."

"I do not accept gifts, sir."

Oh God! Now she was ashen and like to faint.

"Are you ill, Miss Sinclair? Can I help you in any way?"

"No, sir." she was shaking. What had this to do with the book?

"Miss Sinclair, what did you do with my gift?"

"I threw it over the cliff." Her voice was quiet.

"You threw ......a priceless copy!" Richard rose in anger. "It appears you do not want my friendship, Madam. You have shown it in a very clear way. Goodbye, Miss Sinclair."

He pounded up the path to the cliff top, seething with anger. Of all the self-centred, self-important, paranoid, useless, thoughtless specimens of woman kind, she was the worst he had come across. Well he was done with them. They could starve, or freeze, he didn't care any more.

Except he did.

Kitty sat until the shaking stopped and she felt able, then she made her way down the path to the beach. She walked to the area below the house where she had tossed over the book, and she began to search. It took two hours before she found the battered, wet parcel among the stones. She held it close to her, sank to her knees and wept. Had she told him, he would have understood, but how could she tell him?

Chapter 16

Richard missed her. He went down to the cliff face and searched, but not knowing where she had thrown his parcel he found nothing except a pain in his chest.

The weather closed in, the sky grew dark, a storm was brewing.

The little family had never experienced a storm like this. The shutters were closed but still the windows rattled, the candles flamed and flickered. Ferguson brought in all the fuel he could and they lit fires in the bedrooms, the parlour, the range and the boiler for hot water. Still they shivered. The fire in the parlour burned fiercely with the wind. The walls of the house were so cold before, all the heat dissipated into the surrounding structure; they never managed to warm the air in the room. They drank hot drinks, Kitty even took a hot bath and put on all the warm clothing she had. She sat by the fire in the parlour but it was warmer by the range in the kitchen and she moved there. The bed was cold and she slept in her stockings and petticoats under her nightgown, plus a riding jacket over the top. Wrapped in her bed covers she lay and listened to the storm, until the very sound of it lulled her to sleep. It continued into the next day, but had abated enough to fetch in fuel and open the shutter for light.

The sea battered the cliff face, then pulled away, leaving the beach with flotsam strewn over it. Over each high tide more flotsam arrived. Somewhere out to sea, a vessel had come to a bad end.

After the storm came a period of warm, calm weather, an Indian summer, and Kitty took advantage of it. Sitting in her hideout watching the waves gradually subside, the locals from the village scavenging for anything worthwhile

* * *

The storm caused quite some damage, which Richard and his agent had to deal with. A couple of roofs were damaged, a chimney had been blown down. There was flooding where the stream had overflowed, the pressure of water moved some rocks thereby blocking the path of the stream, and changing its course. Where it usually seeped to the cliff edge and tumbled down, taking stones with it and loosening others, it now came out a few yards further along.

The bridge over the stream was damaged; it had to be repaired in great haste or villagers would be cut off from the town. Richard worked with the locals on the repair, the physical exercise being a little relief from the nagging ache in his chest, which had never left him since his confrontation with Miss Sinclair.

A local fisherman, repairing the bridge alongside Richard, remarked on the danger of collapse at the other headland. The cliff had been undermined by the storm and anyone walking above could be in danger. It was near to the town and the possibility for inquisitive onlookers to put themselves in a hazardous position was quite great. Richard spoke with Alwood, and while his agent organised the local repairs, he would ride over and see just how dangerous it was, and what should be done.

The danger at the cliff face was not as great as he had expected. He had left early to spend time checking the whole area, but only a few feet at the far tip of the headland caused a problem. A small fence or a row of poles to show danger would be enough, especially if the townsfolk were warned.

He looked down along the curve of the bay and its sandy shore. It was mid-morning now, the tide had turned and the scavengers had left. The only one there now was Tom Corbin, the local wall builder and cottage repairer, collecting stones to repair the chimney. A strong well built man with a gentle temperament that belied his powerful frame, he was picking stone brought down by the storm. His horse stood obediently by his side as he searched for stone to load onto the dray. He let his gaze wander a little nearer along the cliff. Was she there? The weather was warmer, she could be. The ache in his chest intensified.

The first sign that made him realise something was wrong, was the sound. A deep rumble which seemed to reverberate through the ground. Nothing was amiss at the headland. He searched the bay and noticed Tom's horse and dray speeding towards the sea edge. Where Tom was, there was only a pile of rocks. He was too far away to see. He watched for movement where Tom had been, nothing. From the base of the cliff a figure appeared walking with a steady strong gait; it was the figure of a woman, Miss Elizabeth Sinclair.

He watched Kitty walk towards Tom and saw her move some rocks which must have been heavy for her. She bent down to examine Tom, then she started to do strange things. She was hunting for wood, she made a pile of small lengths and then, lifting her skirt, she began to tear pieces off her petticoat. Tom was alive but injured. The tide was coming in and they were both in danger. He vaulted onto his horse and started along the headland. His horse rode the path, his eyes watched her progress.

She straightened his leg and tied it to a strip of flotsam as a splint. She did the same for his arm; she also spent more time on his arm, wrapping it. She searched around for a larger piece of wood, a particular size? Laying it by his side she slowly slid his body onto the wood.

The path moved away from the cliff edge here and he was unable to see. A little further on he could stop to check. He was near enough to see Tom now.

She was leading the horse and dray back to Tom. The horse was content to go quietly, it trusted her. She positioned the dray near to Tom and then she chocked the dray wheels to prevent him from moving away again. She need not have worried, the horse was under her complete control.

What happened next was nothing less than amazing. She placed a large stone near his head and feet and lifted the wood under his head onto the stone, then she did the same with his feet. He was now off the cold wet ground. More stones, two piles high on each side of him. She lifted the wood and Tom to the greater height. Backing the horse a little until the dray was against Tom's head she climbed onto the dray. The horse stood still as a statue, not moving, as if obeying an instruction from her. Kneeling down on the dray, she lifted the wood under Tom's head and pulled it and the horse backed gently to her command until the wood was leaning on the dray.

She climbed down and chocked the dray wheels and went to the foot of the wood and pushed until it slid and Tom was safely on the dray. It must have been more than her normal strength could handle, because she laid on the dray in clear exhaustion. Richard had no way of getting to them, the only horse access to the beach was from the far end where the village sat just over the headland. He rode hard, over the stream at the new bridge, then down to the cliff again. The horse and dray were being driven smoothly along the beach, avoiding the rough stony areas; soon she would reach the village with her cargo, the village where nobody knew of her existence.

By the time he reached the village and turned to the beach entrance his horse was badly winded. She drove the horse and dray up to the village street where Richard was waiting.

"Madam, as you wish your presence to be a secret, would you like me to take Tom to the appropriate help?"

"Thank you, sir, you are very kind. His leg and arm both seem broken and he is bleeding badly from his wrist. I was unable to hold pressure on it, so I have bound a smooth stone over a bandage. It seems to be effective." She was tired and shaken, but her calm efficiency impressed him. She handed the reins of the horse to Richard, and with a small inclination of her head, she turned back to the beach to walk home.

"Be careful, Miss Sinclair, the tide is advancing."

"I will sir." and then she was gone.

Richard went to the inn where his report of Tom's injury caused a flurry of activity. The dray was taken to Tom's cottage while the doctor was fetched. Tom would never know how lucky he was that the doctor was visiting a village casualty of the storm.

Richard was the hero of the day, which made him extremely uncomfortable.

The only one to question the circumstances was the doctor.

"I would say well done, Richard, but I think you had a little help. That is unless you have taken to wearing ladies' petticoats!" Richard looked rueful.

"It is none of my doing, actually, Bob, but please don't ask me who, for I cannot tell you."

"A secret angel of mercy and an intelligent one. That stone on the pressure point of his wrist saved his life. He may still be in some danger, but he would most certainly have bled to death before I could help him."

"Please, Bob, mention her to no one."

"Nobody to know? Where did she arrive from?"

"Please don't ask. If I could I would tell you, but she needs to remain concealed."

"Ah, one of your intrigues. If you wish it I will say nothing."

"To anyone."

"To no-one, Richard." The doctor had to smile.

It would be weeks before Tom regained any semblance of health, as his head, leg, arm and loss of blood gradually improved. Even longer before he could work again. His family would need to be supported until then or all her effort would have been wasted.

One thing Richard was now sure of, whoever Miss Elizabeth Sinclair was, he now knew he was irrevocably in love with her.

Self-centred, no, self-important, no, useless and thoughtless, definitely not. He just had the paranoid to work at and then she could be his.

To say Kitty was shaken would be an understatement. Binny and Ferguson knew something momentous had happened but she declined to say what.

The evening of the next day, as the fuel was being brought in and the stove lit, Richard arrived at the door and came into the kitchen.

"I wish to speak with Miss Sinclair." Binny eyed him with some misgivings.

"I'll ask."

"Tell her I have news of Tom."

"Yes sir." She disappeared into the parlour, returning a moment later.

"You may go in, sir, she will see you."

He walked into the cold room where she sat in several layers of clothing, wrapped in heavy shawls. She was reading a book. On the side table sat a very battered copy of Dante's Paradise Found.

"I see you have the book. I searched unsuccessfully for it, ma'am."

"I went to retrieve it as soon as you left."

"Then all is well, except for the book which will never recover. Would you like me to send it for repair?" He was gentle and as solicitous as he could be.

"I would very much appreciate that, sir. You are most kind."

"I came to give you news of Tom Colby." She shivered, "It is too cold for you." He opened the door and called to Ferguson, who was hovering just outside.

"It is far too cold in here. Have you not enough fuel? Come, light a fire and when the water boils bring hot tea." He turned to her "I know you have tea, I sent some especially."

Ferguson reacted without thought. He brought a burning log from the kitchen range and put it to the fire which was already laid. Then he strode off into the kitchen to hurry Binny.

"May I sit, Miss Sinclair?"

"Oh, I'm so sorry, of course, please do." He took a chair across the hearth to Kitty's and looked into her strained face.

"So far Tom is doing well. It will be a few days before the doctor can be sure he will not take fever, but he is strong and it is hoped he can overcome it. All of which would be futile if not for you, Miss Sinclair. Your stone on his wrist saved his life; he would have bled to death without that."

"I was only doing what I could at the time, sir."

"You are a remarkable young woman. Most women would swoon at the sight of so much blood."

"I am not remarkable, sir, and it did upset me a great deal."

"It would upset even me, and I have seen men bleed to death. You can have no idea of the horror."

Tears welled in Kitty's eyes, her voice was shaky. "Oh indeed, I can."

"You have seen such horror?"

Her eyes looked hazy as if far away in the past. "I am Medusa, those around me die." Her voice was barely audible.

Well this was a step forward, a glimpse of something that happened in the past.

"Not this time, my dear. Tom is very much alive because of you."

The door opened and Binny brought in a tray of tea and a few biscuits.

"I'm afraid we don't have many biscuits, we don't expect company'" she said quite pointedly.

"Well I am not company, I am landlord and friend, I hope." He smiled up at her.

Turning to Kitty he said "I wish to talk about your horses. They are remarkably fine cattle but need exercise and warmer stabling for the winter. Soon the path into here will be unusable for the coach, so their staying here is not necessary. I could stable them better for you."

"They are not to be seen, Mr Trevane, they are recognisable."

"Indeed they are, a very good pair. I have a little used livery stable where I house visitors' cattle when we have a house party. As I do not intend to hold a party anytime soon, I have excellent grooms with little to do. It would be to both our benefit. Whenever you need them you can call for them and 'John coachman' can visit them if he wishes!" he laughed at her as he said this.

"I believe 'John coachman' is away for some time, sir."

"If you agree, Toby Fuller could take them up, and you need not see anyone who you do not wish to see."

"You are showing me great kindness, sir, after what I did with your book."

"You did not know the present was from me." A statement.

"No, I did not."

"You said you do not accept presents. Is this because of some problem in the past?"

She looked so sad, he wanted to reach across and pull her into his arms. All he received was a small nod.

"I ask no more information of you than you wish to give me, my dear, but I would like to understand what makes you react as you do, if only to save misunderstanding between us. I would like to know something of your past. I may be of some help to you even if only for your peace of mind, someone you can turn to for help."

"I am frightened to be close to anyone, sir. It puts then in great danger." Then she spoke even more quietly. "I fear for you, Mr Trevane."

"You fear for me? Do you mean fear for my safety?"

"Yes, sir."

"Miss Sinclair. Does this mean you fear you would lose me, as you have others?" A silent nod.

"Does it matter to you so much if I am hurt, my dear?"

All she could do was stare at the floor as the tears filled her eyes. He crossed the space between them and knelt before her, pulling her into his arms.

"You mean a great deal to me. I want to help. I need to know. I am not asking you to tell me now, but I want you to think about it and tell me when you are ready. Please, for both our sakes." He held her for a moment and stroked her head, she reacted against his touch, and then relaxed. He ran his fingers through her short hair and stroked the skin, finding places where she was sensitive.

The sound of Binny at the door made him let go of her, and stand up. When Binny collected the tray he was standing before her.

"Are you sure you have enough of everything?"

"Indeed, sir, you are very kind, it is not necessary to keep us in food and fuel."

"You are renting my house, Madam. If the house is too cold to live in during the winter, you will leave, and I will have taken your money under false pretences."

Kitty laughed. "What a ridiculously convoluted argument. It will not stand up, sir."

His heart lurched. He had never seen her laugh before, not even smile, but there it was in her eyes for just a moment. If he needed a cause to make his life worthwhile he now had it. The smile in her eyes would be his whole life's work.

The following day, Toby came to collect the horses in the morning. Kitty put on her cloak and went with him to the stables. She stood with him while he petted them, although they constantly turned their heads toward her for reassurance.

"They be the finest pair of cattle I ever seen, Miss. They'll be looked after good, I'll see to that." She encouraged him to put on the leading reins, then she fussed over them and they nuzzled up to her.

"You've a way with them, miss."

"I have spent a great deal of time with horses, Toby, especially these two. Don't pull them, encourage them and they will follow you. If I am not there, they will trust you."

"If'n you say, miss."

"Off you go to a better place." She patted their rumps to encourage them off. Reluctantly at first, they relaxed at Toby's comforting chatter and followed out to the road and away.

"I shall miss the horses, Binny."

"I expect you will, miss."

"I feel as if my only job here is gone."

"Don't be upset, you will find something else to occupy you. You may not enjoy ladylike embroidery, but a little sewing would help keep down the mending for me. We still have warm clothing to alter for you. You could ask Ferguson to bring you some ribbons to brighten them."

"Why do they need brightening up?"

"Well, you do seem to have attracted a suitor."

"I don't know how much to tell him, Binny."

"How much do you trust him, miss? Tell him as much as you feel you need to. See how he reacts. You will know what to do."

"I hope you are right, I really do."

Chapter 17

Two days later, as they were closing the house for the night, Richard arrived. Binny showed him into the parlour, warm tonight, and then went to make some tea.

"Have you any glasses?" Richard held up a bottle of wine. "I was not sure that you would drink brandy, so I thought this might do instead."

She opened the parlour door and called to Binny.

"Do we have wine glasses?" Ferguson appeared suddenly holding two not matching, indifferent ones.

"These are the best I could find, ma'am." he intoned in his best butler voice.

"Thank you, Ferguson, they will do fine."

"Not quite the best cut glass, but I am afraid they will have to do. At least they are spotlessly clean."

Binny brought in some tea and inquired if Mr Trevane would be staying for dinner.

Richard jumped at the chance.

"It will be rather meagre to what you normally have, I imagine."

"I will be pleased to eat whatever you have, my dear." Richard was convinced her name was not genuine and was loathe to become used to thinking of her as Elizabeth. So, 'my dear' was the best he could do for now.

"Shall we open the wine now, or wait for dinner?"

"Perhaps we should take tea first, since it has been provided." She was quite playful. Would this mood last, he could only hold his breath and hope.

"Mr Trevane."

"Richard."

"Oh! Richard. You wanted to know why I am here and why I threw your book over the cliff."

"I do indeed."

"Then I will tell you some of my past, although you may not believe it."

She started with meeting someone, but mentioned no names. He would never believe it was a prince, and it could give away her identity. She told him of the lost parasol, the present of a parasol she received and the explosion, the deaths and her injuries. Richard listened seriously, then interjected.

"When I stroked your head the other day, you flinched. Was that part of your injury?"

"Yes sir."

"Richard."

"Richard. Some scars are still sensitive. They cut off my hair, it is just growing back."

"That is why you have it so short. I thought it was to be able to dress as 'John coachman'.

She actually smiled at that.

"No, that was just a useful part of the disguise."

"Does Ferguson not drive the carriage?"

"No, he had a bad accident with a horse when he was a boy, and he has never been able to deal with them since."

"And you drove the carriage here?"

She blushed. It was wonderful, it made his heart thump.

"And since then, no presents."

"There is more."

"More?"

"When I returned from my recuperation, there was another present."

"What kind."

"A kitten. Someone had given it something to kill it. Something that made gas."

"It was dead when it arrived, or it died afterwards?"

"It died after it arrived, and it killed my sister."

Richard froze. This was worse than any gothic novel, but was it all true? Had she been mistaken? What kind of gas can a kitten give off that will kill a girl? He accepted that she had been physically damaged, but was it really a bomb, or perhaps a carriage accident? Had she hit her head and now believed her nightmares? Whatever had happened, he now needed to find out the real truth if he was to even contemplate making her his countess.

"You are shocked, sir."

"Richard. Yes I am, who would not be?"

"You do not really believe me, I can see it in your face. I do not blame you, sir, Richard. However, you must not blame me for hiding when someone has twice tried to kill me."

"I do not blame you in the least. All I can do is to offer to keep you safe. And I do."

"Thank you." She was quite moved by his belief in her, even if not in her story.

Binny opened the door and came in to set the small table for them. Dinner, it seemed, was about to be served.

It was a companionable meal, if meagre by his standards. He was, after all, a large, energetic man in his prime. Not to worry, Mrs Levine would find him something when he returned home. He had eaten a great deal less when in France, and that had done him no harm.

He was sorry to leave her alone, after what he had felt between them. As he bid her goodnight, he took her hand in his and held it, looking deeply into her eyes.

* * *

"You could do worse than set your cap at Mr Trevane, miss."

"Binny, you are a matchmaker." Kitty laughed. "How would I marry anyone, Binny. I am not of age, I need my father's permission. Would I marry under an assumed name, would it be legal? We could go to Scotland, but think of the risk of travelling there. If I asked for permission to marry I would need to give my real name and where I was living, which would ruin all our plans."

"Maybe Mr Danvers has caught them!" she sounded hopeful.

"Maybe, Binny. If he has, will papa consent for me to marry a country squire and live buried in the country, so far from everyone?"

"Your papa loves you, miss. He would let you marry anyone you wished."

"But Binny, does Mr Trevane actually want to marry me?"

* * *

Richard could not sleep that night. Did he actually want to marry her? Yes, was the definite answer to that question. Should he marry her? That depended on a variety of problems being solved. Was he prepared to give her up? No. So what should he do about these problems?

Was she willing to marry him? Why not, she needed protection, he could give it. Would that be enough for her? Would she be pleased when she found out he was an Earl? Of course. Or not. Perhaps she would be too overawed. Best not tell her. If she loved him, would his being an Earl matter? Women were romantic creatures. If they were in love, usually nothing else mattered.

So the problems. First and most definitely the greatest was, who was she? He could not take a countess living under a false name. If he found who she was, probably these fears and experiences could be put into perspective. If she turned out to be deranged.... No, do not even think of that. He would rather die than lose her now. One thing was certain, he needed to start searching now, for his own peace of mind. Think back to his days in France.

He is in a foreign country and he needs to discover who someone is, they would never tell him, who does he ask? Those around who know her. Will they tell him? No, probably not, well, not intentionally. How do you find information covertly? No problem.

It was a much warmer day than recently, he had waited for this. His general courtship was going quite well, he thought, she seemed interested, responsive, but still she was holding back. Today she would go to the cliff and he would join her later. For now, Binny.

He watched Miss Sinclair leave for the cliff path, with her basket on her arm and wrapped in her cloak. He waited until she was out of sight, then knocked on the kitchen door calling out "Binny, it's Richard Trevane."

Binny opened the door and let him enter. "Miss has gone down the cliff, sir."

"It's you I came to see, Binny."

"Me, whatever for?" She looked wary.

"I need to know if you will need anything in particular during the next few weeks. I have to go to London on business and would not like to think of you being in need. Miss Sinclair would never tell me, but you might. Food, candles, wood, coal, any clothing for warmth. She is very independent is our Miss Sinclair. Have you been with her long?"

"Oh bless you, I was her nursery maid. (Clue) I have known her all my life."

"Was she a good baby?"

"Oh yes, much better than her brother Jeremy had been, or her little sister." (Brother and younger sister.)

"She has such a sweet temperament, you can tell by the way the horses react to her. They always know."

"She always was good with horses, even before they put her on one they would follow her around." (Rides from a young age.)

"She must be a good driver to have brought the same horses all the way here."

"Well, she has driven around the estate on various horse drawn vehicles from quite a young age. She often drove this carriage to the village, although there was usually a coachman with her." (Use of coach and coachman on an estate!)

"It is a very well maintained coach, even though it is old. It looks comfortable enough." (More than one coachman?)

"Oh it is sir, not as comfortable as the travelling carriage, but my lady preferred it." (Ah, at last - travelling carriage - my lady.) "She felt safe and it could stay with her and not need to go back." (Back where?) "Her father, the ….. sent the luggage in an older one instead. Not that they went anywhere much, except the odd visit to the London house." (Another house in London)

At this point Binny remembered Kitty was just a Miss not a lady and tried to make up some details.

"The house is not that large, sir. Miss Sinclair has no mother, she died years ago, so she runs the house." Binny seemed strained and stopped talking.

Now sort that out, some sounded false, but some true.

Capable of running a house, so unless it happened recently, there is no impairment to normal living. How large a house? Question - who is my lady, if she is a lady with an estate and a father the …..?

"So Binny, please will you decide what you need for while I am gone, and let me know. I will talk to Ferguson and Miss Sinclair, but I doubt she will tell me.

Binny picked up again. If she had said too much perhaps he had not noticed.

"She will not, sir. She is very independent is our Miss." He smiled at her and she relaxed, smiling back.

He called to the cliff during the day. He called that evening, and the next day. He set himself a day for leaving and made sure they had wood, coal, candles and food in store. He spoke to Toby and alerted him that he would be away for a few weeks. Then he came to Kitty.

"Can we talk a little?"

"Goodness you sound serious." She looked a little nervous.

"I have to go to London on business, and I do not like leaving you." She was panicking.

"Why are you going to London?"

"I told you, I have some business to deal with, some of my investments need my attention. I am going to see my agent who deals with them. You look worried, you have no reason. Will you miss me so much?" She nodded and looked embarrassed.

"I hope I have seen to your needs, but if you require anything go to Toby Fuller, you know where his house is."

"Will you be away long?"

"I really cannot say, my dear. I may be back in two weeks, it may be a month or more, it depends on many things, including the state of the roads and the weather."

"You will take care, Richard." He smiled at her.

"It feels so good to hear you say my name. I will take care. You must too, although you have Binny and Ferguson to take care of you."

He took both her hands in his and looked deeply into her eyes. Could he hope, should he hope? He dropped one of her hands and stroked the side of her face. She was so close and he wanted to hold her so much. He dropped her other hand and slid his arms around her waist, pulling her closer to him. He looked down at her face as she looked up into his, he lowered his head and touched his lips against hers. She obviously had no idea how to respond. Her first kiss, and he had had the pleasure. He put his hand behind her to pull her closer and moved his mouth over hers. She responded and, a little surprised, she let her mouth open a little. That was all Richard needed to press his tongue through her lips and caress her mouth. She tasted so sweet, so willing, so innocent. He must be careful not to frighten her.

He pulled back from her mouth to look down into her eyes. It was only then he realised she had her arms around him, holding him. Words were of little use at a time like this. He pulled her closer until her head lay against his chest. How good it felt. It was as if he had waited all his life for this one wonderful moment. Never had he felt so close to anyone. He stroked her hair, now growing to a respectable length, then buried his face in it.

"Take care, my darling girl. I won't stay away too long, I promise." He said it quietly into her ear. Kitty could hardly believe she had heard it. The lump in her throat prevented words, so she just clung to him.

When he had left, Kitty retired to her bed, and cried herself to sleep. The next day she gave herself a lecture on getting ideas that could not happen. It was a sensible plan, if only she could bring herself to accept it. The days would be endless without seeing Richard, but she had no choice but to bear it as best she could.

Chapter 18

If there was anywhere Richard did not want to be, it was London. With the little season already started, his mother would probably be there in his house, with another protégé. She was not expecting him, so perhaps he would have a little respite.

Was Miss Elizabeth Sinclair a lady, the daughter of someone from the ton, or a local squire or baron perhaps? What had Binny said, 'her father the ...' then stopped? She had lived on an estate, quite a big one it sounded like.

Who could he ask for information? Who could help him look? Of course, his old colonel Sir Peter Danvers might be at a loss and needing some cause to enliven him. He never did like being unoccupied.

Depending on when he arrived would it be best to go to his club and make the odd enquiry. She was fearful, running away. He must be circumspect. Listen to the talk, perhaps go to a dinner or two and see what the ton was like, then choose a helpful dowager and ask for help. Or was that too dangerous? Maybe he should start a friendship with a not so young lady and use her to find information. No, that was even more dangerous.

He rode his horse some of the way to keep him occupied. At other times, he sat in his travelling coach and planned and worried.

What if he could find out nothing? What if it turned out she was mentally ill and had just run away. No, he still could not believe that.

Something momentous had happened in her life. She was the reason they were on his land. Who made the arrangements to get them there? Not the servants, they did her bidding. She was 'John Coachman' she had driven them there, organised it. That was not the mind of an imbecile. She was the most remarkable young woman he had met, if all that were true. And he was coming to believe it was.

How real were her stories, her descriptions? If she read gothic novels he would doubt them, but she hated them, had no interest in them.

God, if he could not sort this out soon he would go mad. Every day he wanted her more. Every night he dreamed of her, when he slept that is. His physical wants were becoming a problem during the night and he often awoke clinging to his pillow with both his arms.

He wanted this over, and quickly, he needed to get back to her. He had no idea how she was faring without him but he knew that he was not coping with being away from her. He would marry her if she would have him, and he had to hope that she would.

* * *

Lord Richard Trevane, fifth Earl of Pengarron arrived at his London town house like a thief in the night.

"Elliot, had you all retired?"

"My lord, so good to see you again so soon. We were just preparing to retire, sir."

"Is my mother in residence?"

"Not at present, my lord."

Richard visibly relaxed.

"Thank goodness. I had feared another dinner party, or a lecture in the night. I am somewhat tired."

"It has been a long journey from Cornwall, my lord."

"And done at speed, Elliot. I have urgent business in London."

"Will your Lordship require food?"

"Oh, no. You can lock up now. Once Smithson has the bags in you can secure for the night."

"Thank you my lord."

Richard slept well from sheer exhaustion. The following morning he tackled his butler.

"Where is my mother, Elliot? She is usually in London for the little season."

"She came to visit the modista, but is now staying a few days with the Penfords. I believe they have a daughter just about to be presented."

"Oh God, another one. Tell me Elliot, what will my mother do when I am married? She is in great demand as the mother of an unmarried Earl. Does she have many friends without daughters, do you think?"

"I cannot answer that, my lord."

"If she returns whilst I am here, please let me know before she discovers me, will you."

"Of course, my lord." A corner of his mouth twitched. Could it be that the serious Elliot had a sense of humour?

He took his breakfast at a leisurely pace, not that his insides were feeling leisurely, they were churning. He walked down Bond Street, he walked through the park, although it was mainly nursemaids, he went to Gunter's for an ice. In the end he went to his club for a late lunch. He made sure it was known that he was in London.

Boothby came to speak to him.

"Pengarron, back in London. I thought you had decamped to Cornwall for the winter?"

"I find I have some business in the city, Boothby. Are you here for the whole season?"

"Yes, I expect so. You know wives, no, actually you don't, that's the problem. Have you seen your mother since Highborne?"

"No, and I have to say I would rather avoid her if I can."

"Will you be here long?"

"I really could not say, at this point. I hope to leave fairly soon."

"Avoiding the matchmakers?"

"Not particularly. I am quite happy to be in company, although I have no invitations at present, obviously."

"Have to go to dinner at the Blenkinsops' tonight! Wife accepted it. They have a daughter not taken, and she is getting frantic now. I say, could you fancy an invite to the Blenkinsops'? She would love to have you, I'm sure. So would I, for a little sensible conversation, not just ton rubbish?"

"My dear Boothby, I would be delighted to go if an invitation was forthcoming."

Boothby looked shocked, then delighted.

"Good man! I'll have a word. Men are always in short supply on these occasions."

When Richard returned home later that afternoon, there was indeed an invitation from the Blenkinsops.

He dressed with care that evening. Tonight he began his campaign with all the detailed determination of a military one. He needed to find not the latest on-dits, but the ones from earlier in the year, during the summer season.

Mrs Blenkinsop was indeed exceedingly pleased to have him at her table, and while Boothby tried to talk horses and estate management, Mrs Blenkinsop wanted to talk about her extraordinary and accomplished daughter. Richard just wanted to know about the gossip. Now that was a first.

"So, tell me, madam, what has been the topic of interest this year, it seems I have missed out on the whole year's gossip?"

Several of the ladies tried to speak at once.

"Well it is all about the Prince and his dreadful behaviour."

"His Highness? What has he been doing?" Richard was vaguely amused, knowing the Prince.

"He is beyond any acceptable behaviour."

"He has behaved appallingly."

"Just because of his status he thinks he can do anything."

"He is not fit to represent the Royal House."

"The whole Royal Family should be appalled at his behaviour."

"But they have said nothing, not a word."

"The Prince carries on as if nothing has happened."

"It is not to be borne."

The tirade went on. Blenkinsop broke in to his wife's denunciation of the Prince.

"My dear, Please do be careful, your language is becoming treasonable."

The ladies stopped instantly. Silence reigned and everyone looked rather shaken.

"Well! I did ask, I suppose." Richard tried to make light of the situation, and gradually conversation returned. All in all, he felt as though he had made no progress at all.

He left feeling frustrated at an opportunity lost. Whatever the Prince had done it obviously took precedence over the information he needed.

He escaped the Blenkinsops' as early as was possible. There was only so much he could take of her wonderful daughter.

Returning home, he was met by a somewhat concerned Elliot.

"My lord, there is a gentleman to see you. He insisted on waiting."

"Who?"

"Sir Peter, Sir."

"Danvers, I wonder what he needs to see me for so urgently?"

"I put him in the library, my lord."

"Thank you Elliot, I imagine brandy will be all that we require."

"It was replenished earlier sir."

"Of course, I was not inferring any shortcomings on your part, only that tea will not be required."

"Very good, my lord."

He wished he could make Elliot a little less formal sometimes.

He went into the library with a light heart. He could use his presence to ask for help.

The Danvers who stood to meet him was a very worn and serious one.

"Danvers, to what do I owe this late night visitation? Nothing wrong, I hope. I was hoping to see you while I am here in London."

"Richard, I am more than pleased to see you. I was thinking of sending for you to help. We have a problem which is occupying every man I can muster."

"Good grief, is it France? Has Bonaparte escaped again?"

"No, much worse than that. Treason. Someone, or a group is trying to unseat The Crown."

"What?"

"Exactly. We still have no idea who it is."

"So tell me the problem, what is being done."

"It is very clever, Trevane, someone, or we think quite a few may be involved, are seeding the ton with rumours against the Prince."

"The Prince, I've just been out to dine and all the women are incensed at him. Tell me some of the details."

"He is being accused of one thing after another, it just gets worse. We can find no one source of the rumours, and believe me we have tried. Half the ton are getting to a fever pitch over him. It could bring down The Crown, parliament..." Richard broke in.

"Don't the ton realise, if they ferment insurrection they will bring the whole aristocracy down? England will be like France was, the bloodshed will be immense!"

"That is the problem. It is fuelled and run by the tabbies who live on rumour, not the men who look for facts."

"So tell me about the facts." He poured them both a brandy.

"It started with a rumour that he was involved with a seventeen year old ingénue. First it was an affair, then he was setting her up as his mistress. We are talking daughter of a Duke, Trevane, not some little chit."

"Was any of it true?"

"No, not a word. The first he knew was when his advisers warned him against it. He was livid. He thought she had started the rumours. He went to a ton party especially to give her a real put down, only to find she had no understanding of what he was talking about. Unfortunately that was at a garden party and rather public. Then the rumours were that he had thrown her off, or that she had refused him."

"That's not bad enough to cause treason."

"That was only the beginning. After that he was accused of trying to kill her, or have her killed."

"Good God, what for?"

"You know the ton. Why does there have to be a reason?"

"I presume he did not."

"Of course not. But someone did, and they blamed him."

"How?"

"They sent her a present for her eighteenth birthday and signed it HRH, I can show you part of the label."

A present, no surely not.

"What present?"

"At the garden party someone took her parasol. They sent her a new one, filled with gunpowder."

No, please no. The cold sweat began to run down the back of Richard's neck.

"It blew up?"

"Yes, it killed two maids and injured her quite badly. The Hall windows blew in. That's when I was fetched in. Except for her family and the Prince, no one knew about the present and the name on the label, but the ton did."

God help her.

"It gets worse."

"Go on."

"She went away to recover and when she returned they sent her another present."

Richard picked up his glass and took a huge gulp. He sat forward in his chair and leaned on the table for support.

"Tell me."

"They sent her a kitten. The label said 'A kitty for my Kitty, HRH.' They knew when she was returning. She was late arriving and her younger sister handled the kitten. They had pushed something down its throat that caused a gas, the Foreign Office think. We still don't know how exactly it was done."

"The sister died."

"Horribly. Even worse, Lady Kitty walked in and found her."

Richard was icy cold. He rose and went to the fire, put on another log and squatted down to warm his hands.

"Where is she now?"

"We don't know, neither do they."

"They are searching for her."

"Yes. They can't find her either. Her brother went to check relatives and on the way back, they beat him to a pulp. They wanted to know where she was. Poor chap will possibly never walk again, he definitely will never ride. How he survived, the doctor has no idea, nearly every bone in his body was broken."

"Oh God, no!"

"They have also tried to fire the house, to smoke her out, we presume. We have all the men we can keeping watch on the Hall, and any with ton connections are searching for the sources of the rumours."

There was no doubt about it now, he knew exactly who Miss Elizabeth Sinclair was. Not only was her story true, but she had not told him the half of it.

"Who is she?"

"The girl, Lady Katherine Wellmore, daughter of the Duke of Wenton. They live at Wenton Hall in Oxfordshire, just out on the Windsor road."

"And you say she is missing."

"Yes, we think she organised it herself. She has two retainers with her. She started out to a friend in Norwich, but once on the Great North Road, everyone lost her."

"Who drove her?"

"Their top coachman, William. He was distraught. He fell asleep after breakfast in the coaching inn and awoke hours later to find them gone, a coach ticket and money in his pocket with a letter to her father. She is capable of this; I am in awe of how this young sheltered girl has turned into such an accomplished woman."

145

"Where do we go from here?"

"Meet with a few of us at the Foreign Office tomorrow morning, and we can go over a plan. You are the best I know to find a missing person quickly and quietly. If you can get through the French lines, you can get her back."

"What if she does not want to come?"

"That is the problem we have to sort out tomorrow. Think about it."

With that Danvers stood, patted him on the shoulder and left, nodding to Elliot, the butler, as he took his cloak and hat.

Richard finished his brandy and took himself to bed. Smithson fussed around, picking up clothes as he dropped them, watching his master move as if sleepwalking. He had just had a visitor. What could he have said to make him like this?

It was a select group of Danvers' former operatives which met in his room at the Foreign Office. Each one of them had a different speciality. Danvers opened the discussion.

"I found Trevane in town, I invited him to join us."

"The best man you could get to find someone. You always were the consummate people finder, Trevane." Portman had known him for some time. Others only knew of him through his successes.

"I was not always successful! Don't make me infallible, I'm not."

"You're the best hope we have." Williams was new to him.

"What have you done so far?" Could he say, should he say? He cared too much to bring her into danger, plus he doubted she would come.

They went through all the searches they had made, everywhere they had been. They also reported on what they knew of those following them, who had followed Kitty when she left home.

"Kitty?" He knew really, but he had to ask.

"Lady Kitty, it's what her family and friends call her."

"So Lady Kitty went on a journey to Norwich. Stayed at a coaching inn and went missing. On purpose."

"Yes, where do we start?"

"By telling me why you need her back? What good will it do for her, they have already tried to kill her twice, according to you. How could you keep her safe? What could it achieve?"

"The reason we need her back, Richard, is that the whole country is in danger of tearing itself to pieces. They think she is dead or locked in prison somewhere. We have to prove she is alive and well. She needs to be seen." Danvers was quite animated, not normal for him.

"As for keeping her safe, well all we can do is give her someone to be with her at all times."

"To sleep in her room, stand outside her bedchamber, sit on her windowsill?"

Williams looked at him thoughtfully. "He has a point there. Why would she want to come back? She could be safe overseas somewhere. What if she has gone to the Americas?"

"There would be no hope for England, then." Portman retorted. "We could never get her back in time. The ton would never believe us if we told them, we need proof. We need her, Trevane."

"Would she not come back for her country?" Simister was an idealistic young buck, who had only joined them six months before Waterloo. Not enough time to become as cynical as the rest.

"How would you tell the ton why she had been away? Why would she have gone? It they believe the Prince is behind this, what could have changed to bring her back?" Richard was deliberately leading them.

"A need to see her family."

"Not enough."

"If she came back, they would believe she was still in some way connected to the Prince."

"Then she must be connected to someone else." Well done Simister.

Portman had been thinking quietly.

"What we need, is for her to have a husband. That would give a reason, a break from the Prince and something better for the ton's on-dits," Almost there.

Danvers put a stop to his manipulation.

"I will offer her marriage, if you can find her Richard."

NO! Don't ruin this.

"I bring her back and a marriage is then arranged. What if she refuses you?"

"She will already be here."

"Not married."

"She needs to be married before she comes back."

"You will have to find her, Trevane, and put it to her that Danvers will marry her."

"She may not accept him."

"What a wonderful way to court a young girl. Come back to London and someone you may not want will marry you to save your country. Afterwards you will be married for the rest of your life."

Richard did not need to join in, they were doing it for him.

"Danvers, why do you want to marry her? For England, or do you want a wife? I thought you had no interest in marriage. You have no estate to populate."

Danvers looked at him in despair. "So suggest something."

"I could marry her. I need a wife to be my countess. She sounds delightfully intelligent and I do need an heir. My life is one long escape from my mother's attempts to shackle me to empty headed title hunters. At least it would be a suitable arranged marriage."

"Would you do that, Trevane?" Portman looked shocked, Danvers looked surprised, the others looked astounded.

"Good grief, Richard. You never cease to amaze me."

Danvers stood up and clapped him on the back.

"When did that idea come to you?"

"Last night, after you left me holding your problem. I just needed all the information to see if it was feasible."

"You still have to find her." Simister said.

"Oh he will find her, no doubt about that," Danvers replied, a glimmer of comprehension in his mind.

"We will need to approach her father, she is only eighteen."

"True, I will take you Richard. You can meet her brother while you are there."

The meeting ended with a visit to a nearby bar, the conversation being quite innocuous. Well, these were ex government operatives, spies to you and me, what else would you expect of them?

Chapter 19

Danvers was in no mood to delay. They took Richard's travelling coach, it enabled them to talk on the way though it was only a short journey for such an equipage.

The Duke of Wenton received them with resignation. He was a shadow of his former self. He ran his estates with the help of his estate manager, with the work mainly done by the latter.

He rarely smiled, but looked at the world and everyone in it with great sadness showing in his eyes. Richard was shocked to see such visible signs in a man of his status. Danvers was shocked at his deterioration each time he came.

"Have you anything to cheer me, Danvers?"

"I have brought hope in the person of my colleague, Richard Trevane."

"Trevane, I recognise that name."

"He was my 'people finder'. You may have come across some of his rescue successes."

"Oh! Phillips and his wife. Got caught up on the way through to Portugal for the packet to England."

"Indeed, I did come across the Phillips's when I was working in Spain."

"Behind enemy lines."

"Yes, sir."

"And you are the latest to search for my daughter?"

"I hope I will be the successful one, sir."

The Duke eyed him doubtfully. Danvers waited for the right moment to introduce the reason for their visit.

"Actually, sir, we have come to tell you of out latest discussions, and their surprising conclusions."

"Surprising, eh. Well tell me then."

"We were discussing why Lady Kitty disappeared, and to what advantage it would be for her to reappear. It was thought that if she had been away because she had married, the ton might believe the reason. If we don't find her soon, the crown and structure of England will implode. It is that dangerous."

"That dangerous. So my daughter is to be sacrificed for England."

Richard spoke to reassure him. "Not sacrificed, sir. If she came back now they would kill her; that would be a sacrifice. Marriage is only an option if she agrees."

"Who are you suggesting she marry?"

"Me." Richard said with some enthusiasm.

The Duke looked at Danvers. Danvers smiled.

"I did suggest myself, but Trevane here has much more to offer."

The Duke turned to Richard.

"What do you have to offer, sir?" he asked, in a rather stilted tone.

"I am Lord Richard Trevane, fifth Earl of Pengarron. I have an estate in Cornwall, an estate in Staffordshire, a London House, a hunting box near Norfolk and several houses, most of which are let, as I have no need of them. My funds are good and increasing, in spite of my mother's clothing bills. I have need of an heir, but no wish to marry the empty headed title hunters my mother keeps throwing at me. Your daughter is obviously an intelligent young lady. She must be, if a confirmed bachelor like Danvers was prepared to marry her. I have heard very good accounts of her."

"Good Grief! An Earl running as an operative behind enemy lines."

"Actually, sir, I have several titled gentleman who worked overseas for me." The Duke looked at Danvers with surprise.

"Really, well I am surprised." The conversation lapsed.

"I am not sure my daughter would accept an arranged marriage."

"I would not force it upon her, sir. She would have to agree, but I am not without some powers of persuasion." He smiled and his eyes glinted.

"So it seems, Pengarron. Well I hope you can at least find her. The 'people finder' eh!" A small smile reached his lips, more a softening of them.

Danvers then introduced the practical details.

"She is only eighteen, sir, we need your permission for a licence."

"She's not to marry in London, then. Can I be at her wedding?"

"I am sorry, sir. To maintain her standing she needs to return already married. If you went to her you would be followed and it could put her in danger as they are still searching for her. If the ton thought she was living with someone her reputation would be ruined and more rumours would start."

"Yes, I can see that. I may not like it, but I can understand it. What do you need exactly?"

"A letter agreeing to her marriage to me, sir. Would you like to discuss the settlements now, or with your lawyer present?"

"Oh, of course. A proper agreement. What if she refuses?"

"The settlement will state it is to become effective only if she actually marries me."

The Duke looked at Danvers.

"He is certainly thorough. Well, young man, if you are to be my son-in-law, possibly, you had better call me Wenton."

"Thank you sir.... Wenton."

"Shall we go into my study to discuss terms? They can be sent to my lawyer at a later date. When you have married her. Came across your father at Eton, not in the same year, of course." With that they drifted, relatively companionably, into his study.

Danvers smiled and went to see if Jeremy was well enough to see him.

It took a little time to write the agreement, mostly because they were both so willing to give her whatever the other wanted. Kitty was in danger of becoming the richest countess in England.

Danvers spent his time with Jeremy, overjoyed to have someone to converse with. They covered the lack of information and the presence of Richard downstairs.

"Your 'people finder'. What kind of people?"

"All kinds. Lost travellers in a hostile land, hidden refugees from the French authorities, the odd one hidden by the French for nefarious purposes."

"He got them out?"

"He brought back almost everyone he was asked to find, and a few we knew nothing about until they arrived. He's a pleasant fellow. You would never know his intellect by just talking to him; he hides it well."

"I would expect him to be able to hide a good deal, being one of your agents. He would suit my sister, she has very bluestocking tendencies but you would never think it. Do you believe he can find her?"

Danvers smiled a knowing smile. He knew Richard too well. He had never promised anything before now. He knew something he was not prepared to reveal.

"Oh yes, I am sure he can find her."

The talk then turned to the rest of life in the political sphere, what parliament was doing, who was for and who was against.

Aunt Hetty arrived with tea and delicious biscuits, also with Richard, directed there by the Duke.

Danvers was the one to make the introductions.

"So you are hoping to be my brother-in-law, Pengarron?"

"I am indeed, the agreements have been signed. All I have to do is find her and talk her into marrying me!"

"You need a special licence." Danvers' common sense cut in.

"Yes, I know. I have a letter of agreement for a Bishop."

"I will arrange that, the Prince will be interested to hear the plans, he will give the nod to a Bishop for us."

The talk turned to general information about Richard and where he lived, and Jeremy, how his recovery was going and what the prognosis given by the doctor was. Aunt Hetty returned with an invitation to dinner, country hours, not formal as neither of them had a change of clothes.

Jeremy was now allowed out of bed into a special invalid chair. He could sit out in the morning, rest in the afternoon, then he was brought down to dinner, mainly as company for his father. Dinner which he could now eat with one good hand and one with fingers not yet working well. At least his arms and ribs had healed. It would be some time yet before he could try to put weight on his legs.

They left him to be prepared for dinner, and went to go downstairs to await the Duke and Jeremy. As they left, Aunt Hetty's hand touched Richard's sleeve and he turned to speak to her.

You intend to marry Lady Kitty sir?"

"Indeed I do, Aunt Hetty." His eyes laughed at her.

"I think you will do very well together. You seem compatible, my lord." She smiled a secret smile at him.

"I will take good care of her, I promise you."

"I am sure you will. Please give her my love. I hope she found her cottage."

"I'm sure she did." He took her hand, raised it to his lips and kissed it, looking down into her eyes. She blushed.

"You'll do. Go on with you." And a happy Aunt Hetty went to prepare for dinner.

* * *

"We're invited to a royal audience, so best court dress." Danvers had arrived at Richard's door.

"My mother comes back on Tuesday for the Geralds' ball. How soon can we do this? I want to be away before she returns."

"It depends on the Prince, and if he feels disposed to help. If not we just have to find a Bishop and hope he says nothing about the timing of the licence, when you appear with her."

"I just want to be away."

"I know, but don't forget you are now in their sights. You will be followed."

"I'm sure I will. I intend to lead them a merry dance."

"Good for you. You don't have anything to tell me, do you, Trevane?"

"No."

"Very well. I will await the outcome."

He wore his deep blue coat and grey breeches. His waistcoat was embroidered with flowers, but in muted colours. He was an Earl and needed to look like one. But best not to outdo the Prince with his waistcoat: elegant but not overstated. His stick-pin was the large sapphire he had worn at Highborne. He rarely used it, but he felt it brought out the blue of his eyes.

Smithson eyed him critically "You'll do, my lord. I would have put you in a more colourful waistcoat, but I suppose you know best." He sniffed, meaning he did not believe that.

"Indeed, in this case I do know best, Smithson."

"I hope the Prince appreciates the effort you have taken."

"I doubt it. He will probably barely notice me."

Laughing, he went down to wait for the carriage, the small London one. Thank heaven his mother was not there or he may have been forced to go by hackney!

The palace was alight, the queue of carriages was long and slow. Richard thought he should have brought a book to read. He had forgotten how one had to queue in London.

He had agreed to meet Sir Peter in the outer receiving room and from there they would go in together. The room was seething with people. Who would have expected so many to be invited?

Danvers lurked in a corner, watching for the dark blond hair of Richard who suddenly appeared at his side.

"What a crush, I thought they hated him."

"Where did you spring from?"

Richard laughed. "I am trained for this, you remember."

"What, to appear out of nowhere?"

"If necessary."

"I underestimate you."

"I doubt you do, Danvers."

"Come let's get into the fray or we will never get to speak to him."

"How are we to have any private conversation in this crowd?"

"You underestimate him. No names from now on."

"Of course. General light hearted talk about nothing."

"Not quite nothing." He pointed to where two members of parliament were having a heated argument over some political point. The only clear space was a few feet all around them.

"You look every inch the Earl, today, Richard."

"I tried to look formal, elegant, but not enough to outshine our mutual friend." Danvers laughed out loud and people turned to stare.

"You always surprise me with your insights. Yet I have no idea why as I know you well enough."

It took another half an hour before they reached the Prince as he greeted his guests with a fixed smile on his face and dead eyes.

"Sir Peter Danvers and The Earl of Pengarron." The announcement brought sudden alertness to his eyes.

"Danvers, Pengarron." Danvers looked into his eyes to alert him of the need to speak.

"You know Pengarron, sire?"

"Not recently, I fear. I must renew our acquaintance, Pengarron."

"That would be very good of you, Sire." He looked markedly into his eyes.

"Not at all, Pengarron. Perhaps I may find a few minutes when this deuced receiving line is done."

"I would appreciate that, Sire."

So they moved on to find refreshment and pass the time with acquaintances until the receiving line was deemed to have been there for long enough.

"How do you manage to speak here?"

"The art is to look as if you are having a jovial conversation."

"Will we not be able to see him alone?"

"Oh no. Private conversations are always overheard. There must be something worth listening to. In the centre of a crush, only the recipients understand what is being said. The Prince has made a study of it." Richard laughed. It amazed him the Prince could be so devious.

"May I join the joke, gentlemen?"

"Your Highness."

"Stop bobbing, I'm sick of it. What is new?"

"Not a great deal, Sire, but a decision has been made."

"About?"

"Our lady should marry and reappear as a happy wife."

"Goodness, that's devious! Smile, Pengarron."

"Yes Sire." He put a vague lift to his lips.

"It could work, but is the party willing?"

"We can't know that yet."

"Do we know where?"

"Not yet but I think you should speak with Pengarron."

"Why have I not seen you recently, Pengarron?"

"He has been away on our behalf."

"Oh."

"Richard Trevane is one of mine."

"And an Earl!"

"Yes Your Highness." Richard inclined his head.

"Trevane, I know that name."

"My people finder, Sire."

Understanding dawned on the Prince's face.

"And who is the lucky husband, may I ask?"

"I am." said Richard.

"Then you are a lucky young man."

"Thank you Sire, but we have one problem."

He looked his query.

"We need a special licence from a Bishop we can trust."

"Ah. Yes."

"Do you have one available?"

"Yes indeed. If you follow me vaguely across to the window, I will solicit the Bishop of London to assist. Speak with him when I am gone. A pleasure to meet you, Pengarron." And with that he moved through the throng, which opened up for him as if he were a ship cutting though water. Trying to follow in his wake they were swallowed up by the swell of others doing the same. He appeared to be making for the window alcove. They saw him talking light heartedly, or so it seemed, to a Bishop. When he moved off, the crowd followed after him. They excused themselves from the group of friends they had stopped to speak with, and stood in the alcove.

The Bishop was talking with a very sombre young lady in a seriously drab, if well cut, gown. She appeared to be berating him on a point of detail relating to the dress of ladies with regard to a moral code. The Bishop was having a hard time even getting to speak. In the end he excused himself and came to them.

"The Bishop of London?"

"Indeed, and you are?"

"Richard Trevane, Earl of Pengarron, at your service, your grace."

"Pengarron. I recognise Danvers, we have had dealings before. I gather you need something of me." Speaking to Richard. "Do you rise early, sir?"

"If I need to, your grace."

"Nine o'clock at Lambeth Palace, if you will. I will alert my staff to expect you."

"I thank you, your grace."

"My pleasure, young man. Anything to sort this deuced problem the Prince has." He smiled and walked away.

"It can't be that easy."

"You are too sceptical, Richard. If he wants to help it can be that quickly done."

"Nine o'clock. at Lambeth Palace."

"Then you can leave London and your mother."

"She is getting aggressive with her attempts. At the moment she is at the Penfolds' and not due back until Tuesday. They have a daughter to settle. What's the betting she knows I am in London and will arrive with the Penfolds for a dinner tomorrow evening? She may even be there tonight."

"Then come dine with me, if it will help."

"You, sir, are a gentleman."

"I should hope I am, Richard."

Dinner was a relaxed meal that evening. Both men appreciated the quiet companionship.

Richard returned home fairly late and very relaxed, if now a little inebriated. The house was not free from anxiety. His butler met him, almost wringing his hands.

"My lord, your mother has returned early. She has instructed cook there will be a dinner party here tomorrow evening."

Richard burst out laughing.

"Elliot, I begin to predict my mother. I told Danvers exactly what would happen only a few hours ago. That is why I stayed out for dinner." He gave Elliot his cloak and hat. "Never fear. I have a little business in the morning, then I will be leaving."

A glimmer of a smile showed on the butler's face.

Quietly Richard said. "I doubt she will stay all season with me gone."

"We can but hope, my lord." almost in a whisper.

Smithson was not so overjoyed.

"I have barely unpacked." he complained.

"Well pack again, including some elegant London clothes. You can set out whenever you are ready, you will be taking the travelling carriage, I am riding elsewhere."

"The travelling coach, my lord, just me?"

"Yes Smithson, just you. Nicholls will be your coachman and he is in charge of the journey. I will give him the route to take, you will have nothing to do but enjoy the ride."

"I may leave when I am ready?"

"Yes, but not too late. You will be calling at Highborne Castle. I will give you a letter." He gave a sly smile. "I understand my mother has arrived."

"Oh! Yes, my lord, I will start packing immediately." He was decidedly put out by her presence as she upset any arrangements and walked over everyone's feelings.

"Then the sooner you are packed, the earlier you can leave."

"Before she rises."

"Exactly." Smithson beamed. Escape, and in the travelling carriage, how very agreeable.

"What time would you like to rise, sir?"

"A little before seven, I think. I have your letter to write and must leave a little after eight. Oh, and can you pack me my travelling bags for a few days on horseback? I shall need to pick them up from Elliot when I leave."

"Will that be all for tonight, my lord?"

"Indeed. Goodnight, Smithson, we have a very busy day ahead of us tomorrow."

* * *

"Good morning, your grace."

Richard had entered a private room in Lambeth Palace, sumptuously furnished as befitting a man of the bishop's station. Richard could appreciate the comfort, he lived with it at home.

"Come in, Pengarron. Sit down."

"A comfortable room, your grace."

"Indeed, that is why I have this one for my personal use. Why be a Bishop if not to enjoy the comforts of life a little?" Richard laughed.

"I do appreciate your help in this matter."

"Well I give licences on a regular basis, mostly to the aristocracy, of course. This is a special one, I am led to understand."

"It is the privacy which is most important where this is concerned."

"Relating to this problem of the Prince and the ferment among the ton?"

"We are hoping that her marriage will stop the link between them in the eyes of the ton. The secrecy is how long she has been married. We wish it to appear to be some time ago, to relate to her disappearance."

"How sensible. I can only issue it from today, you understand."

"Of course. Anyone who discovers where she married will be able to find out when, we just need to fool the ton for long enough to stop this madness."

"I need your names."

"My card, for mine. I have a letter of agreement from her father which contains her full name."

"This is a fully approved marriage then."

"Oh yes, your grace. A financial agreement has been signed."

"I am relieved about that. I must admit I was a little concerned that the strict legal procedure might be being ignored. The Prince does tend to expect things done on his terms."

"So I understand." They shared a pleasant laugh.

The Bishop took out the relevant paperwork which he began to fill in.

"You realise I usually have someone fill in the details, I normally only sign it." It amused him.

"Then I am doubly grateful for your help with privacy, your grace." Richard grinned.

"Good luck, my lord. I hope you find her." a gleam in his eye.

"Oh I am sure I can find her, it's getting her consent I am nervous about."

Chapter 20

At a quarter to seven, a bright and breezy Smithson had woken Richard, dutifully clothed him and seen him downstairs. He had packed his travelling bags and collected two letters, one for Carvon at Highborne Castle, the other for the Duke of Wenton, of whom he had never heard. He took to packing the trunks and boxes with real pleasure. He was going home, to Cornwall. He liked that house, he liked the people and even better, her ladyship did not.

It was after ten when the trunk was loaded into the coach. Nicholls the coachman looked fairly serious about the whole expedition,

"I will be but a few moments, His Lordship has given you all the details, I take it."

"Oh yes, I am to stick to them exactly."

"Then you better had. I have two letters. Do you know Wenton Hall?"

"Oh yes. I took him there a couple of days ago."

So Smithson checked the stables had his Lordship's horse to the ready, and the butler had his travelling bag.

Everything seemed to be in order, so he climbed into the coach for a gentle unhurried drive down to Cornwall. When two burly footmen climbed up on the back Smithson was intrigued.

They made good time leaving London, but when they were on the less maintained roads Nicholls never slowed. At one point he heard one of the footmen call to Nicholls, he replied and they picked up speed.

When they pulled into Wenton Hall grounds, Nicholls slowed to let the horses breathe.

The butler at the hall took the letter from Smithson and bade him wait. Shortly after a gentleman, who could only be a Duke, came out to the hallway.

"Smithson, is it?"

"Yes, your grace."

"Come in. Wilson, send the coach around to the stables. Tell them everyone is to be on watch for outsiders, we could have a problem."

"Yes, your grace."

"I take it you know the content of this letter."

"No, my lord."

"Ah, you had better come into my study."

He followed the Duke to the study, where he stood by the desk in some awe. The Duke closed the door.

"Sit down, Smithson, no ceremony today. I need to talk." Smithson sat, rigidly. He worked for an Earl, but this was a Duke and he was in his private study. You did not sit down with a Duke.

"Do you know where you are going?"

"Yes, you ….well not really. I know we are going to Highborne Castle but then I thought Cornwall, to Pengarron Hall."

"You are going to Highborne Castle, that is true. I note you have outrider footmen."

"Yes, your grace, I have no idea why."

"Do you know where Pengarron has gone?"

"No, your grace, he omitted to say."

"I bet he did, Smithson. I presume you are the only one who does not know that you are a decoy. He is expecting you to be followed, and set up the coach to look as if he were in it. Your footmen will be fully armed and on guard. I believe you are the best guarded valet in history."

The Duke was actually amused. Smithson was horrified.

"A decoy. your grace."

"You are now included in an intrigue which you neither know about nor would understand. You will stay here for the night. In the morning you will leave very early by a little used gate and, hopefully, make your way to Highborne without incident and without being followed. If you are followed, you will be assisted in losing them at Highborne."

"Thank you, your grace." He was aghast. "I shall have the trunks unloaded." He rose to leave.

"Not necessary, except for anything you need. The coach is in an enclosed coach house and will be guarded all night. I suggest you go and see Mrs Alford, the housekeeper, who will arrange accommodation and food.

His grace walked to the door and opened it. A totally stunned Smithson went out and was ushered away by a footman.

* * *

Richard stowed the licence and permission in his safe inside pocket. He loaded the bags onto his horse via a back door, bid goodbye to his butler and left through the front door. He hoped the coach had drawn off some of the men watching him, but was still hoping that others, one or two, he would not be able to handle more than that, would follow to allow him to cause confusion as to his destination. He hoped they came to realise the coach was a decoy and following it to Cornwall was not an option.

His first stop was the coaching inn where they had left William the driver. He spoke to the young hostler as well as the landlord. He made friends with the landlord's daughter and complained about being sent on a fool's errand. She was so helpful, remembering the sleeping coachman, the man with him, the woman in black, the ticket in his pocket, and him having money for food. "The lady in black, was she a servant or a lady?" he asked. "Oh, a servant", she assured him. No one saw the lady after they arrived the day before. That meant Kitty was already 'John Coachman'.

Kitty, it suited her. It was good to have a name when he thought of her, and he thought of her all the time. This was a wonderful piece of subterfuge. She would have fitted in as one of Danvers' undercover agents. God, he loved that woman.

The young hostler was a real help. Did he see both women get into the coach, were they both in black? Yes, never noticed the coachman, heard the ladies talking before they left. He did say he was tired of everybody asking.

"Who asked?"

"Well there was several the first few days, then her dad come looking. Nobby cove he was, in his swanky carriage. Stopped on the road, didn't want me to see."

"What, that he was nobby, or his coach?"

Richard knew the Duke had not been out himself.

"Dunno, really."

"What was the coach like?"

"It were a big travelling carriage and six. For one man, six horses!"

"Did it have a coat of arms on it?"

"Oh yes, real fancy it were. Like a 'orse with an 'orn and big animal all furry."

Richard took out his pocketbook and drew a horse.

"No, it stood up." Ah, rampant. "With orn."

A unicorn and facing it?

"Looked like a big furry horse with arms."

Richard drew a rampant bear. "Like this?"

"Yeh, that's it."

The young man was richly rewarded, asked to tell nobody else about the coat of arms, and went back to work feeling very proud of himself.

From the coaching inn, Richard rode on to the next inn, took a room and watched for followers. At least one, probably two. The next morning he rode on to the Norwich road and proceeded at a slow enough pace to be sure they were following him. He turned north towards Thetford Forest. Now he was on home territory.

He rode faster, making them fall behind. Each time he stopped, he made sure they caught up, then moved on again. He rode to the east as if for Kings Lynn or the coast somewhere there, then leaving them behind, he turned into the forest.

It was growing dark now and the forest was difficult to navigate. In places he walked with his horse, careful not to set up any roosting birds which might give away his progress. It was almost pitch black when he walked his horse over the open estate grass belonging to his friend Limburg. He only hoped he was at home.

Limburg's butler was backed by two burly footmen when he opened the door.

"Who are you, what do you want?"

"Richard Trevane, Earl of Pengarron."

"What! Good heavens, my lord, what are you doing out on a cold night like this?"

"Looking for shelter for the night."

"I will fetch Mr Limburg, My lord. Jimmy, walk the Earl's horse round will you?"

Limburg was astounded and pleased to see him.

163

"Why so late on such a cold dark night? You should have taken shelter hours ago."

"Should, but could not risk it. I am being tailed by a couple of men I want to lose. The forest seemed a good place to do it. I was a little later than I expected when I rode into it."

"Have you lost them, do you think?"

"I hope they are on their way to Lynn or somewhere over that way. By the morning I shall be on the way through the west of the forest, and safely away."

"You can't keep away from intrigue, can you?"

"This is not intentional, I fell into this without realising. Now I'm in I must see it through to the end."

"I don't suppose you will tell me anything?"

"Not a chance, Limburg. I wouldn't put you in that much danger. Just tell your household to deny ever seeing me, for their own sakes."

"I will, but now food and a warm bed."

"That sounds wonderful."

It was before light that Richard started down the rides and footpaths through the forest. By the time it was fully light he was almost out. His timing now was critical. He had to be away before his tail reached the great north road and caught sight of him.

Down the road some way he turned off onto the Bedford road. If he was right this would be the road she took.

He stopped at several inns and enquired. Each said they had been asked before. Two admitted that a small black coach with a man servant and a maid driven by a very young coachman had stopped there, and yes, the maid had been in mourning clothes.

Richard grinned. Well done, my lovely future countess. Now all he had to do was get home unseen. That might be almost as difficult as their coach journey had been. He would have to use a variety of places to stop. Friends would give him away accidentally and coaching inns might be traceable. Perhaps if he went over the border into Wales and then southwards from Shrewsbury to Hereford, Gloucester, Cirencester, Swindon, and down to Highborne Castle near Newbury, he could hide his progress.

* * *

Smithson was still bemused when the carriage was prepared in the dark, and they were escorted down a long grassy drive to gates which protested at being opened. They drove through country roads, barely large enough for the travelling carriage. Nicholls knew the way he must take, having had exact directions from William the Duke's coachman. They seemed to be travelling north. Quite early in the journey they stopped at a coaching inn and had a very public meal, the coach being guarded at all times. Smithson found this strange as they were supposed to be going westwards to Highborne Castle, but Nicholls had his orders. They stayed overnight north of Coventry on the route to Stoke.

"Nicholls, are we going to the Stoke house?"

"It certainly looks like it."

"Is that yes, or no?"

"Like I say" Nicholls reiterated "It certainly looks like it."

"If we are a decoy, does that mean we are going elsewhere?"

"You're beginning to understand His Lordship's logic."

"When will we get to where we are going, and don't you dare say 'when we arrive'?"

"Well that depends on the roads."

The weather being cold and Smithson being bored in spite of using the travelling coach, the footmen started to alternate, one now sitting outside with Nicholls and one inside with Smithson. They were less conspicuous than riding as guards. They turned south and Nicholls drove the coach through every puddle he could. When they came to a stream with a small bridge, he tied off the horses, climbed down and took handfuls of mud and threw it at the coach doors. Smithson let down the window and nearly had a face full of mud.

"Nicholls, what are you doing? Look at the state of the coach, it's filthy, you can't see the crest!"

Nicholls grinned.

"Ah, another of his Lordship's instructions."

"You're getting quite intelligent, Smithson."

Smithson sniffed, put up the window and refused to speak to anyone for quite some time.

It was after dark when they arrived at Highborne Castle.

Smithson entered by the servants' entrance and went hunting for the butler.

"I have a letter for his Lordship."

"His Lordship is away from home until tomorrow. I will hand it to him on his return."

So a frustrated Smithson returned to the servants quarters to watch Nicholls and the footmen settle comfortably into the routine of life, leaving him as a valet with no lord to tend and nothing to do.

When the Earl of Carvon returned the following evening, he dutifully read the letter and called for Smithson.

"I presume you know the contents of the letter?"

"No, my lord."

"Ah, he didn't tell you."

"No sir."

"It appears I am hiding you, until it is clear there is no-one following. You need to stay a few days, apparently. Well that is no problem, I'm sure the butler can put you to good use while you're here.

"Yes, My lord."

Oh, unhappy Smithson.

Nicholls, like Smithson, having stayed at Highborne a few weeks before, was known to the servants and spent his time in the stables or the kitchens. One particular housemaid was showing a partiality for him. He was flattered, of course, although she had been more interested in another coachman during the summer house party.

One evening a few days later, the Earl intimated that it would be safe to leave the following morning. That night they enjoyed a last meal below stairs, Nicholls getting more amorous advances that usual. As there were no other guests with coachmen staying, Nicholls had the room over the stables to himself, or so he thought. But that night his bed was especially full.

"No, Daisy, go back to the house."

"Please, Nicholls, you're going in the morning."

"No, Daisy!" her hands and her warm naked body were having a very noticeable effect on Nicholls' libido. She cuddled, stroked and aroused him until he was hard pressed to know what to do.

"No, Daisy, we can't."

"Yes we can, Nicholls, please."

Her hands were skilled as she manipulated him into a very uncomfortable position. She pressed her breasts against his now naked chest, and rubbed her hard nipples against him, moaning in pleasure. He put his hands to push her away and touched the sides of her bust, she sighed a deep sigh, took hold of his shoulders and pulled him over her. This was too much for Nicholls, now laying between her legs, his cock so hard it was painful. She put her legs around his hips and he gave up struggling and thrust into her as she cried with pleasure. He remembered little of the next few minutes except the pleasure of being surrounded by warmth. He thrust with no restraint to empty into her in a huge emotional outpouring. He collapsed, spent and exhausted. When she wriggled, he was aware of moving onto his side.

He slept a deep sleep of contentment, until he was woken by the feel of hands stroking him and warm breath on his chest. He could hear voices in the stables. He tried to rise but a small shapely body pinned him to the bed.

"Not yet" she whispered "afterwards."

"After what?" She put her hand down and started to bring him to full size. He pushed her off, but she went to lean against the door, all naked willingness. He stopped thinking sensibly, only remembering the previous night. He leaned to kiss her upturned face and she put her arms around his neck. He lifted her, his hands under her round soft bottom and, as she put her legs around him, he entered her in one hard thrust. God this was good. He drove with need, just as he had the night before. As he spent himself a voice called.

"You getting up today, Nicholls?" It was a minute or two before he was able to answer.

The personal bags were stowed, the horses hitched and they left Highborne just before dawn. Smithson climbed in sleepily and collapsed into a corner. The two footmen rode outside until it was light and they were on the coach road.

As it grew light, Smithson became aware of not being alone in the carriage. A tightly wrapped cloak held someone in the other corner, also trying to sleep. Another of his Lordship's orders that no one had informed him about. When they pulled in to a coaching inn for a short break, and to allow one of the footmen to come into the carriage for warmth, the small intruder was discovered.

"Nicholls, do you know about this?" the footman called.

"What?"

"This girl in the coach."

"Nicholls leaned in and pulled open the cloak.

"Daisy, what are you doing here?"

"Is she not supposed to be here?"

"No, Smithson, why didn't you say she was here?"

"I though she was another instruction I knew nothing about." He was being rather sulky.

"No, she's another problem."

"Can't we take her with us?"

"No, she belongs at Highborne."

"Please, Nicholls, take me with you."

"No!" Nicholls exited the carriage and leaned against it.

"What are you going to do with her?"

"Take her back."

"Why."

"She is not mine, and I don't want her. She pushed herself onto me." He was angry. What would his Lordship say?

"I'll take a different road back, to make sure the coach is not remembered."

The days being shorter now, dusk was falling when they pulled up at the coach house once again. They left the grooms to unhitch the horses and stow the carriage. Smithson and Nicholls took a tearful Daisy into the house and asked to see the butler.

"Where were you going, Daisy?" He was angry.

"With Nicholls." She was trembling.

"Did he ask you to go?" Silence "Were you given permission to go?" No answer, just tears.

"Are you so unhappy here?" A shake of the head.

Accusations were made and refuted. Nicholls objected to things said to him and about him. To give him his due Smithson stood by him, defending his character.

The Earl was at a loss what to do with Pengarron's servants. A commotion in the hall brought an unexpected late guest.

"Pengarron, Thank God, you can sort out your servants."

A tired Richard was provided with some food and wine and seated in a small parlour. He called in Nicholls, and asked for an account, which he gave, in full.

"Last night, Nicholls, not before."

"No, my lord."

"Was there any liaison between you in August when we were here?"

"No, my lord."

"None?"

"None, my lord, she was walking out with Walcott's coachman. They seemed involved, if you know what I mean." Richard was thoughtful.

"Yes, I do Nicholls. And Walcott left early and rather suddenly."

"Yes, My lord, he did."

"Very well, Nicholls, I will deal with it from now onwards."

"Thank you sir."

"You look relieved." He smiled at him.

"I am, sir. I didn't want to …" He broke off.

"But it is sometimes difficult to resist."

"Indeed it is." he said with feeling.

As Daisy was Carvon's servant, Richard was with him when he asked to see Daisy.

"Why do you want to go with Nicholls?"

"He's kind."

"You don't run off with someone just because he is kind."

He is also strong, intelligent, and very masculine, he thought, but did not say it.

"In August you were walking out with Walcott's coachman. Is that true, Daisy?" Daisy nodded and burst into tears.

"Why do you want to leave Highborne, Daisy?" She looked abjectly sad. Carvon went to speak but Richard held up his hand to silence him. Very gently he said "Daisy, are you with child?" Her tears grew worse.

"Would you rather go with Nicholls, or would you like to be with Walcott's coachman?"

It took her a few minutes to speak. Then she blurted out. "I loves him."

"Who, Walcott's coachman?" A nod.

"And you knew you would be dismissed from Highborne?" Another nod.

"Would you like me to contact Mr Walcott and see if his coachman is still interested in you?"

"Oh yes please, my lord." Her eager face looked up suddenly, covered in blotches from her tears.

"Off you go for now. Don't tell anyone yet, will you?" She shook her head and scuttled off.

Carvon looked at him, a little nonplussed.

"Well I'll be."

"I know my men, Carvon. They know they can tell me the whole truth. Nicholls told me about August. If Walcott had stayed, his coachman may have asked for her. It seems sensible to give him the opportunity, it saves an unwanted child starving and a girl in total poverty, probably living as a street prostitute." Carvon stared at him.

"You care about people, don't you, Pengarron?"

"I've seen too much poverty and cruelty, especially on the continent. Give her a chance, Carvon, it may not have been her fault."

"If he won't take her, I'll find her some outside work."

"Thank you friend. Do you mind if I sleep now? I've been on the road for days."

Carvon thumped his shoulder in friendship and rang for the housekeeper to see him to his room.

Although the days were short, after making the necessary arrangements, he left late in the morning. It was hard to explain to Carvon why he was so eager.

"One day soon, not too far away I hope, you will find out how beneficial you have been to more people than you realise, friend."

"You mean I get to be told something about one of your intrigues?"

"Indeed you will."

Most of the way home he rode in the coach, He was tempted to ride down by horse, but the weather was cold and rainy so he thought better of it. The main joy was, he was going home to his Kitty, he carried a licence in his coat and his heart was starting to sing.

Chapter 21

The weather was cold and wet. Kitty stayed in the house, alternating between hope and hopelessness. In deference to Richard they kept the house as warm as they could. As the days were shorter there were longer hours in which to keep the fires lit, cook hot food, and heat water for warm baths. It used more fuel, of course, and by the time three weeks was coming to an end, Kitty went to Toby Fuller's cottage to ask for fuel.

"Of course, miss, I'll bring some later today. Have you seen his Lordship yet?"

"His Lordship?"

"Lord Trevane, he come back last night."

Kitty didn't know whether to laugh or cry. Lord Trevane, he was back, he was a lord, and he had not told her. She was quite angry that he had not trusted her and pretended to be an ordinary man, plain Mr Trevane.

"Last night, you say!"

"Yes, miss. I seen the Earl's travelling carriage come in, quite late it was."

"Lord Trevane is an Earl!"

"Yes miss, although he don't act like it. Prefers to be Mr Trevane."

"He prefers it."

"Yes miss, He don't like us doing the 'yes Milord, no Milord' all the time, so we just calls him sir."

"Oh, thank you Toby. You won't forget the fuel."

"No miss, I won't."

He was back already. When would he come? He was an Earl. Her father would approve. She was under age. He thought she was a miss, would he want her? Had he heard any of the rumours? Would he ignore her now? When would he come? Why had he lied to her? Lord Trevane! Liked to be called Mr Trevane, but that was by his servants. He thought she was low born, why would he tell her? When would he come?

"Someone to see you miss." Binny grinned as she stood back to admit Richard.

He looked at her with such warmth and affection. The emotion welled in her.

"How dare you not tell me, you're an Earl and you never said." She punched him in the chest.

Richard looked amused at her tantrum, hauled her into his arms, and kissed her hard. She clung to him, shocked.

"Welcome home would have been good."

"Welcome home, *Lord Trevane.*"

"Richard." he said.

"Is there a reason you 'forgot' to tell me you were an Earl, my lord!"

"Richard." he reiterated.

"Did you conclude your business, *My lord*?"

"Richard. And yes I did, very quickly as it happens."

She looked a little contrite.

"I missed you, Richard."

"I missed you too, very much, that is why I came home so soon." He was still holding her close by her shoulders. "Will you do something for me?"

She looked up. "What?"

"Kiss me again, Kitty."

He slid his arms around her waist. She slid her arms over his shoulders and he brought his lips to hers, gently at first, then, growing in need, he pulled her closer and took over her mouth, running his tongue over hers as she tentatively responded with her own exploration. Suddenly she jerked and leapt away from him.

"What did you call me?" Richard smiled. She was angry, confused, upset, adorable.

"I called you by your name, Kitty."

"How did you find out? Is that why you went to London? I could be in danger now, what if you were followed?" She was more distressed than he had ever seen her. "All this will be ruined, just because you had to find out who I was!" She was beginning to panic and her breathing was uneven.

"Kitty, you are in no danger. If you knew the lengths I went to in keeping you safe. If I had just ridden back I would have been here a week ago."

He hauled her close to him and held her until her breathing returned to normal as she was leaning on his chest.

"You didn't have to go. Why did you need to know so desperately? Did you not accept the danger you would put me in?" She pulled away to look into his face.

"No, my love, I did not realise how much danger you were in. Why did I go? Well for one reason, I can't make you my Countess under an assumed name, Miss Sinclair. Another is, I presumed you were not of age to marry without permission."

She stood frozen with shock. "Your Countess!"

"I did not expect to have to ask quite so soon, but yes, Lady Katherine Elizabeth Wellmore, will you do me the honour of marrying me."

"Marry you. Oh Richard."

The door opened and Binny bringing in the tea tray stopped at the scene in front of her, then retreated.

"I could hope for a yes, Kitty." Kitty looked up into his expectant face.

"Yes, Richard."

His arms closed around her as he virtually picked her off the floor to bury his head in her neck, working round until his lips were on hers again. Emotion swept over him, he had never felt so overwhelmed by anything in his life. She had said yes.

"You're mine now" he whispered.

They stood together, Richard holding her close. Then as they moved apart, he took both her hands in his, neither wanting to break the moment.

Binny knocked on the door, tentatively.

"Binny." she opened the door. "Come in Binny."

"I think tea is served, my lady." Richard said bowing.

Turning to Binny he said

"Lady Kitty has just agreed to be my wife, Binny."

"Oh, miss, how lovely." Then she stopped. "Lady Kitty. You know."

"Yes Binny, I know. Probably a great deal more than you two."

"Oh!"

"Do you have any cake or biscuits we could celebrate with?"

"I will bring everything we have, sir, I can cook more later."

"Will you pour, Madam?" Kitty raised herself to her most regal and crossed to the table.

"Indeed, my lord." Then she threw herself into his arms and burst into tears.

Later they sat quietly before the fire.

"How did you find out, who did you ask?"

"No one, actually, although I did intend to. I arrived, went to my club, was invited out to dinner and returned home to find my old colonel waiting for me."

"Your colonel, were you in the army?"

"Not in the normal way, but I was in both Spain and France."

"You were? Why was he waiting for you?"

"When I tell you his name you will understand. Colonel Sir Peter Danvers."

"Danvers! He was your colonel. Then you were…"

"A spy of a kind, yes I was."

"He told you about me."

"No, actually he told me about the Prince and all the trouble brewing with the ton rumours. It was only when he went into detail that I suddenly realised he was talking about you. If it helps, no one realises I know where you are."

"How did you manage that?"

"You are forgetting, my love, I was a spy, I was trained in subterfuge. Although I think Danvers has an inkling. Someone else has more than an inkling I know, and she sends her love."

"She?"

"Aunt Hetty."

"Aunt Hetty, where is she?"

"At Wenton Hall, coping with two heart sore men. They miss you, Kitty."

Over the next few days, Richard Trevane courted Lady Kitty Wellmore. He spent a great deal of time at the house. Mostly they talked.

"Kitty, my darling Kitty. Come let me hold you. She leaned into his chest and put her arms around him. He stroked her hair, her back, massaged the back of her neck, ran his fingers down her spine. She shivered with the pleasure of it all, leaning in to him even closer.

"We can't stand up all day, Kitty. Will you sit on my lap?" Kitty looked askance at him.

"Surely that is not proper?"

"My being alone with you is not proper. My sitting in the cliff was not proper. You living here alone with only two servants, is not proper. I don't want to be proper, Kitty." He nuzzled her neck then towed her across the room. Sitting down in a chair, he pulled her onto his knee. At first she sat stiffly, then bit by bit she relaxed.

As they sat and talked, he let his fingers wander. His thumb brushed the side of her breast. She either did not object, or she had not noticed; he hoped she did not object. His arm around her back, he urged her to lay back onto it, letting his hand just reach to cup the delicious handful. She nuzzled into him. Then he began rubbing his thumb over her nipple. She sat up suddenly.

"Richard, what are you doing?"

"Wishing you had a few less clothes on, my sweet."

"Is this normal?"

"Perfectly normal. Do not forget we are to be married very soon."

"Will you do this after we are married?" she asked.

"Oh yes, all the time, plus a great deal more. Can I show you a little?"

Kitty thought about it.

"I suppose so." She sounded a little hesitant.

He leant her back again with her head on his upper arm, she felt her neckline loosen as if her bodices were undone. His hand ran down the inside of her dress, eventually cupping her left breast and squeezing her gently.

"Oh, Richard!"

"Do you like that?"

"It feels..." she had difficulty finding the word "good." she concluded.

He positioned his fingers over her nipple and gently stroked and squeezed. Her nipples pebbled. Kitty shifted slightly.

"It makes me feel strange."

"Good strange, or bad strange?"

"Good, I think, I don't know."

His right hand closed over her other breast and started squeezing the nipple.

"Oh, Richard, Oh!"

"Good or bad?"

"I feel - I can't say."

"More?"

"Yes, I want..."

"What?"

"I don't know."

He moved his right hand down and pulled up her skirts. Lowering his head, he took her mouth as his fingers stroked up her leg. She shifted and wriggled as he stroked her private curls then slipped his fingers between her legs. She opened willingly to him as he stroked the hot little mound. Her body arched and she made a little cry, then she shook and covered his fingers with the wetness he longed to feel with another part of him.

Soon, oh so soon.

When should he talk about the wedding?

Kitty lay on his arm in complete submission. Her body was replete. He heard Binny talk to Ferguson just outside the door, and suddenly she was upright, the neck of her dress closed. He picked her off his knee, depositing her several feet from him in a chair just as Ferguson opened the door for Binny to bring in the tea tray.

Kitty's face was a picture, her eyes were bright, her body collapsed against the chair back, a bemused but contented smile on her lips. Was this what Petunia had been talking of all that lifetime away in London's parlours?

Binny gave her a funny look.

After that, every time Richard was near her he ran his fingers over her neck or down her back as he passed. He longed to have her completely his, but she was a total innocent and he must be careful not to frighten her.

"Darling Kitty, can we talk about our wedding? Kitty looked confused.

"How can we put up the banns with my real name? In three weeks everyone would know. I'm frightened, Richard."

"Soon you will have me to protect you every minute of every day, sweet. Don't be frightened."

"But until then."

"Until then no one will know anything."

"But the banns, the announcement, Papa's permission." She was clinging to his arm, laying her head against his shoulder.

"I have your Papa's permission. I also have a special licence."

"You do! How?"

"I said I would marry you when I found you, if you would have me, of course."

A very confused Kitty said "You intended to…"

"From long before I went to London."

"And you never said anything!" She beat his chest with her fists. "All that worry that you might not want me."

"Did you want me, then?" He was gently teasing.

"Yes, but I thought it hopeless."

"Nothing is hopeless. I will arrange things, Kitty. For you I will change the stars and the moon."

She laughed, and he pulled her into his arms again.

"Would you like to see the Hall where we will live?"

"Yes, but…"

"Not a visit. Not until we marry, but you can see it from the edge of the woodland. You can walk there from here."

"Oh yes please, Richard."

"If the weather is good enough I shall take you tomorrow then." He was nearly there.

"Kitty, what do you know about marriage? The wedding night that mothers usually tell you about?"

Kitty looked overawed. "Nothing, really. The girls did talk a little, but it was mostly bits they had heard from sisters."

"As you have no mother, and Binny is hardly in a position to know, I will tell you tomorrow as we walk." Tell her, he intended to do more than that.

"Do you have a gown to marry in, a suitable one?"

"Oh, no! That is, I think Binny packed one gown. It may not fit, I shall have to ask her about it."

Binny brought tea and asked if he was staying for dinner.

After Richard left that night, she asked Binny about the dress.

"Did you bring one?"

"Of course I did. I told you there was bound to be a reason to need one. I brought your pale blue with silver lace, miss. It always looked so elegant, it brings out the colour of your eyes so."

"Will it still fit me, Binny? I have lost a great deal of size. Everything is too big."

"I will shake it out now, miss, and you can try it on. Then we will see if it can be altered."

It was very creased after all the weeks in the trunk, but Binny was adamant that she could alter it.

"I shall take the seams down tonight and see what we can do.

"Will it take a lot of work?"

"We shall know when I pin it up, miss."

The next morning saw Binny on her knees, pinning and tucking and humming quietly to herself. Her little lamb was to marry a good man, and the one she wanted. The work on the dress was her greatest pleasure. Housework could wait, a little dust was of no account today.

Richard called for her at ten o'clock, Binny was closeted upstairs somewhere, so he sent Kitty to tell her they would probably be late for lunch. Kitty wondered just how far they would have to walk to see the Hall.

For a while they walked in companionable silence, holding hands as they went. It took almost an hour to reach the rise at the edge of the wood. It was a distant view, but showed the Hall to great advantage. A large solid stone house, what she would have expected for Richard, it was mostly two storeys high with attic rooms above. There was a plethora of chimneys, below which the light caught the windows and made them seem like shining eyes looking over the landscape to espy her where she stood.

"Oh Richard, what a beautiful solid house."

"Yes isn't it. Built for warmth against the sea breezes. You shall see the inside in a couple of days."

"A couple. Oh! Two days! What if the dress is not finished?"

"What a female problem. What is Binny doing with the dress?"

"Altering it to fit. I am somewhat thinner than I was last summer! Last summer, it seems like an age ago."

"A different life to this?"

"Oh yes. Much different." He put his arm around her shoulders and pulled her close to his side. They stayed there for quite some time until he realised she was getting cold.

"Shall we start back?"

"Of course. Where are you going?"

"A different way. Through the woods."

They started down a path in a totally different direction. He had to distract her now.

"Kitty, about the wedding night and what happens."

Kitty looked away from him, rather embarrassed.

"I will tell you first what some mamas tell their daughters. It is not at all helpful for a happy marriage." She looked at him.

"Oh?"

"They tell their daughters things like 'you must lie still and let him do anything he wants', or 'he will lie on top of you and push in between your legs. It will hurt, but you must bear it, it is your duty'. It does not have to be like that at all, Kitty. It is beautiful and fulfilling. But I suppose if a young girl feels no love for her husband it could be painful. Perhaps their mama's were married in an agreed alliance and there was no affection between them. Some men can be less than gentle with their wives. I will never hurt you, nor take you against your will, that I promise you."

Kitty was silent. They had been walking for quite some time, she had lost track of how far. They were entering a clearing.

"Do you know what this place is?"

"A charcoal burners' camp. Look at the house, it's built in stone." She was surprised.

"By Tom Corbin. I have various houses for them in all the forests on my land. They do a necessary job, why should they be cold and wet? Would you like to see inside." He was steering her to the single storey house.

"Oh look, it's a complete house, with chairs and table and beds. Even an indoor fireplace."

"It is a little chill in here, you must be cold after the walk through the forest, I'll light a fire."

"It will make us late, Richard."

"No we have plenty of time. That's why I told Binny we could be late."

He sparked the tinder and a small fire burst into flame as the dry grass burned fiercely. The wood quickly caught and gave the room a glow. Once the fire was burning well, Richard stood and came to where Kitty sat by the table.

"How many charcoal burners are there? I notice there is more than one bed."

"A couple and their teenage son."

"The wife lives here too?"

"Where else would she live, they are always moving. They work as a family."

"How wonderful that the family can live and work together. Do they have no home?"

"No, these are their homes, these stone cottages I provide."

"You really are a caring man, Richard." He pulled her into his arms.

"Will you let me be caring to you, my sweet?" His lips moved over hers gradually taking the kiss deeper, until she was trembling in his arms.

"Come, sit on the bed where I can be close to you." He sat and pulled her down to his side. At first he just stroked her until she relaxed, then he kissed her while his hands loosened the back of her gown. She was unaware what he was doing until her bodice slid down her arms.

"Richard!" He kissed her words away.

He laid her back onto the rough bed, laying beside her on his side.

"I want to show you, Kitty, to teach you how good it can be." He kissed her neck and stroked his fingers down to her now almost naked breast, where he teased and gently pinched. She tried to sit up, but her arms were held by the sleeves of her bodice.

"Oh, you are uncomfortable, let me help you take this off." It was not what she had intended. He pulled the sleeves and removed the bodice completely. He pulled the tie on her chemise and slowly lowered the fine material.

"Oh you are so beautiful, my sweet Kitty." He stroked one of the breasts then put his head down and gently took the nipple into his mouth.

Kitty's body bucked. She thought she was shocked, but not sure what she was feeling. He moved his mouth to her other breast, leaving his fingers where his mouth had been.

Kitty felt the exquisite ache in her, similar to the day before, she wanted more. She moaned in pleasure and need.

"Let me remove some of this excess clothing, my darling one." He was so gentle, how could she fight him.

"May I see your scars, will it embarrass you?"

Kitty shook her head and turned her back to him. He stroked his fingers down the scars, his other hand roaming her breasts.

"How far down do they go?"

"All the way down, they are worse on my shoulders and lower down." He suddenly lifted her and her skirt and petticoats were stripped from her. He eased her chemise down to follow her skirts. Kitty was now blushing all over, and he could see she was, he could see every inch of her.

"Richard!" was all she could say.

He stroked and kissed her back, then turned her and continued on her stomach, his lips travelling from one breast to the other.

When he teased her curls and fondled between her legs, her body arched and kicked under his hands.

"You are so delightfully responsive, sweet. You remember I said the husband went in here." He pushed his finger and rubbed her mound, she was hardly hearing him. "I belong in here, and he slid a finger into her. Her hips bucked and she moaned, then withdrawing, her returned two fingers.

"So tight. It will hurt the first time, Kitty, but I promise it will only be the first time."

"I don't…."

"Not yet. You don't understand yet. I have to break through a thin skin, your maidenhead."

"Oh." She was realising the meaning of the word.

"Yes, you are still a maiden, for a few more minutes." He chuckled and plied his fingers and mouth to bring her to what was an all consuming climax.

"Am I still..." Her voice was quiet and breathy.

"Yes. I want you Kitty. Now I will show you what really happens." He pulled his hand down and unfastened his breeches, rolled onto her and covered her mouth with his.

"Lift your knees, my love."

Kitty did as he asked, mesmerised at what was happening to her. He positioned himself and pushed slowly into her.

"This is the painful part." He pushed through her maidenhead until he was fully seated in her. She tensed at the pain, but he waited until she began to relax, then started to withdraw and thrust. Oh God, how he wanted this. He wanted to drive hard, but he knew he must not, so he stroked her gently inside until she was clinging to him. She cried out in the passion of her second climax and as her body contracted around him

181

he emptied himself into her. Now she was his and he would never ever let her go. This marriage could not be soon enough for him.

Kitty lay there stunned, replete, at peace with the world. "Oh Richard."

"Now that is the way I like to hear you say my name. I will fetch water and wash you."

He went out with the kitchen bowl and returned, putting the bowl into the fire to warm the water. He took out his handkerchief, wet it and cleaned her legs and in between them. He felt he should explain.

"When you are broken, you bleed a little. If I clean you Binny will never know."

"Oh, I didn't realise."

"That is why I am teaching you."

"Why did you not wait until our wedding night?"

"The first time makes you sore for a day or two. On our wedding night I want to make love to you several times!"

"Oh!" He laughed out loud.

"I seem to be able to reduce you to one word, Oh!"

He took his handkerchief, rinsed it and cleaned himself. "I have your blood on me" he explained.

Once clean he dressed himself, then helped her. The fire was dying and the room was growing cold. She let her eyes slide down to his breeches. He took her hand and pressed it onto his still evident erection. "I still want you. In two days time I will be satisfying both of us."

She had no idea how to answer, so she just said "oh!"

It was a slow walk back, she was sore and very aware of his body. He tucked her arm under his and gave her all the support he could save carrying her, which he would willingly have done.

Binny had been so busy she had no idea how long they had been gone. Ferguson had brought in the fuel, filled the water boiler and scrubbed the cooking pots until they shone. He was eating bread and cheese when they returned.

"Ferguson, are you so hungry?"

"Indeed, My lady, I am feeling the need for food."

"I am sure there is no reason not to light the fire during daylight, Ferguson. It is only two days and you will all be up at the Hall."

"Will there be a position there for me, my lord."

"Of course there will, Ferguson, you are part of Lady Kitty's entourage and will become part of mine. Unless you wish to return to Wenton Hall, that is?"

"No, my lord, I am quite content to stay with my lady."

"Good, then be so good as to light the boiler. Lady Kitty has grown a little cold and could benefit from a hot bath."

Ferguson, who enjoyed a firm order he could follow, left his food and went to deal with the boiler. To Kitty, Richard whispered "A bath will help your soreness." Kitty said "Oh" Richard roared with laughter making Kitty laugh too.

Chapter 22

Richard returned home and Kitty had her hot bath. Binny made her try on the dress, pins and all. Some of them stuck into her.

"Ow. How long will it take to finish the dress, Binny?"

"You're in a hurry, miss."

"Richard is talking about a wedding in two days time."

"Heavens, that soon. It will take me every minute to finish that soon."

"Maybe I could help while you are cooking?"

"If you feel able, miss, it would help."

All unnecessary work stopped while the dress was being prepared. It took all the next day, Richard being banished in early evening while Kitty took over the sewing and Binny cooked.

That night Kitty hardly slept. She had one good dress in which to get married, hardly anything else was worthy of a wife, let alone a Countess.

A coach came to fetch them all to Pengarron Hall. The ground being muddy from the house to the lane, a burly footman appeared to carry her to the coach to save her having to put on her boots.

The small family, now to be absorbed into this larger one, was escorted to the chapel inside the Hall. The chapel was full.

She walked down the aisle to where Richard waited, dressed as she had never seen him before. He looked every inch the wealthy Earl.

He gazed in wonder at this beautiful, poised young lady who came down the aisle to him. His chest was filled with pride, his stomach with butterflies. Her dress was everything a Countess should wear. His Countess.

Every eye in the chapel watched her avidly. This unknown woman who had won the heart of their lord, but who they had never seen before. They had known nothing about her until the day before, when he had given orders for a wedding table to be prepared. No guests, only retainers came with her. She was young, slim and every inch a Countess. They hoped she was a good mistress, not a demanding one. The Earl had called the housekeeper and bid her remove his mother's belongings to a guest room.

A trunk had been unpacked with beautiful silk dresses to be put into the countess's rooms. Yet she was alone, no family, no friends.

It was like a dream, the words were said and she was his for the rest of her life. The short ceremony over, the congregation turned to leave but the Earl bid them stay.

"Now you have a new Countess to take care of, and so you all must. Lady Kitty's life had been threatened on more than one occasion forcing her into hiding. She is now under my protection, which also includes my household. If anyone should see or hear of strangers asking questions, tell them nothing and report it to me. Do you all understand?" The stunned household nodded.

"I will speak to the outside staff and visit cook. I cannot stress enough, the continuation of this Earldom depends on your fealty to the house of Pengarron." He turned to the vicar who had preformed the ceremony. "I must include you in this, sir. Show no one the marriage register, and do not discuss it." To all he said "It can be known now that there is a new Countess, but no details please." Then he added "I do not expect this to be the situation for long, but until it is resolved I ask for your help for your new Lady Pengarron." He turned to Kitty and offered her his arm and they walked together out of the chapel and into a new life.

The wedding meal was quite delicious, then once finished she was shown to her new rooms. They were a little over sumptuous for Kitty's taste. The wall and hanging were all extremely flowery in pinks and reds, rather overpowering. Even the bed cover matched.

"This is very" Kitty began "bright" she decided on.

"It is the old Countess's choice." The housekeeper explained. "It was redone less than two years ago, my lady."

"Oh." was all Kitty could think to say.

"It is overpowering is it not, and I guess not to your taste, Kitty." Richard was smiling. "You can change it in any way you care, my love."

"Oh, but the expense."

"There speaks one who ran her father's household for years. These are your rooms, you may have them redecorated, after all they will be yours for a very long time. I intend it to be so." he added to the worried look that crossed her face.

"Come, see your sitting room and dressing room but first of all the door into my bedchamber. He opened the door and drew her into his masculine room, surprisingly light in colours of various blues. The large four poster bed on a plinth had a coat of arms emblazoned in the canopy. The hangings were a tasteful cream and pale blue stripes. The furniture was dark and masculine but not overpowering due to the light colourings.

"A beautiful and tasteful room, my lord." she said.

"Richard." he said.

She grinned at him. He leaned close to her and whispered "I am glad you like it, my love, for you will spend a good amount of time here." Kitty blushed and looked to see if the housekeeper had overheard but she had remained in the Countess's bedchamber.

He led her back through her bedroom where he showed her the concealed bathing area, with its door to allow the hot water to be brought in without disturbing her. Then through to her dressing room, with armoires and chests.

"It will be some time before I have clothes to fill these" she joked. "I have precious few clothes worth wearing." She looked down at her one silk dress.

"We must find a dressmaker for you, Binny cannot do everything." He went to the armoire and opened the doors. Kitty gasped.

"My clothes! Where did they come from?"

"I had them brought down in my coach, via Coventry, Wales and Newbury, all to avoid detection, my lady." He gave a playful bow.

"Oh Richard, I do love you so." She put her arms around him and he held her close. Mrs Pillars withdrew quietly and left them to themselves.

It was soon the talk of below stairs that this was a real love match.

As they retired to bed, Kitty was nervous; she was not quite sure why, after all she already knew what happened. Binny fussed around her preparing her.

"Are you nervous, miss... my lady? I can call you that again can't I? There's no need to be nervous, I'm sure. Lord Richard is a very kind and loving man, he won't hurt you."

"I know that, Binny. Even so it is a big day in my life. I feel all a flutter inside. To be with Richard for the rest of my life, it seems somehow unreal."

"I'm so happy for you, My lady." Binny's eyes filled up with tears.

"Don't cry, Binny."

"I'm so happy for you, miss. We thought you might never find a husband."

"Go downstairs and join the others drinking our health. I bet Ferguson could do with some company."

A reluctant Binny left her to her wedding night and went to bedevil Ferguson and to stop him getting too talkative with the wine.

Richard knocked quietly on the connecting door and opened it gently.

"Did I hear Binny leave?"

"Yes, my lord."

"Richard! Don't start that 'My lord' again."

He wore a dressing robe of blue marl colour. Coming to her he put his arms around her and drew her into a passionate kiss. She trembled in his arms and clung to him. He lifted his head.

"Tonight is our wedding night, Kitty, and I would have you in my bed."

She looked up into his eyes. They held a passionate flame that she had not seen before.

He picked her up in his arms and carried her into his room, lowering her gently onto the sheet, the covers already removed. He returned to close the door and came to stand by the side of the bed. Removing his robe revealed his naked body, strong, well muscled, and rampant.

Kitty blushed.

"Now your turn, my sweet. Let me remove your extremely virginal nightgown. He slid the hem upwards, then lifted it over her hips until her nightgown was a thick wad around her bust.

"Oh, now that is a beautiful sight." He ran his hand down her stomach to play with her curls, and lowered his head to nuzzle into her, then ran his mouth up her stomach to the nightgown.

"Now what is this hiding?" Kitty was looking at him with wide eyes.

He opened the neckline of her gown, and with one hand lifted her as he pulled the gown over her head and dropped it over the side of the bed.

"That's better." He began to stroke one breast then the other as he lay on his side supported on one arm. He leaned over and took one nipple in his mouth and sucked. She arched in pleasure, so he moved to the other one to continue the exquisite torture. His hand moved down to her leg and began to stroke slowly upwards. Her legs parted for him as the aching need from his torture of her breasts brought her body to a high fever pitch. He stroked the curls then slipped his fingers between her open legs to stroke and delve into her. By now she was panting with desire and she was not the only one. He moved two fingers in her as he rubbed the hard little nub with his thumb. She cried out as she fell over the edge, her body gripping his fingers.

"I want that with me in you, my sweet Kitty."

She was trembling but as he continued his stroking, kissing her mouth, her neck, her breasts she began to respond again. He rolled onto her and positioned himself.

"This time there will be no pain, I promise you."

He thrust gently but firmly until he was fully inside her, then he began to ride her slowly but powerfully. She clung to his upper arms as she caught the rhythm and gave herself to the pleasure of it. Then he could hold himself no longer. He increased the speed and the power as he gave in to his need, pounding into her. Her body tightened in climax and he emptied himself into her and collapsed, spent, fulfilled. Realising he was probably too heavy for her, he managed to roll them both to one side.

"Did I hurt you?" He felt guilty, slaking his need so powerfully.

"No. Richard my love, will it always be this wonderful?" He wanted to laugh but was too weary.

"Oh I do hope so, my sweet. Now sleep, for as I promised you, tonight I intend to wake you for a repeat performance."

She snuggled into his arms her head on his chest, and fell into a deep sleep.

She was indeed woken by the feel of his fingers stroking her to arousal. As she grew high, he entered her and rode her a little more gently, until she was begging him. "Please, Richard." at which he let go his restraint and ploughed into her with all control gone. If this was how it continued, married life was going to be wonderful, if somewhat tiring.

She awoke to the feel of Richard carrying her back to her room. He laid her in her bed and leaned over her. "Don't go." she whispered.

"Who said I was going. I thought I might help you warm your bed." Which is what he did. Again trying to be gentle and to take it slowly, again failing, pounding into her as if his life depended on it.

When she fell asleep, he covered her for warmth and went to his room to ring for Smithson. Kitty didn't emerge until late morning, extremely embarrassed that everyone knew why.

The whole week continued to be as pleasurable as they grew closer and understood each other better. It seemed too good to last, which indeed was the case.

At the end of the first week, a letter arrived from his mother. She had decided to bring a party down for a few days and would be arriving at the end of the following week. The staff were to be informed in order to prepare for the guests.

To Richard this was too soon. He wanted more time with her. He knew how much this would hurt her. He longed to be able to shut out the evil of the world and keep her there, just the two of them. But the change was forced upon him and as usual it was by his mother.

"Kitty, come and sit here, I need to talk to you." He led her to a chaise and sat her down.

"What's wrong Richard, you look so serious?"

"This is serious, Kitty and I have no idea how to tell you without hurting you." Kitty turned her head away, fear rising in her.

"At some time, I was aware that we would have to go to London to face the ton."

"No, Richard, please." she whispered.

"You must listen, sweet. I would much prefer to live the rest of our lives here in peace, but it cannot be. Let me tell you what I found in London." He went to the chaise and sat next to her, taking her hand in between his.

"London is full of rumours getting worse by the day. They said you are dead and the Prince must be punished, or that you are imprisoned by him. I went to London to find who you were and gain permission from your father to marry you. This was all so much more than I expected. The ton are about to erupt, parliament will be brought down, the crown could fall and if the people rise, the aristocracy will suffer the same fate as in France.

She was looking at him in horror.

"Because of me!" He put his arm around her shoulders and pulled her close.

"Danvers and his team decided that you must reappear, but to account for your disappearance, you should be married. Danvers offered to marry

189

you. I was desperate not to lose you, but they expect me to return you to London.

"They will try to kill me again!"

"We don't know that, and you have me with you every minute of the day and night. A complete ring of protectors will be around you. If you are ever to be free of fear, my darling one, we have to do this."

"Why now? Why not in a few weeks?"

He rose from the chaise and walked absent mindedly about the room.

"Unfortunately one of the troublesome harpies of the ton is my mother. She knows nothing of our marriage but has sent instructions that she is bringing a party down in a week's time. We can't be here. I won't put you through that."

"I don't want to be Medusa again, Richard, I don't want to lose you."

"You will never lose me, I promise you that. If you are close to me at all times, if they take one of us they take both." He sat down again close to her.

She leaned closer to him.

"I'm sorry Richard. I don't mean to be a coward."

"A coward you most certainly are not, Kitty. You are the bravest woman I know."

"That is not true. I suppose if circumstances say we must go, then it would be good to see Papa and Jeremy, and Aunt Hetty of course."

"We will make sure nobody knows we are arriving to avoid any unwanted presents. There is something you should know though. I have been worrying when would be the best time to tell you." She pulled away a little and looked into his face with some concern.

"Your brother Jeremy."

"Oh no!" She began to curl up in pain.

"Is alive, Kitty." She took a deep breath and sighed in relief.

"But he is injured. They tried to find out where you were. They made rather a mess of him, the doctor was surprised he lived, but he did." Tears were running down her face now.

"No" He pulled her into his arms for comfort.

"He is remarkably cheerful, it must be the stoic nature of your family. Most of his bones have healed and although the doctor thinks he will never walk again, I back Jeremy to prove him wrong. Aunt Hetty is nursing him and that should explain my optimism." Despite herself, Kitty gave a small laugh.

"You know about Aunt Hetty."

"Oh yes, I was told how much she helped you. One day soon you must tell me about everything that happened to bring you here to me. I want to understand, Kitty. We will plan our return and how to avoid any trouble, but not now. Now I just want to hold you, to savour our last days of perfect peace.

The following week should have been the calm before the storm. Not so. They spent long hours discussing the route to use, the time to take on it.

Kitty was worried about upsetting his mother.

"She will be upset whether or not you are here. She wanted to marry me to some empty headed chit she could control."

"Why would she want that? You are her son would she not want you to be happy?"

"No, gentle Kitty. My mother wants control of the Earldom, the houses and the income. I am going to have to curb her expenditure soon and she will not like it."

"What does she spend it on, apart from gowns?"

"Well, take the Countess's rooms, for example."

"Please do, take them away." Kitty laughed.

"You can alter everything if you wish."

"What will happen when she finds I have her rooms?"

"Your rooms. I think perhaps we should lock the door or she will move back in."

"If she wants her furniture and curtains she is welcome to them. Why not put them into her new room. Change everything around." she suggested.

"Not the bed." he insisted.

"Oh no, not the four poster bed, I doubt there would be room with all her ornate furniture. She can have the bed cover. If we take away the curtains there will be little left for her to move into."

"You are a very clever little minx, my love. I can see you are extremely far sighted and sensible."

"I must speak with Mrs Pillars about curtains. If the room was only altered two years ago, maybe the old curtains can be found. They would at least keep out the cold."

"I suggest we do a tour of the house, see if there is anything you would prefer, then you could decide what new items you would like."

"I doubt I will need new furniture, Richard. Curtains and bed hangings, yes, but furniture, I don't think so." Richard laughed.

"I can see you are going to be a very economical Countess."

"I hope so. It is a waste to spend money on fripperies."

"But not on your clothes." Richard was looking at her seriously.

"That would be difficult, the styles are always changing. Even so, I don't see the need for so many gowns. Look at all those in my dressing room; they don't even fit me now. I have ball gowns in the London house which I have never worn. Aunt Jane insisted I needed them, what a waste."

He rose from his chair, sat on the chaise beside her and pulled her into his arms.

"When we are in London you may chose anything you would like for you rooms."

"We would have to be careful, Richard. How can we have anything delivered and feel safe?"

"That is true. We can have everything stored in London until all is safe. Could the curtains be made?"

"Oh yes, if they know the sizes and can have them ready for us."

"Then we must take sizes with us."

"Who made your mother's furnishings? Do you have the bills?" Richard looked at her with understanding.

"I do, indeed. No doubt it will have all the sizes itemised in them. I will look out the bills while you talk to Mrs Pillars. Then we will go in search of your furniture."

Richard did find the itemised bills and the name of the suppliers. Mrs Pillars knew where the old curtains were stored, but it was decided to just exchange the curtains with those in the Dowager Countess's new room. Curtains could be found for the dressing room to enable all trace of his mother to be removed. The walls were a different matter.

The tour started with his mother's new room. The furniture there was a little on the heavy side for Kitty.

"Where will this furniture go when her own is transferred?"

"Well, in a great many other rooms plus some into the attics.

"Oh, we must go there." she exclaimed "Attics are a treasure trove. I found much of my winter clothing there, as well as 'John Coachman's' which had been Jeremy's." She laughed up into Richard's face. Mrs Pillars looked confused but Richard was not about to explain.

Each bedroom they visited held a piece she might like, a chair, a commode, a bureau.

"Mrs Pillars, were there not two of these commodes?"

"Yes there were, my lord. We may find the other in the attic." which they did. It had a little damage, possibly done in the move, but it could be repaired.

They also found a dressing table with only some small marks on it.

"This is not the furniture that was your mother's previously, this was your grandmother's. Lady Pengarron had it removed and replaced long ago."

"I remember it when I was young, then mother had everything changed. This was made in Cornwall, that's why she hated it so. If it didn't come from London it was cheap."

"I love this style, it's Hepplewhites design isn't it?"

"'You could be right, my dear. Would you like to have it repaired? I am sure we have a catalogue in the library."

"Oh yes. I prefer this to the new styles. If it is Hepplewhite's design perhaps we can find a local furniture maker to repair it, and make other pieces to match. If I pick out a fabric we could have the chairs recovered by him."

"We will pick out all the pieces we have found, my lady. Where shall we have them stored?"

"I will contact a good furniture maker to have them fetched. Keep them in the Countess's rooms until they come for them." Turning to Kitty he said "You do realise how unusual you are, Kitty, not wanting everything new." Richard was enjoying the new experience of someone who did not care how much anything cost, usually only to prove how rich they were.

They continued to check all the rooms for any other suitable furniture.

"Thank you, Mrs Pillars, you have been most helpful."

"I am glad to have been of assistance, my lady." She curtsied and left to continue her work elsewhere.

Later, after lunch, they returned to the library where they discussed the project while Richard searched for the catalogue.

"Now, Kitty darling, what will our peaceful tomorrow hold for us? We have not finished discussing our journey. I will need to send letters to London, but we need to know when we will arrive. You must decide if you want fabric from London or from Bath, or Bristol on the way. We could even go by Plymouth and Exeter, they should have quite as good a selection as London."

"It depends on the bills, if they have the sizes on them."

The next day was almost as busy as the previous one. Richard wrote to furniture makers in Exeter asking for repair and refurbishment to pieces in Hepplewhite's design. It was also decided to stay more than one night to pick fabrics and wall coverings whilst there. It would save the worry of being recognised in London, or having to wait a long time before it was safe to order. Richard wanted the rooms ready when they eventually returned home to Cornwall.

They planned their journey and the day they would arrive at Wenton Hall. Richard wrote to both the Duke and Danvers, in a quite cryptic way, so that anyone other then those it was meant for would not understand the message.

On the third day she worked with Binny, deciding which dresses fit her well enough to take. By lunch time she was tired, and Richard noticed.

"Kitty, you look weary. Am I too strong for you?" she looked confused. "Are our night time exertions too much for you? If they are you must tell me. I will not force you to anything."

"Richard, how can you think that." she put her arms around him and cuddled him. "I love our nights together. It is trying on every dress I own that has tired me. If you think I look too tired, then after lunch I will rest. But only if you come with me."

He laughed. "Then it will be no rest for either of us, my little minx."

It was decided that Binny and Ferguson would take Smithson in the Wenton carriage, driven by Phillips. The carriage was fetched to the Hall, not without some difficulty due to the state of the field, to be cleaned, checked and prepared.

The horses were brought up in to the Hall stables. They were calm, well fed, well exercised, in fact ready for any long journey. The grooms found it unusual to use one pair of horses and never change them. They were used to riding horses being cared about, but not carriage horses, but the grooms at the overflow stables had come with them and remarked how attached to one person they became. They were sad to see them go.

The second coachman, Phillips, was discussing this unusual behaviour when the usually quiet animals became excited. They whinnied, shook their heads and stamped their hooves. Voices were heard as visitors arrived. The Earl and Countess appeared in the doorway. The Countess moved purposely forward to the two carriage horses. She patted and stroked their ears and they nuzzled their noses around her neck. All the time she was crooning to them.

"You will smell of horses, my lady." Phillips started to advise.

"No matter, Phillips, these are her Ladyship's horses, can't you see how they respond to her." Phillips looked a little sheepish.

"Phillips, I want you to learn about these horses and how to treat them. They will be your responsibility on your journey to London, and perhaps longer. They are not to be over driven, must be rested regularly, and never ever changed." He then proceeded to tell of her Ladyship's arrival in Cornwall, having driven this pair for three weeks for several hundred miles. He did not go into detail, but made him realise how much care he must take with them.

Kitty moved closer to the conversation.

"I have driven this pair of cattle since I was quite young, they are very dear to me, Phillips. I entrust them to you, be gentle with them and they will respond well to you.

Phillips gave a mumbled reply with a bow of the head and stood aside as the couple walked to the other horses and spoke with the grooms, the stable master and Nicholls, his chief coachman.

The Earl took Nicholls and the stable master aside while Kitty spoke with the grooms.

"Are we ready, Nicholls?"

"I believe so, my lord. We can have the trunks in and away fast if any of the party arrive early."

"Do the rest know what to say?"

"Oh yes, sir. Basically, nothing, act dumb."

Richard laughed. "Good, we are relying on everyone to stay vigilant. Not just with the Dowager Countess but all the visitors and coachmen they bring."

"What you said to them, that meant a lot, sir. They like the new Countess and she likes horses. They won't say anything, cos the tales might get back to someone bad. They wouldn't like to see her hurt."

195

So the few days went by quickly and were anything but calm. Richard made sure that was the case, to prevent Kitty from fretting about what was to come.

On the morning his mother was due to arrive, the coaches were packed, food was packed in hampers, as if they were going on a picnic, extra in the small coach for the ever hungry Ferguson. They may start out together, but they would not keep together all the time as Phillips had to nurse Kitty's cattle. While she and Richard were staying in Exeter it would give the smaller coach time to catch up with them.

Chapter 23

They left mid morning, aiming to be on the coaching road before they would risk meeting any of the expected arrivals. They stayed overnight near Plymouth then continued on to Exeter, to stay at an inn from where they could visit the various tradesmen they required.

To Kitty this was all so new never having stayed anywhere except London, and never shopped for anything but clothing. She had not realised how much was out there to be seen. Richard watched the delight on her face and enjoyed every moment.

They visited the furniture maker who was to repair and refurbish the furniture, found a beautiful fabric for recovering the chairs, in pale pink with a delicate cream pattern in it, for curtains a slightly contrasting one in cream with deeper pink flower motif including pale green leaves. There were to be curtain ties and edging for the furniture in the pale green. She also chose a chaise to be made and upholstered to match. It took two days to find and visit everywhere they needed.

The small coach had arrived and been sent ahead. They would all require two more nights at coaching inns.

The nearer they came to London, the more tense Kitty became, so to distract her he started to ask questions.

"Tell me about what happened, Kitty, from the beginning."

"From the beginning, when exactly?"

"When you first went to London for your come out."

So she started with her first outing, meeting Emily Weston, about Robert Fitzwilliam and being presented to the Prince at the ball. She told of the visit to Kew Gardens and the Prince coming in from the rain. She explained how the ton had seemed to disapprove of her, then that awful garden party.

After the garden party, being shunned by almost everyone, except horrible men with reputations who were the only ones wanting to dance with her. She explained about Aunt Jane not understanding what was happening and Jeremy coming to rescue her and take her home.

The further into her tale, the more upset she became. When they stopped for lunch he plied her with wine in the hope it would relax her. It probably did, for he pushed her on through the first attempt on her life. Although he knew most of this, what surprised him was the reaction of her aunts, and the pain it caused.

"How could your aunts be so dreadful to you? How could they think such awful lies when you are their family? No wonder Aunt Hetty is so precious to you.

"Without her I would never have been strong enough to cope. I fear for her, of anyone finding out how much she means to me."

"So you came home, and were caught in a storm. Then what?"

"Richard they knew I was going home."

"I know, my love, Danvers told me."

"No, listen Richard. They knew when I left and could be expected to arrive home. Only I knew that. The storm slowed us, so we were late arriving, but they didn't know about the storm, therefore they were aware of out departure and worked out when we would arrived. If they knew that early they must have known where I was. Why did they not kill me there if they wanted me dead?"

Richard stared hard at her, turned away and thought deeply.

"Did you not send to your father or to an inn for a room to be reserved?"

"No. I just left in the morning, the only ones who knew the night before were Binny, William the coachman and my aunts. Unless a footman or stable lad heard and told an outsider, then someone saw me leave. Why not kill me there, Richard?"

"Kitty, I go cold when I even think about it. It makes no sense does it?" He took her hand in his. "There is so much we don't understand. If all of this is supposed to be against the Prince, perhaps it has to happen in the London area where he could be seen to be involved."

"So I was not in danger in Cornwall."

"I wouldn't guarantee that, sweet. They were seriously angry at losing you." He was holding her hand so tightly it was beginning to hurt. She moved her arm. "Richard." He loosed his grip. "I'm sorry, Kitty. We need to talk to Danvers about this."

"Shall I go on," He lifted her hand, turned it over and kissed her wrist above her glove.

"Go on." Richard thought he was distracting Kitty, instead he was becoming more anxious himself. His young Countess meant more to him than he had ever expected.

She was so distressed at the second incident that he took her onto his knee and held her close. When she told him what the ton ladies had said at the funeral he made a mental note to speak to Danvers to see if he knew any names. He was angry enough to retaliate in some way, women like that must be open to rumours against them. He would remember that idea.

"How did you leave William behind at the inn?"

"Ferguson put a small amount of laudanum in his ale. We bought him a ticket to London, left him some money to get to the Hall plus a letter to my father. Getting into the coach was the most difficult. I talked to Binny out of sight of the young hostler, she went to go into it, twice. Ferguson distracted the lad and I climbed onto the driving seat and away. None of us breathed out until we were well away."

"I knew there must have been only three of you in the coach but everyone was looking for four. They thought you had been abducted, or at least someone was with you to drive the coach."

"That was the idea. I was terrified we would be followed. We used all kinds of tricks to put anyone off our trail." He stroked her neck and back, it soothed both of them.

"It worked. I found the inn you stayed in on the Great North Road, then the ones you stopped at on the Bedford road."

"Goodness. If you found me, why didn't they?"

"They were looking for four people, I was looking for a male and a female servant, with a very young coachman. When I knew how you had done it I came home, via Wales."

"Wales, you went right over there."

"I told you, I had to keep you safe."

She leaned close into his arms, snuggling her head into his neck. His heart lurched *I love you so much* but he did not actually say it.

"You know the rest."

"No I don't. Which way down did you come?"

So she told him the route, of Morton-in-Marsh and what she saw there. How they worried about Bodmin Moor, what everyone had said, what actually happened and how relieved they were to arrive at Bodmin. When she described their search for a house, all the characters they met, he began to laugh with her.

"I am so very glad you came to my land, to me. Although I would probably have met you at some time in the investigation, Danvers was about to send for me."

"Would you have found me had I been somewhere else, like Scotland?"

"Oh yes, eventually. The only place we worried about was if you had taken ship to the Americas."

"Goodness me, I would never have had the nerve, nor enough money." He cuddled her close.

"I am so glad you came to me." and he sincerely meant it.

They allowed for a slow drive that gave time for the small coach to catch up each evening. It was only because they were on a coaching road and carried a footman guard that it was safe for them to travel for longer in the dark. Even so, it was beginning to be dim light when the two carriages pulled into the grounds of Wenton Hall. As the travelling carriage stopped by the front door it opened immediately. The footman opened the carriage door and put down the step. Richard climbed down, then helped Kitty out. As she reached the front door a host of people seemed to be coming towards her. The butler was beaming, the Duke striding down the hallway, and Aunt Hetty was coming down the stairs so quickly she had to be steadied by a footman to prevent her from falling. Kitty didn't know who to hug first. Richard made the decision for her by greeting the Duke and taking his hand so Aunt Hetty had the first hug. Everyone seemed in tears, the Duke included. Richard stood aside to allow Kitty to embrace her father, a hug which lasted long enough for them both to take control of their tears.

While the coaches were unpacked and bags taken to their room, tea was served in the main parlour. The small parlour had not yet been refurbished. Everyone tried to speak at the same time. Kitty held up her hand.

"Papa, I am sorry to have caused you so much worry. I did what I thought was best for all of us. Can you forgive me?"

The Duke was quite overcome; it took him some minutes before he could reply.

"You did what was best child. If you had stayed, who knows what could have happened. If it kept you alive then I am pleased you went." It must have been hard for him to admit, but he had been thinking a great deal since Richard had left, about her safety and how they could ensure it.

"I sent a letter to Danvers, so no doubt he will arrive within a day or so."

"If it was as cryptic as the one you sent me, I can only hope he understood it."

Kitty broke in "What did you say to papa, Richard?"

"I sent a formal enquiry hoping it was acceptable for the Earl and Countess of Pengarron to pay their respects on their way to London."

"It took me a few minutes to realise what it meant. I had this dreadful thought you had married someone else. It was Jeremy who realised why it was worded like that."

Kitty leaned forward. "How is he, can I see him?"

"He is doing remarkably well, according to the doctor, and you can see him when he comes down to dinner."

"Would you like to go up to your room and freshen up before dinner?" Aunt Hetty suggested.

Richard rose to go with her but Aunt Hetty said "It's all right, I'll take her."

"No, Aunt Hetty" Kitty said "Wherever I go, Richard goes. That's the way it must be." Hetty looked up at Richard, who smiled at her. "Don't worry Aunt Hetty, it is not a reflection on you, just a promise I have made to Kitty to protect her at all times."

Both Hetty and the Duke looked surprised.

"How will you protect her during the night, my lord?"

"Aunt Hetty, my name is Richard, and I hope you have not given us two rooms, for we need only one."

"But" she said and he laughed. "No arguments please" and followed Kitty out of the room.

They had indeed been given two rooms. Kitty had been put into her old room, but after a discussion about the strength of her bed, which caused them much laughter and not a little experimentation, Richard's room was chosen as the most suitable.

Binny completely understood, even if it was inconvenient. Smithson was quite put out. An arrangement had to be made for each to be assisted in dressing. Although embarrassed, Binny was prepared to help her mistress dress with Richard there. With Smithson, it was inappropriate for Binny to be there, so most of Richard's dressing was achieved with only Kitty there, often helping, occasionally hindering.

There was a little delay in descending to dinner due to the discussions, removals and not a little hindrance from Kitty.

Jeremy was already waiting rather impatiently when they arrived. He could not stand or walk even though he had permission to try for a few minutes each day. His fingers were also improving gradually.

"Jeremy!" Kitty bent to hug him where he sat.

"Kitty, you look a picture of health. I think married life must be suiting you." Kitty blushed.

"That and the sea air."

"Sea air, where have you been?"

"In Cornwall on a cliff top." She laughed at the face he pulled.

"You on a cliff top?"

Dinner was announced at that moment and they went in, the Duke with Kitty, Richard offering his arm to Aunt Hetty. Jeremy was pushed in by the footman. Family only being present, they were in the small dining room and close enough for everyone to be involved in the discussion.

Jeremy opened the conversation.

"So, you were by the sea, how did you like it? I expect you have never seen the ocean before."

"The sea is wonderful, so big, you can see forever. So many things happen on the beach. We had a very big storm, the windows rattled even though we closed the shutters. It made the candles flicker and the fire flare up; it went on all night. The next day the waves on the sea were huge, and people came to collect whatever had been washed up onto the beach. More and more came in on each tide, there must have been a shipwreck somewhere as there was a great deal of wood. The day after that I could not believe how clear the sky was and how warm and calm the air, even while the waves were pounding.

"Shall I tell them about Tom Colby?" Richard grinned at her. She blushed "No please don't." Everyone looked intrigued. Jeremy said "Don't stop now. We are all agog, Richard." So he told of his inability to reach Tom, but of how Kitty had splinted him and stopped the bleeding.

"The most amazing thing was how she raised him up on stones to pull him onto the dray.. He is a big man, a heavy one. She pulled him onto a long piece of wood washed up on the beach, lifted the wood onto a stone top and bottom, then piled up two stones top at either end and continued until she had his head level with the dray. The she pulled him onto it. I have no idea how she managed to make the horse stand so still, and where she found the strength. It would have taxed mine. While she lay exhausted, I rode hard to another point where I could see them, and would you believe it she was driving the horse and dray to the village. She saved Tom's life, the doctor was extremely impressed, even though I couldn't tell him who she was."

Kitty, who was purple in the face with embarrassment, looked up sharply. "She! How did he know it was not you?" Richard laughed. "I don't wear petticoats to tear up for bandages, my sweet." "Oh." was all she could say.

They avoided discussing Jeremy's attack until the next day. Jeremy was allowed to try to stand and use his legs, although it was impossible to do it. Richard and Kitty went to sit with him in the library where he spent much of his day sat before the fire.

"Do you have no idea who it was?" Richard asked him. "Have you remembered nothing more?"

"No, the ones I saw, and it was extremely dark, they were rough men, not really recognisable. I vaguely remember a more cultured voice asking over and over where you were."

"But you didn't know!" Kitty said.

"No, but they didn't believe me. I wish I could remember what it was about that voice that struck me so. It is so frustrating not being able to remember."

"It may come back, you should not worry so, old chap." Richard said, trying to calm him down.

"Not so much of the old." Jeremy laughed "although I do feel like an old man, not being able to even stand."

"Do you have crutches of any kind?" Richard asked.

"Yes, they made me some, but my ribs and arms had to heal before I could use them. I am just starting to now."

"Well then, let's get to it. Kitty, ring for a footman to fetch the crutches and we will have a try."

"Now just a moment!" Jeremy laughed.

"No time like the present, Jeremy. Let's see how you get on, then we can make a programme of exercise to improve you." Kitty looked at him in surprise.

"Richard, have you had experience of such injuries before?" she asked.

"A little." Richard answered non-committally.

The footman arrived and was sent to get the crutches. Richard was in quite high spirits.

"Kitty if you had seen him when I came, that was only a few weeks ago and a long time after it happened. He was still a mess."

"Thank you!" Jeremy retorted.

"It's true, if you could see the improvement in him you would be amazed. I bet you can't see it." he said to Jeremy.

"Well I know the fingers work better and I can lift myself about with my arms."

"You'll be surprised when you start with your legs. The improvement will be slow but you'll make it, however long it takes."

"I like your optimism, Pengarron. I'll send for you when I need my spirits lifting."

"I have no doubt we shall be here regularly, Kitty is not going to be kept away from you all now she is back."

Jeremy looked serious. "Can you protect her?"

"With my life, plus a whole army under Danvers."

"Ah, Danvers, we don't see him often."

"Well I expect that will change, now we are here to stir up everything."

"Do you know Danvers offered to marry you, Kitty?"

She looked up at Richard, who answered for her. "For a reason, but it was never going to happen, she was mine!" Richard was suddenly a little intense.

"Ah, I began to wonder about your confidence in finding her. It didn't take long, did it?"

Richard looked rueful. "No time at all. It was persuading her to marry me that I expected to take the time. I had to be sure it was for the right reason, I didn't want her unhappy in her marriage."

Before the conversation became more complex than Richard wanted, he jumped to his feet. "Exercise time, fetch the footman in Kitty, with one either side we'll have you up in no time." So Kitty called the footman in and they lifted Jeremy out of his chair and put the crutches under his arms, holding him upright.

"Put your feet down to the ground if you can."

His legs felt useless, his feet not sitting on the floor. Kitty knelt down and turned his feet into the right position and straightened each leg until his feet were on the floor, sort of.

"Balance is going to be the first problem. If I loosen my grip on you try to lean on the crutch and your left leg." Jeremy looked doubtful. He leaned to the side a little and wobbled. Richard held him. "Put your crutch a little further away and try to put your foot down firmly. He pulled the crutch a little to the side and in front of Jeremy, then eased his hold. "Now try." With support to stop him putting down his whole weight, Richard held him while the footman on the other side copied what Richard had done. Suspended with some support, Jeremy's face was a picture of concentration.

"Try to bend your left leg and lift your foot off the ground."

"Don't grit your teeth so hard "Kitty laughed "You'll break your teeth."

"Good grief, I can't break anything else!" Everyone laughed and it broke the tension of the moment, helping Jeremy relax. His feet extended to the floor, rather like a puppet on strings. He tried it a few times until Richard saw the sweat on his face and decided that was enough for now.

"We'll try again later in the day and see if we can work out some exercises for you to do while sitting down to strengthen your legs and ankles. Jeremy was just happy to be sitting down again.

"I have a horrible feeling that this process is not going to be painless!"

"It will be worth it, I'm sure." Kitty assured him.

Kitty and Richard stayed several days at Wenton Hall. They talked, laughed and exercised Jeremy, sometimes against his inclination. Kitty was gratified to see the improvement in her father. They were loath to leave, but a little surprised at the lack of a visit from Danvers. It could only be put down to his not wanting to draw attention to their presence there.

The first to leave were Binny and Ferguson in the small carriage with Smithson and a guard riding with Phillips. They were to alert the staff at Trevane House to expect the Earl and Countess a little later in the day.

There were almost as many tears in leaving as there had been when they arrived.

"We're only going to London, we shall not be far away." But Richard knew his words fell on deaf ears.

"Come and visit often, Kitty, and you too Pengarron. Keep her safe"

"I will, sir. It is in my own interest as well as everyone else's. I have my perfect wife and Countess, I am not willing to lose her."

Chapter 24

The arrival of the small coach with Binny, Smithson and Ferguson threw the whole household into a frenzy of activity. A new Countess, and his mother still used the Countess's rooms. The old Countess's belongings had to be removed and the room swarmed with maids as they cleaned and polished, dusted and remade the bed. Luckily the Earl's room was always held in readiness. The previous occupant of the Countess's room had the least attention they could safely give while still keeping their position.

Mrs Brent presided over all. Cook was alerted to provide a meal fit to impress a new Countess. Binny fussed over her trunks while Smithson was his usual superior self, calmly unpacking his Lordships clothes.

Shortly after lunch the travelling carriage arrived. Richard ushered everyone into the hallway as he could not risk standing outside the front door while all the introductions were made. It was a squeeze and while the staff looked uncomfortable, Kitty looked around and smiled at everyone saying "How delightfully cosy" and making Richard laugh.

"This is Lady Katherine Trevane, your new Countess of Pengarron, who I know you will soon love as much as I do. She is usually referred to as Lady Kitty. I would ask that her presence here be kept secret until she has had gowns made and I take her into society. This is a serious request for all your safety. From now on, no one accepts a present from anyone, do you understand!" Much nodding of heads.

This is Elliot, well trained in helping me to avoid my mother. Mrs Brent is our housekeeper; you two will no doubt become well acquainted." Kitty greeted each as they were introduced.

"You can see the house a little later. I think tea in the parlour is the first requirement of you please, Mrs Brent."

They entered the parlour, all gold and white covered furniture with embossed wallpaper and curtains.

"Oh dear, I suppose this house is going to be like your mother's bedroom throughout."

"Not completely, but as she spent more time here I'm afraid the main rooms and her bedroom, yours now, are to her taste. When my father was alive he kept her expenditure limited, but since he died and I was away in France so much she has run riot with her redecoration. You may change everything. This is your house now."

The first room for her to be shown was her bedroom and to see the removal of all his mother's clothing and personal items to another room already being done. Binny was trying to unpack her trunk in the dressing room while the maids worked in the bedroom. Kitty thought it a bit of a waste of effort as she would be in Richard's room most of the time.

"Your mother has left behind more dresses than I own." Kitty laughed.

"Then we must rectify that. Your outfits must show your position as a Countess, that is how the ton sees it. Am I right?"

"Yes, you are."

"Then your outfits must be the best. Not more than you need but of the best quality. They have dared to look down on you, now you must be seen to be above them."

"Richard!"

"No, my love, this is part of how I see our campaign against the ton and whoever is manipulating it."

"Oh, I see 'military tactics'"

He laughed. "In a way, yes. We need to order your clothes quickly before anyone knows you are here."

"If I go to Madam Lefite she will recognise me and tell everyone."

"Then we must use another modista. My mother uses Madam Julienne. She always said she was the best because she never told anyone her little secrets, whatever they are, or the styles and colours she chose. That way she was at the forefront of fashion and became a leader. I think as my mother is in Cornwall, a visit to her modista may be in order. We should be accorded preferential treatment and have your gowns made with priority."

"If I am not to be seen by the ton, then an early morning appointment would be best. Would she see me at nine o'clock do you think?"

"I can try. I will send a note this afternoon requesting an appointment tomorrow morning. We shall await the outcome." Richard left her to go to his study.

"Mrs Brent, would you show me the rest of the bedrooms while we are upstairs?"

"Of course, my lady." They wandered from room to room.

"This one has been decorated to the Countess's style, the Dowager Countess, that is. She gave the room to her special guests." She looked around and sniffed. "Mostly men." she concluded.

Kitty looked at her in some surprise. "Really?"

"Oh yes, likes the gentlemen she does." Suddenly realising what she had said, Mrs Brent became a little flustered.

"Thank you for telling me, Mrs Brent. One cannot have too much information when dealing with the ladies of the ton." She smiled at her sweetly. "Especially when they tell lies and try to ruin your life." Mrs Brent's eyes opened wide and looked at the firm set of the new Countess's mouth.

"If you have any questions, my lady, it would he my pleasure to answer them." It seemed they understood each other perfectly, especially in relation to the Dowager.

The following morning saw Richard waiting in the hallway for Kitty to don her cloak and hat. He stared at her.

"Where did they come from?"

"Binny found them when they were moving your mother's clothes. The hat with the veil is particularly useful as anyone who sees me will think you are accompanying your mother."

"I said you were a clever minx."

They went in the London coach which waited a little down the road. Madam Julienne, probably Miss Julie, was quite obsequious until she took off the hat.

"Madam, this is my new Countess who cannot be presented to the ton until she is adequately clothed for her position. Some items will be required as early as possible. As my lady has not used you before, I hesitate to ask you to alter the dresses she already owns."

Kitty took over to assist him. "Madam Lefite made all the gowns for my come out, but most are white, of course, and I hesitate to go to her as she is not discreet. You, I understand, are very discreet. I do not wish it to be known that we are in London until I am suitably dressed. You do understand I am sure."

Madam Julienne nodded. A new Countess, all her gowns!

Richard added "That request also includes my mother should she come to London."

A bemused Madam showed her styles and brought out her best fabrics. "You do not appear to favour frills, My lady."

"No, I am not very fond of them. Perhaps on the hem or down one side as an added ornament. I always think frills take away from the form of the woman and the quality of the materials. But perhaps that is the whole reason for them" She smiled at Madam, who smiled back. It seemed they both understood her meaning.

Richard could not believe the speed with which Kitty chose styles, some similar but with ornamentation, fabrics of the very best silk, satin and lace for ball gowns, day dresses and carriage dresses in heavier winter weights, nightgowns, chemises plus cloaks for day and evening. Two ball gowns and three day dresses were to be rushed through as priority. They took her into the fitting room to be measured with efficiency.

A beaming Madam Julienne saw them away in record time.

"Now where to?"

"Shoes for evening wear."

"You need new boots too. What about a riding habit?"

"I don't think it is going to be safe for me to ride out in London, do you?"

"No, you are right. All we have to do now is contact Danvers and decide on a plan of action. We also need more protection in and around the house. I don't want to leave you at any time, but while we establish ourselves it may be necessary for me to visit my club or go to dinner somewhere in order to receive invitations to the ballrooms. It is nearing the Christmas break and there will not be many more."

"Here we are, lets see how quick I can be!"

Less than half an hour and she had all the footwear she needed plus a couple of bonnets, and they were on their way home before most of the ton were out of bed. Even the new arrivals with their mamas were only just arriving.

"What a pity I can't take you to Gunters." Richard mused "It would have rounded off the morning. We shall have to return home to have our tea and cakes, let's hope cook has made some especially tempting."

After lunch, Richard penned a note to Danvers requesting a plan of action, then joined Kitty in the library.

"You have a good selection of books, Richard. With your mother here so often, I am surprised there are none of the modern horrors."

"No, the books here are to my taste, my mother never reads. I sometimes wonder what she does with her time." Kitty smiled. After her afternoon with Mrs Brent, she had quite a good idea. Richard noticed her smile.

"Ah, I see you have as good an imagination as I."

"Let me just say Mrs Brent and I have struck up an accord."

Richard raised his eyebrows. "Not just my imagination, then."

"Have you any books in Latin?" she changed the subject.

"Latin, I see you were sincere about reading Latin."

"I was, although I am a little out of practice after the last few months."

"I will show you the different sections in here, they are quite distinct." He walked to an area on the far wall. "This area holds foreign books, divided into each language. They are not in any order of content as there are insufficient of each, except for Latin, where the sections are marked. The rest of the library is in distinct order." She was walking along the shelves.

"Even the novels are divided into ages and alphabetical within them. How organised. Richard I am so impressed. Whenever you lose me you will know where to look."

"Each time I came back from France it was difficult to sleep or relax, especially with mother and her machinations, so I used to come in here and catalogue then rearrange them. Normally only the staff knew I was here."

"It was your space."

"Yes it was. I have never had enough time to start on Pengarron Hall library but I would like to."

"Then that is something we can plan to do together."

It felt good. It gave them a positive future to look forward to at such a difficult time.

Danvers appeared the following morning. On minute he was not there, the next he was. No knock on the front door, no announcement from the butler.

"Good grief, Danvers, where did you come from?"

"I would have thought you would be more secure, Trevane."

211

Richard's face was one of horror.

"Calm down, Richard. Don't forget it is my man covering your back. This one recognised me, some of them don't know me that well. It can be a problem; I have to take special care."

Richard had stood to shake his hand. "Can I get you a drink, I certainly need one?" Kitty smiled at Danvers.

"Lady Kitty, it is indeed a pleasure to see you again, and looking so well. I hope he is a good husband to you, or I could become a little upset."

"He is the best husband I could have, Sir Peter. I would not change him for anyone, not even you." she said with laughter in her eyes.

"Ah, he told you did he? Well I am still a little bemused as to why he was so adamant about why it should be him, but I have my own thoughts about that."

Richard brought Danvers a glass of brandy and suggested they all go into the study where they could talk more privately.

"So, now we need a plan. How to keep Kitty safe out on the street and at ton balls."

"Out on the street could be the most difficult. However many men we have there could always be a gunshot or carriage accident." Turning to Kitty, he said "I trust you are not intending to ride in the park, ma'am."

"Most definitely not, Danvers. If it were summer that might cause some talk as it is expected to be seen in the park, but in the winter that is not the case. I am quite happy not to go anywhere you cannot protect me."

"Well that makes life a little easier. In the ton I have ten gentlemen who can watch over you at a ball. Going out to houses in the daytime is difficult, so are dinner parties. It may become easier as I infiltrate guards into certain houses, acting as footmen. That depends on the cooperation of the family, of course. We are gradually increasing the number of outside men watching buildings, or as at Wenton Hall, integrated with the gamekeepers."

Kitty looked astonished. "Have you really, does Papa know?"

Danvers smiled. "Not necessarily. We have, of course, had watchers on your house here ever since I knew you were coming back."

"Do you have a plan, Danvers?" Richard asked. "I don't fancy sitting here for several months waiting to be attacked. I had hoped we could take the offensive line."

"Probably the best way is to introduce Lady Kitty back into the ton. Of course, you will have no invitation as you never go and are seldom here. What about your club? Could you use it to let it be known you are here?"

"I am not prepared to leave Kitty alone, at any time!"

"It should be safe while her presence here is not known. But I agree, she must have protection or be hidden when you go out. How do you feel about that ma'am?"

Kitty was not sure whether to be frightened, angry or amused. "I hope you have no intention of shutting me in a priest hole?"

Richard was also perturbed. "No Kitty. Unless we can find a private room where you would be safe, I would not leave you. Even so, it could only be until you attended your first ball." He leaned across to take Kitty's hand. "You are trembling, my love."

"So would you be Trevane, if you were in her position. We are asking a great deal of you, Lady Kitty."

"I'm sure we can find a way to hide me. I managed it to escape you all." Richard sat back and smiled. "Danvers doesn't know about that. It could work in this situation."

"Would one of you mind explaining?" Kitty leaned over and patted his hand. "Stay to lunch, Danvers, and you will find explanations to several questions."

So cook was informed of one extra for lunch by Kitty, who took Binny with her to her room to dress her as 'John Coachman'.

The butler was a little upset when he knocked on the door of the study. "My lord, there is a young coachman asking to speak to you. I do not understand how he managed to enter the house, but he says you will want to speak with him."

"Is his name John, by any chance?"

"Yes My lord, it is."

"Show him in here, I am expecting him."

Elliot withdrew and returned a moment later. He could be heard talking to the coachman in a stern voice. "You mind your manners, my lad." The young man was shown in.

Both men looked at the newcomer, Danvers was disturbed, someone had bypassed his security, Richard was on the verge of laughter.

"Now John, have you news for me?" Kitty grunted in her deepest voice. "Speak up lad." Danvers said. Richard called her to him turned her round and looked. "Your hair is getting longer, you may need a better hat soon."

"Trevane, who is this and why is he here?" Richard removed Kitty's hat and slowly turned her to face Danvers. "May I introduce you to John

213

Coachman who drove two servants in a black coach several hundred miles over three weeks, from the Great North Road to Cornwall, to a cottage on my Cornwall estate."

"Good God, Lady Kitty." He was speechless.

"I think like this I could hide in a room below stairs and not be found. Don't you?"

Danvers left after lunch to search out more men for their security. He advised Richard to show himself a little, maybe at his club, in the hope of the much needed invitation.

Late afternoon brought a note from Madam Julienne asking for a visit to finalise the first of the ball gowns. She suggested another early appointment.

"Is that wise?" Richard wondered.

"I would rather go to her than have her come here. It needs to be done, Richard. How are we to get the gowns home, I will not accept a delivery?"

"No, of course not. Someone will have to fetch then on your behalf, someone we trust."

"Ferguson." she decided.

Ferguson was glad to be of service. He was new to this household and had yet to find his place in it. As the messenger for Lady Pengarron it gave him more status than as an extra help with the menial tasks. They had yet to learn of his importance to Kitty.

They arrived early the following morning. Ferguson stayed with the coach until called. The fitting was very quick, Madam Julienne had worked well from the measurement and only the setting of the hemline was needed. The rose satin hung superbly in the simple design, showing off her slim figure to perfection. The frill of cream lace down one side of the skirt made it that more unique, just as it should be for a Countess. The others similarly needed only to set the hems.

The gowns would be ready later that day. At this point Ferguson was called in.

"This is my man Ferguson. Would you and any available staff come forward to meet him? He, and only he, can fetch my gowns. No other will ever come and please do not send anything other than a note as a parcel will be refused. If anyone other than Ferguson comes, do not trust them for my safety is in jeopardy." Madam Julienne looked a little shocked.

Ferguson stepped closer to meet the girls and Madam. Was it her imagination or was there an instant rapport with Madam Julienne, she was certainly blushing, Kitty had never seen him so attentive. So it was a light-hearted Ferguson who willingly undertook the return visit later that afternoon.

Richard was preparing to visit his club to elicit the invitation when a message arrived from Danvers. He was invited to dinner that evening at the Sugdens', but preferred not to go. They had a marriageable daughter and would gladly accept the Earl of Pengarron in his place.

Smithson was still not pleased at having Kitty in the bedroom as he dressed Richard. Blue superfine coat, buff breeches, a cream waistcoat and the sapphire stick-pin in his cravat. Kitty wanted to touch him, to stroke his chest, his arms, ruffle his hair. Richard was amused. Smithson was embarrassed.

It was a different feeling altogether, Richard decided, going out to dinner as a married man, lacking the need to guard against anything that would be done to entrap him. He was quite looking forward to it, the only sadness was being apart from Kitty, and the pull in his chest when away from her was still there even though she was now his wife.

Mrs Sugden was everything he expected of a ton wife and mother. A pleasant enough woman even if she did have a daughter to see married, and like all mamas of the ton, a titled son-in-law was definitely to be preferred. He was relieved she had not placed him next to Miss Sugden but across the table where he could look at her but have conversation with others. Clever mother, what conversation can a young girl have with a man of his experience?

The conversation ranged from this years harvest, the government debates in which Richard had taken no part, to the current state of Europe. He asked questions with genuine interest. He was also interested in the recent ton rumours but was too wary to ask directly. These people did at least not rail against the Prince. The discussion took a turn when someone mentioned the treasonous ideas circulating around in the ton, was he one of Danvers' gentlemen?

"I have to admit, when I was at the Blenkinsops' earlier in the year, George did have to warn his wife against treason as the ladies were full of ire. I did wonder why they were so incensed; they usually enjoy their little tales."

"Not little, old man." Sugden broke in. "Believe me they are bitter and acrimonious, not in the usual way of on-dits."

"Are they treasonous?"

"Oh yes, I dare not think where such treason is leading." They fell silent.

"I hope not as in France." Parsons remarked. The silence spread.

Mrs Sugden as a good hostess should, changed the subject completely thus breaking the atmosphere of gloom.

"I had heard you went to the Blenkinsops' my lord. She was convinced you were on the point of offering for her daughter. You must beware for she means to trap you." Richard laughed. "And you do not, ma'am?" She looked at him a little sharply. "Not against your will, I hope. But she will try her tricks when she next sees you."

"At a ball? I have no invitation so that is hardly likely."

"If you found yourself a wife, Pengarron, none of this would happen." Woolcote said.

"Ah, but I have a wife, Woolcote."

"What!" issued from various sources. "You're married?" Woolcote had to check he had heard correctly. "Yes, for some time now. We have not been in town and told no one, especially not my mother, or you would have all known."

"Why did you not announce it?"

"What, and have my mother trying to interfere in her life as well as mine? No, we married quietly. I intend her to find her own place in the ton if that is to her taste and if not, we shall go home to Cornwall and take up residence in the library."

"Why did you not bring her tonight?" Philpott asked pointedly.

"Insufficient suitable clothing. The modista is doing her best but the first dresses only arrived this afternoon. You ladies do like to be dressed in the height of fashion."

Miss Sugden found her voice for the first time. "She has no suitable dress, my lord, is she not from the ton?" He knew this could arise. How to keep from telling who she was and still give her position? "Indeed she has been presented to the ton but found it not to her liking. She may enjoy it more as a married lady." He could see everyone musing over what he had just said.

Mrs Sugden again restarted the conversation. "My lord, you said you do not have any invitations, I am sure you would be welcome without one." Her eyes were dancing. "It is the Tunstalls' ball in two days, I could have a word with Lady Tunstall, I'm sure she would oblige you. Mrs Blenkinsop and her daughter will be there, I will make sure they know of your attendance."

"Oh, Mrs Sugden, what a delightfully wicked idea."

"I have to admit, she is not my favourite acquaintance, she belittles everyone's daughters to make hers seem a paragon of virtue with accomplishments she does not possess. Is it too cruel of me to see her little humiliated? She has talked of you with such assurance of success."

"Then we will let her cause her own downfall. I hold no affection for her or her daughter after that tedious dinner party."

The men being bored with ton talk the discussions turned to other subjects. Richard was very pleased with his evening, he had found others not willing to follow the rumours, possible friendship for Kitty, plus the all important ball invitation.

Chapter 25

The invitation arrived from Lady Tunstall addressed to the Earl of Pengarron. In fact a second arrived for The Countess of Pengarron. Kitty was surprised until they realised it was actually meant for his mother. "Who cares who it was meant for? It is addressed to The Countess of Pengarron, which is who you are, therefore it is for you. Who can complain? Believe me my sweet, they will be more eager to see you than my mother, I assure you."

Kitty put her hands on his chest and leaned her head on him. He enclosed her with his arms. "Are you frightened, sweet?" Kitty nodded. "It's not going to be easy for you, this first ball will be the worst. If it is unacceptable we will find some other way. Don't forget I will be close to you all the time." He drew a list from his coat pocket. "There are ten names on this list and all of them will be there for your safety. Read the list and see how many of the names you already know."

She took the list and tried to put faces to those names she knew, most she did not. "I know so few of them, Richard. How will I know who to turn to?

"Me, you turn to me, Kitty."

"What if we are separated?"

"Then I will leave you with others. I will ensure there are at least two you recognise at all times. The only time I will leave you is to play my trick on Mrs Blenkinsop." She looked up at him. "What trick?" she asked.

"Well, my dearest wife, she is intending to trap me into marriage with her daughter. It appears half the ton knows about it. I intend to give her the opportunity to spring her trap in front of the ton. How will she look when I bring forth the wife I already have?"

"Will it not make the ton more angry with me?"

"No, quite the opposite I expect. Most of the ladies are tired of her airs and graces and her invented claims for her daughter. They will be delighted I am sure." He stroked her head and massaged her shoulders and neck. "What time are we eating?"

"Oh, Richard, don't expect me to eat. I feel ill enough now."

"You must eat something bland that will not upset you. If you have nothing, you may be ill from the lack of food and the pressure of worry. Promise me you will try to eat something." She saw the concern in his face and smiled at him.

"I will try." was all she could promise.

They ate at six o'clock, country hours, she was bathed and ready but not fully dressed. The meal over, they went up to finish her dressing.

"How will you wear your hair?"

"I thought as it is not long enough to dress yet, I would wear ribbons and lace to match my dress woven into the crown, with pieces hanging down instead of curls."

"Have you jewels? I have never thought to buy you any yet. It is very remiss of me. Most of the family jewels are still with my mother, of course. It will not be easy persuading her to give them up."

"I normally wear very little jewellery as you know. I did bring what I have with me from Wenton Hall. You can help me choose what suits the gown when I am dressed."

Richard was ready first. As Smithson wanted to preen and flutter over him it was useful to have a reason to dismiss him. Kitty had seen him looking just like this as she had walked the aisle of the chapel on her wedding day. The sight of him made her heart bear faster. He was hers and tonight they would all find that out.

Richard watched Binny pinning the ribbons into her hair, it was quite an art. The lace hung down by one ear, finishing by her jaw line. When she arose to put on her dress she banished him from her dressing room to wait in the bedroom. The effect on him could not be mistaken as she entered. She looked exquisite. He had never seen her dressed in such finery before and it took away his breath. He took her hand in his and leaned close. "You look superb, my love, could we not just stay at home and retire to bed?" Kitty laughed. "I wish we could. My insides are in such turmoil."

He walked around her just taking in the sight of this beautiful young woman who was all his.

"I have these pearl ear bobs my father bought me for my birthday, this necklace is rather simple but the pearl matches them." Richard took the simple chain with the hanging pearl and carefully placed it around her throat. It hung just low enough to enhance her décolletage. She looked every inch his innocent Countess but as speaking had become difficult he offered his arm and in a husky voice said "Shall we, my lady?" Kitty picked up her reticule, placed her hand on his arm and with Binny following with the cloak they went down to the hallway to await the carriage.

The timing of the arrival was critical. Too early and there would be insufficient to mingle, too late and everyone would note their arrival as they were introduced. They had to be in the centre of the melee where everyone was busy talking to those around them, not really interested in arrivals they did not recognise. Kitty kept her face towards Richard in order not to be recognised too early. The announcement came just as Richard laughed with some gentleman she did not recognise. The gentleman spoke with Lady Tunstall as Richard propelled Kitty to Lord Tunstall, and then they were through the line and inside.

The ballroom was dressed for early Christmas. Greenery was entwined with holly berries and red flowers all tied with white satin ribbons. The effect was entrancing, the candlelight reflecting in the glass making the greenery shine and glitter. Kitty had never been to a ball like this. There were still young ladies wearing white but more were now dressed in much richer colours. Kitty drifted through the throng with Richard close by her. She was introduced to several youngish men, a Mr Williams asked her for a dance, which she accepted when Richard nodded. The gentleman who distracted Lady Tunstall was Lord Wolfstone, both of whom stayed close by.

Richard danced the first waltz with her, it was their first dance together and it felt wonderful, or it would have if she could control her increasing panic. They stayed near the windows in an alcove where she was shielded from the eyes of many. The next waltz (Richard had suggested she dance only the waltz as her partner could keep her better protected) she danced with Mr Williams. When it came near to supper time, Richard indicated he was going outside to smoke a cheroot, with the possibility of enticing the Blenkinsops. Kitty, with Wolfstone and Williams moved closer to the terrace doors leaving her protective alcove. Richard walked to the edge of the terrace and lit his cheroot, then turned to lean on the balustrade. He looked around to see where Kitty was and who else may be watching.

Several of the ladies seemed to be urging their partners to the terrace and it was becoming quite busy. The doors opened and Mrs Blenkinsop pushed her daughter out, whispering to her she urged her forward.

Richard leaned back with his cheroot held almost behind him as Miss Blenkinsop lifted the front of her skirt and launched herself at him. He held her away from him by her shoulder and laughed down at her as her mother flew out of the doors screeching. Everyone turned to see Richard laughing.

"How dare you, sir, you have ruined my daughter, who will want her now. I demand you do the honourable and marry her. I am so mortified." Richard continued to laugh. "A good try Mrs Blenkinsop but we all know what happened."

"You have defiled her, look he had his hand under her skirts. I knew you were interested in her but this…. and in public too."

"My dear Mrs Blenkinsop, I have never been interested in your daughter, and if you note my hand, it would have been painful if not dangerous for your daughter. He lifted his hand high to show the lighted cheroot. He pushed the girl away and went to walk down the terrace. An uproar was occurring just inside the doors and everyone's attention was transferred. He heard Wolfstone's voice arguing and then a shrill voice calling "Richard!"

He pushed people aside to see two burly footmen holding Kitty by the arms and trying to drag her away. Wolfstone was holding one of the footmen to prevent him.

"Let go of her!" he heard Wolfstone. "Can't sir, have to evict her she was not invited." Someone in the crowd said "We don't want her sort here."

Richard saw red. He stood in front of them and bellowed at the top of his voice "UNHAND MY WIFE!" The footmen looked perplexed "But…."

"IS THIS HOW YOU TREAT A COUNTESS?" They let her go so suddenly she almost fell. Richard caught her and held her close.

All those close to them were silent, some like Mrs Blenkinsop and her ladies were white with the shock. He looked straight into her face and said "If your daughter is considered ruined it is by your hand madam." With that he picked up the trembling Kitty and carried her out into the hall to request her cloak and his carriage.

Lady Tunstall came rushing towards them "My lord." He interrupted her. "Whose idea was this?"

"Well I was just told."

"Who told you?"

"Several of the ladies said she was not one of our class."

"Since when has the daughter of a Duke and wife of an Earl not been of 'our class?' Who were they? A Mrs this and a Miss that, little minded harpies of the ton. Beware who you listen to Lady Tunstall, in France it cost them their heads."

The cloak having been fetched, he was glad to be out in the night air to cool his temper.

The following day the Earl had a visitor, Lord Tunstall, a younger son with a courtesy title who had married a Miss Phillips, daughter of a vicar. If he could have grovelled on the floor he would have.

"Pengarron, I hardly know what to say. When I found out what had happened I was mortified. My wife has cried through most of the night. She would visit the Countess herself but I doubt she will be well enough, her face will need to be veiled for the next week."

Richard held to the insulted Earl demeanour. "Did your wife tell you who gave her the information?"

"No, I did ask but she refused to say." Richard walked to the bureau with the decanter. "Brandy?"

"Yes, if you would." He poured two and handed one to Tunstall. "You look as if you need it."

"Indeed, nothing like this has ever happened before, I don't know how we can hold our heads up in society."

"Get used to it or learn to deal with your wife."

"She said some strange things although some were hard to make sense of."

Richard looked him directly in the eye. "Tell me what they said and I will see if I can interpret for you."

"They said she was a fallen woman."

"Not so, she came to me an innocent maid, and I should know if she were not. Go on."

"That she killed her sister, but that can't be true."

"No it most definitely is not. But her sister was killed, by a present to my wife which arrived too early to kill her." Tunstall stared in horror. "If you knew what my wife has been through, you would be horrified, much of it caused by the ladies of the ton with lies and rumours. Why and who started it I want to know." Tunstall had hardly realised he had a glass in his hand, he remained frozen. "Do whatever you can to find out the names for me, Tunstall. This is more important than you can know. I told Lady Tunstall to be careful who she listened to, in France it cost them their heads." Tunstall stared into his glass. "You mean these rumours the ladies are whipping up are that dangerous? There must be someone behind this!"

"Indeed there is a who and a why but we don't know either yet. If you can extract names from your wife, if you hear anyone at your club inciting uprising of any kind, let me know."

"Uprising, yes I suppose it could become that." He looked up shocked "But that would be treason!"

"Yes, Lord Tunstall, treason. I need names."

"I will do my best, indeed I will."

"Take care, tell no one else, they are prepared to murder, three have already died, a fourth is badly injured and my wife was injured and is lucky to be alive, do not become another victim."

A silent and shaken Tunstall left the town house to return home. It would be some time before he was calm enough to speak even to his servants.

After the fiasco of the ball, all Richard could do was hold Kitty close. Making love to her was out of the question as she was so locked into her emotional pain. "Darling Kitty, I should have known something like this would happen but I have to say I never expected it to be so blatant." He waited but she said nothing. "Forgive me, Kitty, please forgive me." She clung closer but when she went to speak nothing came out. Was this what it had been like before? They did say she never spoke for days. He didn't think he could stand that, he felt like going out to fight someone. All he could do was sleep with her in his arms. She had remained dry eyed, not a single tear had fallen.

After Lord Tunstall had left, Richard wrote to Danvers with a long and detailed account of what had happened the previous night. Then he went to help Binny in dressing Kitty. He escorted her to the parlour and ordered tea which they drank while he told her of Lord Tunstall's visit, of his letter to Danvers and that there would be no more ton balls. Now everyone knew of her, she could receive visitors if she wished but he would always be there with her. He would escort her anywhere she wished to go; it would be her decision from now onwards.

The afternoon brought Danvers. "What in God's name... I apologise Lady Kitty. What did she think she was doing? Without her husband's knowledge? Those ladies must be very powerful."

"Is it them or their husbands orchestrating this?" Richard exclaimed. Danvers looked at Kitty; she was sitting quietly looking vaguely in their direction. He looked at Richard and raised his eyebrows. Richard shook his head. Danvers held his head in his hands and whispered "Oh God!"

"I know, but where do we go from here? If Tunstall can get names out of his wife it would help." Richard was at a loss. Danvers suddenly looked up. "The ton, or part of it, must be seen to approve of her. I'll send out to those of my men who have wives, sisters or mothers to start visiting. If Lady Kitty is unable to speak to them it matters not, they will have visited and others will know. I believe we can cause a revolt on Lady Kitty's behalf."

A knock on the front door brought the butler to inform them a Miss Weston had called and was Lady Kitty at home. Well it had to start sometime. "Why not, Elliot, show her in."

They neither of them knew Miss Weston nor why she had come, so they were surprised when a young girl of Kitty's age rushed into the room in a most unladylike manner, took one look at Kitty and threw her arms around her.

"Kitty I heard about last night, how awful. You must feel dreadful, if I could get hold of them, I would scratch their eyes out."

When Kitty did not answer she looked into her face and said. "Is it like before when you could not speak for a while?" Kitty gave a small nod. "Never mind, I will do the talking if it will help you." She suddenly realised there were others in the room.

"Oh, I'm sorry, I completely ignored you, I do apologise." Danvers looked amused, Richard looked thoughtful. "Miss Emily Weston of Norwich, I presume."

"Yes, indeed I am."

"Oh, I see," Danvers suddenly realised. "Lady Kitty's friend who she corresponded with."

"Yes, she wrote to tell me everything that happened, so when I heard about this I wondered if she was having trouble speaking. You see ladies will call and someone has to talk to them." she concluded as if she had just solved the problems of the world.

"Miss Weston, I think you have just solved our little problem. We do indeed expect ladies to call; indeed I am about to request friends' wives to do just that. Your help would be invaluable."

"Oh," she blushed "Which of you is Richard, I mean the Earl?" she corrected.

"I am." Richard answered. If he could have any amusement in this situation, she was the cause of it.

"Who are you?" she looked at Danvers.

"I am so sorry, we have not been introduced. My name is Sir Peter Danvers."

"Danvers, are you the spymaster?" Danvers looked uncomfortable, Richard smiled.

"I am in charge of the investigations, I admit."

"I've always wondered what a spy looked like."

"And now you have met two."

"Two!" she looked from one to the other, putting her fingers over her mouth as her eyes grew large. Danvers had to laugh.

The butler arrived at the door with a card in his hand. "A Mrs Sugden to see Lady Trevane."

"Show her in Elliot."

Mrs. Sugden was a little concerned about her reception but Richard put her at her ease. "Mrs Sugden, I am so pleased you called." she looked at Kitty.

"My dear, how awful for you. If I can help in any way.....you look as shocked as I know I would be." Turning to Richard she said "If I had any idea what would happen I would not have encouraged you to go. I feel responsible for all this." She waved her hands about in helplessness.

"My dear Mrs Sugden, this is in no way any responsibility of yours. Whichever ball we attended this would have happened, or something like it. My wife is indeed extremely shocked but I am sure will recover soon."

Emily, feeling she was Kitty's voice burst in "Shall I order tea?"

"Yes indeed." Richard responded smiling at her innocent help.

Dinner that evening was a silent affair. Richard tried to encourage her but she ate very little. They retired early, Richard taking a book to help him while away the sleepless night he expected. Kitty however, had other ideas. She pulled him close, her hands roaming beneath his robe. "Kitty, do you want me closer, if so I cannot promise to restrain myself." She pulled him towards the bed. "So be it, my darling girl."

He had intended to be gentle and persuasive but as she came to a climax a small whisper in his ear said "Oh Richard."

The relief was intensive, his resolve broke and as his emotions became uncontrollable he rode her like a stallion unable to contain the passion that poured though him. He lay spent, her arms still around his neck. He pulled her head into his shoulder and they both slept a deep and restorative sleep.

For the next few days Emily came to be with Kitty as she received more and more callers, sometimes only ladies, sometimes accompanied by their husbands, not all of them were Danvers' men.

They received a letter from her father reminding them he was expecting them to come to Wenton Hall for Christmas. After conferring with Danvers, they replied that they would arrive in three days time. Binny and Ferguson were alerted, Binny to pack, Ferguson to check all was in place with the carriages and horses and that the mews staff were keeping a close eye on the equipage.

Chapter 26

It should have been a simple journey, only about an hour in the coach, yet it had to be planned like a military offensive. The luggage was in the hallway, the small coach brought round and loaded. Smithson, Binny and Ferguson went with Phillips driving and a footman guard. They were sent ahead for their safety. Richard intended to leave about half an hour after them. A carriage drew up at the front of the house which Kitty presumed was the Earl's travelling carriage and rose to prepare herself. The voices in the hall said otherwise.

"Mother, what are you doing here, I presumed you were with friends for Christmas?" She was quite white around her lips.

"How dare you pollute the Earldom with that woman?"

Realising that Kitty could probably hear, he towed her down the corridor and into his study.

"Now mother, what has you so angry?"

"That appalling girl and you married her!"

"You mean my wife, of course I married her, I happen to love her."

"You said you didn't want to get married, then you do this behind my back."

"No mother, I said I didn't want you finding me a wife. There is a great difference."

"You have no idea what you have done, how could I live in the same house as that ……whore!" Richard drew a deep breath. He was shouting at her now.

"HOW DARE YOU INSULT MY WIFE, YOU WHO RUN AFTER ALL YOUR FRIENDS' HUSBANDS!" She went to answer. "How dare you. Yes I know your habits."

"I am a widow; I am free to indulge my inclinations. She was unmarried, do you know what she did, who her lover was?!"

"There was no lover, I should know, she was a maid when she came to me. Everything you believe has been made up by you and your cronies."

"I don't make up things, I just repeat what is true. When Maria told me who you had married I could have fainted."

"You, faint, never. Maria Campbell I presume."

"She sent a note to tell me how you had paraded that woman around at the Tunstalls' ball. I am so embarrassed."

"No, mother, this is not acceptable. All of Kitty's problems have been caused by the harpies of the ton, and you are one of them. NO MORE." He held up his hand. "Listen to me clearly and note that this is not a request it is an order." She breathed in ready to speak. He stepped forwards to place a hand over her mouth. "You defiled the Earldom when my father was still alive; you flirted with every man you met even in front of him and his friends. You have tried to match me to any empty headed chit you could and now you insult my wife with the lies you have invented. My houses look like they belong to a courtesan, which I suppose is what you are.

You have an income from my father's estate and your patrimony which he never touched, but you continue to live in my houses with my staff and send your clothing bills to me. Well no more. Choose one of my empty houses if you wish, or buy one for yourself, because from now onwards you pay your own expenses. You are no longer welcome in any house of mine."

She was vicious in her reply. "You will pay for this. I will make her wish she had never been born."

"You try that mother and I will start a rumour of my own, and I mean it. 'How dreadful it is to have a mother who is so depraved she will sleep with anyone especially friends' husbands,' which is true, 'and now she has contracted syphilis and cares not who she infects with it.'" She stared at him. "You would not dare!"

"Oh yes I would, mother. I think I will find a new name to use, mother does not seem appropriate. I could call you old lady Pengarron, or my father's whore. I must give it some thought. So should you before you try any of your tricks. Remember, I have the Government, the Crown and the Foreign Office working on my behalf and that of my wife. Who do you have that you can trust? Will you still be popular now your son the Earl is married? How many of your friends will stand by you when they know I have thrown you off?"

He opened the door and pushed her into the hall. "When you find yourself a house of your own to live in, I will have your belongings parcelled up and sent to you. Oh and I expect the Pengarron jewellery to be returned. You can, of course, keep anything that was bought especially for you."

They had reached the front door. "Elliot, The Dowager is leaving, see to it she never has entry here again." The butler opened the front door. "Yes My lord." and to his mother "Goodbye ma'am."

The Dowager was distraught over the confrontation with her son. She had never expected to lose an argument with him, he was always so amenable when she saw him, which she had to admit was not often. That woman had bewitched him; she would find a way to win him over as she needed his support to live the life she expected. Her own money would not support her clothing bills, never mind the cost of a house.

The carriage with the Earl's crest on the side was travelling west towards Falcombe Hall, the home of her friend Lady Falcombe and her husband with whom she was spending Christmas. Her coachman was the first to notice that he was being followed. He made a short detour to avoid them but still they were there. Knowing he would be vulnerable on the open country road to Falcombe Hall he turned south towards Walcott's house which was nearer. He was almost there when the highwaymen appeared in the road, two of them blocking his way, their pistols trained on him. As the coach stopped another came from behind and opened the carriage door. "Get out" he growled. "How dare you" she began but stopped as she saw his pistol pointed at her. "Get out". She had to comply. "What do you want?" she simpered, "I have very little, I am only a poor widow." The highwayman looked at the others. One of them said "Who is she?"

"Who are you?"

The Countess of Pengarron was not officially her title now and she refused to use the name Dowager unless she had to. Better to be of lower status. She could never be a Mrs so she said "Lady Trevane."

"Why are you in the Earl's carriage?"

"He was my son, he gave it to me."

"Was?"

"We no longer communicate."

"She's too old, it doesn't really matter who she is."

They turned their horses and rode away. The Dowager stood trembling with fear and cold. Her man climbed down and helped her into the coach which as they were close to Walcott's house is where they headed. Walcott was not overtly friendly, although when he heard her tale he was sympathetic.

"They took nothing?" She was almost tearful, almost! "They said I was too old." This caused him some amusement.

"Well, my dear, you are hardly in your prime. Did they ask you for anything?"

"They asked why I was in the Earl's carriage. It's mine, Henry."

"Yes but you insisted on having one with the coat of arms on the side which is strictly not the thing. Do you not think you ought to tell Pengarron what happened, they obviously thought it was the Earl and Countess inside?"

She looked askance at him. "No I will not. If they get shot it is their own affair. I have nothing to do with him any more." Walcott raised his eyebrows. "He threw me off, Henry, his mother, in favour of the whoring little chit he married."

Walcott was silent "If that is your attitude to his wife, I am surprised he has not cut off your allowance."

"He couldn't do that, it was in the will."

"You'd be surprised what an Earl can do, especially when you insult his wife in that way."

"Are you on his side, Walcott?"

"Let's just say I do not spite myself just to hurt others."

"I do not hurt others." His look was incredulous.

"I doubt there is a single soul you have met you have not hurt. All those families, hoping to marry their daughters to your son. Did you care if you hurt them, made them feel dreadful when you abandoned them? What of your so called friends you talk about with others behind their backs, plus those whose husbands you covet." He shook his head at her disbelief. "I suggest you climb back into your coach and go to your Christmas party at Falcombe Hall and don't bother coming back here."

A very sad and heart sore Walcott watched the coach draw away. He was possibly the most hurt of all, but the person to whom you give your heart is not always the most suitable recipient.

He went to his library and penned a note to Pengarron. Meanwhile less than a quarter of an hour after his mother left, the Earl and Countess with outriders drove to Wenton Hall and encountered no problems whatsoever. Now though, he had a possible name, Maria Campbell, could this be the first breakthrough?

Christmas was going to be different this year. For one thing there were very few of the older generation there, only a couple of her late mother's aunts who came with two single daughters. The Duke had invited a couple of friends and their wives who were bringing some young people to liven up the festivities. It would seem strange with so few there. Kitty herself did not feel filled with Christmas joy. There were still days to go, maybe she would feel different in a day or two. They arrived for a late lunch with only the three family members and although the staff had dressed the house in the normal way, Kitty had always had Carina to help in adding extra decorations, making it different every year. It was painful to think of it.

It became obvious that everyone felt the need to talk. Richard explained exactly what had happened at the Tunstalls' ball, how it had been timed exactly for when he was not close to her. Who would have been involved? Not Lady Tunstall, Danvers had visited them only to find she had retired to family in Scotland, fled might be a better description. He had a man travelling there now to ask for names in the hope her family would encourage her. Marie Campbell's name was brought up but only Richard knew anything of her. They found it strange their journey had been so uneventful; it worried all of them there might be an attack on the house as there had been none on the road.

The days being short, it was dark when the messenger from the Earl's London house arrived with two messages. The first was an invitation to a New Year house party to begin on the thirtieth of December for four days. The invitation was from Lord and Lady Stone. Neither Kitty nor Richard knew them well, they had barely met, perhaps they were showing their support or could this be the next move. Richard was not prepared to make any decision without Danvers' advice.

The second message was the note from Walcott. Richard gave a sarcastic laugh. "Well this answers our questions of earlier. My mother in her carriage with the Pengarron coat of arms was accosted by three highwaymen on her way to Falcombe Hall, they took nothing, asked who she was, told her she was too old and let her go."

"Why go to Walcott's house?" Kitty knew of the failed romance and wondered if she might be regretting it. "I gather the coachman knew he was being followed and tried to make safety." The Duke was curious. "Were they following her all the way do you think?"

"Yes I expect so. She came to see me and was most unpleasant, I'm afraid I threw her out. Her coach left shortly before we did."

"No wonder we had such a trouble free drive." Kitty mused.

Bright and early the next morning Richard sent two notes, one to Walcott thanking him for the information which was helpful to them, the second to Danvers detailing all that had happened and asking for his advice. Early afternoon brought the first visitors, two elderly aunts of her mother's, one a Miss Sinclair, like her grandmother's maiden name, the other her widowed sister Mrs James with two unmarried daughters, both older than her father. They were so completely opposite to her father's family. They were worried about her health, about the upset to her, they talked of the terrible lies and how distressed they were, how sad at the loss of Carina and the horror of the injuries suffered by Jeremy. Jeremy had to be fetched to assure them he was healing well; he even stood on his crutches alone, if a little unsteady. Kitty was not one to cry but the sheer love and care they showed moved her enormously.

While Kitty was with the arrivals, Richard sat in discussion with the Duke over a letter from Danvers which came by a very fast messenger. His advice was to refuse the offer but not in a way that would prevent them from offering again. If they were genuine they would accept the refusal but if it was a ploy then they would ask again. He must not accept unless Danvers could get protection inside the house as well as outside.

"If it can be arranged, would you let Kitty go?" The Duke was worried after the latest upset to her. Richard was worried also. "I will need to speak to her. She must make the decision. It might be genuine, but it feels wrong somehow. If this is a trap then she must choose. The answer to your question, sir, is no I don't want her to go, but we came back to clear up this problem so until it is solved she will always be in danger. I know she is finding it hard, but believe me I am having difficulty myself watching her suffer when I just want to take her somewhere safe."

Voices in the hall announced the arrival of the Simpkins with their daughter Jane. Everyone converged on the hallway to greet them until order was restored and the housekeeper ushered them away to their rooms.

Calm returned for the next hour until the Arnotts' coach drew another flurry of activity as their girls Julie and Sarah chattered excitedly.

Dinner was a more formal affair, the ladies then leaving the gentleman to their port.

"A bad year for you Wenton." Simpkin remarked. "Yes indeed." the Duke replied. "The worry never leaves us." Richard had left the Duke to talk with his old friends. Arnott asked "Has no one any idea who it doing this? There has to be some reason. You never seemed to make enemies, everyone liked you."

"Many of us were quite envious of your popularity at Eton." Simpkin noted.

"I am only grateful you accepted my invitation, many would rather not take the risk." the Duke remarked.

"Were others invited?"

"There were a couple but I won't hold it against them in the circumstances."

"I presume you have men alerted for problems."

"Oh yes, Ask Pengarron if you want the details."

Richard leaned forward to join in "There are quite a few specially trained men in with the gamekeeper and his staff."

"Have we really?" Jeremy was surprised, "I had no idea."

When they joined the ladies, Jeremy still being wheeled in the chair, the young girls were intrigued. "What happened to you?" Jane Simpkin asked. She was a pretty girl of sixteen with light brown hair and pale eyes behind darker eyelashes. Nor overly tall, she still had a little puppy fat.

"I was attacked."

"Will you get better?" Sarah Arnott was only fifteen and rather over confident. "I hope so. I am much better than I was. I could hardly use my hands until a few weeks ago. I do things to make them stronger."

"What?" A general interest.

"I play cards. Richard, is there a pack of cards over by the window?" Richard walked over and found the pack, bringing them over he was intrigued. "Cards, Jeremy?"

"Yes I have been teaching myself tricks to exercise my fingers."

"Good for you. I would never have thought of that."

A quiet voice, that of Julie Arnott asked "Will you show us some tricks?" Jeremy looked up into the face of the seventeen year old and her blush amused him.

"Richard, push me nearer the table and I will show you my tricks."

In the end it was not only the girls who watched as Jeremy entertained them.

The following morning was bright and clear and although it was not that warm, it was possible for the girls to go out with Kitty. Richard followed at a distance, unhappy at being so far away from her when out of doors. "I think we need more decoration in the house. "Kitty explained.

"Oh yes." "How can we cut it?" "What shall we collect?" General excitement ensued. Kitty beckoned to a gardener who was watching them. "We need clippers to cut greenery." He was loath to leave but Richard walked closer and the gardener nodded and went. Kitty looked at Richard, then at the retreating gardener. "Oh, I see."

"Can I help ladies?" There was much giggling from the younger two. "Shall we choose what to cut?" he suggested

Eventually the gardener returned with clippers.

They chose various greenery that could be tied with ribbons to make posies. The only awkward moment came when Sarah looked at one of the topiary bushes. "What shape is that supposed to be, it looks dreadful!" Kitty looked at the floor, not knowing what to say, again Richard stepped in. "It was damaged in an accident earlier in the summer, it will grow back in a year or two and look like all the others."

"Then we can cut some branches from it without spoiling it." Oh the innocence of a young girl.

"Yes I suppose we can." Kitty found her composure. Richard knew he would make sure that this greenery was put nowhere that Kitty would see and be reminded.

Sarah was one of those chatty girls who joined in an adult conversation if she could. "We had a wonderful day today. We cut greenery then found ribbons to make posies. I think it brightens up the place." Her parents were proud of her until she continued. "It's a pity we can't ride, there are plenty of horses in the stables, we would be in no danger with all those men in the woods."

Her mother started a conversation on a different subject.

"What did I say?" she asked her sister quietly.

"I'll tell you later."

After dinner Lady Simpkin suggested charades, most of them could join in.

This morning being Christmas Day, the whole party dressed for church. It took several carriages to convey everyone to the service. The church was full to overflowing with the estate tenants. Jeremy chose not to go due to the problems he would face; one of those was the memory of Carina's funeral.

Kitty felt she was living in a nightmare even with Richard by her side. He sensed her dismay and pulled her arm under his to enable him to hold her hand tightly. On returning to the Hall, Sarah did it again. "Why did all those men on horseback who went with us not come into church?"

In the evening the young ladies played the piano. Kitty tried to be excused as she had not played for months but simple music was found and she was forced to comply. Richard was surprised. "You play well, Kitty, I had no idea you could play. My darling wife, you continue to surprise me."

Sarah played a jig with not too many wrong notes. Julie was the most proficient, her performance giving great pleasure. Jane said she was not that good but would play another day if they wanted to dance.

The biggest surprise was when Jeremy asked Kitty to play a duet with him. "We used to play this years ago, can you still play the cello?"

"I have been practising. I thought if I had to spend my life in a chair I should have some way to entertain myself."

"I thought you were getting better." Sarah again.

He might not be very good yet, but everyone felt the lump in their throat as he played.

Four days after Christmas, the Stones renewed their invitation. A fast rider was sent to Danvers whose reply came quickly. Richard took Kitty into the study to discuss the request. "I cannot fault you if you choose not to go, my love, I myself would prefer not to. It is obviously some ploy by whoever they are. The Stones may be involved. I will not force you into anything."

"Richard, I am frightened I admit, but how long can we keep all these men to protect me and my family? If this will help catch someone then I will go."

"If you are sure. Danvers can cover the grounds and already has men inside. I will stick to you until you are tired of me."

"I can never be tired of you, Richard. I love you too much. Especially now you know how to deal with my shock." She was a little pink. It took a minute for Richard to realise. "Really!"

The rider was sent back to Danvers confirming their willingness to attend and the need for cover. An acceptance was sent to the Stones early the following day, confirming that they would arrive late afternoon. Binny was to pack her best satin and silk gowns, Nicholls was given instructions about the route to take and the Duke insisted the second carriage with Binny, Ferguson, Smithson and the luggage should be his travelling carriage with William driving. Both carriages were to have outriders.

Chapter 27

The house party was already in progress when they arrived.

The hostess was insincerely obsequious. Some of the guests were cool, others downright icy. Richard longed to push them against a wall and plant his fist in their faces; however this was a spying mission which he would carry out as he had every other. The difference this time was that it was not only his life in danger.

Kitty dressed for dinner as befitted a Countess; she was, after all, the most high born lady attending. Her dress of ice blue silk with satin ribbon edging in a scallop design showed off her youthful figure to perfection. For jewellery, she wore only ear bobs, without a necklace to spoil the perfect creamy skin of her neck and upper breasts. If they were going to look at her in hatred then why not include jealousy, Kitty thought. Most of the ladies were somewhat older than her; maybe their husbands would not be so cold.

The discussions at the dinner table were mundane to the point of boring. When the ladies rose to leave, Richard eschewed the port and followed his wife through the hall where a footman touched his arm as he passed. They made eye contact and he nodded his head. One of Danvers' men.

They arose to a rather dismal day and breakfasted almost alone. A few of the men were around, some already in the billiard room. Most of the ladies had not yet risen, or not come down which could be more accurate. Well if they avoided her at least it saved her having to be civil. The less people there the less people of whom to beware.

Most arrived shortly before lunch which was taken in the small dining room and served as a cold collation, in spite of the miserable weather outside. It had stopped raining, however the terrace was awash and the extensive lawn looked positively soggy. It was obvious nobody wanted to converse with them so they discussed the layout of the parkland, which gave them a reason to look out of the window whilst they searched for signs of Danvers' men. When Lord Stone passed them Richard posed a question about the extent of the woods he could see. Now he was in a position to ask his real question.

"Lord Stone, why did you invite us? It is quite evident no one wants us here."

He turned a little pink. "It was my wife who wished to invite you, she insisted."

"It was against your will, Lord Stone?"

"No, of course not. I merely meant it was her particular wish." He looked very disconcerted.

"You keep a large staff, I am surprised."

"Not normally, we have to hire in extra for house parties."

"Do you hold them often?"

"Not very often, they are usually only my wife's friends; why she insisted on you I shall never know. I can only hope the atmosphere improves."

"Oh, you feel it too." Kitty remarked.

"Indeed I do, Countess." He gave a nod of his head and scuttled off to the farthest corner of the room.

The afternoon became a bore. Wherever they went there was little conversation with the other guests before each excused themselves and moved away.

"I think I will propose a toast tonight." he had a determined expression on his face. "To the truth, and God help those who tell lies and those who believe them."

"I think you will shock them."

"I hope they ask me to explain!"

"The ladies seem worse than the men."

"Yes they do, several men have tried to converse but have been called away by their wives..."

Tea would be served in the large parlour, all were instructed to attend, especially the Pengarrons. This immediately put Richard on his guard. "Stay close, Kitty, I have a feeling something is about to happen."

"If they give me anything I will refuse it."

"Good, just be on your guard."

As they approached the parlour Richard looked at the footman. "Be ready." was all he said.

"Yes sir." the footman quietly replied.

Teatime was nothing unusual, the tea was handed round, cakes and pastries were the same as normal and it was not until all was nearly over that they brought in the cake. Lady Stone rose to speak.

"As we have a young couple with us, I thought it would be appropriate to have a cake made to celebrate their recent wedding."

Kitty's stomach lurched. Richard leapt in to interrupt her.

"Who made the cake, Lady Stone?" She looked taken aback.

"It was made by the Palace's own cake makers." She was almost belligerent.

"I see it is on a metal stand with a crest on it."

She was definitely annoyed. "I'll have you know it is one of the Palaces own stands."

Richard looked at the metal knife and made a decision. He walked to the door and beckoned in the footman. Lady Stone picked up the knife.

"Well if you will not cut it, then I will." Richard grabbed the knife out of her hand.

"Nobody is to touch it."

He went to the terrace doors and flung them open. Beckoning the footman they each took a side of the wooden tray holding the cake on its stand, lifted it and Richard said curtly "Outside" and inclined his head.

Lady Stone stepped forward to intervene but Kitty saw the danger and caught her arm to pull her away.

Between them Richard and Danvers footman carried the cake carefully over the terrace and across the lawn, a very long way from the house. Placing it on the ground, Richard shouted to the men hidden in the trees but it was impossible to hear what he said from the house. By this time the house party guests were spilling onto the terrace to see the proceedings which meant Richard had to drive them back into the house. As he shut the glass terrace doors the noise of a shot rang out.

With a great whooshing noise, fire billowed into the air and the windows rattled, soil raining down onto the terrace. The aftermath was silence, both outside and inside.

He strode to Kitty and held her tightly in his arms until she stopped the worst of her trembling. "Are you alright, my sweet?" she nodded. "Can you speak?" She looked up and very quietly said "Yes, I think so." He half smiled at her. "That is progress then."

He turned to look at the stunned faces. One elderly lady had fainted and was being lifted into a chair, several clung to each other and were shaking.

"Will you all please sit?" Richard ordered.

Lady Stone went to take charge but was shushed by him. He looked at the footman, who appeared just as stunned. "Are you alone?"

"No, sir. I'll fetch help, shall I?" With a nod Richard turned to Lady Stone who was confused but still standing. Taking a spare straight backed chair, he placed it in the centre of the room.

"Sit here." he instructed her. She went to argue but thought better of it when she looked at his expression.

"Lady Stone, I am going to ask you questions and for your own sake, please answer them." She stared. "Tell me about the cake, who sent it?"

"I ordered it."

"From the royal cake makers?"

"Yes."

"When?"

She was silent. "When did you place the order Lady Stone."

"I don't see...." she began. Richard raised his voice.

"When, Mrs Stone, before or after Christmas.?"

"Before."

"Who suggested it?" She looked panicked.

"Whose idea was it?"

"Mine." Not very convincing with her lack of confidence.

"With a cook and kitchen here you decided before Christmas to order a cake and then we turned down your invitation." Somebody murmured about them being there so they hadn't.

"What would have happened to the cake had we not come?"

"Well I cancelled it."

"You cancelled it, then why is it here?"

"They obviously didn't get my message."

"You cancelled the cake but it arrived, who fetched it?"

"No one, they delivered it by coach this morning."

"Who were they?"

"Well they were in livery so I thought it was...." she stopped and Lord Stone broke in.

"Now look here Pengarron."

"No, Stone, you look there at the deep hole in your lawn, at the terrace covered with soil. If that had happened in this room everyone here would be dead and the house probably burned down."

One of the ladies began to sob.

"I want to know who knew we would be here."

"Tell him what you know, my dear." She looked at her husband.

"Well I was surprised when the cake arrived, having cancelled it. I would have reordered it but you didn't accept until the last minute and then there was no time."

A movement caught Richard's eye and he turned to see Portman standing quietly. "Portman, good, I may need your help." Turning back to Lady Stone he said "So ostensibly the cake arrived unexpectedly." She nodded. "Who knew we would be here?"

"Well those here, of course."

"Any one else? Who suggested the second invitation?"

"Well it was just an idea I had." She was definitely lying now, covering up some details.

"Lady Stone." He was getting frustrated and impatient. "Do you know the livery of the men who delivered the cake?"

"Yes."

"Was it the Prince's livery?"

"Yes." Gasps from one or two guests.

"And the stand had the Prince's coat of arms."

"Yes."

"So you presumed it came from the Prince?"

"Of course it did."

"No Lady Stone, the Prince believes us to be at Wenton Hall until the New Year, why would he send a cake here?"

"He wanted to..." she stopped.

"You know who suggested the cake and the invitation, who was it?"

"I will not tell you anything more."

"Very well then, Portman, do you have handcuffs?"

"Indeed I do. Order the carriage Trevane, I'll take over now."

He stepped forward pulling handcuffs from his pocket.

"You can't take my wife away, I won't allow it."

"Oh don't worry Lord Stone, you will be going too, after all as her husband you are ultimately responsible for your wife."

"I am the local magistrate, you can't drag us away like common criminals, I am the law here."

Mrs Stone lifted her chin. "We have friends in high places, they will not allow us to be subjected to a mere magistrate, you overstep yourself."

Richard came to stand by Portman.

"Lady Stone, sit down a moment while I inform you. Whoever did this knew we would be here and intended us all to die, you included. You cannot testify against him if you are dead and the only information the staff would have was the livery of those who delivered it. You were meant to die as part of his plan, if you tell us his name we will be lenient with you, if you do not then you are being taken to The Tower which is where we take anyone suspected of treason."

"Treason!" Most of those in the room said the word. Then there was uproar, everyone talking at once.

Richard and Portman stood silently until their very stillness quieted them.

"This is all made up rubbish." One of the guests said.

Kitty rose from her chair and asked "May I speak?" They looked at her as she held up her hand. "You all think badly of me because of lies. I have met the Prince only three times, all of those in public, the third you might have been there. The Prince had been told of the rumours and that I had started them, which was not true. He was angry, I was upset and confused. Whoever started those rumours has influenced the ton to make them hate the Prince and they are using me to do it. This is the third time they have tried to kill me and blame the Prince. Now they wanted to kill all of you too," she turned to Lady Stone "and you are prepared to hang for treason to protect him. Have you no children to inherit? How will they live when your house, your lands, your money and your title are taken away, because that is what happens when you are hanged for treason. Your family will be destitute outcasts, all for the sake of concealing the name of a traitor who wanted you dead."

"But he is one of my oldest friends, he would not do this it must be a mistake.

"Mary, just tell them his name." Her best friend had just realised her life was included in the attempt.

Portman stepped forward "No my lady, it is no mistake. I work for the Prince and the government in trying to stop this treason. I can assure you the Prince has no idea the Pengarrons are here, he wants this ton madness stopped, it is bad for the country. Your kind of arrogance is what caused the uprising in France. If you bring down the Crown you bring down England."

Everyone stared at him in horror. Lady Stone clung to her husband's arm. "It was Sir William," she said, "Sir William Forster."

"Thank you, Lady Stone." Portman said. "Trevane, everyone is to stay within the house until I return. Not even servants are allowed to leave. I'll have the men come in closer to be sure they don't. I will take a couple of men with me to Danvers, we have fast horses stationed ready. Lock your door!" He bowed to Kitty." Lady Kitty, let us hope this is the finale to the evil that has befallen you. You can be sure you have protection all around you." Kitty inclined her head in acknowledgement. Two footmen standing inside the door acknowledged him as he left.

"If you will excuse us, we will go to our room." Richard took Kitty's arm, leading her from the room.

Being isolated with Richard did mean Kitty had him all to herself for a few hours during the early evening. "What did Danvers actually say, why did he want us to come?"

"Apparently after we turned down the invitation he set up a trap. Each of the Prince's advisers was given different information about where you would be. No one has been told we are here and the Prince definitely doesn't know. He said he could enjoy Christmas knowing you were safe with your family."

"How would it spring a trap?"

"If anyone tells the Prince we are here we will know who is behind this." She looked confused.

"Explain, I feel dull witted over this."

"No one knows we were invited a second time, there was not time between our acceptance and our arrival so Lady Stone or her friends could not alert an outsider. Whoever knew we were here was responsible for suggesting it.

"You knew Lady Stone has been used, like me."

"Oh yes. I feel sorry for her in a way. Someone she has probably known all her life has used her to attack you, and after her help was prepared to cover his actions by killing her also. She may not be a strong minded lady but she did not deserve this from a close friend."

"The trail of humiliated ton ladies is growing."

"I believe there will be a great many more when all the details are known.

In the morning Lord Stone organised everyone into the parlour. His request was that Richard explain what had happened and why they had become involved.

Richard was more than willing to comply. These were ton members who could carry away the message. First he told of Kitty's innocent meetings with the Prince. Kitty added that Sir William had been with him on all occasions. He told of the rumours accusing the ton of appalling behaviour in their treatment of Kitty, the attempted murders, the killings and the injuries caused. All eyes were on Kitty as he described her suffering, her recovery while the ton invented more lies about her.

"Someone has been trying to unseat the Crown using the ton on-dits to whip up hatred. For this they picked an innocent girl of high status to use, believing her murder would incite the aristocracy against the Prince. What we do not know yet is why. Any knowledge you have will save England becoming like France. We will all suffer if that happens. Who do you know who is so adamant about these lies? Were any of you at the Tunstall's ball, are you able to give us names of the ladies who caused the problem? Rest assured, if anyone is just misguided in their beliefs it will be understood, but the ton leaders will be charged with treason. Bear in mind if you are one of them, Sir William wanted you to die last night."

Tea and other stronger drinks were brought and the whole group discussed among themselves while Kitty and Richard stood by the windows and looked out at the devastation Lord Stone was also contemplating.

Portman returned to give them permission to leave. Some took the chance to speak with him. Kitty and Richard had their carriages brought and returned to the relative safety of Wenton Hall.

"Well this is a surprise, Danvers, I hadn't realised you were invited."

"I am not, Your Highness, I am here over our problem."

"News on New Years Eve?"

"Not exactly. Has anyone told you where the Pengarron's are?"

"I know where they are, you told me."

"Has anyone intimated they are elsewhere?"

"Well, Forster thought they were somewhere else, I don't remember where exactly."

"Lord and Lady Stone's."

"That's it. Why?"

"They were at the Stones when a cake was delivered on a silver stand with your coat of arms, by men in your livery. There is a very large crater in their lawn. Trevane was vigilant enough. Their invitation and the cake were at the behest of Lady Stone's old friend, Sir William Forster.

"Have you men guarding the entrances?"

"Yes, sire."

"Don't let him escape, Danvers."

"No, Your Highness."

Chapter 28

A range of emotions swept everyone at the Hall. Relief, disbelief, confusion. How could he have managed this alone? His family and other friends must be involved, he had used Lady Stone why not others? The relief was obvious, disbelief that it was all over, that depended on what Danvers found out and it was still hard to relax. The confusion was not yet knowing why, why he wanted to bring down the Royal House, why he picked on Kitty, indeed why he used the ton rather than whipping up the general populace. After all, there were a great many out of work soldiers who had come back from France, many of them starving. In the north there was already unrest due to changes in industry, why not use these to ferment a revolution, using the ton made no sense.

A week into the New Year Richard and Kitty returned to their London house in the hope of life returning to the peaceful atmosphere of Cornwall. Danvers was a frequent visitor. He had found a few contacts of Sir William's whose names Portman had been given by guests at the Stone's house party. Lady Tunstall had also reluctantly given up her secret, but none of this was proof, none of it gave an answer as to why. The ton was in shock with the incarceration of Sir William Forster in The Tower. The rumours were much reduced, everyone fearful of being seen as a traitor.

By the middle of February the first ball invitations arrived for them. The Spencers would he honoured to receive The Earl and Countess of Pengarron at a ball to be held at the end of February. Kitty's insides felt strange, fluttering and roiling. She was not sure whether she wanted to go or not, if she wanted to be part of the ton or not. Richard watched her emotions flit across her face.

"Sweet, you don't have to go, but how will we know if they accept you if you stay away."

"Do you think they might resent me?"

"It is possible. We have gone to a great deal of trouble to clear your name, now let's see if it worked."

"I doubt it; they hold their opinions for a long time. Some are never accepted back."

"It may show up those who have been the instigators of the rumours. I think we have a great many supporters now."

Was having more than a week to anticipate it a good or a bad thing? Kitty had plenty of time to prepare, however it also gave plenty of time to worry.

The ball was not one of the largest, being in the early part of the season when everyone had not yet returned, which also made it less crowded. The Spencer's ballroom was not over large and at this time of year the terrace was not an option.

Mrs Spencer had decorated in a bouquet of colours to brighten the dismal weather. Mr Spencer being a wealthy man she could afford the variety of hothouse flowers which made for a very pleasant atmosphere. Although spring was a long way off the overall colours were pink and yellow with the odd splash of red.

Kitty wore a long sleeved gown of delicate pink with a half overskirt of lace adorned with tiny satin bows in deep pink sprinkled over it. As usual she wore little jewellery but Richard had bought her a choker necklace of small rubies in a gold setting, not too large to overpower the ethereal effect she gave.

"Kitty, you look exquisite as usual. Every man there will envy me."

"I don't feel exquisite, I am in turmoil inside; I shall be glad when this is over."

"Smile, my love, you are being admired." So she smiled and nodded and they smiled and nodded back. She danced the first waltz with Richard then several more dances with those who asked. She was aware most of them were Danvers' men but there were one or two, mainly older men, who came to speak and asked her to dance. One young man asked, which she thought amusing, as she had seen his friends daring him to dance with the notorious Countess. A little after the supper interval Richard waltzed with her again.

"Are you tired, my love, you do look as if you are wilting?"

"I am, Richard, I have to admit."

"Then we will leave early."

They found Mrs Spencer and thanked her for inviting them, the carriage was called and Kitty sat back on the squabs and breathed out with a great sigh.

"I am so glad that is over."

"You did so well, my dear, you must be pleased with their response to you."

"I am, but it is so early in the season, many have not yet returned."

Richard sent a note to Danvers regarding the ton's attitude to Kitty and asking him about those names he had, suggesting dinner, which Danvers accepted. It was unusual to have a dinner party with only one guest so Portman and Dinsdale were included in the invitations. There were no ladies Kitty could invite because of the need for private conversation.

Little was said during the dinner when the footmen were there, mostly they discussed the government and the food, which was delicious. Portman was very taken with the apple tart with cook's own cream sauce. He was sure there was a flavour of alcohol, which was possible. They took the port to the library where they could talk more privately. When tea was brought for Kitty they fell silent until they were alone again.

"Those whose names you have, how many of them can be traced to Forster?"

"Only a few. We know some were friends, like Lady Stone, most of them easily manipulated."

"That does not sound like the leaders of the pack, they seemed to be much more powerful and crafty in using others."

"Can you find any common connection between them?"

"No, only some of them. Of course we may not know of the main instigators yet."

"What did you find out about Maria Campbell?"

"Your mother's friend, she has no connection to any that I can see. She just seems to be a vicious woman."

"Like my mother."

"I wasn't going to say that."

"You don't need to. I still expect her to do something; she is not one to give up easily."

"The problem is, most of the ton is related in some way, it makes it hard to see if it is coming from one family or another, who started it and who is carrying it on."

"So we are really no nearer finding out why. I suppose Forster is not talking."

"That is the most worrying of all. He seems prepared to die rather than give away anything."

"Do you think he is the only one or one of several?"

"I certainly think if he had a personal reason for this he would be shouting about it. It's as if it were not his campaign and he is only an operative who is completely loyal."

"So there is still a central person or people, with Forster just running the campaign against the Prince using Kitty?"

"I can't even be sure of that. With him in The Tower who knows where this will go now?"

"So we keep watching and listening."

"I'm afraid so, I'll keep looking for connections, there's nothing else we can do."

The next ball was the following week. Mrs Spicer, a widow, had a newly married son and wished to throw a ball on their behalf. There were a few more of the ton returned as parliament was debating a controversial bill, the ladies accompanying their husbands. Kitty was just as nervous as the last time; her insides never had the chance to settle down. Tonight she wore a deep blue satin gown in a very simple uncluttered style. There were times when she wished she could wear off the shoulder gowns, but that was impossible with the scars on the back of her shoulders so she had to be satisfied with a low neckline.

The overall friendliness was similar, although there was a little knot of ladies who seemed hostile. A few more gentlemen asked her to dance including a couple of young bucks, probably because of a wager. It was an uncomfortable night but for no particular reason. Richard felt the same.

"Who were the young men I danced with?"

"Don't you remember?"

"I was too tense to remember their names."

"Wilkinson was the one trying to grow a moustache, the other was the Roberts' youngest."

"They seemed nice enough even if it was done for a bet. They had that bravado about them."

Richard laughed. "You are probably right about that."

Danvers did not wait to be told, he came the following afternoon to ask. "My men took a few more names last night, there was the odd connection but nothing much. A couple were cousins of some kind to Maria Campbell, so we shall have to keep an eye on her. Do you have an invitation to the Falkirks' next Tuesday?"

"Yes, is there a reason?"

"I have a suspicion there may be some contacts being made at certain balls, I believe this is one of them. Don't ask me, I just have a feeling there are some extra arrangements being made to attend this ball for no real reason. We'll have a full contingent there so you are in no danger."

Richard wrote to the Falkirks to accept their invitation.

Kitty wore her blue silk with scalloped satin ribbon edging. She wore only ear bobs and looked magnificent, Richard thought she glowed. They arrived fairly early in order to watch for knots of conspirators as they formed. By now more men were prepared to ask Kitty for a dance, although she was not feeling sufficiently settled to dance all the country dances. She did dance with one young buck of about twenty who asked for a waltz. He seemed filled with bravado as the others had been but with a more quiet and detached arrogance than usual.

The waltz started as normal, they barely spoke, there seemed something different about the way he held himself aloof. At first she was light hearted with him but he was not inclined to flirt with her as they usually did. Kitty decided he must be a very serious young man and smiled up into his face in encouragement. Then a strange thing happened. As he looked down into her face his eyes changed. It was as if he woke up and for the first time saw the real woman he was dancing with. The shock showed in his eyes, which grew large. His steps faltered, he stopped dancing and stared into her eyes with a strange look on his face. Then he shook himself, apologised under his breath and began to waltz again just as the music concluded. He escorted her back to Richard and virtually fled. Kitty though it was a good job she was already married as she could easily have fallen into those remarkable eyes with all their intensity.

"How was your waltz with young Hurst?"

"Quite strange, he really is a very intense young man. He completely stopped dancing when he looked into my eyes."

Richard laughed. "I know the feeling. I can hardly blame Martin for falling for you, especially tonight."

Chapter 29

Danvers came with Portman the next afternoon. Kitty had callers and had to leave them to discuss on their own.

"There was a definite grouping there to meet and assess the situation. When you go into who married whom you find more connections. There are one or two old dowager dragons involved, they may possibly be the female power."

"So do we still have to wait? I just wish we could force their hand, make them do what we want."

"That would definitely sort out the who if not the why."

"It is the arrogance of them, making all of us watch and worry while they hold the upper hand."

"It is difficult to be arrogant when they hold all the cards."

Richard thought while he poured them all a drink. "How about if we were arrogant? That should make them angry."

"What sort of arrogance?"

"Suppose we held a ball or party to celebrate the end of our problems, freedom from fear, something like that."

"Impossible to control everything in this house."

"How about at the Hall, just invited guests?"

"We could guard the hall, we already do, how were you envisaging it?"

"A grand carriage ride to the party. They stopped my mother's carriage, it's the way they think."

"They would attack the carriage unless it had outriders."

"I told you, arrogance, no outriders."

"Are you mad, Richard?"

"They see us get into the coach, but they don't see others already in there, heavily armed."

"It's risky."

"I know."

"It could work. Let me think about it."

"It could work. If we had someone riding footman at the back to see them coming, armed of course, two more inside with Lady Kitty. She would have to lie on the floor for safety so we could take one side each."

""We?"

"You're not leaving me out of this now. We've come this far I want to see it through."

"What about Nicholls my coachman, anyone with him?"

"Not your coachman, I'll provide the driver, he needs to be trained to drive and shoot at the same time."

"What if they don't bite?"

"We have to find a way to make them."

Danvers took the idea of a party or dance to the Duke, not giving the real reason, just a celebration.

"You mean an end of hostilities party with music or dancing?"

"Yes, a dance would be good, not too many, family and a few close friends, a small house party."

"Is there a specific reason for this or it is more military tactics?"

"The war is never over until the enemy is completely vanquished, we learned that with Napoleon."

"I see, or perhaps it's better I don't see!"

"Just so, Your Grace."

Aunt Hetty and Jeremy organised the weekend party in record time, less than two weeks would see everyone invited arriving on the Friday for the weekend. Richard and Kitty in the armed coach would go on Saturday morning. The timing was critical, it must be early enough so no one saw the preparations but full light when they left London for the country roads. The main problem would be letting them know of the arrangements and making it plausible. Kitty was told of the plan, this time not an option for her to veto it.

"Where would you like to go, I wish to take you out?"

"Whatever for?"

"To be seen. We have to be relaxed and confident."

"I don't feel confident."

"Nor do I, but this is part of the plan, relaxed arrogance."

"And we need to be seen out and about? A walk down Bond Street, a visit to the bookshop, either would do, I suppose."

"We'll do both, at the busiest time when everyone is out and about."

Bond Street made her feel very vulnerable, relaxing even on Richard's arm was difficult.

"What if..." he silenced her. "Don't worry we have protection all around us."

"Oh." she was not convinced. The bookshop was easier, she had a distraction with her real interest in the books. She bought several which Richard carried for her.

"Would you like to go to Gunters? I've always wanted to be able to take you there."

Kitty looked up at him. "Is there a special reason?"

"There are always so many interesting people there to overhear your conversation."

"Ah, a part of the plan."

"It seems a good idea, let's see, shall we."

The simple idea became a major military tactic shortly afterwards when Richard spotted his mother and one of her gentlemen friends walking close by.

"Look up at me and say something about Gunters." Richard whispered.

"Oh, yes." Then louder "Oh, Richard, we are so near Gunters, may we go there?"

"That is exactly where I am taking you, my love."

They strolled gently onwards as if unconcerned at who might have heard. True to his expectations his mother steered her companion in that direction. Richard found Kitty a table where they could be seen and heard making sure his mother and her companion would have the chance of a seat nearby. Tea and cakes were ordered during which time Richard quietly asked her to follow his direction in the coming deception.

His mother walked beside her companion in a manner she thought hid her from his view and took a table near them, her back to Richard.

"I hope you are not angry, my love, I know you expected to go to Wenton Hall on Friday, I had not realised the dinner was this weekend when I accepted."

Kitty looked at him. He mouthed silently, Saturday.

"Well I am a little upset I have to admit. This is a celebration for us and we are not there until Saturday."

"Well the dance is not until Saturday and we can leave early enough to be there well before lunch. Most of the ladies will not have risen."

"I suppose that is true. Saturday can be our special day. A new life together, free from all the fear."

Richard beamed at her inventiveness.

"If you wish we can leave London afterwards. It would be my pleasure to take you anywhere you wish to go."

"What a lovely thought, there are places I have always wanted to visit. I will decide which." Her eyes sparked at him.

"We could visit several, maybe do a European tour."

"Oh, Richard, what a wonderful idea." They were both full of mirth, enjoying the extent of the deception.

"I have a book on Venice and the art in Italy, maybe we could go there."

"I could take you to see Greece, perhaps."

Maybe they should calm down a little; they were in danger of becoming too outrageous.

"Some of Spain and Portugal is very beautiful. I don't think France yet, perhaps later. There are places I went that I would like to see as a visitor now the fighting has ceased." That should do it.

They finished their tea and cakes and left his mother preening over her illicit information. She would act on it he was sure, the added departure should force whoever it was to attack this weekend.

On Friday they prepared. Kitty had never seen some of the guns before. He put a small pistol in her hand.

"Could you fire this? Would you if you needed it?"

She held it like it would blow up.

"It isn't loaded."

"Oh."

"It's a ladies' pistol."

"They make them for us."

"Yes, although they have been around like this for a while. I had one in France, they fit in the pocket without showing."

"Show me what to do with it."

He turned the gun in her hand and showed her how to cock it and pull the trigger.

"Why do I do that first?"

"That's a safety mechanism to stop it going off in your pocket."

"Are all the bigger ones the same?"

"More or less, the newer ones are better than the old blunderbuss which had not such good accuracy."

"I've seen the shotgun for hunting game before, Papa and Jeremy use them. Jeremy showed me how to load them."

Richard thought for a little. "We are taking several guns each, but if we needed to reload, could you do it Kitty?"

"Well I don't see why not, you'll have to teach me."

They spent several hours loading the guns, some Richard discharged into the ground in the garden, so she could refill them when still warm. Eventually he declared himself satisfied. All the firearms were loaded and carefully stored in the carriage seat, the carriage checked and secured in the mews with constant cover by the grooms and a cavalry officer brought in by Danvers.

Smithson and Binny laid out their clothes for the following day and left in the small carriage. Ferguson was upset to be sent on ahead, unable to protect Kitty. Nicholls and Phillips both went on the small coach with all the luggage.

Kitty was not sure how to cope with her fear that night. Richard ate a little dinner but she hardly touched anything.

"I know it's hard, my love, but you should eat something.

"I notice you are not exactly hungry, we might as well have told cook not to bother. It's a good job we have you two." She turned to Danvers and Dinsdale.

"How could we not eat such delicious food, ma'am?" Dinsdale said.

"Did we manage to find a footman's livery to fit you?"

"Eventually, ma'am, luckily Pelman will be covered by a coachman's cloak; it would have been more difficult in his case."

"Oh I don't know." was Richard's rejoinder. "Have you looked at the muscles on Nicholls!"

Not much alcohol was consumed that night. These were special agents used to being guarded in their habits, and this was definitely a military operation.

Saturday started early for everyone. The three men were up early checking everything was ready. Danvers made it out to the mews before daylight, where he checked all was in order with the cavalry officer who had spent a peaceful night with the carriage horses.

Kitty had her breakfast, what she could eat of it, in her room before dressing. Dinsdale waited in the hallway with the butler. Richard paced the corridor from the study to the hallway. As time grew nearer he worried that Kitty had not come down. He sent a maid up to check all was well, but was told she would be there in time and to stop worrying.

The carriage was rolled out, Danvers sitting on the floor, and the horses harnessed, for arrogance six of them. The carriage pulled up at the front door and Kitty came slowly down the stairs already tightly wrapped in her cloak and carrying a bag. The butler stepped forward to open the door and Richard leaned forward to offer her his arm. "Do you have your little pistol?"

"Of course I do, stop worrying, Richard."

She eschewed his arm, looking up to give him a beaming smile as she brushed past him, out to the carriage where she climbed in unaided. Richard was a little surprised at her demeanour, she was stiffly upright and controlled, he only hoped she was going to cope with the coming drive. He climbed into the Carriage; Dinsdale lifted the step and closed the door as a footman should, then climbed up at the rear. Richard tapped the roof for the coachman to pull away just as the sun broke through the clouds to give a bright day.

Danvers stayed on the floor of the coach until they were away from the ton houses, then sat opposite them.

"At least the sun is out and we can see them coming."

"Have you told your man to take it steady through London?"

"Oh yes, we won't rush until we see them, after all we want this confrontation, we are not about to speed past."

Kitty, now feeling it was safe, put down her hood and opened up her cloak to reveal her coachman's outfit beneath. Richard and Danvers stared at her.

"Well I don't intend to lie on the floor loading guns in a ball gown, what did you expect?"

Richard started to laugh. "I should have known you were up to something, you were too secretive this morning."

She finished removing her cloak, folded it and laid it on the seat by Danvers.

"I can lay on it on the floor if I need to, I don't expect it is very comfortable there." She looked at both their faces.

"This was good enough to get me to Cornwall, it seems only sensible for this drive."

Danvers grinned, the look he gave Richard was filled with appreciation with which Richard was not best pleased. Opening the bag she carried she seated the coachman's hat to hide her hair and tapped her left pocket.

"Your ladies' pistol?" Danvers enquired.

"And I am not frightened to use it after all they have done to me!"

They were away from habitation apart from the occasional hamlet, the roads becoming narrower. When they were about two miles from Wenton Hall gates they passed through Wenton village, rather small and spread along the road. A shout from Dinsdale brought them all to their posts. A mounted man concealed between the houses.

The two men took one side door each and opened the window. Kitty laid on the floor. The seat was lifted and she prepared for the reloading. The coach put on speed.

As they passed another house Danvers saw a second man on horseback and shouted to Dinsdale, but as he passed the rider fired at him. Dinsdale was firing back but it was an exposed seat and he had been wounded.

There was a short area of tall hedges before the next house and Dinsdale was able to slide over the roof and appear head first in the window. Richard pulled him in with much grunting from the pain as his leg was bleeding badly. Kitty opened her bag once more and produced a strip of bandage with which she bound his leg tightly.

The guns now needed reloading. It was not comfortable with the pistol in her left pocket as she was laying on her left side to leave the right arm free, so she changed the pistol to her right hand pocket. Dinsdale was breathing better now.

"I'm pretty sure I hit the one that shot me, but I don't know how badly, he certainly fell."

A shout from Danvers as another horseman appeared at the side of the carriage. A volley of shots from both sides and they pulled free of the village.

"You all right, Danvers?"

"They hit my right forearm. I'm not sure I can hold a gun."

Kitty drew out another bandage and wrapped it to stop the worst of the bleeding.

"Can you shoot with your left hand?"

"Yes but not very accurately."

"Let me come to that window." Dinsdale said. He tried to slide over the seat to help. "I think I hit him, or at least his horse." Danvers was gritting his teeth.

They were now coming to an open field. As they almost reached it a fourth mounted gunman moved out ahead of them and aimed for their coachman, then galloped away over the field.

They could now see two horsemen across the field. Not close enough. The horses were running wild with the shooting, the coach shaking.

"I think he hit Pelman, there's no one driving."

It was an extremely dangerous position to be in. They were passing the church, the vicarage came next with high hedges. The horsemen were no longer close to them and as they came to the tall hedges the horses gradually slowed coming almost to a stop.

While Richard helped Danvers and Dinsdale to change places, Kitty leapt for the door, opened it and jumped down. She heard Richard shout after her but continued running for the driver's box.

How she made it up there with Pelman laying in the way she could never remember. She pushed Pelman along and pulled the reins from his lax fingers. Although not used to using a whip on six horses, she used it now to encourage the tired and frightened cattle past the vicarage and around the curve in the road that led towards the narrow bridge over the stream.

Kitty had to slow a little to negotiate the bridge as she was only used to a small carriage with two horses but on clearing the bridge she whipped them up. She heard more shots, someone had obviously caught up.

The road here traversed a field in a large curve to enable the coach to enter the Hall gates easily. The guns were now shotguns but she was unaware if anyone was injured, she had enough to cope with, all her attention was on the problem now ahead of her.

From across the field the fourth rider, now realising there was another driver, was crossing the shorter diagonal distance on a powerful horse. He was riding a large bay hunter who was fast and she was not sure she could make the gates.

Putting all the reins into her stronger right hand the better to hold six horses she reached her left hand over to take the pistol from her right pocket, cocked it and hung onto the horses as best she could. She had no experience of driving a travelling coach with six horses through gates and had hoped she could have slowed a little but that was not going to be an option.

The bay was now in front of her and turning in her direction, closing fast on her right hand side. The rider waited until he was within range then lifted his gun and looked at his target, directly into her eyes. And froze.

Kitty was also as shocked as he but she pulled the trigger. He fell. She had no idea where or how badly she had shot him, only that she was still alive.

She also knew she would have recognised those eyes anywhere.

She made it though the gates, the horses straining at full speed. She tried to pull them in hand but she had little enough strength left.

There were people in the path in front of the Hall. It felt like a nightmare.

She was pulling on the reins as hard as she could, praying they would see.

Someone heard them and shouted and guests of all ages were running for safety.

She slewed the carriage round in front of the door and the horses came to a halt, totally blown.

Chapter 30

Men came running; someone lifted her down from the box. Doors were opening, male voices were talking, Richard's voice, her father's voice. Richard's arm came around her and she looked up into his face.

"Pelman didn't make it, by the looks of it." Grooms were unhitching the distressed horses. "Well done Kitty." People seemed to be running in all direction, orders were being given. Portman seemed to be involved. Danvers voice said. "I'm all right, it's just my forearm. Have you arranged a search?" "Yes sir, they're saddling up now." "Make sure they are adequately armed. There were four of them altogether. At least two were down, a third may have been hit, or it may have been his horse."

"We'll look for them."

The Duke's voice said "Bring them inside, someone has already gone for the doctor."

Kitty went to lean on Richard's shoulder. "Careful sweet, I seem to have taken a hit in my left shoulder, nothing too bad, I can still use my arm." He added as the horror showed on her face.

The men were taken upstairs where their wounds were exposed and cleaned. Richard insisted Kitty change and go downstairs for tea.

She was walking in a haze and went with Aunt Hetty without argument.

It seemed a long time before the doctor arrived. While he was there she was not allowed to go up to Richard.

By the time the doctor appeared Kitty was a little calmer, her composure returning.

"Countess Pengarron, I have to reassure you your husband is well, he has lost a little blood when I removed the bullet but apart from keeping his arm in a sling he will do well enough."

"Thank you so much, doctor. How are the others?"

"Dinsdale is the worst, he won't be out of bed for a good few days. Danvers has been patched up, stopping his bleeding was the most difficult. They all need to take it easy for a while."

When the search party returned they were empty handed. They had searched the whole area but found only blood.

In the circumstances lunch was extremely informal. While everyone wanted to know what had happened they realised the need to wait until everyone was willing and able to talk.

After the excitement, the shock, the pain, their dismay began to overtake them. The only one who could not move about was Dinsdale who was confined to bed. Gradually they all drifted into his room. Danvers sat in a chair, his arm out of the sling and resting on the chair arm, Richard sat on a small chaise, his arm still in the sling with Kitty by his side leaning close to him. Portman, the only uninjured among them, leaned against the wall. All were silent, thoughtful, depressed.

"We still have no idea who they are."

A knock on the door brought Jeremy, struggling along on his crutches. Cheerfully he asked "Is this the gathering of the fallen and if so may I join you?"

"Come in Jeremy, Portman can you bring a chair from the corridor?"

"You all look so down hearted."

"All this and we still have no clue who they are."

Kitty said "I..."

"Were they roughnecks?"

"No."

"Could you not recognise any of them?"

"No they wore kerchiefs."

"Kitty said "I...."

"What about their horses?"

"They were good fast hunters."

"So we're talking about well heeled men."

"Yes."

Kitty said "I...."

"They took everyone away, dead or injured."

"So we couldn't identify them."

Kitty opened her mouth but closed it again and gave up. Let them talk it out and then she could have her say.

"Can I be devil's advocate?" Jeremy asked

"Go ahead if you feel it would do any good."

Jeremy looked around. "How did they know you were coming?"

"We made it quite public."

"But how did they know when, everyone else came yesterday?"

"Ah, I think that may be due to my mother." Richard ventured. They all turned and looked at him. "We deliberately lured her into Gunters and talked, she thought we hadn't seen her."

"So ask your mother, or Danvers could ask her."

"She will probably have gone to Maria Campbell. She'll deny it anyway."

"Campbell, why do I know that name?" Jeremy queried. "How did they know your route, you could have come in by a different gate?"

"I presume we were followed, we have been before and it's not as if we were trying to avoid them."

"How could this be attributed to the Prince?" Portman asked.

"I'm not sure, it could be a personal vendetta now."

Kitty managed to say "We intimated we were going abroad after this weekend."

"Good grief, are you really, Kitty?" Jeremy looked surprised and concerned.

"No, of course not, it was to force them to act this weekend."

"Oh, thank goodness for that. I don't want to lose you again so soon."

Everyone sat quiet for a minute until Dinsdale asked "Why don't we just go through everything that has happened, from the beginning, to see if we can notice a pattern or a particular name that might give us an idea or a connection?"

"Could be helpful, I suppose."

"Shall I do it?" Kitty suggested. "After all I appear to be involved at every point except Jeremy's attack."

"That's true enough." Richard agreed. "We can add information as we go along."

"I'm sure there are details I don't know." Dinsdale said, Portman added "Nor me, I suspect."

Kitty started with her arrival in London, giving all the details she had given Richard on the journey from Cornwall. She detailed the change in the ton, the accusation of the Prince and the loss of her parasol. Her relief at the arrival of Jeremy prompted him to tell his findings in his London club. When she told of the present and the explosion the room was heavy with emotion.

"I hadn't realised just how dreadful it had been for you, Lady Kitty." Dinsdale was really shocked. When she told of her journey to the aunts for recovery, Jeremy sat with his head in his hands. The others were appalled. She told of the difficult journey home, the storm and their delay.

"You see it was hard to make you understand that nobody knew I was coming home. How could it be they expected me here before I arrived, late because of the storm? They must have been near me on the first or second day, then ridden ahead to arrange the present not knowing I was delayed."

"Good grief, they calculated when you expected to arrive. They must have been watching you the whole time." Portman was seriously adjusting his understanding of the situation at the time.

"Why did they not kill me then?"

"I don't know." Danvers pondered.

"Was it because you were not near the ton?" Dinsdale enquired.

"Everyone there knew the ton rumours about me, why should the ton not hear if I was killed?"

"It had to be a certain way, something that would enrage the ton, an attack by the Prince." Portman concluded.

"Today wasn't."

"That's true, but I think we made them desperate with talk of going abroad." Kitty concluded.

"It must be personal then." Richard looked down in sadness.

"It is now." Danvers decided.

They sat quiet for a moment. "Go on, Lady Kitty."

"Oh, yes, of course." The next part, the death of her sister was quite traumatic for both her and Jeremy. When they related what they had heard the ton ladies saying at the funeral Danvers was able to add what he had heard also.

"Why so vicious?" Dinsdale queried.

"That's what has troubled me for so long." Danvers mused.

Her escape to Cornwall was more light hearted with all the funny things that happened, what it felt like to be free of ladylike constraints. The proposition by the young lady in Moreton caused much hilarity and helped to lighten the atmosphere.

Richard could now tell them of this Miss Sinclair he found on his land, plus the débâcle of the book thrown over the cliff.

"You knew her, why didn't you say. All that subterfuge. I think we operatives are all finding it hard to be open with anyone outside the Foreign Office." Portman mused.

Richard grimaced "I was desperate when Danvers here decided to be the chosen husband."

"Serves you right, you could have said." Danvers had no sympathy.

"I couldn't risk it. What if she had declined me and I had given away where her secluded retreat was."

"I'm glad you succeeded." Danvers said.

"So am I." Jeremy added.

"So am I," Kitty whispered. Richard tightened his arm around her. "It was not a happy return with Jeremy so injured."

"Yes, your input please." Danvers requested.

"Well I know there is more to tell but I just can't remember."

"There were four again."

"Yes but roughnecks. There was that one voice, cultured, like I should recognise it."

"Any accent?" Danvers queried.

"Yes, that's a thought, it could have been Eton."

"Well that's something new."

"He said something before I blacked out."

"Someone kicked you in the head."

"I wouldn't know, I just remember the voice."

"Shall I go on?" Kitty wanted to finish this, she had to lead them to comprehend the information she had to impart.

Richard gave an account of his mother's attack and the mention of Maria Campbell. "They must have been watching for the coach to leave, so they knew we were going. It was because of her coach they stopped her, it had my crest on it. Oh, the crest! My God I can't believe I forgot."

"What?" Everyone sat up to attention.

"When I left you all to go back to Kitty I went over her route asking questions of all those everyone else had spoken to. One young hostler told me about her father who came looking but I knew the Duke had never left Wenton Hall. He described a coat of arms on a coach waiting down the road, not in the inn yard. A unicorn and a bear rampant it sounded like, I don't know if it means anything to any of you."

"It could," Danvers said" we can check it easily enough."

"Of course it could turn out to be another friend."

"That's true."

"And that's it until today."

Kitty jumped in. "Not really Richard, can I finish. I want to tell you about the balls and what it was like.

"The first ball was a nightmare for me. After Christmas it was somewhat better but being so early in the season there were few there, not a good feeling but men did ask me to dance, not all of them to oblige you, Danvers." She smiled towards him. "The young ones were the most interesting, they were obviously doing it for a wager, dancing with the notorious Countess! The Falkirks' was the most interesting. One young buck of about twenty waltzed with me. You remember, Richard."

"Oh yes, the youngest Hurst, Martin."

"That was a strange dance, he was aloof until I tried to put him at his ease and smiled up at him. I told Richard at the time, his eyes changed as if he had just woken up. He froze, stopped dancing and looked totally confused."

"I can imagine you having that effect on a great many young men." Danvers laughed.

"I remembered Martin Hurst coming to Eton as I was about to leave, a very serious young man, wanted to join the army." Jeremy looked troubled for some reason.

"I have seen those eyes since then."

"Where, at Gunter's?" Richard suggested.

"No, the fourth rider came at me ready to shoot, looked into my eyes and froze, just like at the Falkirks'; they were the same eyes, the same look. I fired, he didn't. That's the only reason I am still alive."

The atmosphere was suddenly alive with questions and anticipation.

"Martin Hurst, I don't know much about him." Dinsdale queried.

"He's the youngest of four, the sons of the Duke of Lyndford." Danvers informed him.

Jeremy began to describe them. "They all went to Eton, I knew them all. Lyndford Hall is only about half an hour away. I had problems all through Eton, they were so arrogant, even the masters hated them. The worst was the eldest, Stewart. The whole of my time there he never let me pass without calling me 'a snivelling little wimp', then he'd clout me across the head."

He stopped. "THE BASTARD! That's who it was, the voice. He said you always were a snivelling little wimp, there was a pain in my head and I blacked out."

Everyone held their breaths.

"The Hurst boys, four of them. How do we prove anything?"

"I think I hit one of their horses."

"At least one of them could be dead or badly wounded."

Kitty said "He rode a bay hunter, could someone pretend to want to buy it?" All eyes turned to her. "That would give us clarification it was them, but no real proof. Still no why."

"Do you know anything more about them, Jeremy?"

"Apart from them being arrogant bastards, you mean?"

"What are the rest of the family like, do you know any of them? I have to admit the Hursts have not appeared at any time in the investigation."

"The only other one I knew was younger than I was, a cousin or great nephew, he didn't have much affection for them."

"Was he a Hurst?"

"No, Jimmy Campbell, his father was a cousin of some sort. Jimmy used to laugh at them, they were so superior, he used to tell really tall tales about them."

Everyone was staring at him.

"Campbell?"

"Yes."

"Did he have a mother or aunt named Maria?"

"I don't know, I never heard him mention her, he hated being invited to Lyndford Hall."

"Tell us any of his tall tales if you can remember them, Jeremy" Danvers was leaning forward intently.

"They were only made up to make us laugh." He said.

"Please, Jeremy." Kitty also was giving him her whole attention.

"Well, the best one was that when the Duke had the library altered and refurbished they found a concealed compartment with old papers locked in a box. They were supposed to be proof that they were the rightful Kings of England, he even said he had been shown some but ......God NO!"

Danvers was the first to utter a whisper.

"We've got them. Now we know the why."

Kitty leaned into Richard's good shoulder and tears began to course down her cheeks.

"I for one need a drink." Richard said "Pull the chord will you Portman?"

For an agreed hour they silently ate and drank tea and something stronger for the men. They moved about the house and thought through their own emotions. After the hour they returned to Dinsdale's room to plan. Danvers took charge.

"Someone needs to go to London before they can cover up any evidence. You're the only one standing, Portman, it will have to be you."

"Of course, but who do I go to, magistrate, Foreign Office, Prime Minister?"

"I think we need a magistrate to approve this. Who can we trust?"

"The chief magistrate Wentworth is usually trustworthy. I know the Prime Minister trusts him." Dinsdale added.

"Then go there but …"

"What?"

Danvers finished his sentence. "This is too important. In this case I would say trust no one."

"We need the proof." Richard insisted "That idea of Kitty's sounded useful. Could we use someone to get into the estate? How about your cavalry officer, could he do it?"

"More than that, we need to enclose the whole estate, keep word from getting out." Danvers was thinking hard.

"Then we need a whole regiment, where would we get one now the war is over and they are disbanded?" Portman queried.

"Colonel Mathers, he has a whole regiment of regulars kicking their heels near Windsor. The Queen has not come down yet. If Phillips can find the evidence, have you a trustworthy man who could get there fast?"

"Yes sir. Lyndford is closer to Windsor than we are. Can he act on your word?"

"My word on behalf of the Crown, Portman. I have that power."

"I'll go to Major Phillips first to send him to visit 'Just passing, wondered if he wanted to sell.' I'll have him look for a wounded horse. Any distinguishing marks?"

"A chestnut hunter is all I can say. I was too busy defending myself. Go to the chief magistrate, see what he suggests, I'll send a letter with you.

Don't mention the possible use of the regiment, wouldn't want to give away tactics until we can be sure of him."

"No, sir. I'll call in a few operatives first to cover the situation."

"Right, let's get that letter written."

Danvers rose from his chair just as Dinsdale asked. "Is it safe, won't they have the roads watched?"

"Damn! Sorry Lady Kitty. Is there a safe way out?" He turned to Jeremy, both he and Kitty said "Oh yes." then laughed. Danvers raised his eyebrows.

"While I write this letter, you could just tell Portman if you would."

Kitty nodded to Jeremy and led Danvers down to the Duke's library to write his note. She found him paper, pen and ink then went to a small drawer and took out a quite substantial key, which she took back to Dinsdale's meeting room.

Jeremy was drawing a plan in his notebook with Portman watching avidly.

So much needed to be done. Another rider had to be alerted, horses readied and instruction given.

"I still don't know how to get out safely."

Danvers had the finished letter, Burns had been alerted to travel with Portman, the route had been described, just the safe exit remained. Kitty looked at Jeremy and produced the large key.

"When we were younger we used to sneak out to Molton village. It's nearer than Wenton but not on the main road. There are gates that we rarely open, they squeak dreadfully. Near them is a small wooden gate, big enough to lead a horse through. The lane leads to Molton. Jeremy has told you which road to take from the village. Just in case anyone is watching, don't use the main grass ride to the gates, go toward the gamekeeper's coverts. Once inside the trees a path leads towards the wall, you will only be able to go in single file. When you come to the wall turn left, across the gates and the carriage ride, about a hundred yards further on is the gate. Please lock it after you. Go left and you will come into Molton."

"Why the subterfuge, Lady Kitty, why not down the drive?"

"You would draw attention if you went straight down. Who knows, there may be spies watching. You need to appear to just be out for an evening ride."

"Richard have you been training your wife?"

Richard laughed. "I don't need to train her, she is capable of working it out on her own."

"Actually we always did that, to make sure we weren't seen. We were not supposed to go out by ourselves, Carina and I." She looked suddenly so sad. "Make this work Portman, for Carina." she whispered, turning her head into Richard's chest.

The two riders left before it would be thought too late to go out riding. There was still nearly an hour's light left. They needed to travel in daylight to avoid any unseen attackers. Following Kitty's plan, Portman even asked where the gamekeeper's coverts were in order to visit them. The path just inside the wood was a little overgrown with lack of use but not enough to cause them trouble. They inspected the somewhat rusted gates as they crossed the grass ride.

The access to the wooden gate was clear, possibly someone else from the estate had a key as it was clearly used. They had to dismount to lead the horses through, but no one appeared to be about. The small road was deserted and obviously little used. It had probably been put in as an alternative route to the estate. It seemed to go nowhere in particular. Portman thought he would not have liked to take a team of horses out onto it in the rain because it would have been extremely hazardous for a carriage.

They reached Molton, a small village with only a couple of shops. "We go right here. Then down to the coach road to London."

Portman and Burns reached London as dusk was turning to dark. Saturday night, there would be a ball for those of the ton, perhaps the Major too. The Chief Magistrate could wait until they were ready, even if it meant waiting for him to return from an evening out.

The major was indeed preparing for an evening out. He was surprised to see Portman and Burns.

"We have an assignment for you."

"Is this relating to the Pengarrons' problem?"

"Yes, I don't know how much you know?"

"Danvers told me enough. Was anyone injured?"

"Yes all three of the men, and the driver was killed."

"Pelman, he was a good driver, did they get any of them?"

"That's what we need to know.'A bay hunter is he willing to sell it?', that's the cover story. The rider was shot, possibly another, a large chestnut hunter was possibly shot. See if you can find out if they have the bay, is the chestnut wounded and how many of them are injured or dead."

"How many of them were there?"

"Four, we think brothers, they all rode hunters, big powerful horseflesh."

"Where?"

"Lyndford Hall, half an hour or so this side of Windsor."

"Lyndford, the Duke of Lyndford's place."

"Yes."

"Then we're talking about the Hurst brothers."

"Yes."

"Arrogant bastards, well the older ones are, the younger one isn't so bad."

"He may be dead, or at least injured, the Countess shot him at close range but she was using her left hand."

Major Phillips looked perplexed. "What was she doing with her right hand?"

"Driving the coach."

"What! With six cattle?"

Portman laughed. "You have no idea what the Countess is capable of, you would be amazed."

"But she's not very old."

"Only eighteen. Age does not always mean much, think of some of your men in the war."

"When pushed."

"Exactly."

"You can count on me. What time do I arrive?"

"No later than ten, we don't want to give them time to cover up. Take any news to Wenton Hall but be careful, we think they have spies all around it." He clapped the Major on the shoulder and left knowing he could rely on that part of the plan to work as it should.

The next task was to call in operatives. He needed cover. He visited a few of the slightly older men who were less likely to be on the town. Some were due at a ball but Binton was not married, not interested in the marriage mart and was growing bored with his quiet life.

"I need men around to keep an eye out."

"Do you need general watchers or Bow Street muscle?"

"I'm not exactly sure at the moment."

"Just men around to be useful. I can find two or three fairly easily, where do you want to meet?"

"Where is the best food around here, neither or us has had any dinner?"

"The Black Boar is pretty safe to eat in. I'll meet you there when I have the men."

Portman nodded. "We'll talk later."

Portman and Burns ate their hearty meal at the Black Boar. He would remember this place and thank Binton later.

They had finished eating and moved into the tap when Binton joined them.

"I see they all arrived." He looked around and nodded to a group of three drinking at a table close by. "I don't recognise any of them."

"They all know Danvers, I can vouch for them."

Portman moved to the window and spoke in a low voice. "I need a general watch kept on anyone leaving or arriving. No information is to leak out. This is vital to England and the Crown. I'm not expecting any problem but this is too important to take any risk. Watch the servants, if they try to leave, take them in to the office, but keep watching, if one leaves another my follow. You may have a quiet night or it may be extremely busy, stay alert." He turned to his companion. "Burns, stay with them. I'll take you with me Binton, you're more ton than I am."

"The Chief Magistrate, why do you mistrust him?"

"This is so important I dare not take any chances. You'll see when you hear what happened."

By the time all was in place it was nearing ten o'clock at night. He knocked on the door, waiting what seemed an age for the butler to open it.

"My lord is about to retire, is it necessary to see him tonight?"

"Yes, it is extremely important."

"Who shall I say is calling?"

"A messenger from Sir Peter Danvers."

When the butler returned to show them in he was somewhat friendlier.

"Come in, come in. How is Danvers these days?"

"Wounded at the moment."

"Wounded! Do we know who?"

"Yes, My lord. This is a complex case which he has been working on for some time. He believes we can bring them in but you should be informed, Sir."

"So, he will bring them in, will he, well why not wait until I see them in court."

"They won't be in court, My lord, they will be going to The Tower."

"The Tower, are we talking about this treason case?"

"Yes, we now have reason to believe Sir William was working for them."

"I am intrigued." So was Binton.

Portman outlined the problem that had arisen, the attacks and rumour-mongering against the Prince, the attack that morning which injured three and killed the driver. When he came to the possible evidence of treason, their belief in the Kingship of the family, they were both speechless.

"This is the greatest treason we have ever had to face. Can you prove it?"

"We are trying to get the evidence now. At least two are wounded or killed, the extent of the treason in the ton is not yet known but we know several ladies have been working on their behalf to whip up the ton against the crown. We believe them to be family members."

"Who is this arrogant family may I ask?"

"The Hursts, the Duke of Lyndford and his family."

"Lyndford, are you sure. Good God!" He had turned pale.

"We are ascertaining that they are the four men involved in the attack today. It is of course imperative they know nothing of what is happening or they could flee abroad. We need a warrant from you and any advice you can give."

"Yes, of course. Do you need it tonight?"

"Yes Sir. Danvers sent me for it."

"Very well." He rose, rather reluctantly to Portman's feeling, went into his study and emerged a short time later with the warrant in his hand.

"Thank you sir, goodnight."

They left a very quiet man behind them.

"Is it my imagination?" Binton started.

"No, I don't think it is."

"He was with us until you gave the name."

"Yes that was interesting. He took a long time writing the warrant. Let's check the men shall we."

"Burns are you alone?"

"Yes sir, for the moment. It took two of them to keep the footman from yelling out. When he is in custody they will be back."

"We'll stay with you until they do. You stay here, Binton, I'll double up at the front."

The night passed off quietly until the early hours of the morning. When they noted the footman had not returned a second footman was sent but was again taken to be temporarily detained. From both of them a message was retrieved. It warned Lyndford to leave England.

Chapter 31

Portman now had the warrant in his possession although he was very wary. This being the morning after the ton ball, more of Danvers' ton men would be available, which enabled him to maintain the cordon around Wentworth's house. They could not prevent him from going to his chambers on Monday, but this was still Sunday and they could keep the servants from taking messages. So he was not surprised when Burns arrived with another note from Wentworth. This one was addressed to Danvers at Wenton Hall.

He was currently with Williams, one of Danvers' close associates.

"Williams, Danvers took you from the military, what rank were you?"

"Major."

"I don't suppose you know Colonel Mathers."

"I have met him at the occasional soiree when military made up most of the gentlemen. We are not always acceptable unless we can prove our heritage, especially now there are so many half pay officers. Is there a problem, he seemed sound to me?"

"No problem, if everything goes according to the plan his regulars could be asked to surround Lyndford Hall tonight. I need a messenger, preferably one the Colonel knows and will believe."

"Fine, if you need me. He's down by Windsor I believe."

"Yes, a couple of hours away, or even less with a fast horse. I'll explain the details, no one is going to like this."

It took very little time for Williams to absorb the details. "I only hope he has enough men. We need the whole operation keeping very quiet, no servants to leave, no messengers. There could be any number of spies and roughnecks out there, they seem to have spread a very wide net of surveillance, so be careful. Good luck Williams."

"And you, I can take precautions. How will you report back to Danvers, can you get in easily?"

"I have the key to a small gate but Wentworth knows about that now, I may have to be inventive."

He moved towards the front door to leave and encountered Mrs Williams descending the stairs."

"Good morning ma'am. You are an early riser. I understood all ton ladies stayed above stairs until late."

She laughed "Not all ladies, sir. We were not out late last night, it was not a ball. We attended the theatre."

"Ah. Not to my taste, ma'am, all that playacting."

"It was exceedingly good, I'll have you know." She was still laughing. "The plot made it extremely believable."

Portman was by the front door. He shook Williams' hand. "Good day to you ma'am." She inclined her head in acknowledgement as she entered the parlour.

"Good luck." Both knew they needed it but in their previous capacity working mainly in France they had become accustomed to the dangers.

* * *

The house looked silent, the curtains closed. Major Phillips went to the front entrance but decided not to knock. Working his way around to the stables he found the grooms quiet and closeted in the tack room. He tied his horse outside and walked silently along the stable block. A large bay hunter stamping his hooves restlessly. A whole stable of hunters, no chestnut. He came to the only activity which was in the end stable.

"Is it bad enough to put him down? Lord Robert will be devastated, he is so fond of him."

Phillips moved to a position where he could see into the stable from a safe distance. A chestnut, wounded.

"It's hard to say, we took the bullet out but it was quite deep." The groom was saying.

Phillips moved quietly away and returned to his horse. Pretending to have just arrived he called "Hello my man, anyone here?"

A groom appeared from the tack room. "What yer want?"

"That's no way to speak to a gentleman, lad, I'm here to see Lord Martin."

The young man stared up at him. "He's dead." was all he said.

"Good grief, how?"

"He was shot, so were Lord Phillip."

"Are they both dead?" he nodded. "No wonder the house is so quiet."

"Who are you?" The head groom came purposefully towards him. "What do you want?"

"Major Phillips. I came to see Martin, Lord Martin, he has a bay hunter I fancied and since I was passing I wondered if I might persuade him into selling it."

"A friend of Lord Martin are you?"

"An acquaintance, yes. Has he really been shot dead?" He put his head into his hands to pretend shock.

"I don't know if they'll want you up at the house."

"I wouldn't dream of intruding at a time like this. I'll just be on my way." and seemingly to himself "Martin, good heavens."

He rode his horse at a slow walk down the drive. So long as he could make it to Wenton Hall safely, that was the problem. From Lyndford to Wenton was only about thirty minutes ride, but not the way Major Phillips rode. He took any cover he could find, walked his horse through woods, waited behind hedges and went in the wrong directions when he became aware of anyone near. It must have been the most tortuous route ever. When he came close to Wenton village he rode around it until he came to the wall further along, which he then followed closely to avoid being seen. Eventually he reached the gates. Once inside two men with shotguns confronted him.

"Major Phillips to see Danvers." he said tersely. He was waved on but they watched him carefully until he reached the front door.

* * *

Portman went to his rooms. He was tired, no, more weary, having had no sleep. He took a cold wash and went to look out a set of clothes. What persona was he to take, roughneck, working man or gentleman, which would be safest? He lay on the bed to rest while he decided. He was in no danger of falling asleep, his heart was beating too fast, there was too much to do. Had the enemy enough trained men to be a problem to him? How would he best get through enemy lines? Either undercover of darkness, not an option, or walk through casually. He recalled Mrs Williams' description of the players being believable because of the plot.

Half an hour later he took his breakfast while his horse was being saddled. Then the dutiful grandson, hat covering his face but very recognisable with his pale breeches, deep red coat and bright blue waistcoat set out for Wenton Hall to escort his grandmother and elderly aunts home to London.

The nearer he was to the Hall the slower he rode. He walked his horse through Wenton Village doffing his hat and talking with everyone he met. He encountered the vicar and his wife leaving the church after the morning service. He seemed to have timed it exactly right so that everyone took note of him.

"Good morning, vicar, a good turn out for the service, I hope."

"The usual, not from the Hall though, that is not normal for them. I believe there was a dance last night."

"Indeed I am come to escort my elderly relatives home. They do so enjoy an outing like this, even at their age." He doffed his hat and rode on. Behind him he heard the vicar's wife remark "What an attentive young man, if only all the young cared for their elderly relatives." The hedge blocked out the rest of her praise. He smiled to himself.

On the bridge he stopped to contemplate the gentle flow of the water carrying a little detritus, then a slow walk around the field to the gateway. Everyone should have taken note of him now. He passed through the gates and was ordered to one side.

"Who are you?"

"Jones, am I so unrecognisable?"

"Goodness Mr Portman, I didn't know you dressed like that."

"No, Jones, that is the whole point. I'm glad to see you are so efficient."

Jones beamed "Thank you sir."

He went down the long drive at a slow trot, a gentleman at his ease, so much so that when he arrived at the front door the groom was already there to take his horse.

"Oh it's you Mr Portman!"

"Indeed."

"I thought it was some toff."

"That's the idea." He slapped the lad on his back and went to the already open front door. "Good day to you Wilson. Do you think there will be any lunch left, I am starving hungry?"

"Welcome, sir. I am sure there is enough to feed even you. I know you are eagerly awaited.

"Did you get the warrant?"

"Yes."

"What happened?"

"I put Phillips on to searching out the bay the way Lady Kitty suggested. He should have been here by now."

"He arrived an hour ago. Everything as we suspected. Two dead, even the chestnut with the bullet in him. Go on."

"Binton pulled in some men to watch while we went into Wentworth's house. He was with us all the way until I mentioned the name, then he visibly paled. He gave me the warrant but we've taken two footmen so far with notes to Lyndford telling him to leave England. He sent this message this morning with another footman. At this rate he'll have no staff left, the office is getting quite full." He handed the note to Danvers.

"You were right to be cautious. We're working so high in the ton it is going to be difficult to control. The sooner we have them in The Tower the better. They can argue from there." Danvers sat back. "We need to get a request to Colonel Mathers."

"I sent Williams to alert him, give him some details, apparently he knows the Colonel. It just needs instructions from you and he should be ready to move."

"Well done, Portman, that was excellent thinking. And Williams there as well."

"I'll get the message written. They'll have to be restrained and heavily guarded."

"They won't like it."

"Who said they would?"

Jeremy added "I didn't like it. I still don't but I have to live with this because of them."

A quiet voice said "Carina and Aleen didn't like it at all."

"The question is, are we under threat here, if so how do we get out?" Richard was being practical.

"We need another magistrate, more than one in the circumstances. Perhaps a meeting with the Prime Minister."

"Good thinking Danvers, I wish I could go with you."

"Poor Dinsdale." Kitty patted his good leg. "We'll tell you all about it."

"I have a plan in hand as it happens." Portman began, then laughed. "You probably won't like this either. It was at Williams' house, when his wife talked about the theatre and being plausible." Danvers lifted his eyebrows. "I came very slowly and talked to everyone in the village including the vicar and his wife. Told everyone I was coming to take my elderly relatives home from the party."

"Is that why you're dressed like a bunch of flowers?"

"I had to be noticed, but not by my face."

"You're dressed up like in a play. So you can get out but how can we?"

"Well, they are expecting me to escort my elderly lady relatives."

Kitty nearly fell off the chaise with laughing. "Where do we find clothes to fit these hulking men?" Richard looked askance at her.

"How dressed do we need to be?"

"They decided they only needed to fool anyone watching from a distance, so no detail was needed, although in the coach they would need shawls and bonnets.

"What does the note from Wentworth say, sir?" Dinsdale was not involved in the idea of dressing up.

"Oh this, yes. It's from Wentworth. 'Lord Jeremy and Lady Katherine are in danger and need to hide. I have arranged a carriage at Molton gate tonight at ten o'clock. Wentworth.'

"They must have sent news out somehow, how did Wentworth know especially about that gate?"

"That's my fault, I mentioned the back route." Portman noted ruefully. "He asked how I got out."

"The Tower could be quite full by the time we've finished. Obviously you two aren't going, we need both of you in London. We'll send a couple of decoys. Don't want to warn them off before we know Mathers has them." Danvers was thinking out loud.

"More clothes to find? How soon do we need to leave?"

"In an hour I would say. No later than five o'clock."

The jobs were allocated. The orders for Colonel Mathers were to secure the estate exits, then arrest those inside. He was warned to watch out for attacks but mainly about the importance of guarding the library. They must not be in a position to destroy or hide any documents. Clothes for the elderly ladies, especially bonnets plus clothes for those who would play

Kitty and Jeremy. A watch needed to be set on the back road to allow them to follow. "We could do with another battalion." Danvers moaned.

"We have men surrounding Wenton Hall, use some of them." Portman suggested.

"How many are there?"

"We sent eight in the beginning but they have trained the Duke's men."

"We could use them, they know the area. We can also ask Mathers for a few to be sent straight here."

Kitty was having fun with Binny. They searched the attics for large skirts, jackets, shawls, anything big enough. They found a couple of dresses from a very pregnant ancestor. Shawls they could find, bonnets proved a little harder, although when they realised they could be wildly out of fashion it became easier. Jeremy was a problem. How was he to reach the coach without his crutches and how was someone to impersonate him without crutches? The compromise was that they each had one. Jeremy's could be loaded in the stables and he would be supported into the coach like an ailing old lady. Jeremy was not impressed at being likened to an old lady. Fletcher offered himself to play Lady Kitty, being tiny enough for one of her shapeless Cornwall dresses with her grey cloak. A wig from a previous era covered his fair hair. Wigglesworth was a similar size and colouring to Jeremy and was given tutoring on how to walk with one of his crutches.

It was a difficult and busy hour. When they were all dressed, armed and ready, the staff, Binny in particular, were in fits of laughter. Then someone realised Kitty looked wrong. She was too small, she showed up their size.

"Oh, dear. This is a disaster, I never thought of this." Binny took her in hand. "No matter Lady Kitty." turning to the men she said "Give me about ten minutes." It was just a little over when Kitty came down the stairs.

"Don't you dare laugh." she warned. She wore the outfit of a young girl with a shorter skirt, stockings and child's soft white cotton bonnet with flowers on it. She also carried a doll. Richard had to turn away before he burst.

Climbing into the carriage took some time, as it would do with elderly ladies. The problem was Jeremy. From a distance he would look like a rather inebriated old lady. When they were settled William drove the black unmarked carriage at a sedate speed, Portman accompanying them on horseback. They faced inwards as they traversed the narrow country roads. Anyone seeing their faces would be close enough to know they were men. It was a slow and tension filled drive as Portman chatted with the locals, still playing the part of the attentive young man.

Once on the coaching road Portman left them to ride ahead to the Prime Minister's house with some trepidation. What if he was not at home, what if everything had gone wrong, if he didn't believe them? It was a relief to find not only was he at home, he was surrounded by magistrates who had been harassed by ladies all afternoon.

"Portman is this important, you can see I am besieged at the moment..."
"I have come from Danvers, they are on their way. We can sort this problem you have." He bowed to the others. "If you will wait about half an hour for the coach to arrive we will answer all your questions."
"Why a coach?"
"I am the only one uninjured, sir. None of the others can ride." Their interest was held. The prime minister's butler brought drinks to keep them occupied.

The coach arrived in a flurry of anticipation in the house. The occupants disgorged to the incredulity of all including the staff. Two large elderly ladies, one crippled old lady being helped in, plus one young girl. Kitty had to help as none of them had two good arms. She removed Danvers' bonnet and shawl and untied his skirts.
They stared at them. "Good afternoon gentlemen. If you can just wait while we disrobe. I can't think how ladies cope tied up in all this material." Kitty had almost finished Richard. She took the two slings from her bag and insisted they put them on.

"Excuse me," Jeremy began.
"I'm coming."
Jeremy was sat on a chair while she removed his hat and shawl. Undoing his dress, she motioned to the other two to lift him while she removed it onto the floor around his feet. "What a to-do, I'm glad I'm a man, that's all I can say."

Danvers began to tell how the Prime Minister had called him in on behalf of the Prince. Kitty then began the story, telling of the ton, the presents, the deaths. Danvers explained his dealings with the Prince and how they had avoided telling him details until they isolated Sir William Forster as the viper in the palace. Richard told of those who were trying to find Kitty, of the young hostler who remembered the coach purporting to contain her father. "A rampant unicorn and possibly a bear." One magistrate was white, "That's Forster's arms. I thought you had made an error, I was most upset for Sir William."

The return to the ton ball and what had transpired made everyone angry.

Richard told of his argument with his mother at Christmas and her mention of Maria Campbell. Finbury interrupted. "She came to see me a short while ago, she wanted Wenton arrested for murder."

"We are coming to that. My mother left just before us, her carriage has my coat of arms. She was stopped by well spoken highwaymen who declared her too old to be the Countess and let her go." The Prime Minister laughed. "Oh, Lady Amelia would not appreciate that." Richard had to grin. "I don't believe she did."

Danvers introduced the dealings with Lord and Lady Stones, the wedding cake and her subsequent confession that it was Sir William, a lifelong friend, who instigated both their presence and the cake.

Everyone joined in the final journey, from the laying of the trap to the attack by four men, kerchiefs over their faces, riding fast hunters. They each told of the fight as they saw it, the injury to Danvers, the death of Pelman the driver. Danvers thought he had hit if not the man then at least his chestnut hunter. Richard told of Kitty's heroism in driving the coach home but left her to describe the shooting of the man on the big bay hunter.

"Have you no idea, no proof who they were?"

"Kitty was sure, tell them, my love." He was very solicitous to his wife.

It was easy enough to retell the ballroom meeting but she was quite overcome when talking of killing a man while he was frozen with shock. She knew who he was.

"Who was he?" One of the magistrates was enthralled.

"His name was Martin Hurst."

Silence held for a short minute until one said "Are you sure Lady Katherine?"

Danvers stepped forward to take over.

"We have Colonel Mathers' regiment containing Lyndford Hall. I have two notes here. One from Major Phillips, he called on our behalf and confirmed a bay hunter, a chestnut injured by a bullet and two sons dead, Martin and Phillip. I also have other evidence plus a disturbing occurrence."

Portman told of his visit to Chief Magistrate Wentworth for a warrant, the subsequent notes to Lyndford and then handed the Prime Minister the last note addressed to Wenton Hall.

"Why have they done all this? It makes no sense."

"Perhaps Lord Jeremy can help here." He went to stand.

"No, stay sat young man. I know, but perhaps you need to enlighten my colleagues about what happened." With a nod Jeremy started on the harrowing tale of the attack on him, the voice he could remember but not what we said. "Until Kitty mentioned the Hursts. They were the bane of my life at Eton, Stewart the oldest particularly. He used to say I was a snivelling little wimp and clout me around the head. Then I remembered the voice and what he had said 'you always were a snivelling little wimp' then a pain in the head and I lost consciousness." Someone brought Jeremy a drink to help his distress.

"They asked me about the family and I remembered Jimmy Campbell, a relation of some sort. We thought he made up the tale about them having found papers which proved they were the rightful Kings of England."

"What?" Two of the magistrates were on their feet.

"We have had no chance yet to search." Danvers said. "It might be helpful if we found Jimmy Campbell before they do. It could save us dismantling half the house. We sent Colonel Mathers and the regiment to guard it."

"Are the family still there?"

"No, hopefully in The Tower."

"We need to ascertain they are safely there before we go to search."

"You intend to accompany us, sir."

"Indeed I do. The more witnesses the better to verify the facts, especially ones of good standing.

It is not easy, they discovered, to find the whereabouts of a young man without anyone realising. Discussions were held that evening to decide who could ask around. Richard, being the people finder, was looked to for inspiration. As Jeremy was the only one who knew Jimmy, he was the most obvious, but that was impossible, not just for his mobility but as a person known by the ton to be involved. Others had to be used, those known by Jeremy who were themselves at Eton and also knew Jimmy. Jeremy could not even remember where he lived.

Since his visit to Whites, Jeremy had seen none of his friends so it was with some trepidation that Jeremy accompanied by Richard and Danvers arrived at Phillip Moreton's bachelor flat late that evening. Moreton's man assured him he was indeed at home preparing to visit friends.

"I will inform him you are here, My lord." he intoned.

"Don't leave him on the doorstep, can't you see his condition!" Richard was quite angry.

"I'll wait in the carriage." Jeremy began.

"Not after the effort to remove you from it."

Turning to the manservant Danvers said. "Perhaps you should also tell him Sir Peter Danvers from the Foreign Office is with him." Richard and Danvers propelled Jeremy forward backing the man further into the hallway. He opened a door.

"If you would like to wait in here."

He shot off at a great rate to find his master. Phillip Moreton strolled nonchalantly into the room having obviously come down the stairs with all speed.

"Wellmore, what brings you here?" he began. "Good God man, what happened!" The concern for his friend was obvious. Danvers stood and held out his hand.

"Danvers from the Foreign Office." Moreton looked at him in surprise but took his hand. "What is this about?" Danvers was the one that answered.

"I am investigating a very serious case which has been the cause of physical injury to Lord Wellmore, his sister Lady Katherine and the death of his youngest sister. Others have died and as you can see Lord Trevane and I are both casualties. We need your help in tracing someone."

He looked from one to the other stunned. "Why me?"

Jeremy answered "Because I can't do it. We need to know where to find Jimmy Campbell."

"What, Crazy Jimmy from Eton?"

Everyone looked at him expectantly. "How am I supposed to do that?"

"Go gambling, Moreton, ask about Jimmy but don't make it seem a definite request. No one must be alerted."

Danvers stepped in. "We need information from him quickly. If we ask we could put him in danger. That's why you must be surreptitious in your enquiry."

He looked perplexed. Richard stood and eased his shoulder. "You don't have to go, we just need to know his whereabouts."

"Is there only me, do I have to go alone, I was on the way to meet Carstairs?"

"What a good idea." Jeremy said. "You could be having a discussion about Eton and mention him, ask around those near, you know, how we used to find out where the boys were going."

"Oh, nothing more than that, I see. Is it really that important?"

"Look at me, Moreton. They did this to me, we need evidence."

"And you think Campbell can give it."

"We would not be asking if we didn't." Richard and Danvers were both standing, they looked impressive in the small room, no, intimidating.

"Believe me, Moreton, this is bigger than you could imagine. Lives depend on it."

"Well I'll try but I'm no spy. I'll speak to Carstairs when I get to him." Jeremy went to struggle to his feet to leave. "Thanks old friend." Moreton was visibly moved. Danvers grinned. "You should have seen him at the start. The doctor said he wouldn't live, when he did, that he would never walk again. I'd lay a wager on Jeremy and win." They moved slowly to the door. "Send a note to me at the Foreign Office if you find out anything." With a nod he went to leave.

Richard held out his hand "We were never introduced. Richard Trevane, Earl of Pengarron married to Jeremy's sister Kitty."

Moreton watched them slowly assist his friend out into the coach. He could hear Jeremy remarking about sleeping tonight.

What were the Foreign Office doing investigating, they dealt with the war and France didn't they? The war was over so what were they investigating? Spying?

Bloody Hell! What had he got himself involved in?

Carstairs thought it a lark. Not having seen Jeremy or felt the power of those with him he was inclined to treat it as a game. It was only when he told him it was for the Foreign Office and they could put Campbell in danger if they were not careful that he began to comprehend.

They toured the gaming hells, trying not to become too inebriated. In the end they struck lucky when they met some other Etonians they knew. They started their conversation again. "We were talking about Jimmy Campbell, do you remember crazy Jimmy with his tales? I wonder what became of him, he's never been around town?" Richards who was from a northern family replied "Crazy Jimmy, didn't you know, his family refused to keep him for some reason. He became a lawyer in York. He never did like his cousins, they were an obnoxious lot. Can you remember the trouble Wellmore had with them?" Moreton and Carstairs looked at each other.

On the way home in the hackney they merely said "Jimmy Campbell, the Hurst brothers, Jeremy Wellmore beaten up. Leave it to them, we did our bit."

Chapter 32

Wigglesworth and Fletcher, the stand-in Kitty and Jeremy, were taken to the gate on a pony and trap fairly early before the coach arrived. Men were stationed in the bushes at both ends of the small road. Someone was near the gate to take a message to either end as needed. The pony cart moved away a safe distance, the gate unlocked.

As the small carriage pulled up they opened the gate and 'Jeremy' spoke to the driver. "Where are we going?" He was quite a rough fellow. "Somewhere nobody will find you."

The carriage set off northwards away from London. The messenger took word to Molton which way they had gone, all the horsemen now following in pursuit. There seemed to be no guard with the carriage, only the driver. They travelled until the early hours of the morning and while not moving fast, the horses were well beyond time for rest or to be changed. Wigglesworth was growing more concerned as the time went on.

"Why are we still on country roads, with no guard or cover? We could be picked off in an ambush. If a highwayman killed the driver we have only ourselves to rely on for protection." he whispered. Fletcher agreed. "I don't think we are going anywhere except into a trap. Keep your guns to hand, I expect us to need them very soon."

The following men were perplexed. "Where are they going?" "I'm not sure but we came this way an hour ago. If I'm right he's taking a circular route to waste time. I'll station men around to see if it happens again. It will spare our horses if we can wait them out at strategic points."

By the fourth time around the coach horses were tired and all road turnings were covered. Eventually the driver turned them south towards the coaching road. It was just showing a glimmer of light when a group of highwaymen stopped the coach.

"Everything going to plan?"

"Yes."

"We'll deal with them, you take yourself off."

"Right, thanks." Inside the coach Wigglesworth and Fletcher took a window each. Someone opened the door and ordered "OUT!" Wigglesworth fired. "Get her out!" a man at the other door.

Fletcher fired. How many of them are there, he wondered. Hooves pounding down the road, could be the driver escaping. Then more shots, another man at the door, Wigglesworth fired his second pistol.

All was quiet until a voice said "You all right in there Fletcher?"

"Major Phillips, is that you?"

"You were hard to keep track of in the end." He came to the door.

"We're not injured, just tired of being bounced around in this awful box of a carriage."

Phillips laughed. "It looks a little basic, it could be hired."

"Should we take it back with us?"

"I would think so."

At which point a voice inside the carriage said "Well if you think I'm riding a horse dressed like this you can think again."

Wigglesworth laughed. "Shall I drive your carriage for you, my lady?" He climbed up onto the box. Where does this road lead?"

"Not sure, let's go and see shall we?"

It led to Lyndford Hall.

"Halt."

"Major Phillips to see Colonel Mathers."

A voice whispered "Who's on duty? Go and get backup." The sound of quiet footfall running through the grass.

They waited until several armed soldiers appeared looking serious. "Military, thank God for that. Is Colonel Mathers here?"

"Who's in the carriage?"

"Lady Katherine Wellmore and the driver is Lord Jeremy Wellmore." The officer in charge took them on foot to a hut and some tents in a clearing.

"I'm sorry to wake you sir. We have more of them." A rumpled and sleepy Colonel Mathers came out of the tent and glared at them. The major stepped forward. "Major Phillips, sir, working with Sir Peter Danvers on a decoy mission." Mathers looked around at them. "Is the one before one of yours?"

"No sir, he was driving the coach and was part of the abduction."

"Major, it's early, barely light, we've had a very busy night and I've had no breakfast, can I just have a simple explanation?" He noticed Fletcher. "Who is she?"

"Fletcher, sir." he said removing his wig "decoy for Lady Katherine.," He looked at Wigglesworth. "You are?" "Wigglesworth, decoy for Lord Jeremy."

Phillips asked "You mentioned a previous rider, sir, has he been held? He was driving the coach to an ambush. We shot the rest, he escaped."

"Yes, we have him."

"Good, Danvers will need him. We've been up all night sir, is there somewhere we can rest? We'll stay until full light, than return to Wenton Hall."

"Jones, get the coach under cover."

"Are the family in custody, Colonel?"

"Oh yes. No trouble. It helped being the middle of the night, they were all drunk. I can't blame them with two of them dead. We took them in their own coach with a dozen men riding shot. Everything as requested. Do you have any idea how long we may be here?"

"No idea at all. They're all in London at present."

"You're falling asleep on your feet, man. Come and rest." The Major went willingly into the tent and lay on the bed provided.

"Jones, get him a drink and some breakfast."

He never ate it; when it arrived the Major was fast asleep.

Richard and Jeremy were home later than they expected but Richard knew Kitty would not retire without him even with Burns and Portman in the house guarding her.

Nobody could have slept through the noise of Jeremy falling in the front door.

"I can't cope with only one crutch, and you're not much help with only one arm."

"You need a drink."

"I need a whole bottle."

Portman came to give a hand. "The library?"

"Lady Kitty is in the parlour."

They both said "The parlour."

Kitty blinked at them. "I'm sorry, I fell asleep. I seem so tired these days."

"It's been a very busy day, my love."

"I second that." came from Jeremy.

Whilst they tried to discuss the evening's events it was clear everyone was wilting. "Are you two staying here? Binny did ask Mrs Brent to organise it."

"Good, tomorrow could be busy for all of us." He leaned into the hallway. "Elliott, can we have some footmen to escort Lord Wellmore upstairs?"

"We have our own house, you know."

"Who's there to look after you?"

"Point taken." A sleepy Jeremy was assisted upstairs, while Mrs Brent showed the others their rooms. Richard lifted a tired Kitty against him with his good arm and carried her to bed.

Monday morning came too soon for most of them. Danvers had several things to do, one of the first was to visit the Prime Minister's office.

"I have sent a note to Wentworth asking him to see me at some urgency. I hope he is not unwise enough to run."

"I've had a word with my men on watch, they will stick with him, he won't get far."

"Coffee?"

"Please. After last night there's so much to do and little enough time. I've sent for a report on the decoy situation. I hope there were no more fatalities. I have confirmation the Hursts arrived at The Tower and are safely incarcerated. I also sent a messenger to Colonel Mathers stressing the importance of protecting the library. You never know which servants are loyal and well informed."

About an hour later Danvers sat hidden in a side room while the Prime Minister held a prearranged meeting. When Wentworth arrived he stayed in Willoughby's office. "Do you know what this is about?" Wentworth was definitely jumpy. He must have known the footmen who carried messages had not returned.

Eventually the Prime Minister managed to curtail the long winded discussions he was embroiled in and called Wentworth into his office. "Willoughby, fetch Danvers will you?"

"Now Wentworth, there is a dangerous treason being perpetrated."

"So I understand, I issued the arrest warrant, you know."

"Indeed I do. Come in Danvers." He came and stood close to them both, just a little intimidating. "I understand you sent this note to Danvers."

He looked puzzled. "Yes, I was very worried for them." Danvers asked "Where were you taking them?"

"I have a house in the north I thought would be safe."

Danvers leaned forward. "What about these notes?" He held out an open note. Wentworth put his head in his hands. "I didn't know what to do. We've been such good friends all our lives."

"You do realise the seriousness of this." The Prime Minister asked. Wentworth nodded. "I'm finished."

"That depends on what happened to the coach you sent."

"I asked one of my men to organise it."

"I'm afraid we will have to put you under arrest until we know what happened." Wentworth said nothing, he stared at the floor. His whole life's work ruined by one night's madness in defence of a friend.

When Danvers returned to his office he found a message from Moreton. He needed to speak to Richard and Jeremy so Pengarron House was his destination, where he also found all his missing men, eating a late breakfast.

"Have you eaten? Don't stand there salivating, come and eat." Danvers needed no further invitation.

"We've pulled in Wentworth and I've sent to Wenton Hall to hear what happened last night."

"Last night at Lyndford Hall?"

"No, they are now in rather secure accommodation, I meant the decoys, He says he sent them to a house up north. It must have been a busy road, we had enough men tailing them. Portman, how are you feeling?"

"Very well, sir. A good night's sleep can do wonders."

"Good, fancy a trip to York?"

"York, what's at York?"

"A lawyer by the name of Jimmy Campbell."

"They found him!" Jeremy was elated.

"I only hope no-one else gets to him first." Danvers looked serious.

"When do you want me to start?"

"As soon as you can, but go home and change those awful clothes first."

"Yes sir."

Kitty joined Richard in the parlour. "You slept late, my sweet." She looked around. "Where is everyone, have they all left?"

"No, Jeremy, Burns and Danvers are in the library, Portman on his way to York." He explained the latest developments. "Are you sure you are well, you look pale?"

"I think all the excitement has upset my stomach again, I do seem to be suffering at the moment. I hope I don't turn into one of those over sensitive ladies who have the vapours." Richard laughed and pulled her close.

"I shall be glad when this shoulder heals and I can put both arms around you again." Kitty sighed "I miss that, especially at night." She snuggled up to him. "Then we will have to be a little more adventurous." he nuzzled his face into her neck. "What do you mean?" "You'll find out tonight."

Burns interrupted by sticking his head in through the doorway to bid them goodbye. "Not staying for lunch, Burns?"

"No, sir. Work to do." With that he left in a hurry.

"I shall not be sad to have a quiet day." She was clinging to his hand. "I am not leaving you for a moment today. You look quite frail."

Jeremy was clunking down the corridor, a footman helping. "It must be lunchtime soon."

"After that late breakfast?"

"You forget, I missed dinner last night."

"So did we all."

Danvers followed him in. "I really should leave."

"Before lunch? You missed dinner as well yesterday."

The four of them sat down to a hearty lunch, the cook was in her element having all these energetic young men to feed. Kitty ate little. As they were leaving the dining room the front door knocker was applied with force. The men stood by as Elliot opened the door but the caller was Major Phillips. "Come in Major. Elliot, see if cook can find some lunch for the Major, we must have left something he can have."

Danvers strode forward and shook his hand. "I take it you have news for me. Come into the library." He turned to the others. "I'll bring him in when he's eaten." They disappeared down the corridor to the library. There were other arrivals behind him, Binny, Smithson, Ferguson and the luggage.

"Binny, I'm so pleased to have you here." Kitty said "Ferguson, oh, that is so welcome." In his hand he was holding Jeremy's second crutch.

The hullabaloo now over the three of them sat peacefully in the parlour. "Your Smithson brought me clothes, I'm afraid you'll have to share him for a few days."

Richard did not mind in the least. "An Earl and a Ducal Heir, Smithson will be in heaven. Be prepared to be turned out like a mannequin."

Danvers brought Major Phillips into the parlour to tell the news.

"What a relief!" was Kitty's reaction. Perhaps her insides would calm down now.

"I think my wife has been concerned for Wigglesworth and Fletcher. You say an ambush that led back to Lyndford."

"Yes, either our Chief Magistrate is in it up to his ears or he has men on his staff who are. I need to deal with this now, so I'll take my leave." He nodded to everyone. "Lady Kitty." He gave a bow.

Major Phillips added "I shall be off home, I have a message from Williams for his wife, so if you will please excuse me."

"And then there were only three of us left." Jeremy observed, leaning back in his chair.

The peace did not last long. The butler announced "A Miss Weston to see you, my lady, are you at home?" Behind him a voice said "Of course she is, don't be a nodcock, just let me in." She glanced around to locate Kitty, then strode across the room and hugged her so hard Kitty had to protest. Richard rose to greet her while Jeremy struggled out of his chair. Emily beamed at Kitty, beamed at Richard then turned to Jeremy and her face dropped. "Oh you poor dear, are you injured?" Jeremy was staring at this bundle of life, his eyes wide with amusement and admiration. "Do sit down again. Now Kitty, they said you were dead. I called yesterday but your butler could tell me nothing. I'm so relieved." She turned to Richard. "Oh, you are injured too."

"Come and sit with me, Emily." Kitty drew her down onto the chaise so the men could sit.

"Emily?" Jeremy raised his eyebrows at Richard. "Emily Weston of Norwich." Richard said pointedly.

"Oh! Kitty's friend she didn't visit." Richard nodded.

Emily was chatting to Kitty about the upcoming wedding of her cousin Robert Fitzwilliam to Miss Jane Arbuthnot. Kitty was interested but tired.

"Kitty are you not well? You look pale and tired. Are you increasing?"

Kitty looked at her bewildered. Emily looked at the others guiltily. Jeremy looked intrigued, Richard looked enlightened, a grin gradually infusing his face. Richard leaned forward. "Thank you, Miss Weston, I will explain it to my wife later." His eyes smiled at her and she lost her guilty look.

Jeremy broke in "Could I perhaps be introduced?"

"Oh, I'm sorry Jeremy, I forgot you had not met. Miss Emily Weston, this is my brother, Lord Jeremy Wellmore." Jeremy went to rise again. "Oh no, my lord, please don't get up."

"It's good for him." Richard remarked. "He sits down for too long."

"I'm sure that is not the case, my lord."

"Oh for goodness sake Miss Weston, stop my lording me and call me Jeremy. So you are the friend who came to help Kitty after the Tunstalls' fiasco. I am grateful to you."

Emily looked embarrassed. "What happened to you, or were you born like this?"

Jeremy smiled at her. "Do you always go straight to the point?"

"I suppose I do. My mama despairs of me. She says I will never catch a husband that way."

"Catch! Should I beware of you Miss Weston?"

"No, of course not. My mama just thinks that way."

Kitty remembered the unnamed young man she had been pursuing last summer. "Emily, the house party last summer. Did the young man not come up to scratch?"

Emily sat up regally. "He did, but I refused him. He was not what he seemed, they seldom are it appears."

Jeremy was enjoying this young woman's chatter. "Are you damming all men then? Are we considered all the same?"

She looked confused. "No, of course not."

"But he was what, precisely?" Richard wanted her to finish explaining.

"He was attentive, wanting to be with me all the time, until the house party. All he talked of there was hunting, riding, gambling, and I accidentally heard him telling his friends he had no intention of changing after his marriage. He intended to keep his mistress, his wife was to run his house and provide children, nothing more."

"So you gave him his congé."

Jeremy's mouth was having a hard time from grinning.

"I did indeed. He's not the only one I refused. Papa was not angry but mama was. She thinks any wealthy man will do."

"And you don't?"

"Of course not. We are not a wealthy family, why should I expect to marry for money. I would rather care for a less wealthy husband than marry a rich one I cared nothing for." Kitty pulled the chord for tea.

"I admire your determination, Miss Weston."

"Emily. If I am to call you Jeremy, my lord, you must call me Emily. You never answered my question."

He looked bewildered. "Which one?" She pointed to his sticks. "Ah, this is due to the same people who tried to kill Kitty. They thought I knew where she was so they beat me senseless. It was a few months ago, I'm quite healed now."

She looked at him with round eyes. "If this is healed, what were you like at the beginning?"

Jeremy looked embarrassed, so Richard answered. "A mess. They broke near every bone in his body, kicked him unconscious and left him for dead."

Emily looked at Kitty a little perplexed. "Why didn't you tell me this?"

"It was a while before I knew and it was too painful. If I wrote it down it would be more real than I could cope with."

Emily went to Kitty and put a hand on her arm to comfort her, Kitty's head was low and she was on the verge of tears.

The tea tray arrived and the tension was broken.

"Shall I pour?" Emily took over efficiently handing round the cups. Jeremy had difficulty balancing his cup and saucer in his left hand. She looked pointedly at his fingers.

"They broke them." He said.

"Oh no! Do they work at all? Do you do exercises?"

"I am practising the cello."

"Oh, how lovely. I play the piano a little but music was never a priority in our house."

"What is a priority, Miss Emily?"

"I help papa with the estate books and mama with the housekeeping. I have a young brother and sister who need attention, their governess is not very efficient, but we are not a family to attract the best servants. We have to make do with those we can employ."

"Why would good servants not wish to work for you?"

"It's the cold wind and the damp, especially in the winter." She became thoughtful.

"You would rather not stay in Norwich when you marry."

"I hope not. It depends if papa decides to give me to a neighbour."

Horror swept over Jeremy's face. This bright and beautiful girl given away without thought for her happiness was too much.

The tea tray was removed and everyone sat in silent contemplation. Richard broke the silence. "You asked Jeremy if he did any exercises. Do you have knowledge of such?"

"We have accidents with the workers sometimes, and the housekeeper broke her right arm. I had to do all the housekeeping. Her arm took so long to mend the doctor suggested I exercise it for her."

"Show me." Jeremy suggested. She fetched a footstool and sat on it at the side of him. Taking his left hand in hers she began to massage the fingers. The pleasure showed on his face.

"Is it that good, Jeremy?" Richard raised his eyebrows.

"It is. You would think I would be used to the pain by now. The relief is enormous. I could let you do this all day, Miss Emily." Emily blushed. Jeremy relaxed. Richard grinned. Kitty opened her mouth and stared.

Richard caught her eye and his eyes twinkled at her. She closed her mouth and knowingly beamed. Oh my!

Chapter 33

It was a relief to have Binny and Smithson there to assist. Kitty was tired and Richard's shoulder made disrobing slow and difficult. He also needed a fresh dressing. It always felt better when freshly cleaned and salved. Tonight, however, it was not his shoulder that gave him the most pain. He lay on his back supported by pillows, Kitty cuddled up to his side, her head on his chest. It was pure torture. After a few minutes Kitty said "You're not asleep." "No." "What did you mean earlier about showing me later?" He pulled her closer and kissed her hair, gently stroking her back. "I meant, just because I can't bed you does not mean you can't bed me." Kitty's eyes opened wide. "That is, if you want to."

She ran her fingers down his chest. "Mmm. I like that." "You do?" "Oh yes, I like you touching me anywhere you want to." "Can I kiss you?" "Anywhere you like."

She slid up to be able to reach his mouth. She was eager. Yes, he thought, he could probably talk her into doing this. She kissed his chest and stroked him, gradually moving downwards.

"It's very difficult with one hand isn't it? I keep rolling away." That had been his reason for not holding her at his side.

"You could always sit astride me and use both hands."

"Oh." she said wriggling her leg across his waist.

She stroked his chest and leaned against him to reach his mouth, rubbing her nipples on him in the process. He now had a free hand with which to cup her left breast and squeeze the nipple. Kitty forgot what she was doing. "Sit up and I can reach the other one." She dutifully obeyed. How could one hand do such wonderful things to her? She was wriggling in need not knowing what to do next. "Put your hands on my chest and slide your body down onto me." "Onto you?" "You'll see." He stroked her soft bottom as she slid down him until she met his fully engorged erection.

"Don't stop now, sweet, this is the best part." He urged her down using his good hand to position himself, and pressed her lower back to impale her on him.

"Oh Richard!" He was no longer capable of speech, his body was pressing upwards into hers. Feeling the pleasure of him in her she moved to his rhythm, more and more urgently. When she could hold on no longer, her body racked with wave after wave of release as she clung to him. He cried out as he emptied himself into her.

"Oh Richard." She murmured as she collapsed onto his chest and, still in that position, both of them sank into a deep and peaceful sleep.

The next morning saw the arrival of Portman with Jimmy Campbell. Everyone met in the Prime Minister's office at midday. Jimmy had to be informed of the reason he had been fetched. Everything swung on him being willing to help in opposition to his family.

The magistrate began. "We will keep your name out of this. We just need information about the hidden papers." Jimmy was wary. A clopping noise outside announced the arrival of Richard and Jeremy. They all turned to the door as they entered.

"Wellmore. What the hell happened to you?"

"Your cousin Stewart Hurst and his thugs. They left me for dead."

Jimmy looked around at them, saw Richard and Danvers also injured. "You two as well?"

"Two days ago. They tried to take us all, they were dressed as highwaymen."

"Is this all that blasted business of those papers?"

Jeremy answered. "Yes it looks like it. We didn't believe you when we were at Eton."

"I know, you called me crazy Jimmy. Luckily that's what stopped me from being part of their schemes. They always had schemes, the whole family. I suppose they see me as the black sheep."

Danvers wanted to move on. "Will you help us? Can you remember where they were kept?"

"I should be able to. They may have moved them but I know most of the hiding places at Lyndford. They're going to stop us if they can."

"They are at the moment under guard at The Tower."

"The Tower!"

"You have not been keeping up with the ton on-dits. They've whipped up hatred for the Crown using the Wellmores. Lady Katherine was attacked three times and Lady Carina, her sister, was killed in her place. You've seen what they did to Jeremy. All of it done in the name of the Prince who knew nothing about it. I presume the ladies of the family were included in these schemes."

"Oh yes, the Dowager, my great aunt and Aunt Maria especially were."

Everyone looked at Richard.

"I was right then."

"So it seems."

"Where is Lady Kitty, I expected her here?"

"She is not feeling well. I left her with a full guard." He laughed. "I would bet on her friend Emily Weston against all comers." He grinned at Jeremy who was a little peeved at being dragged away as soon as she had arrived.

The Prime Minister suggested they had lunch and met in an hour's time. Carriage places were organised and when preparations were completed they all left. Danvers was not inclined to let Jimmy Campbell out of his sight but as he was more Jeremy's friend they all went in the Earl's travelling coach.

"HALT! Bloody Hell, fetch the Colonel, we're being invaded."

"No need to swear, my man." chided the magistrate. Men came running.

"Sir Peter Danvers to see Colonel Mathers."

"Danvers, I wondered when you would remember us." He held out a hand, Danvers offered his left hand. "You were injured, I heard about that from Major Phillips.

"We've come to search the library."

"I'll bring a few men with me. Some of the servants are a little troublesome."

The coaches arrived at the front door surrounded by horsemen. The soldier on door duty was keen to let them in. "We've several locked in one of the cellars with a watch on them, just in case there's a secret passage."

The library was not only guarded outside, it also had soldiers inside guarding the windows. Jimmy walked around it. "It has changed a bit but not significantly. It was more than ten years ago, I was only about eleven at the time. I think it was somewhere here." He fetched the library steps and reached up to the top shelf at the side of the fireplace.

"Why by the fireplace, do you think?" The magistrate asked Richard.

"Could be to keep the paper dry. I really have no idea."

The books were handed down leaving the shelf clear.

"I can feel where it is but I don't remember how to open it." He changed places with Richard. "Run your hands along the cornice."

"Oh, yes. I can feel the edges."

Between them they pushed and pulled anything that could be a handle.

"It could just be stuck, it is quite old." Jeremy remarked.

"OH!" In his frustration Richard thumped the panel, which duly gave a crack and bounced out a little. Not much, but enough to prise it open. A box sat in the recess. Richard handed it down to Danvers who laid it on the library table. Richard came down the steps and they all stood and stared at it.

"It's locked." Jimmy said in despair "I have no idea where the key is." Danvers, Portman and Richard began to laugh. "Mr Campbell, do you have any idea who we are, what we did during the war?" He shook his head. "I'll let you tell him, Mathers."

Colonel Mathers put an arm around Jimmy and led him slightly away from the box while they dealt with the lock.

"All of them!" Jeremy was grinning at him.

"Come and see. God I hope this is it."

Inside the box were various old and not so old papers and parchments. They started with the oldest, complete with seal. It certainly gave them status, but not kingship. However one or two more did, they even had seals on them. As they opened the other papers, Jeremy scrutinised the oldest.

"This, I think is real, hundreds of years old I would say, genuinely so. Look at the age of this parchment, it's more modern." He held up the old parchment to the light, then the newer one. This is much newer. Look at the signature, it's a copy. A different signature I would have accepted, but not the same one. The seal is too perfect, in most old documents the seal was not always perfect."

Danvers broke the spell. "Keep looking."

"This is definitely newer, it's a letter."

"What does it say?"

"It's addressed to the eighth Duke of Lyndford. That's the present Duke's father isn't it?"

"Yes, who from?"

"The Duke of Wenton."

"My grandfather probably. Read it."

"Dear cousin."

"Cousin!"

"I hate to disappoint you but apart from the first document I believe the rest are well constructed forgeries. If you look to our grandfather, I recall a hoax being mentioned. I purport these are the papers from the hoax. I beg you not to take this too seriously, if anyone saw these papers it could be seen as treason. I advise you to destroy them. Keep the oldest if you wish, I believe that to be genuine, Wenton."

"What do you know about your grandfather, or even his father, it could be either, we need to check?"

"I know he was a scholar like me. If he had not been a Duke he would have been a don at Oxford."

"So he knew what he was talking about."

"Oh yes, definitely."

Danvers finished putting the papers in the box. "I will take these to London to the Privy Council. Colonel Mathers, I believe we need a military escort in the circumstances."

"Yes, Sir Peter, with the greatest of pleasure."

"Richard, will you see to Campbell for me. A few days holiday concealed in London are in order."

"My pleasure."

The magistrate rode with Danvers, Portman and Williams on horseback with the escort. The soldiers were ordered back to their Windsor base to await the arrival of the Queen. The servants were ordered to close up the house, several of them being taken into custody.

The Earl of Pengarron with Lord Jeremy and Mr James Campbell rode comfortably back to London.

"You sure you would not prefer Wenton Hall, Jeremy?" Richard queried in a mocking jest.

"London please."

"What about the Duke?"

"I'll write to him."

"Has this anything to do with a rather helpful young lady?" Jeremy made a growling noise but eventually looked up.

"It could."

Can we just go through the women in your family who supported the Duke? His mother the Dowager, her sister Dowager Lady Campbell, her son Lord Campbell and his wife Lady Maria Campbell. Who else, any brothers and sisters?"

"My parents were included but not very enthusiastic. I was too young really, I thought it all a game. In the end they withdrew my funding for Eton and Oxford and I was articled to a lawyer. I believe my parents turned away from them then. I know they have a little money but not enough to live well. I hope to make enough to help them."

"Do they never go out into society?" Kitty asked.

"Not really, only to the local landowners. He augments his income helping the smaller landowners with their estate management."

"We know there were several Dowagers, real leaders of the ton's on-dits. Maria Campbell we have heard about before. She seems good at whipping up others to do her nasty business."

"If you arrest them others will be angry on their behalf."

"We need to manipulate the ton."

Emily Weston was gently massaging Jeremy's fingers. "You don't understand the ton ladies at all, do you? If anyone is accused everyone joins in, like with Kitty, but if they were accused of treason they would desert them like rats from a sinking ship. They need to feel the fear of being implicated, that's why they deserted Kitty in the ballroom. What happens outside doesn't matter. It's what is said in the ballroom that counts."

"Are you saying we should arrest them in a ballroom?"

"Oh, wouldn't that be wonderful." Kitty was quite animated. "March the army in and drag them out to The Tower."

"You're getting vindictive, Kitty." Jeremy said.

"No." Danvers said. "She's right. A small platoon of soldiers in full uniform, to inform them they were to go to The Tower for treason and I believe the others would desert them. I feel much more hopeful now that we can deal with the ton and free Lady Kitty from their lies. Once we put out the whole story you will be the most celebrated lady in London."

"No thank you! I shall retire to Cornwall again and hide."

A check was made on each of the ladies, to be sure they would be at the Pertwoods' ball. The Prince relinquished his personal guard for the evening. In full dress uniform with Danvers also in uniform and a Privy Councillor in attendance they sealed the exits before they entered.

The ton would never forget this spectacle as they marched in and the names and charges were read out. Maria tried to escape, some tried to defend her, then she pretended to swoon. The Dowagers held their heads high and tried to bluff it out, after all, they believed they were royalty. They at least walked out, Maria was half dragged between two very large soldiers. Her pleas and flirtation were to no avail.

"So now we know who, why and also why us. I'm not sure I shall know what to do with myself now."

"Of course you will, Jeremy. You have to practice walking. Your fingers seem to be improving. You should ask your Miss Emily to massage your legs."

"My legs?" Jeremy said, his eyes laughing. Richard was roaring with laughter. Kitty looked bemused. "His legs?"

"It's not just his legs Jeremy is imagining her massaging."

Within a few days Dinsdale came calling. He was walking badly using a walking stick.

"How is the leg doing?" Richard enquired.

"Well the damage has healed but it will not hold my weight too well." Jeremy knew how he felt.

"What does the doctor say?"

He shifted in his chair to ease the stiffness. "Good, really. He thinks it will strengthen in time. I heard about a special doctor in Bath who uses the hot springs to help cases like mine. I wondered if you might accompany me, Jeremy."

Jeremy looked unconvinced. "I doubt it would help me."

Kitty looked sadly at him. "Why not try it, perhaps it would help if only a little?"

Richard looked hard at him. "Is that the real reason or does another come to mind?"

Jeremy looked a little rueful. "It is a rather inopportune moment, Dinsdale, but I will keep it in mind."

Kitty smiled at Dinsdale. "It was good of you to think of Jeremy."

He looked at bit embarrassed. "Well actually, when I said where I was going it was the Duke who encouraged me to persuade you. Surely any improvement would be good."

"Oh I am improving but only slowly. I just prefer not to leave London at this time."

The knock on the door announced the arrival of the doctor to see the Countess. Everyone rose as Richard requested the men accompany him to his study. "Elliot, no callers for Lady Kitty until the doctor leaves." The butler bowed. "Of course, my lord."

In the study Richard insisted Dinsdale wrote down all the information for Jeremy in the event that he changed his mind. Jeremy was now in a strange mood. He hated being reminded of his inability to do normal everyday tasks. His hand was stronger, his fingers more flexible but how long would the solicitous attention of the delectable Miss Emily Weston continue?

Meanwhile, Elliot was unsure how to proceed. "Miss Weston, I am afraid everyone is occupied with visitors at the moment, would you care to wait in the library until the Earl can see you?" The library being the only available room at the moment, Miss Weston was definitely not her usual bubbly self. "Yes, may I wait please, Elliot." He escorted her to the empty library. "I will tell their Lordships when their visitor leaves, miss." She gave him a very watery smile. "Thank you."

Emily wandered around the library but was having problems controlling her tears. She had no wish for them to see her like this, she must pull herself out of this somehow. She heard voices and retreated to a large chair facing the window where she curled herself into an unhappy ball. Someone was opening the door and entering.

"How long do you think the doctor will be?" Jeremy's voice.

"Not long, I hope." Richard's voice. "Why are you suddenly in such low spirits, my friend?" She heard Jeremy reach a chair and sit, the sound of the crutches ceased. "These" he obviously pushed them aside. "I can never have what you have, Pengarron. I can never walk to her and hold her against me. I can never look into her eyes as I lower my head to kiss her. I can never bed her as a husband should. What have I to offer?"

Richard was silent for a while. "Jeremy I never knew you felt this badly. Why don't you talk to her, I'm sure she cares for you. She has already helped you, maybe in time everything will come right again."

"What can I offer her, I'm a wreck of a man, she deserves so much more." At that point Emily's tears became too much to hold. Her heart felt as if it were breaking.

The door then opened and the doctor was admitted. "Congratulations, my lord, it is as you suspected. In the early autumn I expect you to be a father."

Richard breathed out in a huge sigh of relief. "Is everything well with her?"

"Indeed she is healthy, there is nothing out of the ordinary, she should lose the queasiness and tiredness in the next few weeks."

Jeremy stood and thumped him on the back. "Well done, you lucky man."

"I will see you out, doctor." As they left Emily heard Jeremy's crutches, took her handkerchief out of her reticule to wipe her eyes and blow her nose, presuming she was alone.

"Who's there?" Jeremy stood clumsily. Emily rose, trying to keep her face away from him.

"I'm sorry, My lord, I had no intention of eavesdropping. I was just avoiding seeing anyone for a moment.

"Emily look at me. Are you crying?" This brought another wave of tears which she struggled to stop. "Why are you crying?"

"I came to say goodbye, My lord."

"What happened to the 'Jeremy' Where are you going?"

"My mother has discovered I have been visiting here and has forbidden me to call again. We are to go back to Norwich tomorrow."

"When will you return?"

"I doubt she will allow me to London again. She intends I should marry Mr Wilkes." Jeremy turned his head away in pain. He reached out a hand risking falling in the need to touch her. Taking her hand he pulled her towards him and lifted her fingers to his lips. It was thus they were discovered when the door opened and Mrs Weston pushed past Richard.

"You wicked girl, I told you not to come here again. You have disobeyed me for the last time, miss." She grabbed Emily's arm and pulled her out of the library. "I came to say goodbye, mama." As she towed her down the corridor to where her sister Mrs Linton waited, they heard her admonitions continuing. "Good grief, girl, he's a cripple. You don't seriously think we would allow you to have any liaison with him." They were through the front door. Elliot was trying to explain but Richard was only interested in Jeremy and the damage this had done to his recovery.

The next day Emily Weston was taken home to her father with instruction from her mother that he stop dallying about and arrange the match with Mr Wilkes. His usually bubbly daughter was quiet and withdrawn. Her mother insisted she take over her duties in the household. Mr Weston wondered if his wife wished the match to enable Emily to manage both households, Mr Wilkes's being only small.

A few days after the débâcle, Jeremy stated his intentions of joining Dinsdale in Bath and embroiled Ferguson in his plans, together with his valet, to manage the move.

Now the country waited.

The evidence of treason was overwhelming, they had been so confident of success they had misread avarice of servants and hirelings for genuine adherence. When their lives were in jeopardy, they were vociferous in protesting they were only following orders. Some, like the decoy driver and several of Chief Magistrate Wentworth's servants, all provided by his friend Lyndford, were deported. Others were hanged for their crimes.

The Dowager Duchess of Lyndford refused to accept she was not the Queen Mother. Her husband may have known the truth of the hoax papers but if so he took the information to his grave, never speaking of it with his wife. Lady Maria Campbell became ever more vicious and vindictive in her panic.

Good can sometimes come out of the jaws of evil. The Dowager Lady Campbell, her son and daughter-in-law Maria being removed from the family's estate, it fell to Jimmy Campbell's parents to take over the running of it, Jimmy thus being raised to a gentleman with expectations.

Lyndford Hall and all their lands became the property of the Crown and were left vacant to await allocation.

The statement and proof were printed for the information of all, and distributed widely throughout the country. One place it did not reach was the Wilsons' house in Norwich, where Mrs Weston continued to tongue lash her daughter over the cripple called Jeremy, and her husband for not having arranged Emily's marriage.

For the Duke of Wenton, the pressure was lifted, his daughter cleared and happily married. In such an atmosphere of relief he was open to Richard's suggestion that he hold a house party for family, friends and all those who had been of assistance through this terrible year.

Aunt Hetty, working with the Duke, made lists with a little input from Richard. Rooms were counted, prepared and allocated. Menus discussed all preparations made, invitations sent. The event was eagerly anticipated.

Epilogue

A month later

The Westons sat at luncheon together, Mrs Weston admonishing Emily for not having completed all her chores. In this atmosphere Mr Weston began to talk of a letter he had received that morning which included the official statement from the Crown. He insisted on reading it in its entirety. Mrs Weston was unmoved.

"I take it this young lady is the one you considered not suitable as a friend for Emily?"

"Well how was I to know, you could hear what they were saying."

"Did you think to ask, ma'am? Emily knew her innocence. Presumably you will wish to refuse the invitation to the Wenton Hall house party."

"Well I don't know what good it will do."

After lunch he called Emily into his study. "Now tell me, my dear. Would you wish to go?" Conflicting emotions showed on her face. "This young man your mother keeps mentioning. His name was Jeremy, is that right?" Emily nodded and blushed. Her father patted her hand. "I will reply to the Duke. A little aristocratic arrogance may put your mother in her place and stop her harassment of you, my dear, and I should like to meet your friends." Emily went to her room, buried her face in her pillow and sobbed until she had no more tears left. What if they didn't want her there, if they were too upset over her mother's behaviour? How could she face him after what her mama had called him?

The day of arrival was the usual chaos, only in this case some of the arrivals turned into helpers until many newcomers were not sure who were staff and who were guests.

This was no ordinary house party. There were few entertainments arranged and the guests were encouraged to organise their own. They were from a variety of backgrounds, some ton, some not. Some second or third sons working for Danvers, some titled, many not. Mrs Weston was at a loss who to call what, in the end she called all the men 'Sir.'

Danvers approached Emily and her father. "It it good to see you here Miss Weston." Emily smiled up at him.

"Oh, Mr Danvers, how nice to see you again, may I introduce my papa?" They shook hands.

"Danvers, where do you fit in, I am rather removed from all that happened, not even having been in London." Danvers smiled at him.

"It must be confusing, sir, most of us already know each other. I am Sir Peter Danvers, I headed the investigation." Mr Weston looked surprised.

Emily leaned forward and whispered. "He's the spymaster, papa."

"Good heavens and you know my little Emily."

"Indeed several of us have had the pleasure of knowing her. Have you seen Lady Kitty yet?" He asked.

"No, not yet."

"Then come and introduce your papa to them, I see Richard over there." He led them across the room.

"Richard?" Mr Weston queried.

"Lord Richard Trevane, the Earl of Pengarron. He married my friend Kitty, Lady Katherine Wellmore who became Lady Katherine Trevane, Countess of Pengarron."

As they reached them, Danvers said "Look who I found." Kitty turned, saw Emily and threw her arms around her.

"Oh Emily, I'm so pleased you came. Richard was not sure you would be allowed." Emily extracted herself from Kitty and introduced her father.

"I was not willing to allow that to happen." he said. Richard smiled with understanding and shook his hand.

Dinner was announced and the chaos occurred again as everyone tried to give pride of place to another. The evening was spent in general introduction and questions. The only upset came when a young lady, Miss Julie Arnott touched a young man on the arm and said "Lord Jeremy?" Everyone turned including Wigglesworth. "Oh. I'm sorry." He smiled at her. "I am, or I was Lord Jeremy but only as a decoy, Miss ...." "Arnott, Julie Arnott." "George Wigglesworth." All would have been well if Sarah Arnott had not said "Don't be silly, Lord Jeremy is in a wheelchair." As the room fell silent she said "Did I do it again!" looking around with large eyes.

There was only one thing wrong with the party, No Jeremy.

Her mother made it worse the following morning at breakfast by remarking to Emily and her father in front of others that she expected Lord Jeremy was not there as nobody would want to see a cripple. Mr Weston took her by the arm and hurried her from the room leaving Emily purple in the face with embarrassment and mortification. It had to be explained to her mother that Lord Jeremy was not a cripple and last seen, by herself, had been walking with crutches.

Over the next few days Emily relaxed, made friends and regained much of her good spirits. Thursday morning Kitty, still a little delicate in the mornings, was sat with Emily as the Duke approached. Emily jumped up to curtsey. "None of that, my dear. I understand you have been a great help to both my children." Emily blushed not knowing what to say. Kitty reproached her. "Come Emily, where is all that spirit. Richard said he would back you against any assassin that came and you were so good with Jeremy's fingers." The Duke looked down at her.

"I seem to have had a few problems since then." He patted her hand. "Never mind, my dear, when you are married your mama will have no say any more." He chuckled.

"Oh but that is not so, Your Grace, I am expected to marry Mr Wilkes who lives very close and I am to continue my housekeeping at home also."

The Duke looked quite shocked. "Is this marriage finalised, are the settlements made?"

"No, I do not believe so, although mama exhorts papa daily to arrange it." The Duke nodded a goodbye and went thoughtfully in search of Mr Weston.

Many of the young men were in the billiard room when George Weston left his wife in the care of several keen eyed matrons. He was fast coming to realise that most of these young and not quite so young men were employees of the Foreign Office, many having served abroad. They were, in fact, spies for England helping to win the war. How could his wife be so misunderstanding of these exuberant young fellows, to any one of which he would cheerfully have given his daughter's hand in marriage?

He wandered into the orangery with its heavy citrus scent and sat studying the estate through the window. It was sat thus that the Duke came upon him. He went to rise. "No, stay where you are. I will join you, it is a pleasant spot even on a drab day. Your daughter seems a very intelligent girl."

"Indeed she is; I let her help me with the estate and the workers. It saves her mother making her into a total drudge."

"I understand she is expected to marry a Mr Wilkins, is it?"

"Not if I have anything to say about it."

"I understood the settlements had been prepared."

"No, definitely not. I know it is her mother's wish but the man is twenty five years her senior. I have seen what my wife has done to my bright girl. The change in her is so great, her manner sad and dutiful. I hardly know how to help her. If I had not insisted I doubt she would have come here."

The Duke looked worried. "That is not good, Weston. We must see what we can do to revitalise her. There are enough young men here to catch her eye, are there not?" George Weston smiled at the Duke but his heart knew how great the problem was.

Tea was served on the terrace with the doors open for anyone who wished to sit inside if they were not sufficiently warm. In the distance one or two noticed the arrival of a carriage. Several of the men went in to meet the new arrivals. One of them was Dinsdale. Portman was talking with Kitty and Emily when he saw the first to appear.

"Dinsdale, how are you?" Many turned to look at him.

"You see. I'm walking perfectly normally again."

"That is excellent news." Kitty walked forward to greet him. "So all has ended well for you Dinsdale, I am so pleased."

"Thank you Lady Kitty, it is good to be back to normal and among friends." Emily hung back as she had never met Dinsdale. "I brought a surprise for you, Lady Kitty, but you must wait until later for it. Tea. I am starving hungry."

"I never knew one of Danvers' men who wasn't." Kitty laughed. "I await your surprise eagerly, go and eat."

The ladies retired early to dress for dinner. George Weston was reticent in going up to his wife. A door on the corridor opened and a young man walking slowly with the aid of a walking stick came into the corridor followed closely by the Duke. "Weston, can I introduce you to my son Jeremy." He held out his hand. "George Weston, Emily's father." Jeremy beamed at him. "I am pleased to meet you, sir. I hope we will get to know each other better before you leave. I understand Miss Weston is still unmarried."

"And will remain so unless I am certain of her happiness, Lord Jeremy." Jeremy looked closely to judge his meaning. "Weston, call me Jeremy or Wellmore if you will but please, leave out the Lord. We are at home here."

Weston stood close to his daughter while waiting to go in to dinner, the better to monitor her reactions. She was facing away from the door when Jeremy approached her from behind. "Miss Emily." Emily turned shocked, surprised, her face turning bright red. "Jeremy! Lord Jeremy. I had no idea you were here."

"Then this is my surprise, may I lead you in to dinner?"

"Jeremy, your crutches."

"Are gone. I need only a stick to help my balance now. Who knows, in the future, maybe not even that."

Dinner was announced and Emily floated in on a cloud. Kitty grinned at her. Richard's eyes twinkled at her. Her mother stared in shock and her father began to glow inside.

Saturday was to be a grand ball preceded by a dinner. All was set, the housekeeper was in evidence more than usual, normally it was Aunt Hetty bustling around. The Duke was beside himself with an inner happiness Kitty had never seen before.

The ladies retired to dress leaving the men a little time to themselves.

"Mr Weston, may I have a word." Jeremy was nervous and it showed. He led him to the Duke's study but when Weston sat Jeremy remained standing. "I thought I had been through the worst times my life could hold but I find this the most nerve racking." He took a deep breath. "I would ask for your permission to pay my addresses to your daughter, sir." Weston was quiet for a moment.

"Will you make her happy Wellmore?"

"I will do my best, sir"

"If my daughter will have you, then I will happily give her to you." They shook hands warmly. "When will you ask her?" "During the ball if I can get her alone sir." "Then I will arrange to keep her ever interfering mother away for a while."

The dinner over, they proceeded to the ballroom where neighbours were already arriving. It had been so long since they had held a full ball, the visitors were intrigued to see inside the house.

The musicians were playing the introduction to a waltz, Portman was waiting for Emily to solicit her hand when Jeremy slapped his stick across his chest. "Hold this, old man, if you will." He walked a little unsteadily to Emily. "May I perhaps have this dance, Miss Emily?" She looked up at him. "Can you dance, are you able?" "We will find that out in a moment. I may need a little support from you." "I will give you any support you need, you know that, sir." He took her in his arms and very carefully moved her around the periphery of the floor, other dancers being careful to avoid them. It was not until later on the terrace that he managed to hold her again. He leaned against the house wall for balance. Emily looked warily at the doors.

"What is wrong?"

"I am expecting mama to burst out at any moment."

"No, you are quite safe, your papa is restraining her." She had to laugh at the image that induced.

"Emily." He pulled her close into his arms. "Do you know how much I care for you?" She blushed, although it was hard to see it in the dark of the terrace. He lowered his head and touched his lips to hers. She trembled and pressed her lips in response. He moved his mouth to force hers to open a little and slid his tongue around the inside of her lips. Lifting his lips from hers to look down into her eyes he stroked her back gently. She leaned closer. "Emily, my lovely Emily, will you marry me?" Emily clung to him, her mind whirling. Had he just asked for her hand in marriage? "Emily, please, put me out of my misery. Will you?" Her eyes filled with tears. "Yes please, Jeremy." Then the tears were running down her face. "This is the second time I have had you this close and both times you were crying. I hope to make you happy, my love, not make you cry." "I am happy, Jeremy these are tears of happiness."

For Love of Kitty

Others were now walking on the terrace and coming close to seeing them. "Shall we go in then and put your papa out of his misery."

The rest of the evening passed in a dream. Jeremy drew his father aside to give him the news. He agreed to announce it at supper.

Emily thought the dancing would never end. Kitty felt the same. Richard urged her to sit at the side but not to leave until after supper.

Supper time arrived. The Duke stood and held up his hand. Eventually everyone noticed and fell quiet. "I have a couple of announcements to make." Everyone was silent. Kitty looked at Richard who smiled. Was he going to announce her condition? She hoped not.

"I have to announce the engagement of my son Jeremy Wellmore to Miss Emily Weston." Noise erupted, people clapped, her mother cried out in frustration, her father glowed with pleasure.

Kitty thought her happiness was now complete, her best friend and her beloved brother.

Eventually they realised the Duke was still holding up his hand. They quieted again. "The second announcement is that Mrs Henrietta Winslow has agreed to become my new duchess."

Aunt Hetty and her father, now her happiness was truly complete. Tears rolled down her cheeks. Richard took her hand.

"Is this a good ending to all the terrible troubles?"

"It is the best there could be."

"You look so tired, my sweet."

"I am. Take me to bed, Richard."

"With the greatest of pleasure, my love." His eyes sparkled at her so then there was only one thing she could say.

"Oh Richard."

Lightning Source UK Ltd.
Milton Keynes UK
UKOW05f2101160614

233532UK00002B/65/P